AMULET

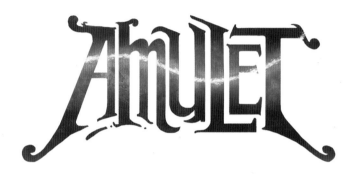

Library of Congress Control Number: 2017955789

ISBN 978-0-545-85002-5 (hardcover)
ISBN 978-0-545-82860-4 (paperback)

10 9 8 7 6 5 4 3 2 1   18 19 20 21 22

Printed in China   62
First edition, October 2018
Edited by Cassandra Pelham Fulton
Book design by Kazu Kibuishi and Phil Falco
Creative Director: David Saylor

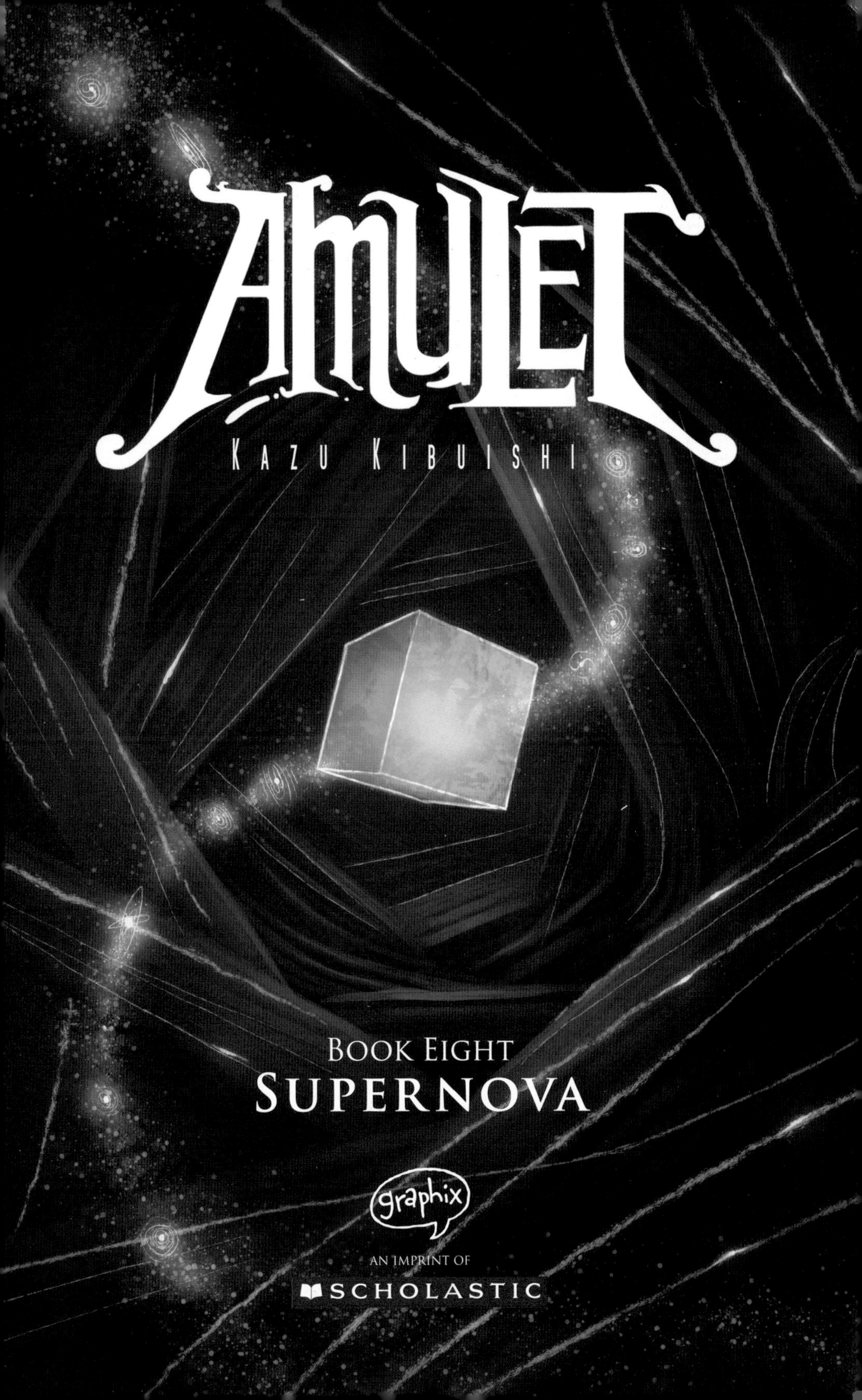

AMULET

KAZU KIBUISHI

BOOK EIGHT

SUPERNOVA

graphix

AN IMPRINT OF

SCHOLASTIC

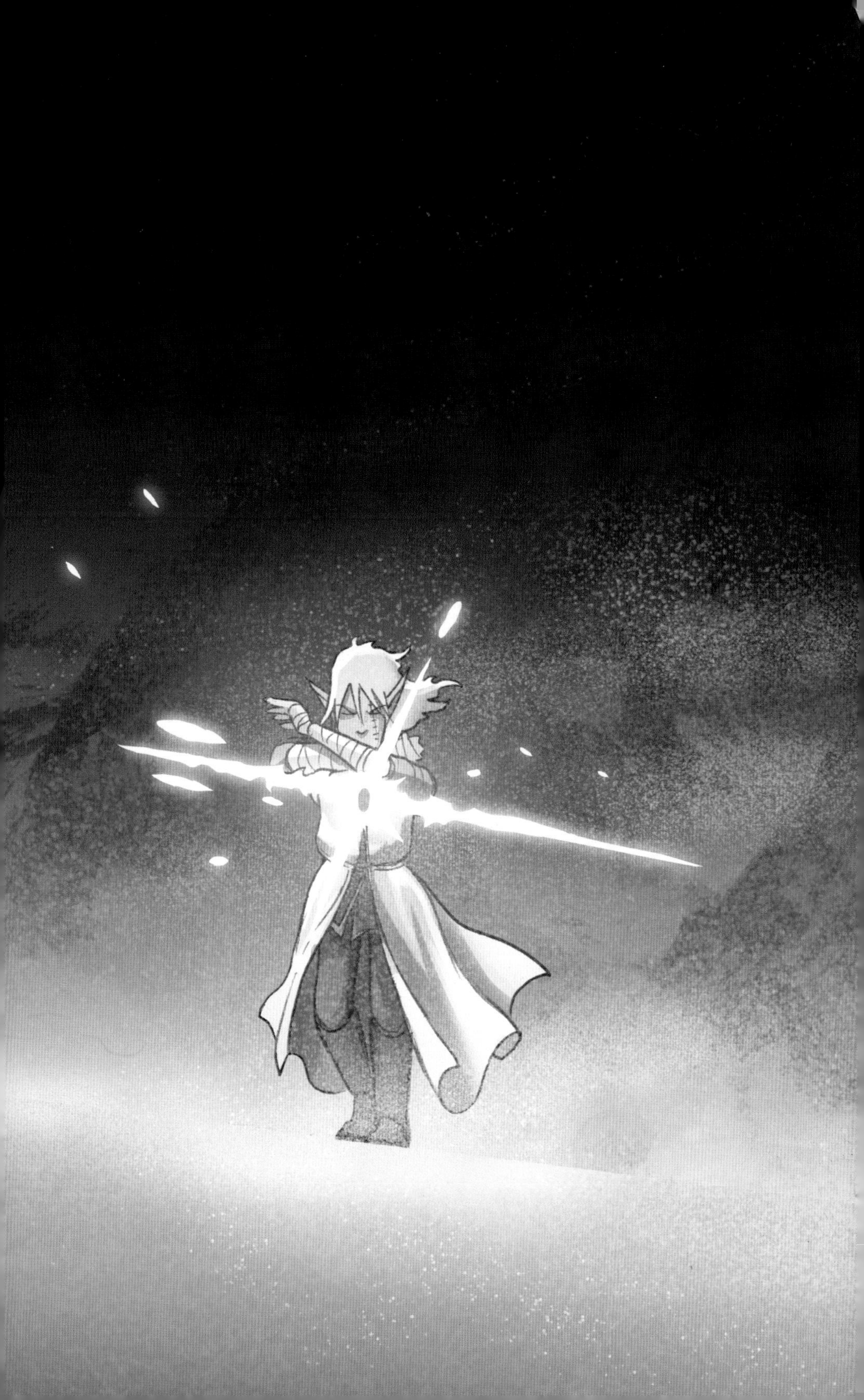

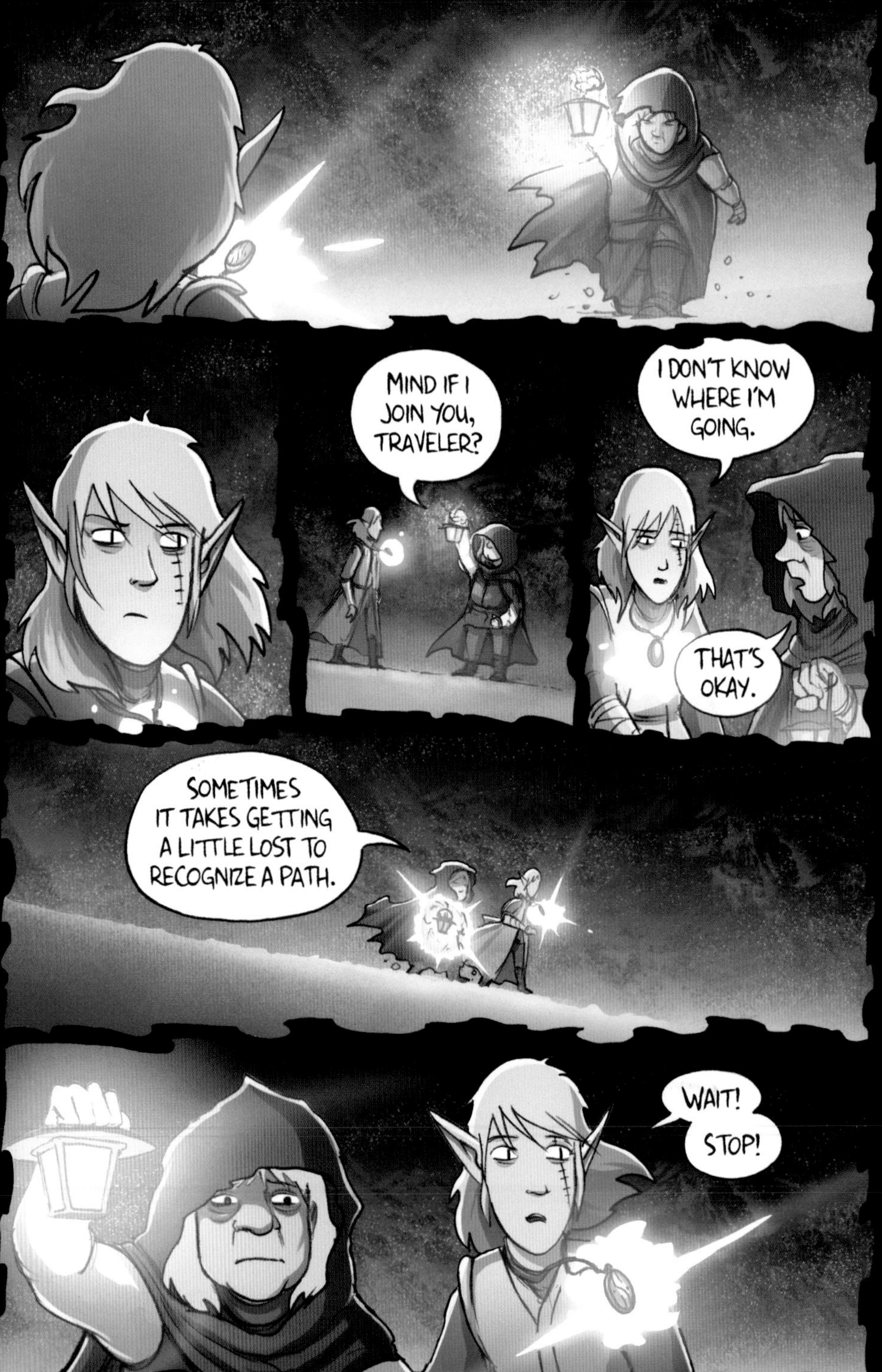
MIND IF I JOIN YOU, TRAVELER?
I DON'T KNOW WHERE I'M GOING.
THAT'S OKAY.
SOMETIMES IT TAKES GETTING A LITTLE LOST TO RECOGNIZE A PATH.
WAIT!
STOP!

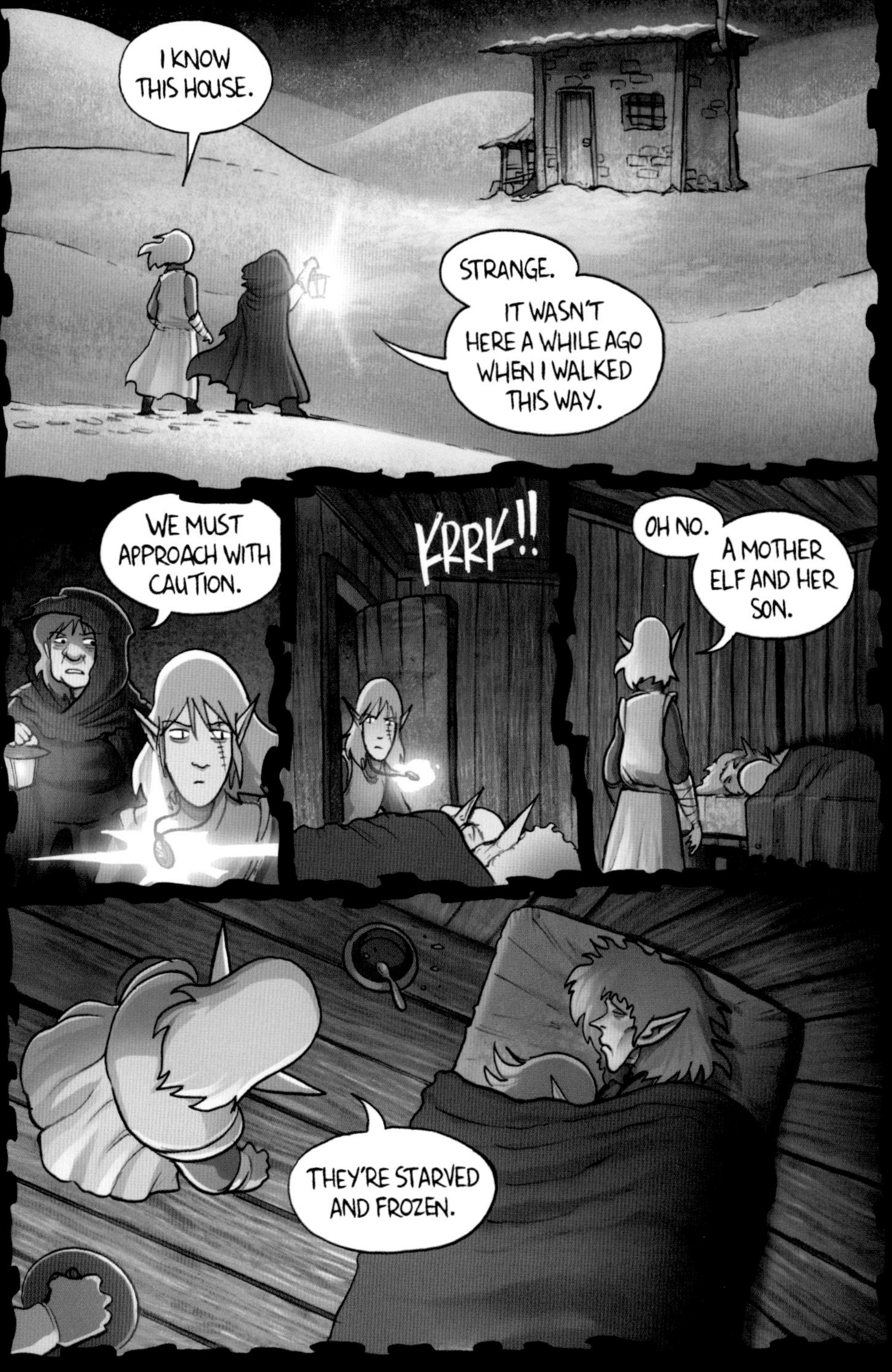
I KNOW THIS HOUSE.
STRANGE.
IT WASN'T HERE A WHILE AGO WHEN I WALKED THIS WAY.
WE MUST APPROACH WITH CAUTION.
KRRK!!
OH NO.
A MOTHER ELF AND HER SON.
THEY'RE STARVED AND FROZEN.

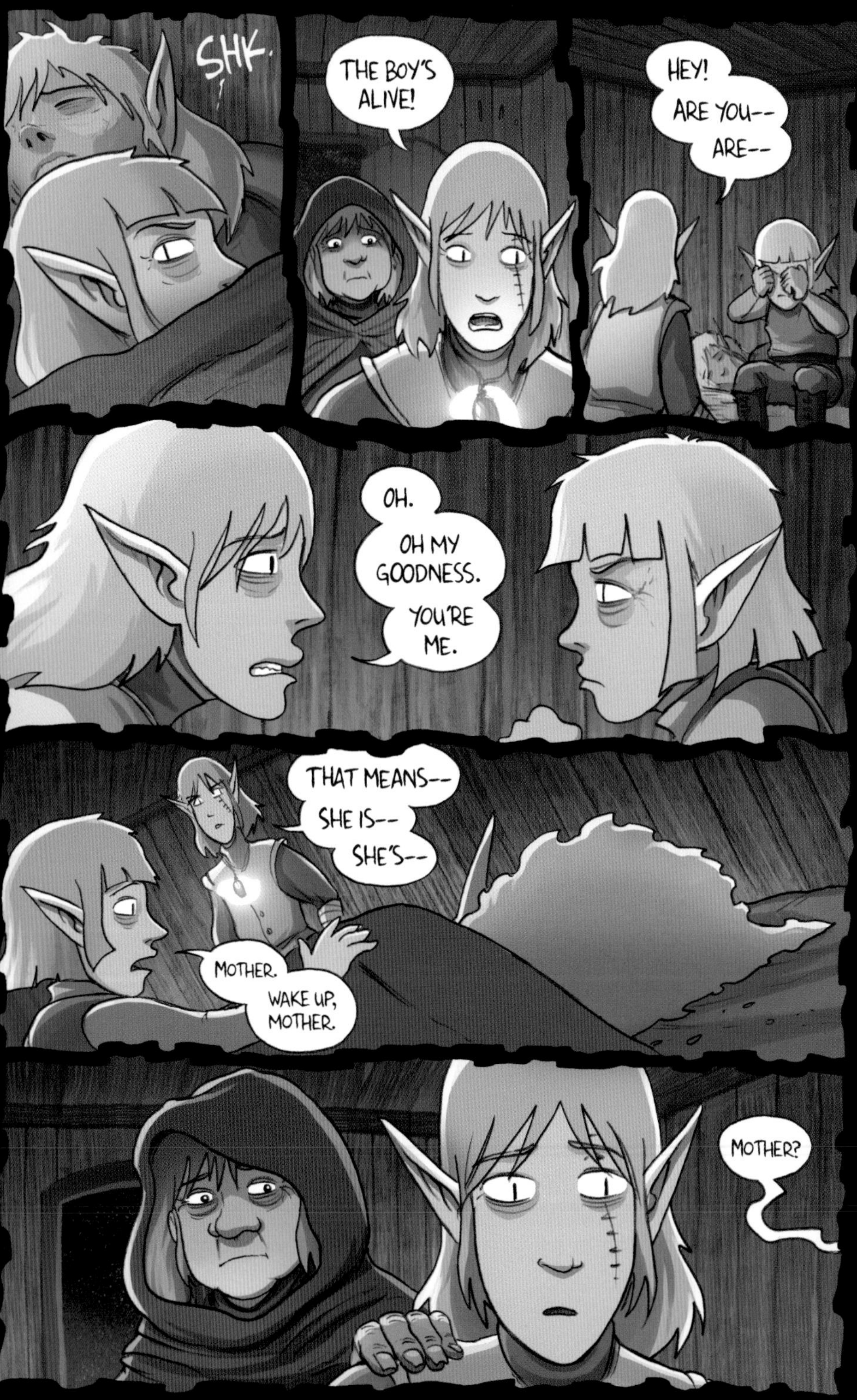
SHK.
THE BOY'S ALIVE!
HEY!
ARE YOU--
ARE--
OH.
OH MY GOODNESS.
YOU'RE ME.
THAT MEANS--
SHE IS--
SHE'S--
MOTHER.
WAKE UP, MOTHER.
MOTHER?

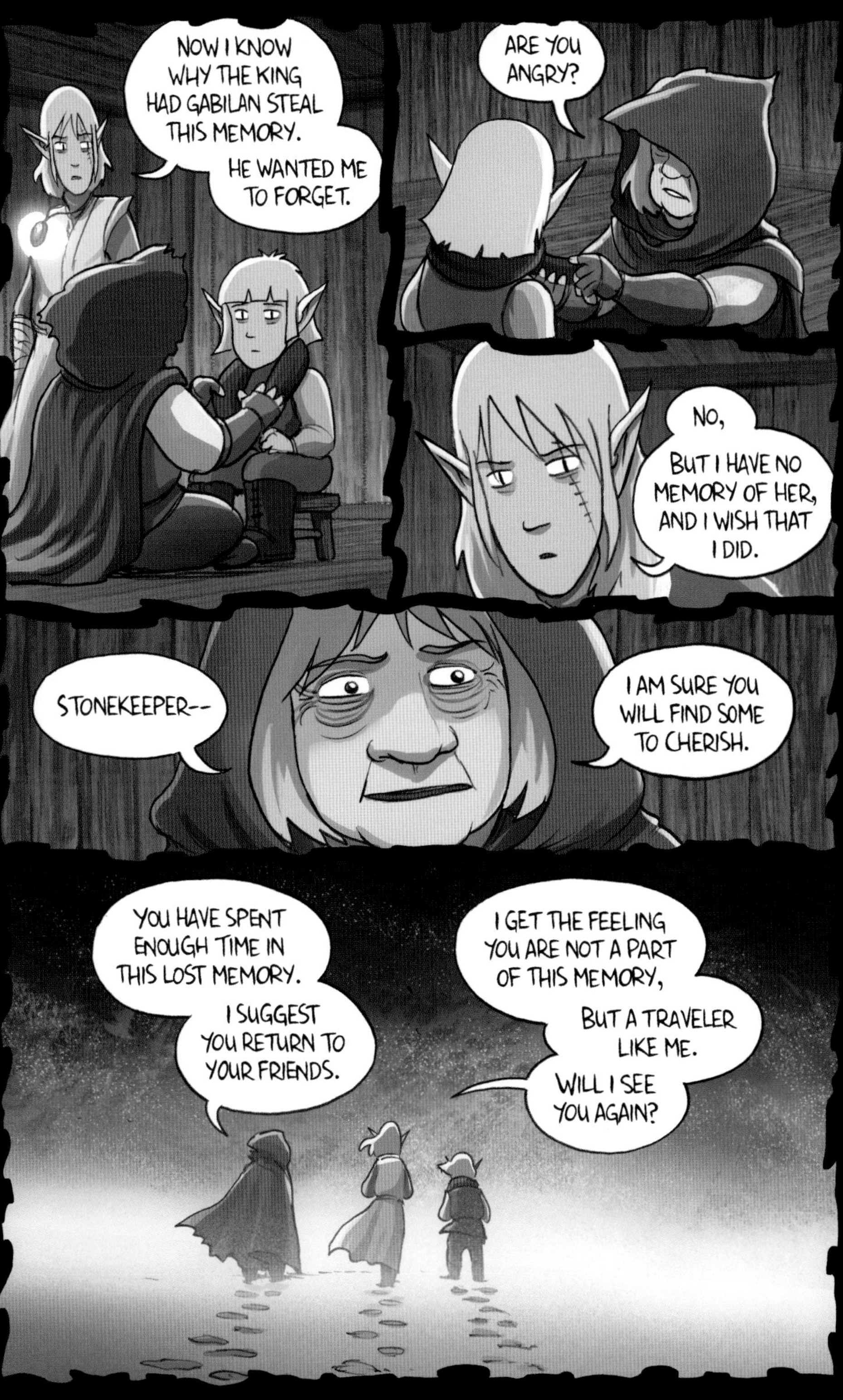
NOW I KNOW WHY THE KING HAD GABILAN STEAL THIS MEMORY.
HE WANTED ME TO FORGET.
ARE YOU ANGRY?
NO,
BUT I HAVE NO MEMORY OF HER, AND I WISH THAT I DID.
STONEKEEPER--
I AM SURE YOU WILL FIND SOME TO CHERISH.
YOU HAVE SPENT ENOUGH TIME IN THIS LOST MEMORY.
I SUGGEST YOU RETURN TO YOUR FRIENDS.
I GET THE FEELING YOU ARE NOT A PART OF THIS MEMORY,
BUT A TRAVELER LIKE ME.
WILL I SEE YOU AGAIN?

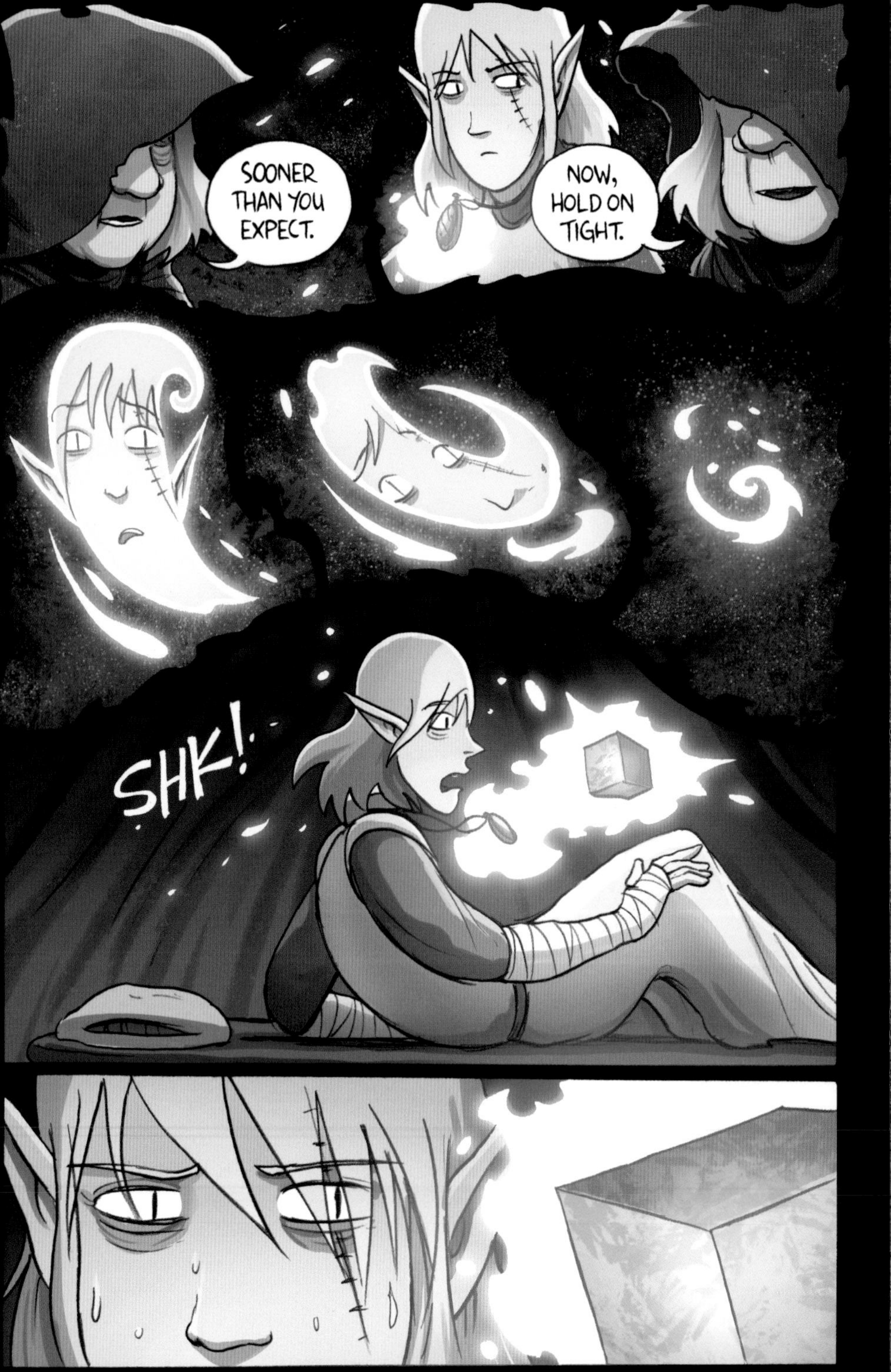
SOONER THAN YOU EXPECT.
NOW, HOLD ON TIGHT.
SHK!

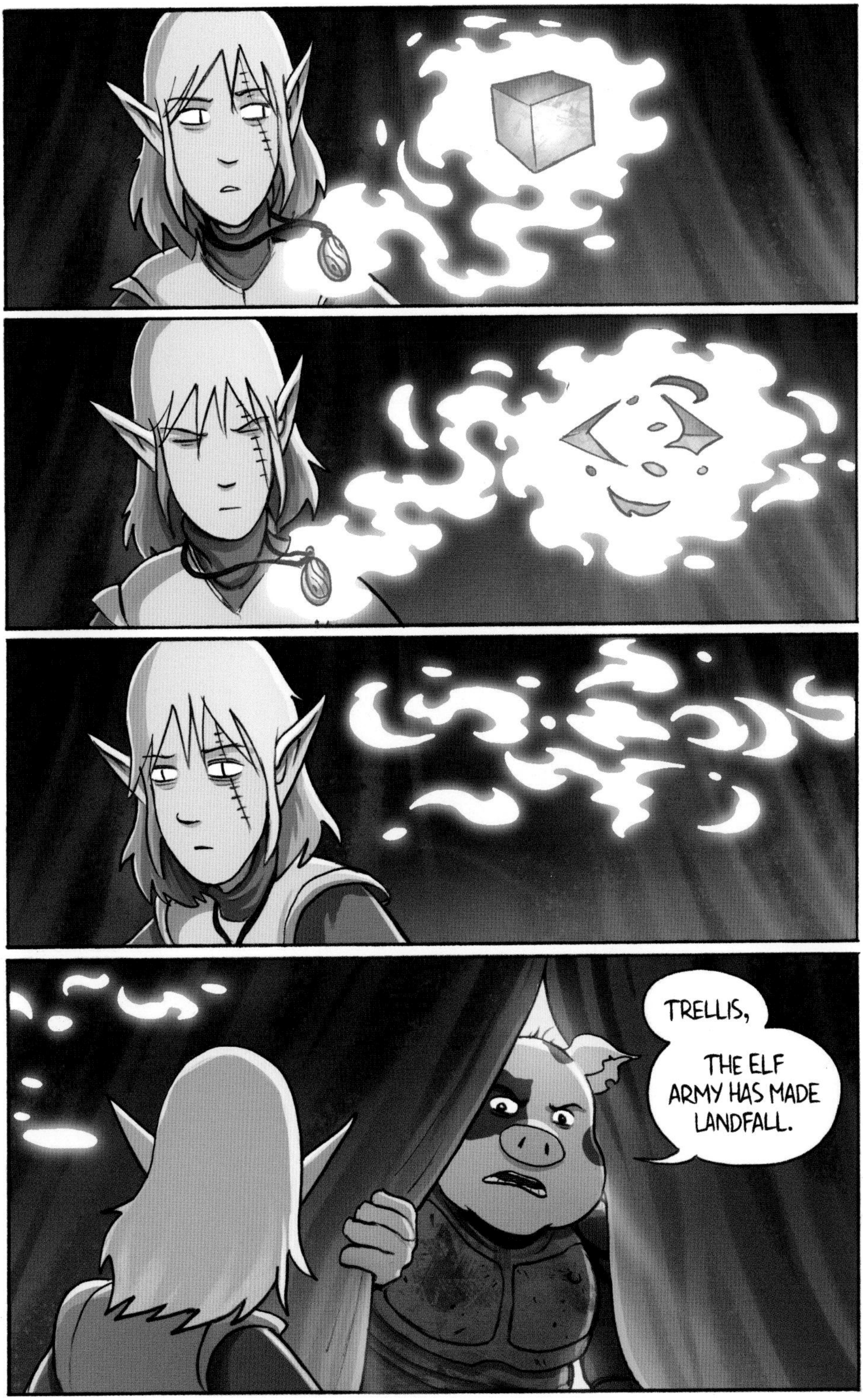
TRELLIS,
THE ELF ARMY HAS MADE LANDFALL.

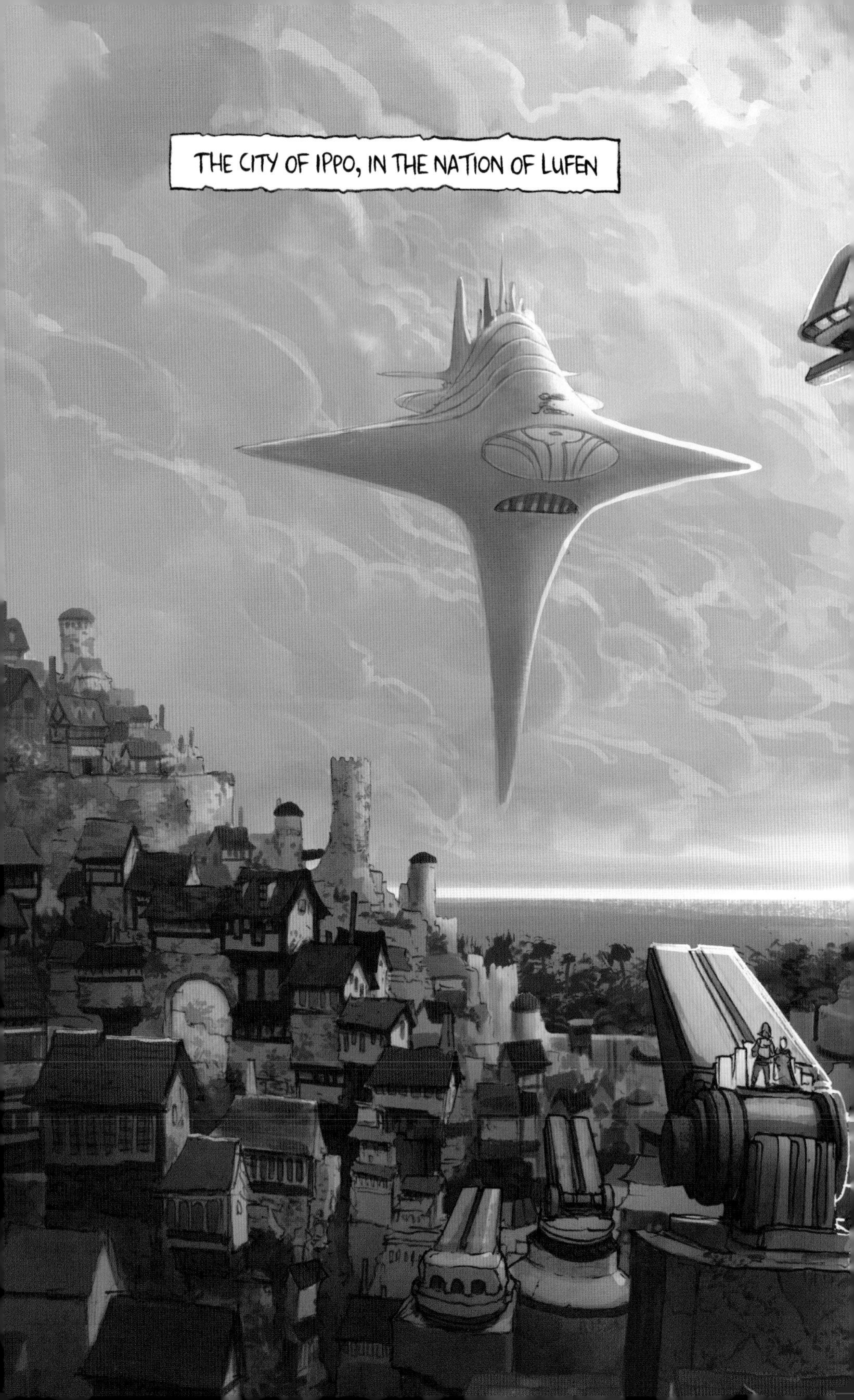
THE CITY OF IPPO, IN THE NATION OF LUFEN

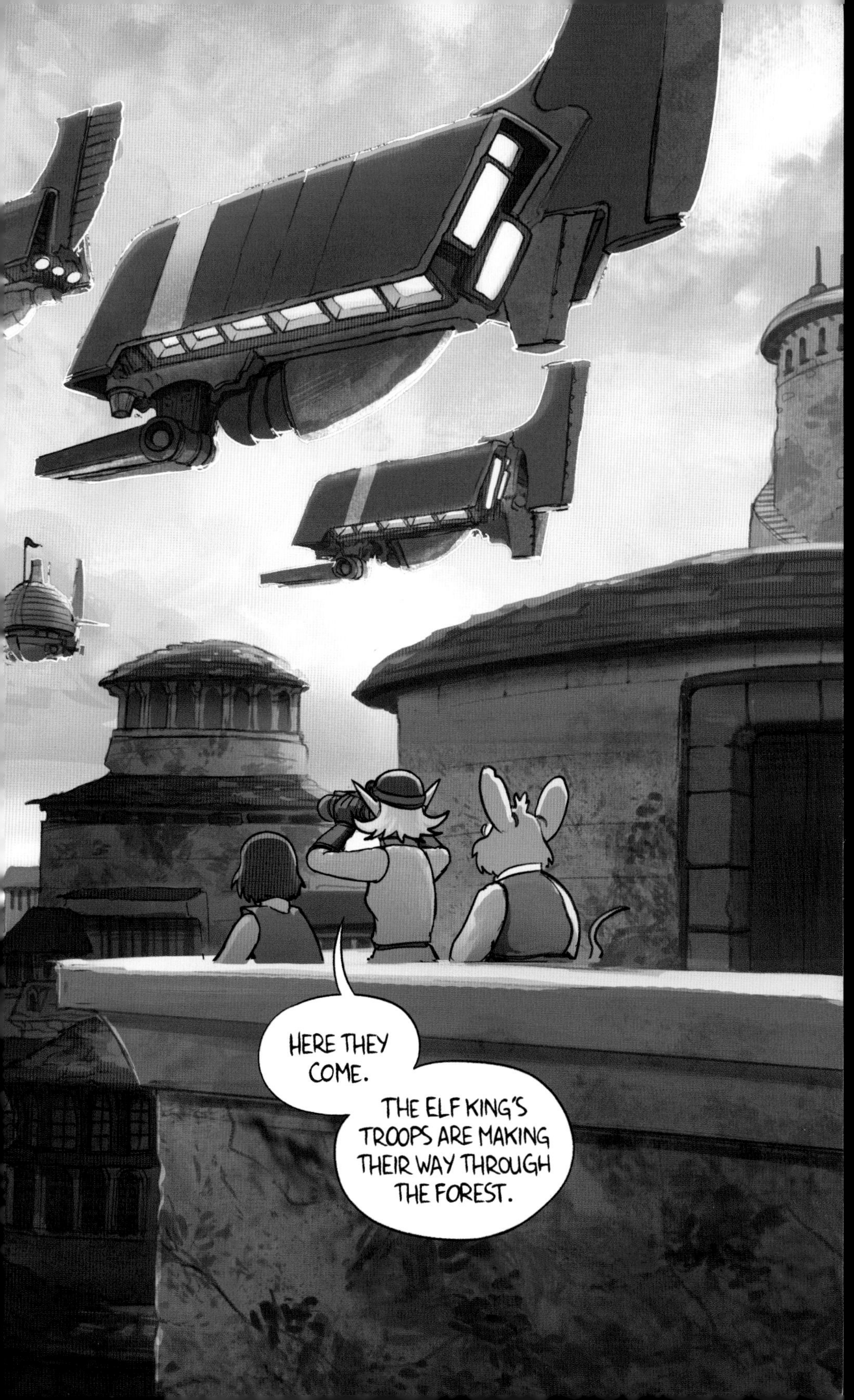
HERE THEY COME.
THE ELF KING'S TROOPS ARE MAKING THEIR WAY THROUGH THE FOREST.

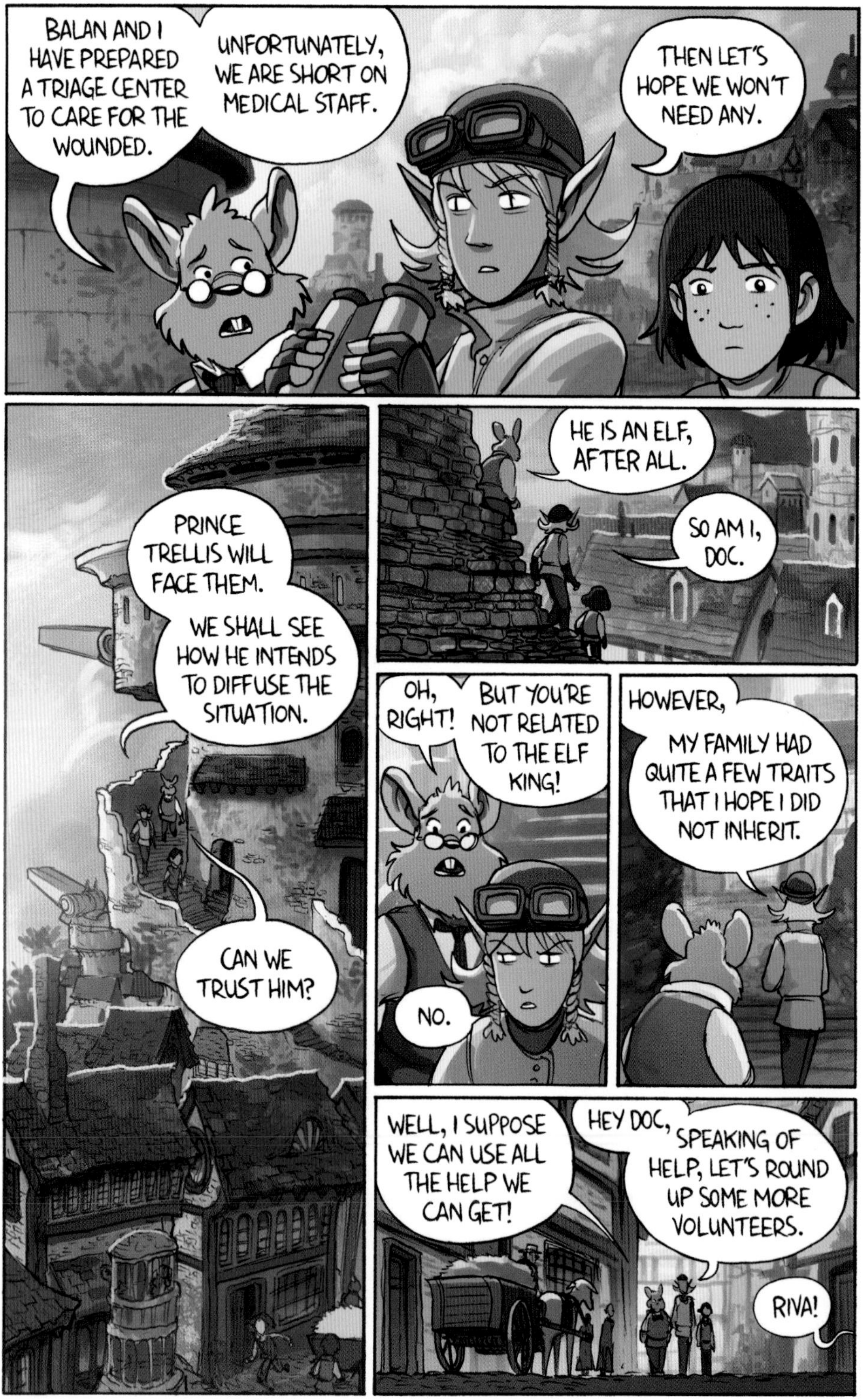
BALAN AND I HAVE PREPARED A TRIAGE CENTER TO CARE FOR THE WOUNDED.
UNFORTUNATELY, WE ARE SHORT ON MEDICAL STAFF.
THEN LET'S HOPE WE WON'T NEED ANY.
PRINCE TRELLIS WILL FACE THEM.
WE SHALL SEE HOW HE INTENDS TO DIFFUSE THE SITUATION.
CAN WE TRUST HIM?
HE IS AN ELF, AFTER ALL.
SO AM I, DOC.
OH, RIGHT!
BUT YOU'RE NOT RELATED TO THE ELF KING!
NO.
HOWEVER,
MY FAMILY HAD QUITE A FEW TRAITS THAT I HOPE I DID NOT INHERIT.
WELL, I SUPPOSE WE CAN USE ALL THE HELP WE CAN GET!
HEY DOC,
SPEAKING OF HELP, LET'S ROUND UP SOME MORE VOLUNTEERS.
RIVA!

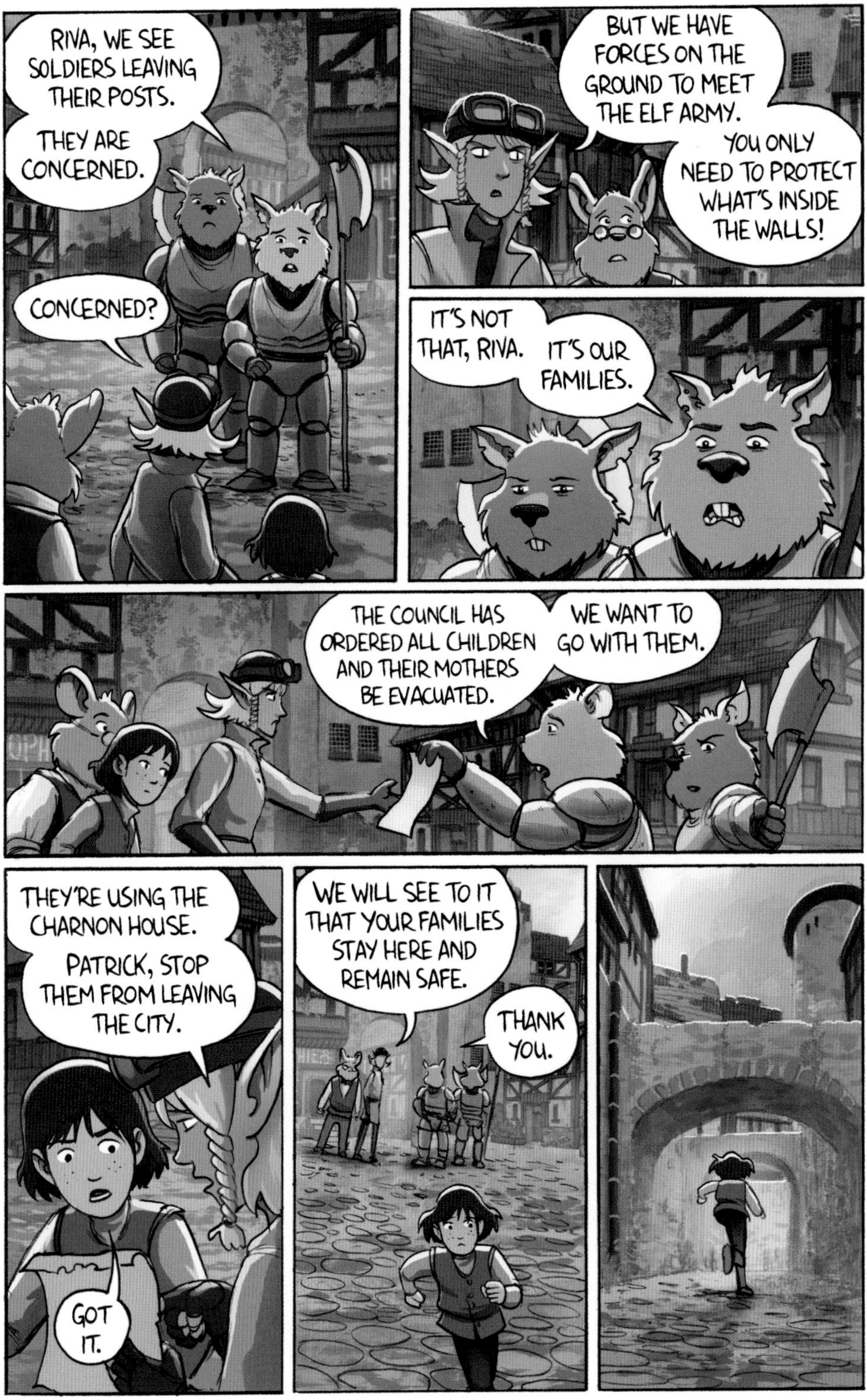
RIVA, WE SEE SOLDIERS LEAVING THEIR POSTS.
THEY ARE CONCERNED.
CONCERNED?
BUT WE HAVE FORCES ON THE GROUND TO MEET THE ELF ARMY.
YOU ONLY NEED TO PROTECT WHAT'S INSIDE THE WALLS!
IT'S NOT THAT, RIVA.
IT'S OUR FAMILIES.
THE COUNCIL HAS ORDERED ALL CHILDREN AND THEIR MOTHERS BE EVACUATED.
WE WANT TO GO WITH THEM.
THEY'RE USING THE CHARNON HOUSE.
PATRICK, STOP THEM FROM LEAVING THE CITY.
GOT IT.
WE WILL SEE TO IT THAT YOUR FAMILIES STAY HERE AND REMAIN SAFE.
THANK YOU.

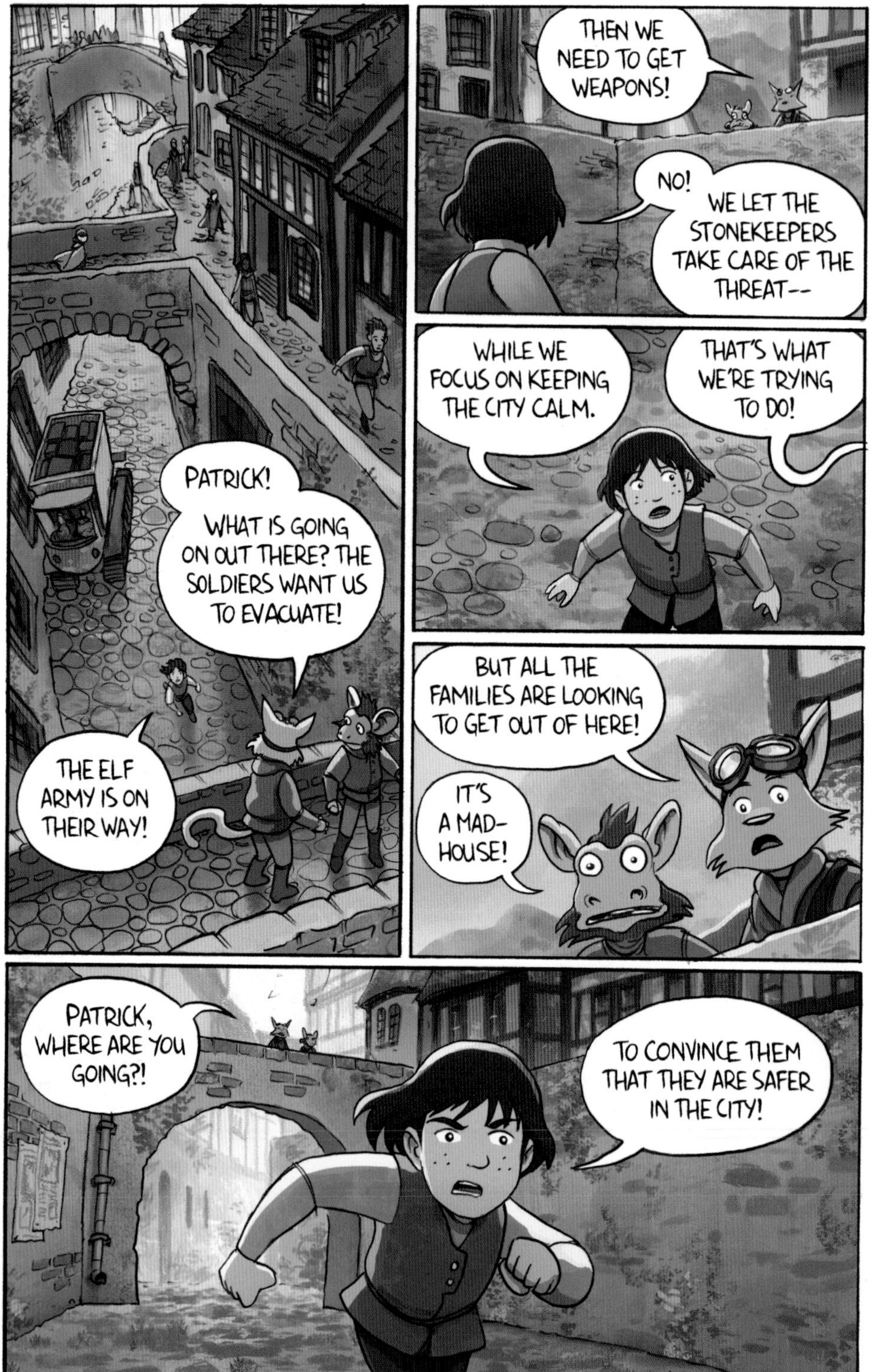
PATRICK!
WHAT IS GOING ON OUT THERE? THE SOLDIERS WANT US TO EVACUATE!
THE ELF ARMY IS ON THEIR WAY!
THEN WE NEED TO GET WEAPONS!
NO!
WE LET THE STONEKEEPERS TAKE CARE OF THE THREAT--
WHILE WE FOCUS ON KEEPING THE CITY CALM.
THAT'S WHAT WE'RE TRYING TO DO!
BUT ALL THE FAMILIES ARE LOOKING TO GET OUT OF HERE!
IT'S A MAD-HOUSE!
PATRICK, WHERE ARE YOU GOING?!
TO CONVINCE THEM THAT THEY ARE SAFER IN THE CITY!

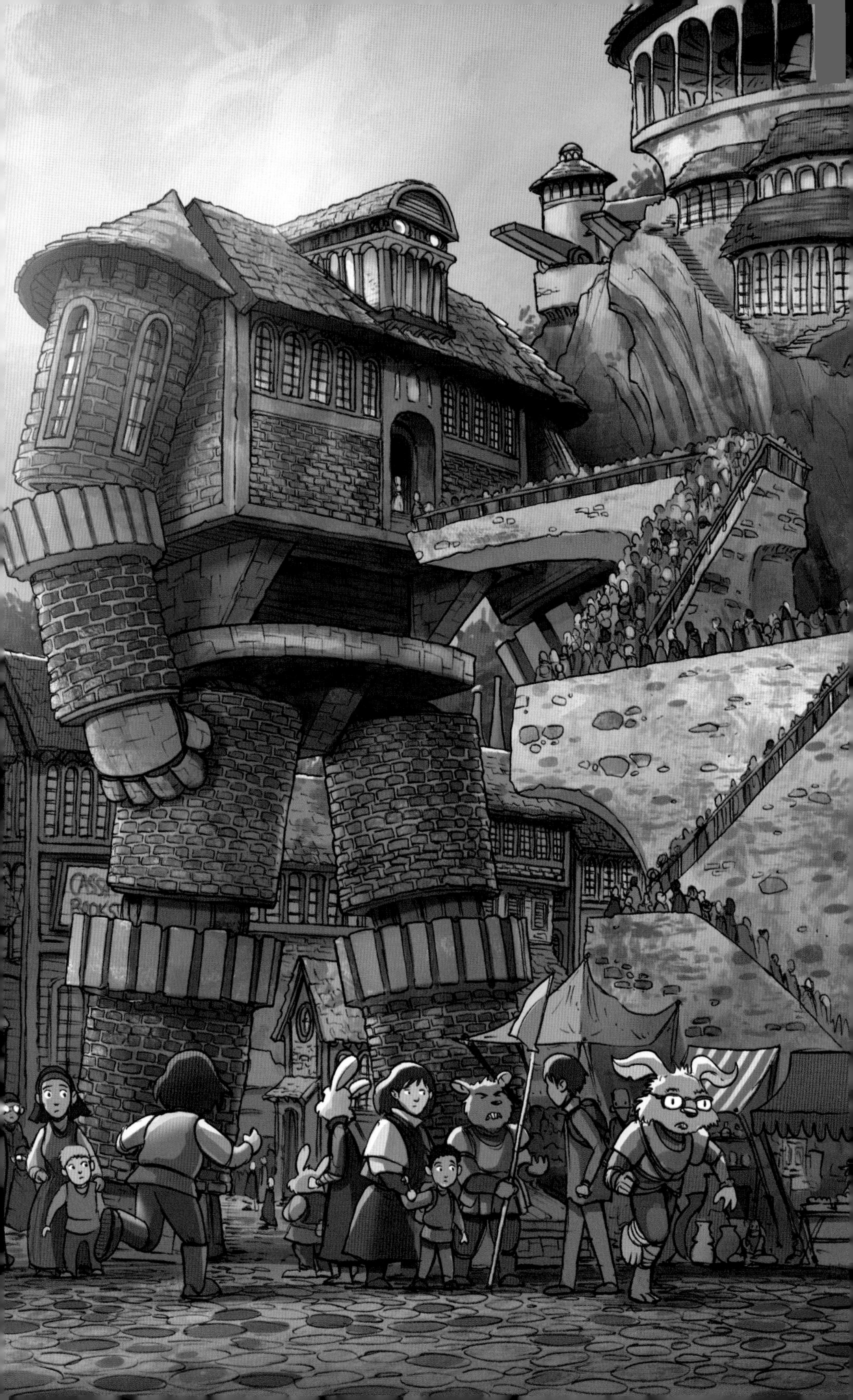

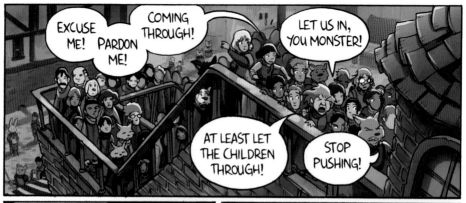

EXCUSE ME! PARDON ME!

COMING THROUGH!

LET US IN, YOU MONSTER!

AT LEAST LET THE CHILDREN THROUGH!

STOP PUSHING!

EVERYONE PLEASE STAY CALM!

THE HOUSE IS TOO FULL, BUT WE WILL FIND A WAY TO GET EVERYONE ON BOARD!

LIAR!

MORRIE! TELL EVERYONE TO RETURN TO THEIR HOMES!

WE'RE NOT GOING ANYWHERE, KID!

I WAS TOLD TO BRING ABOARD ALL WOMEN AND CHILDREN!

BUT THEY CAN'T ALL FIT IN THE CHARNON HOUSE, AND IT'S JUST CAUSING THEM TO PANIC.

EVERYONE NEEDS TO GO BACK TO THEIR HOMES.

EASIER SAID THAN DONE, PATRICK!

WE HAVE A LOT OF PASSENGERS ON BOARD!

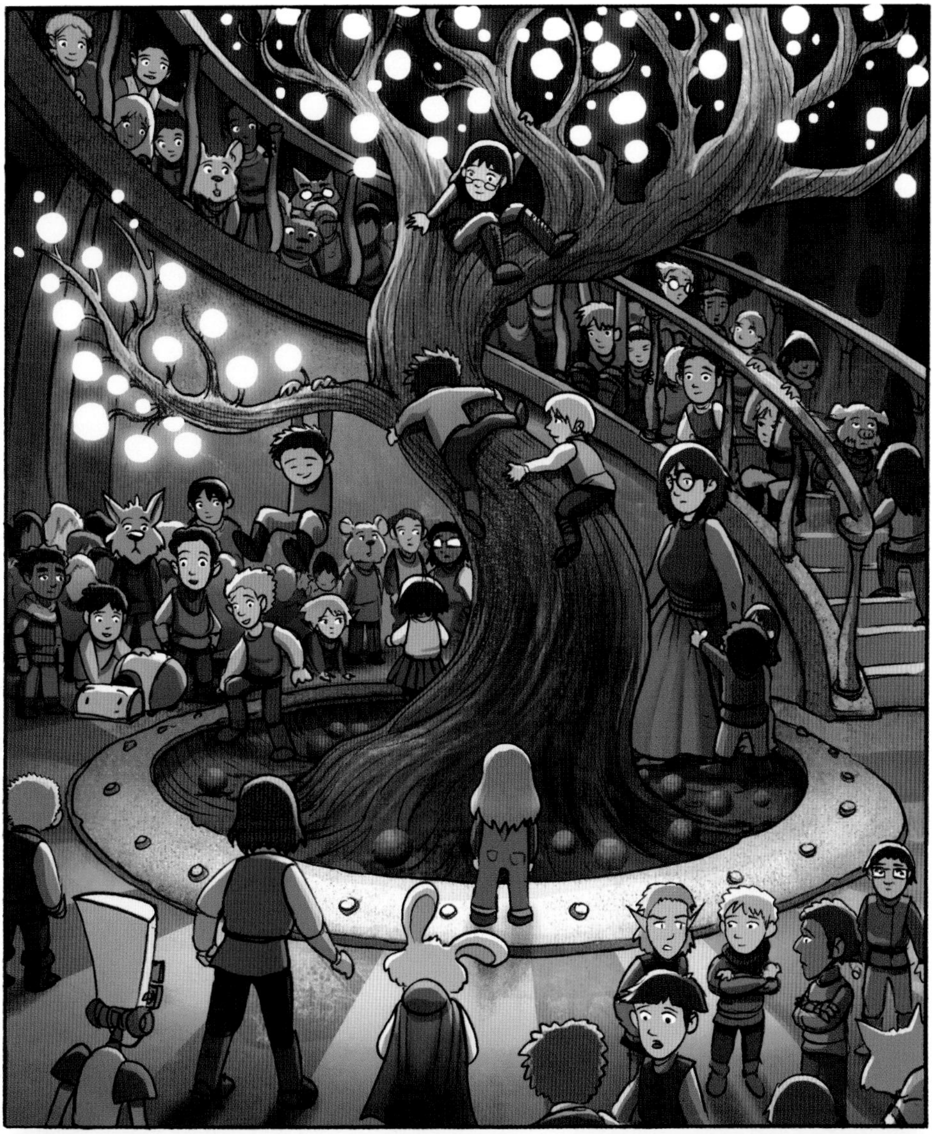

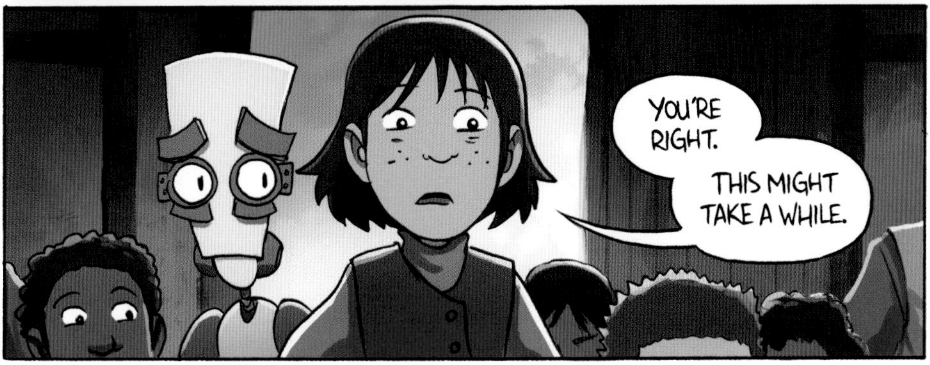
YOU'RE RIGHT.
THIS MIGHT TAKE A WHILE.

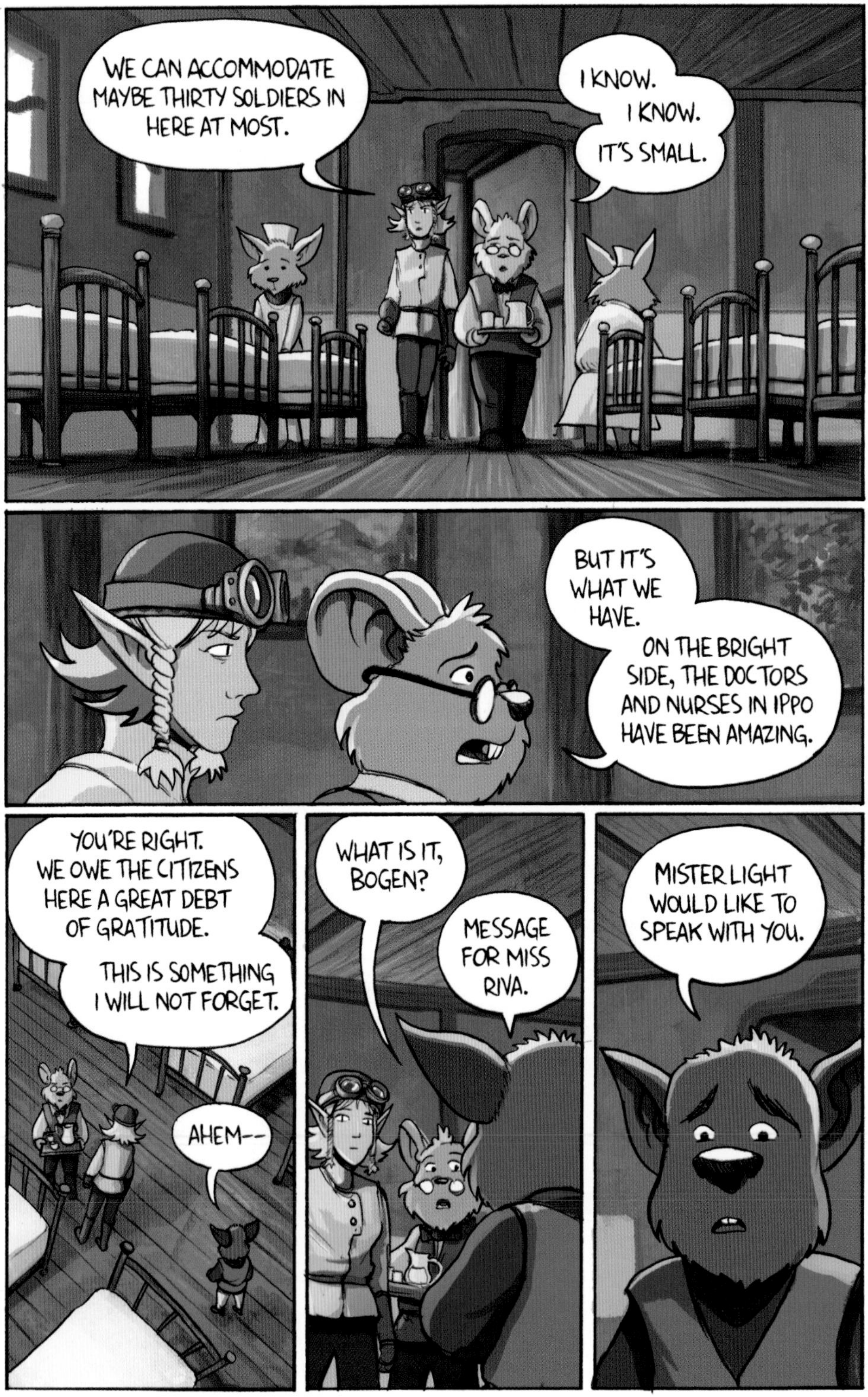
WE CAN ACCOMMODATE MAYBE THIRTY SOLDIERS IN HERE AT MOST.
I KNOW. I KNOW. IT'S SMALL.
BUT IT'S WHAT WE HAVE.
ON THE BRIGHT SIDE, THE DOCTORS AND NURSES IN IPPO HAVE BEEN AMAZING.
YOU'RE RIGHT. WE OWE THE CITIZENS HERE A GREAT DEBT OF GRATITUDE.
THIS IS SOMETHING I WILL NOT FORGET.
AHEM--
WHAT IS IT, BOGEN?
MESSAGE FOR MISS RIVA.
MISTER LIGHT WOULD LIKE TO SPEAK WITH YOU.

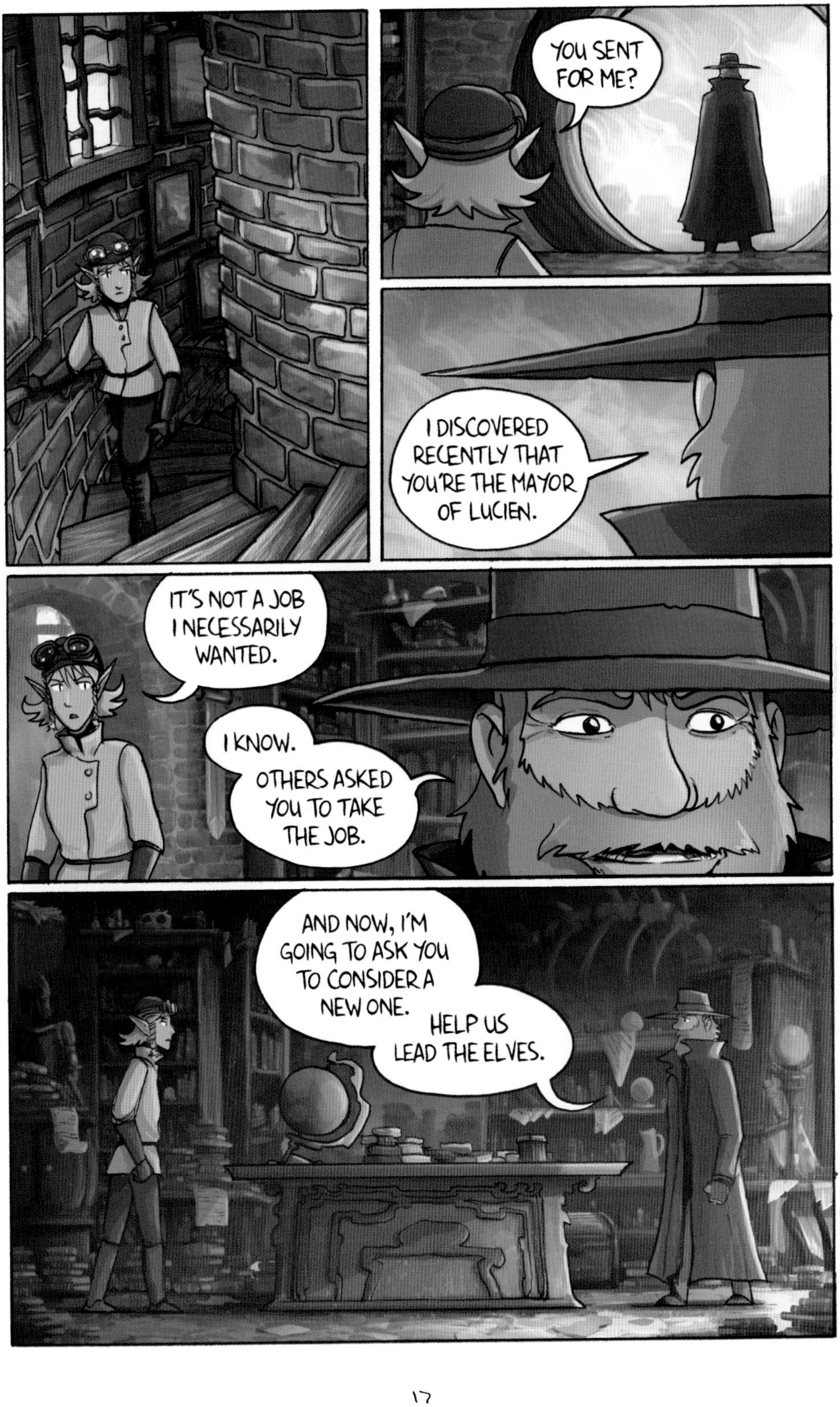
YOU SENT FOR ME?
I DISCOVERED RECENTLY THAT YOU'RE THE MAYOR OF LUCIEN.
IT'S NOT A JOB I NECESSARILY WANTED.
I KNOW.
OTHERS ASKED YOU TO TAKE THE JOB.
AND NOW, I'M GOING TO ASK YOU TO CONSIDER A NEW ONE.
HELP US LEAD THE ELVES.

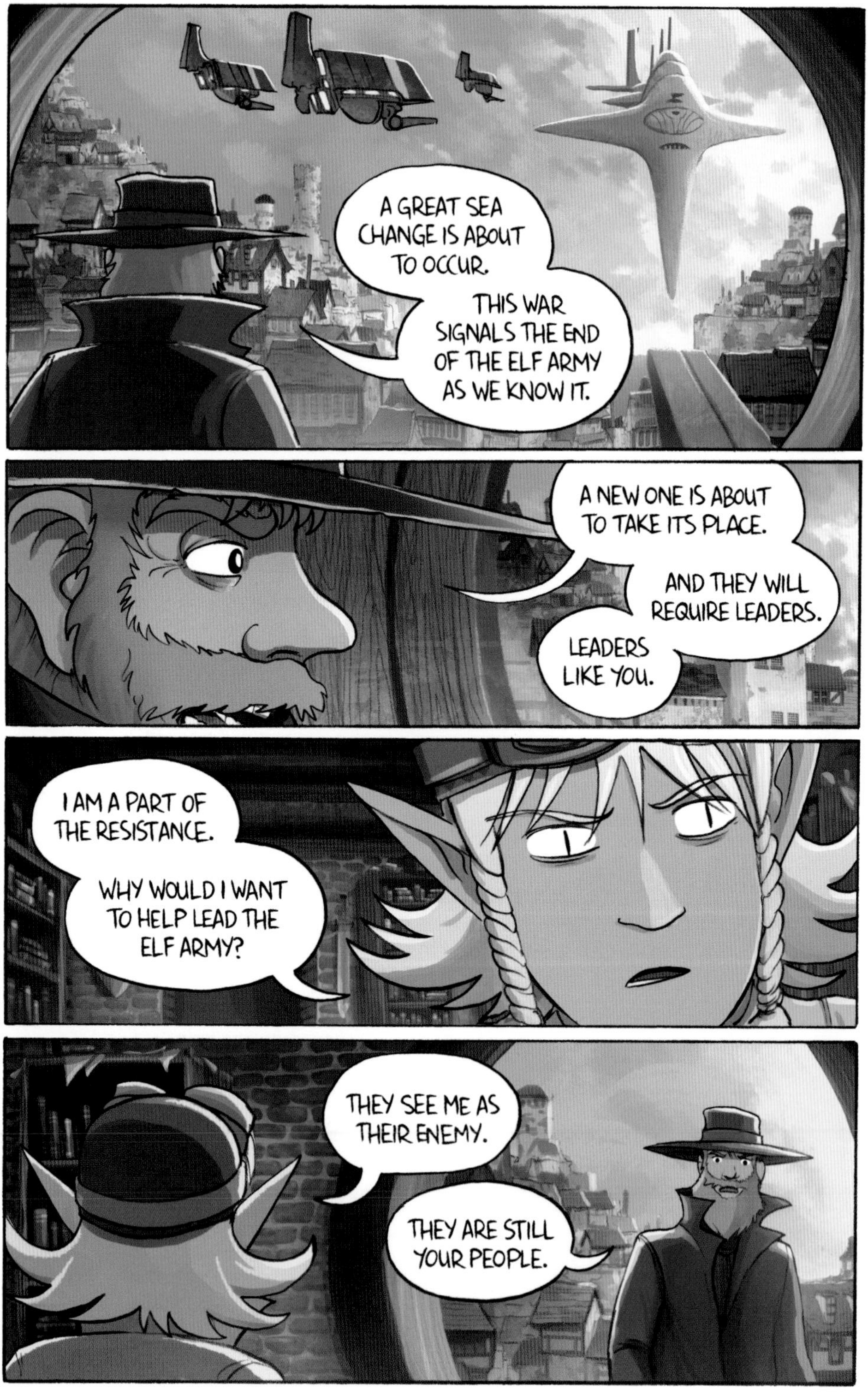
A GREAT SEA CHANGE IS ABOUT TO OCCUR.
THIS WAR SIGNALS THE END OF THE ELF ARMY AS WE KNOW IT.
A NEW ONE IS ABOUT TO TAKE ITS PLACE.
AND THEY WILL REQUIRE LEADERS.
LEADERS LIKE YOU.
I AM A PART OF THE RESISTANCE.
WHY WOULD I WANT TO HELP LEAD THE ELF ARMY?
THEY SEE ME AS THEIR ENEMY.
THEY ARE STILL YOUR PEOPLE.

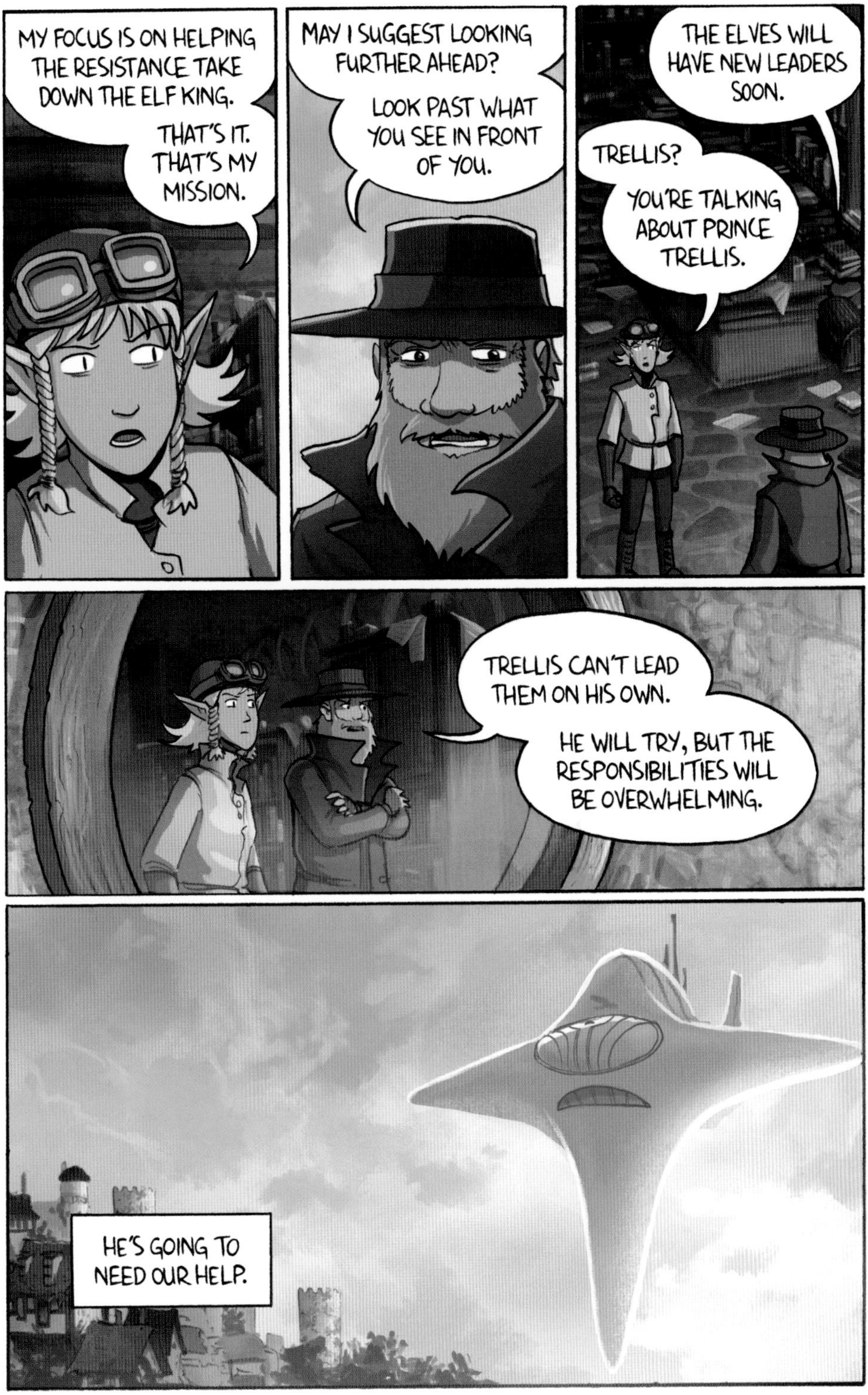
MY FOCUS IS ON HELPING THE RESISTANCE TAKE DOWN THE ELF KING.
THAT'S IT. THAT'S MY MISSION.
MAY I SUGGEST LOOKING FURTHER AHEAD?
LOOK PAST WHAT YOU SEE IN FRONT OF YOU.
THE ELVES WILL HAVE NEW LEADERS SOON.
TRELLIS?
YOU'RE TALKING ABOUT PRINCE TRELLIS.
TRELLIS CAN'T LEAD THEM ON HIS OWN.
HE WILL TRY, BUT THE RESPONSIBILITIES WILL BE OVERWHELMING.
HE'S GOING TO NEED OUR HELP.

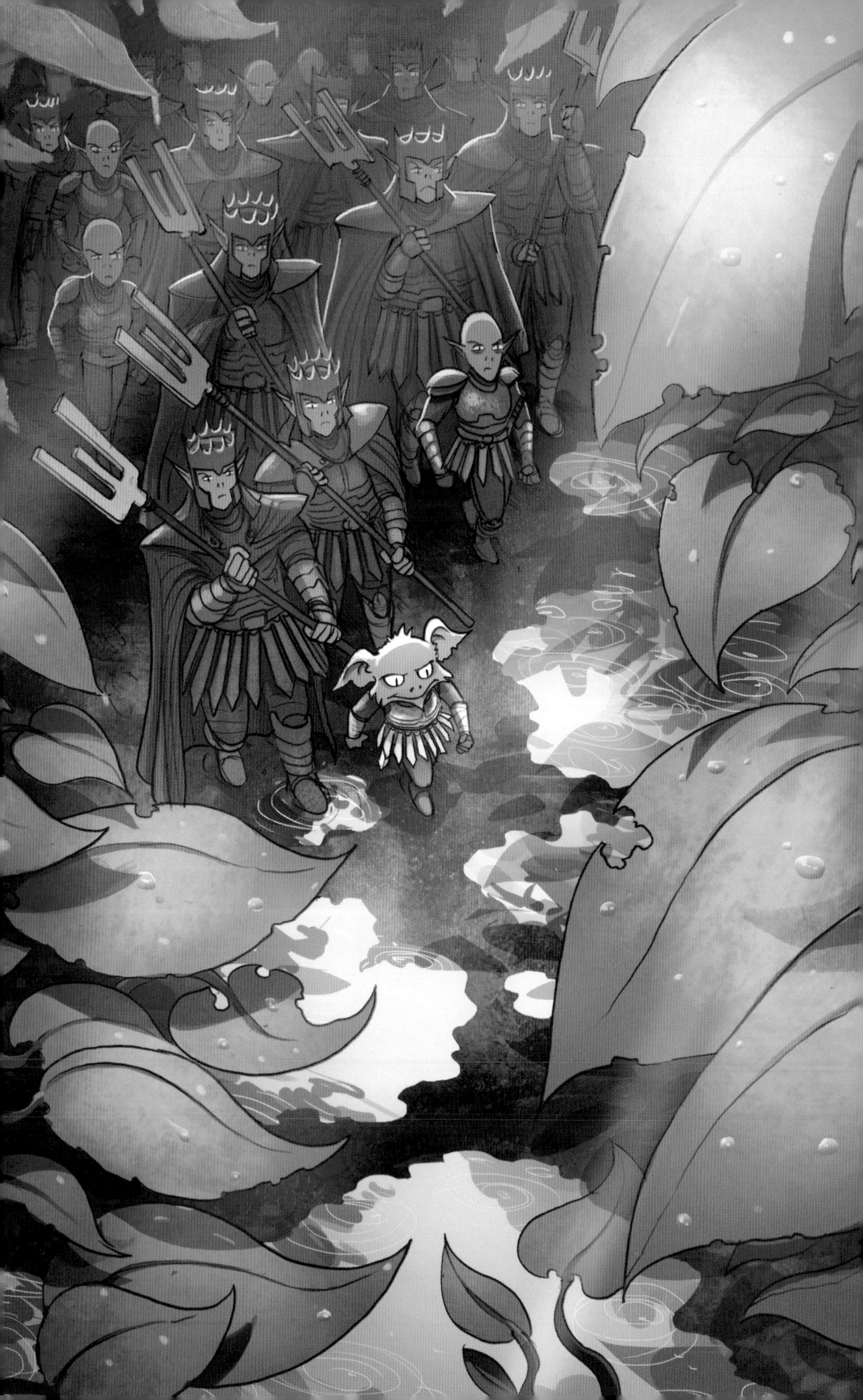

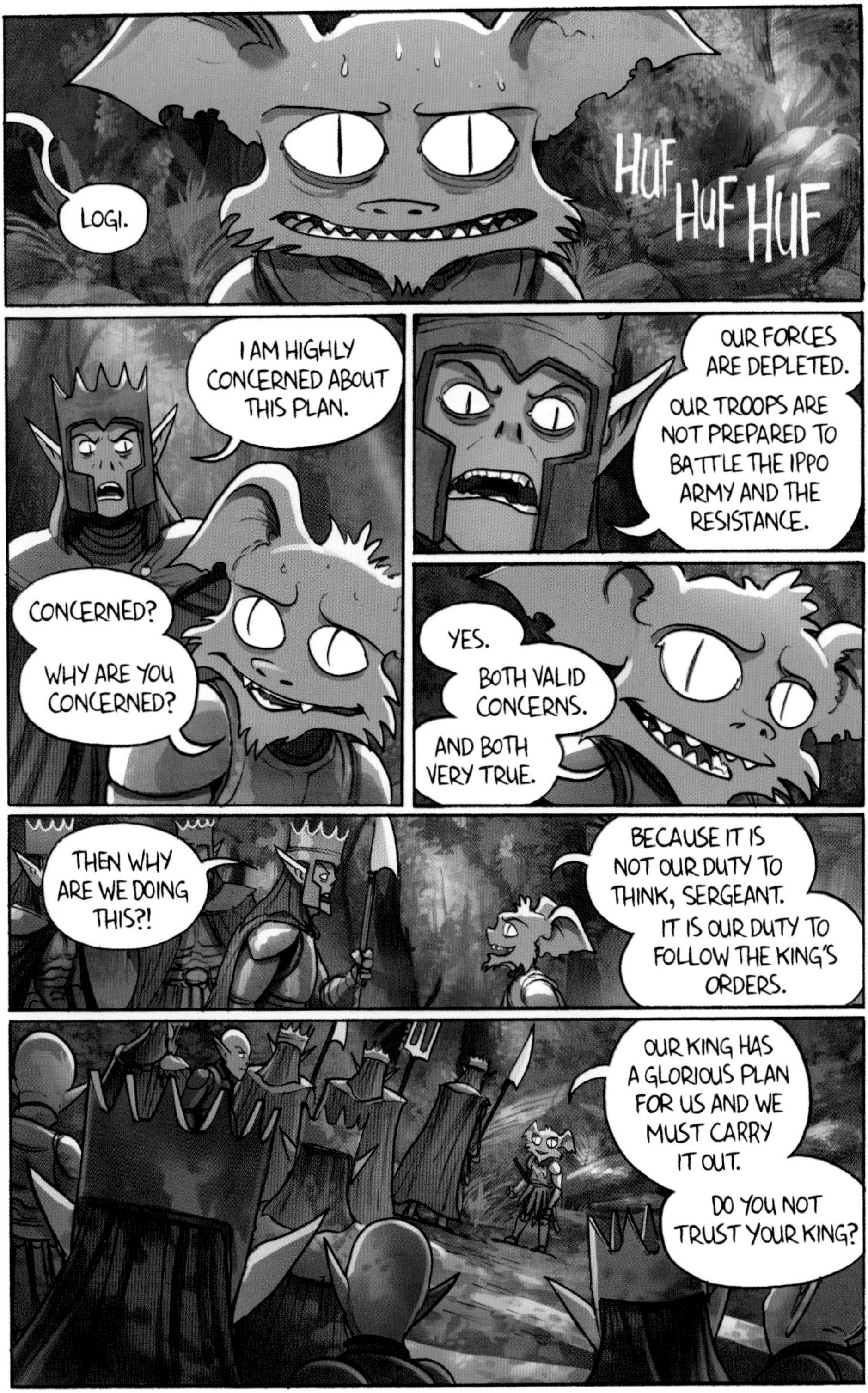
LOGI.
HUF HUF HUF
I AM HIGHLY CONCERNED ABOUT THIS PLAN.
OUR FORCES ARE DEPLETED.
OUR TROOPS ARE NOT PREPARED TO BATTLE THE IPPO ARMY AND THE RESISTANCE.
CONCERNED?
WHY ARE YOU CONCERNED?
YES.
BOTH VALID CONCERNS.
AND BOTH VERY TRUE.
THEN WHY ARE WE DOING THIS?!
BECAUSE IT IS NOT OUR DUTY TO THINK, SERGEANT.
IT IS OUR DUTY TO FOLLOW THE KING'S ORDERS.
OUR KING HAS A GLORIOUS PLAN FOR US AND WE MUST CARRY IT OUT.
DO YOU NOT TRUST YOUR KING?

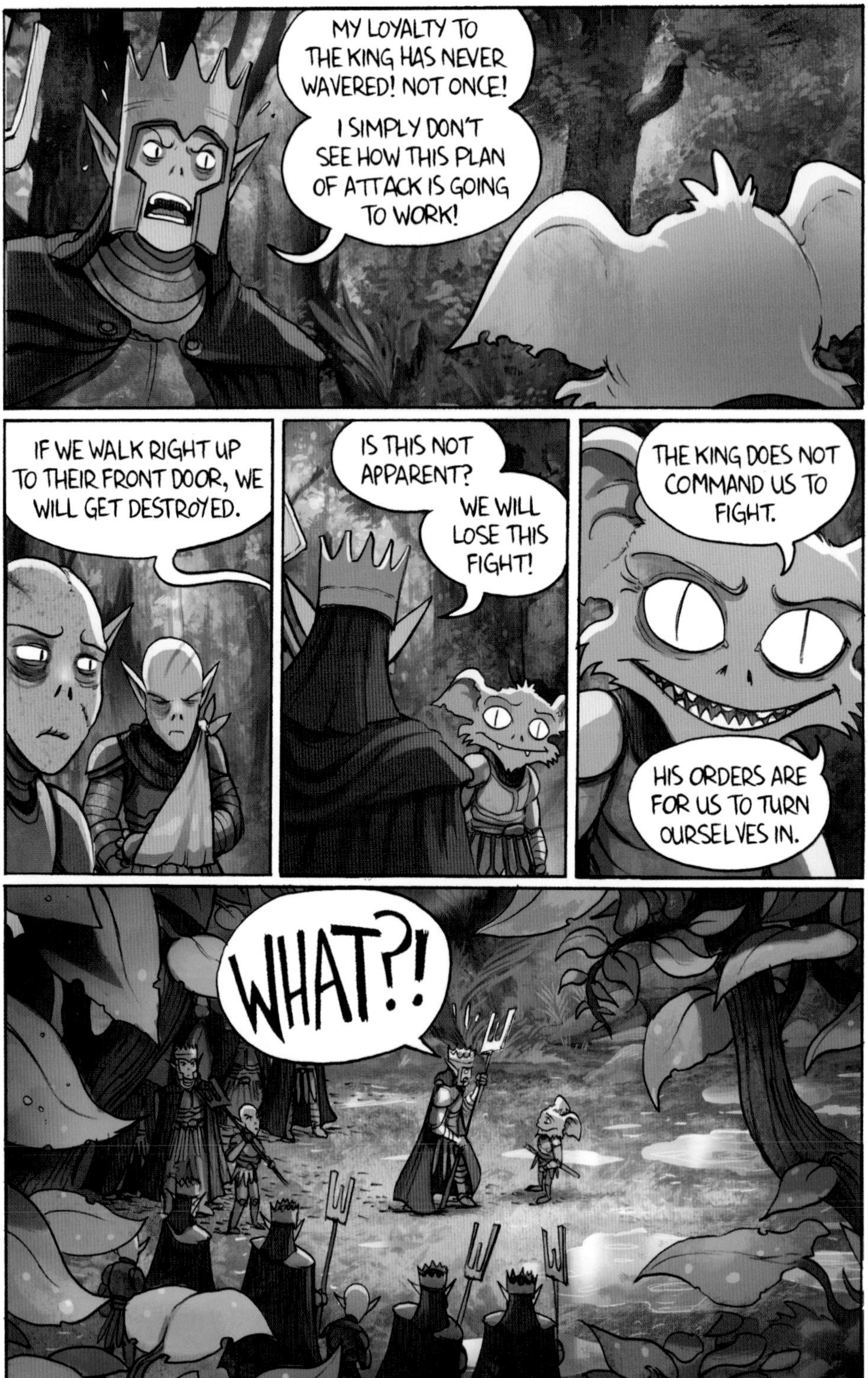
MY LOYALTY TO THE KING HAS NEVER WAVERED! NOT ONCE!
I SIMPLY DON'T SEE HOW THIS PLAN OF ATTACK IS GOING TO WORK!
IF WE WALK RIGHT UP TO THEIR FRONT DOOR, WE WILL GET DESTROYED.
IS THIS NOT APPARENT?
WE WILL LOSE THIS FIGHT!
THE KING DOES NOT COMMAND US TO FIGHT.
HIS ORDERS ARE FOR US TO TURN OURSELVES IN.
WHAT?!

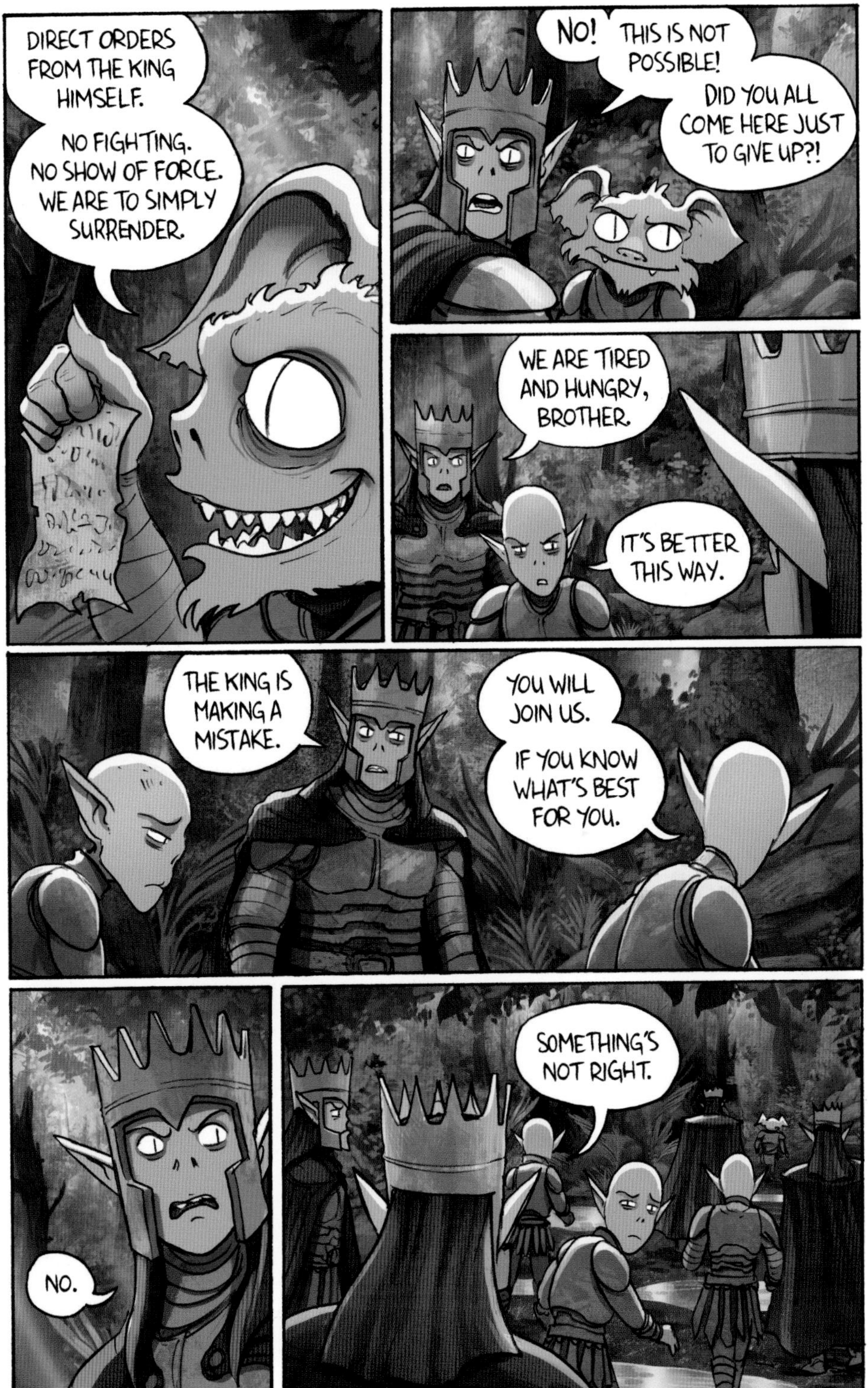
DIRECT ORDERS FROM THE KING HIMSELF.
NO FIGHTING. NO SHOW OF FORCE. WE ARE TO SIMPLY SURRENDER.
NO!
THIS IS NOT POSSIBLE!
DID YOU ALL COME HERE JUST TO GIVE UP?!
WE ARE TIRED AND HUNGRY, BROTHER.
IT'S BETTER THIS WAY.
THE KING IS MAKING A MISTAKE.
YOU WILL JOIN US.
IF YOU KNOW WHAT'S BEST FOR YOU.
NO.
SOMETHING'S NOT RIGHT.

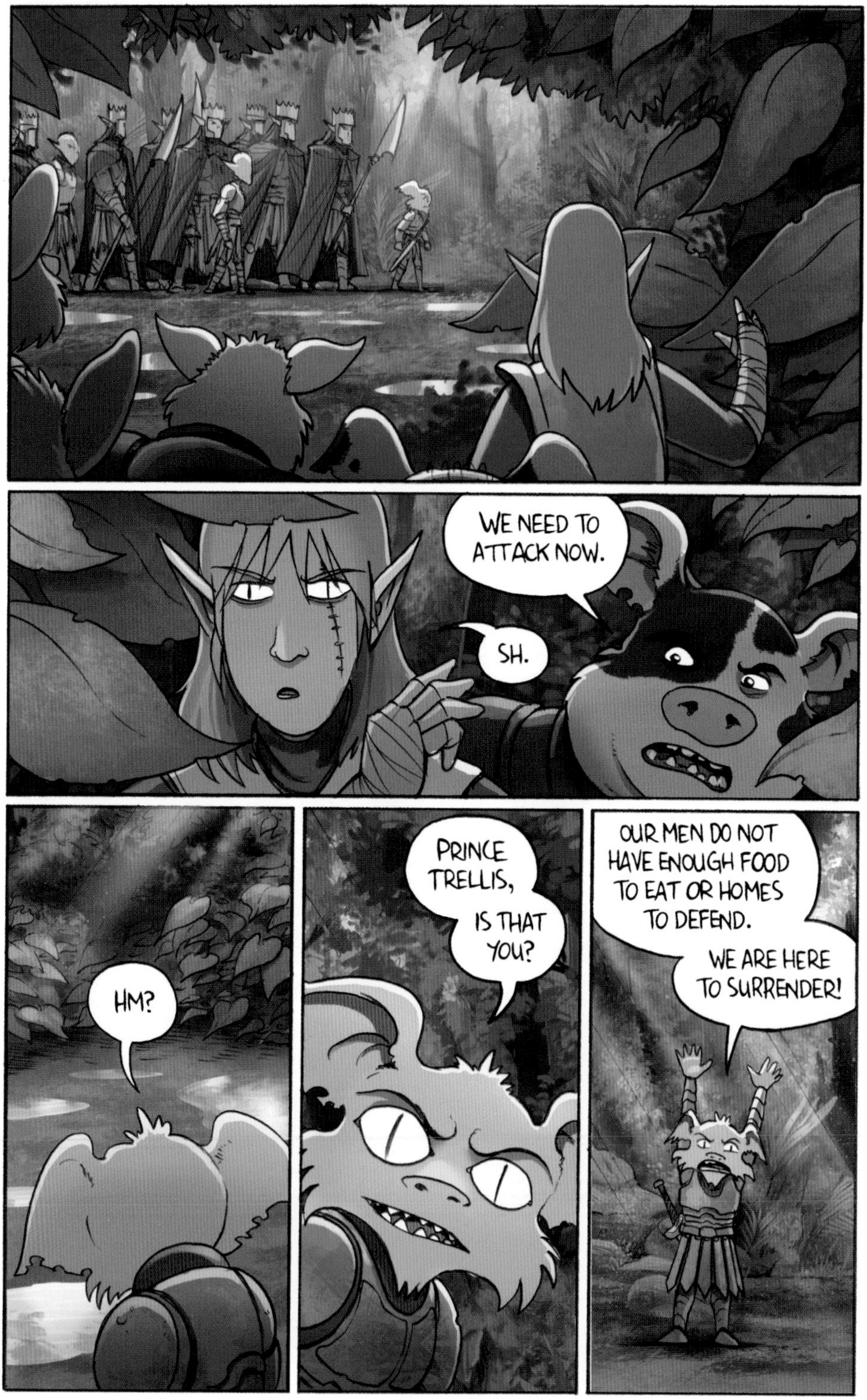
WE NEED TO ATTACK NOW.
SH.
HM?
PRINCE TRELLIS,
IS THAT YOU?
OUR MEN DO NOT HAVE ENOUGH FOOD TO EAT OR HOMES TO DEFEND.
WE ARE HERE TO SURRENDER!

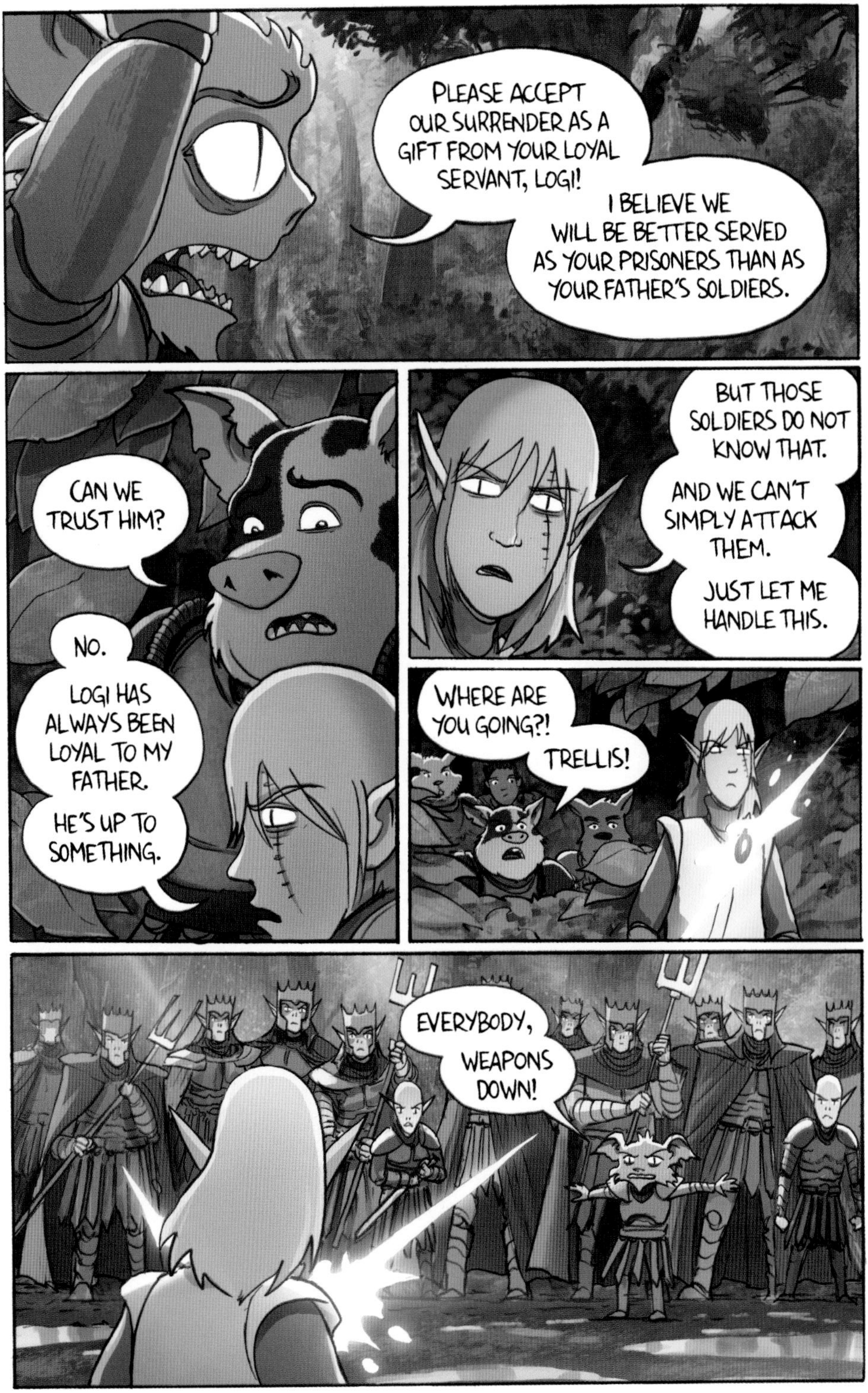
PLEASE ACCEPT OUR SURRENDER AS A GIFT FROM YOUR LOYAL SERVANT, LOGI!
I BELIEVE WE WILL BE BETTER SERVED AS YOUR PRISONERS THAN AS YOUR FATHER'S SOLDIERS.
CAN WE TRUST HIM?
NO.
LOGI HAS ALWAYS BEEN LOYAL TO MY FATHER.
HE'S UP TO SOMETHING.
BUT THOSE SOLDIERS DO NOT KNOW THAT.
AND WE CAN'T SIMPLY ATTACK THEM.
JUST LET ME HANDLE THIS.
WHERE ARE YOU GOING?!
TRELLIS!
EVERYBODY, WEAPONS DOWN!

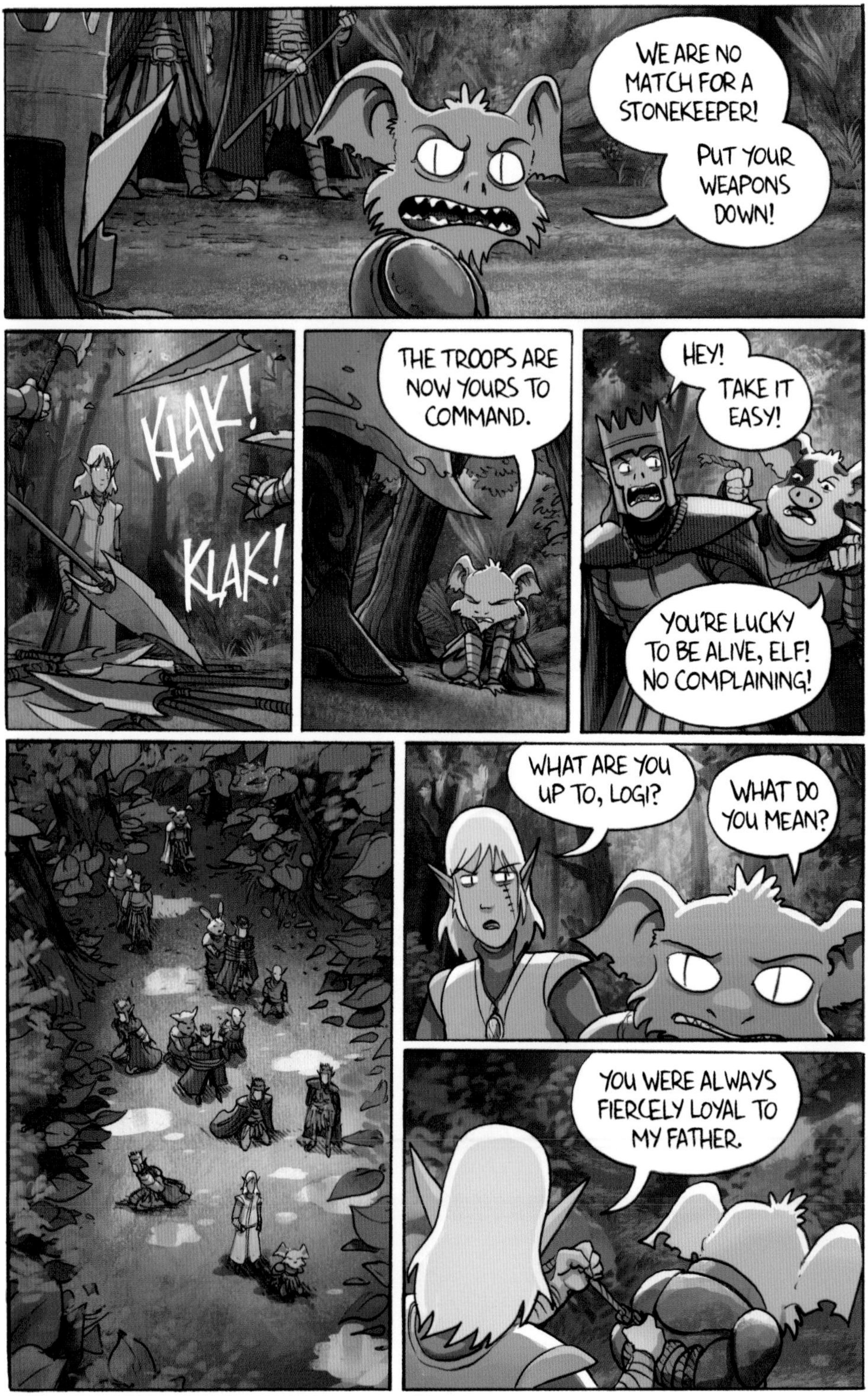
WE ARE NO MATCH FOR A STONEKEEPER!
PUT YOUR WEAPONS DOWN!
KLAK!
KLAK!
THE TROOPS ARE NOW YOURS TO COMMAND.
HEY!
TAKE IT EASY!
YOU'RE LUCKY TO BE ALIVE, ELF! NO COMPLAINING!
WHAT ARE YOU UP TO, LOGI?
WHAT DO YOU MEAN?
YOU WERE ALWAYS FIERCELY LOYAL TO MY FATHER.

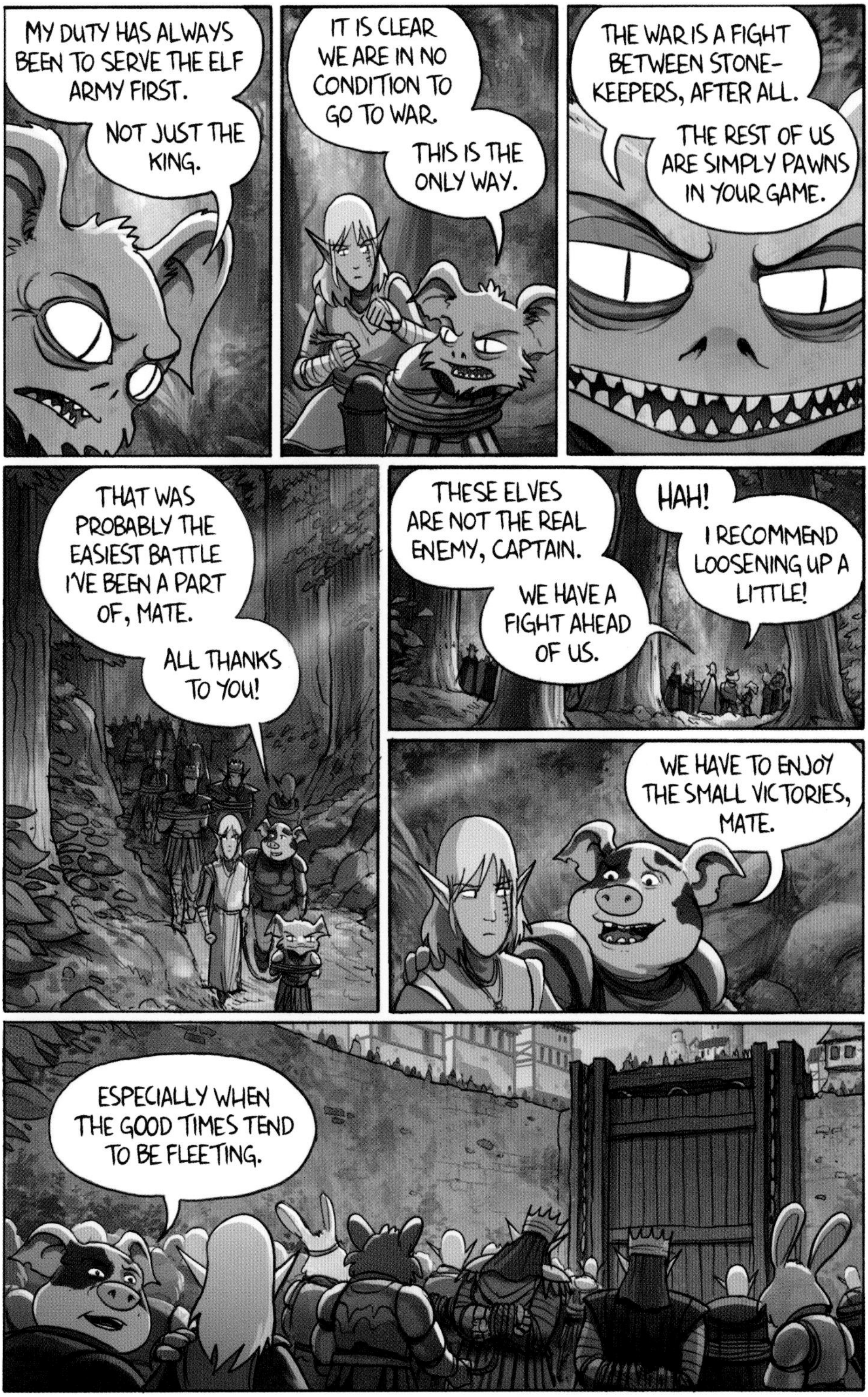
MY DUTY HAS ALWAYS BEEN TO SERVE THE ELF ARMY FIRST.
NOT JUST THE KING.
IT IS CLEAR WE ARE IN NO CONDITION TO GO TO WAR.
THIS IS THE ONLY WAY.
THE WAR IS A FIGHT BETWEEN STONE-KEEPERS, AFTER ALL.
THE REST OF US ARE SIMPLY PAWNS IN YOUR GAME.
THAT WAS PROBABLY THE EASIEST BATTLE I'VE BEEN A PART OF, MATE.
ALL THANKS TO YOU!
THESE ELVES ARE NOT THE REAL ENEMY, CAPTAIN.
WE HAVE A FIGHT AHEAD OF US.
HAH!
I RECOMMEND LOOSENING UP A LITTLE!
WE HAVE TO ENJOY THE SMALL VICTORIES, MATE.
ESPECIALLY WHEN THE GOOD TIMES TEND TO BE FLEETING.

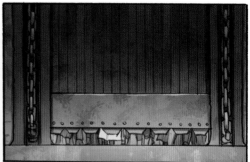

THEY'RE BACK!

OPEN THE GATES!

THE ELF ARMY HAS SURRENDERED!

HM.

SURRENDERED?

THE ELF PRINCE REALLY DID IT.

HE SAVED US!

LET THE WARDEN KNOW TO PREPARE FOR A LARGE INFLUX OF PRISONERS.

YES, COMMANDER.

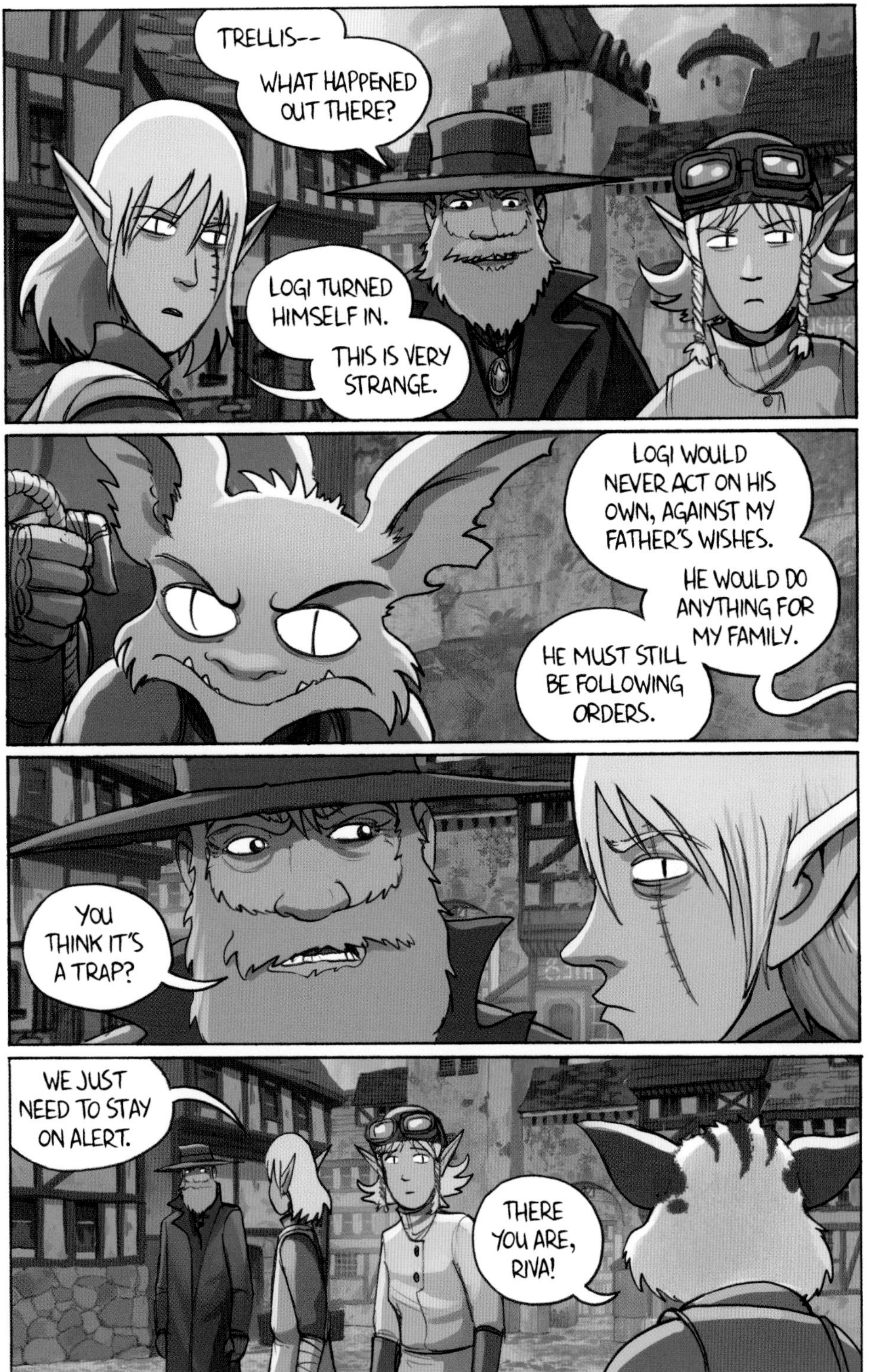
TRELLIS--
WHAT HAPPENED OUT THERE?
LOGI TURNED HIMSELF IN.
THIS IS VERY STRANGE.
LOGI WOULD NEVER ACT ON HIS OWN, AGAINST MY FATHER'S WISHES.
HE WOULD DO ANYTHING FOR MY FAMILY.
HE MUST STILL BE FOLLOWING ORDERS.
YOU THINK IT'S A TRAP?
WE JUST NEED TO STAY ON ALERT.
THERE YOU ARE, RIVA!

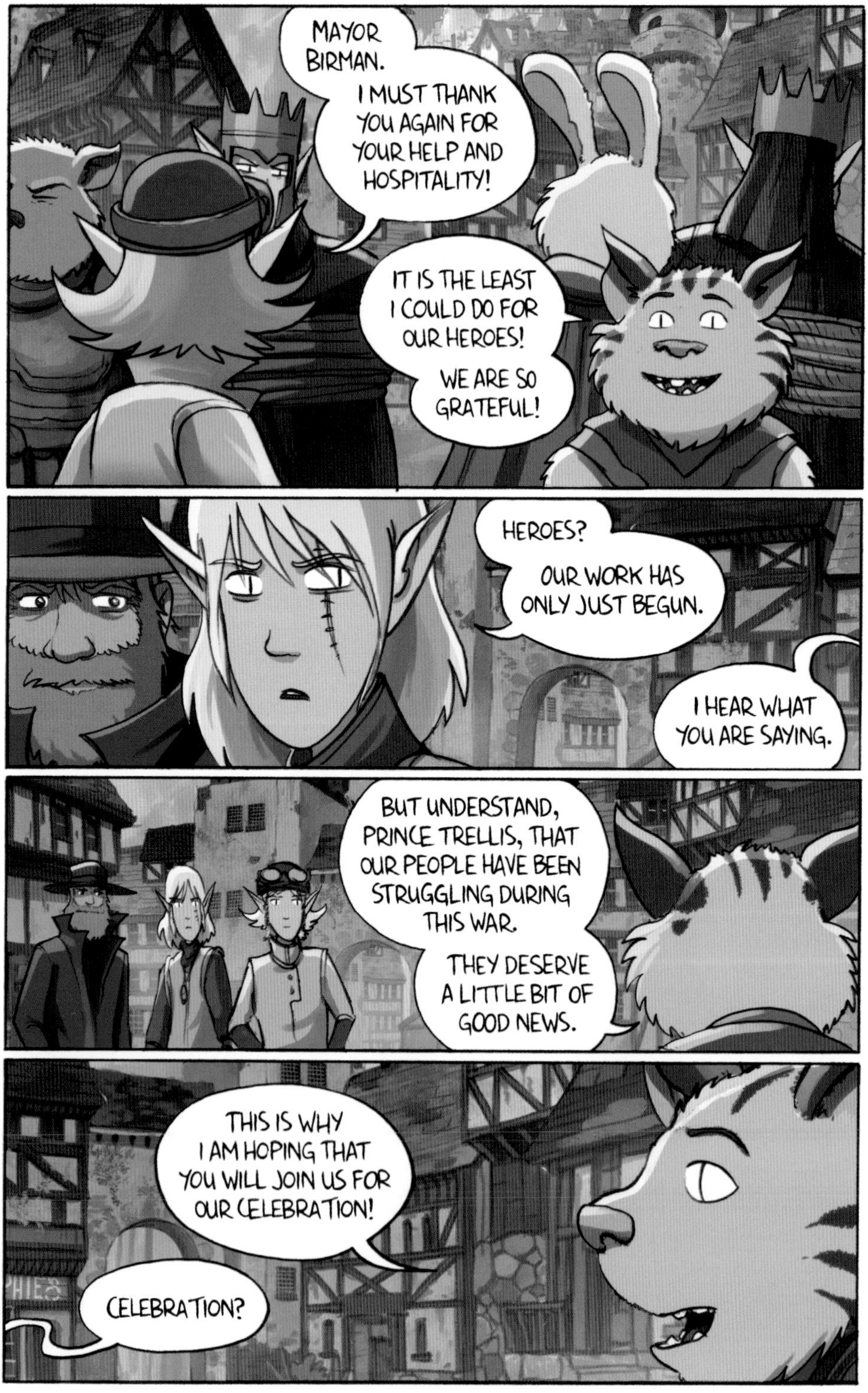
MAYOR BIRMAN.
I MUST THANK YOU AGAIN FOR YOUR HELP AND HOSPITALITY!
IT IS THE LEAST I COULD DO FOR OUR HEROES!
WE ARE SO GRATEFUL!
HEROES?
OUR WORK HAS ONLY JUST BEGUN.
I HEAR WHAT YOU ARE SAYING.
BUT UNDERSTAND, PRINCE TRELLIS, THAT OUR PEOPLE HAVE BEEN STRUGGLING DURING THIS WAR.
THEY DESERVE A LITTLE BIT OF GOOD NEWS.
THIS IS WHY I AM HOPING THAT YOU WILL JOIN US FOR OUR CELEBRATION!
CELEBRATION?

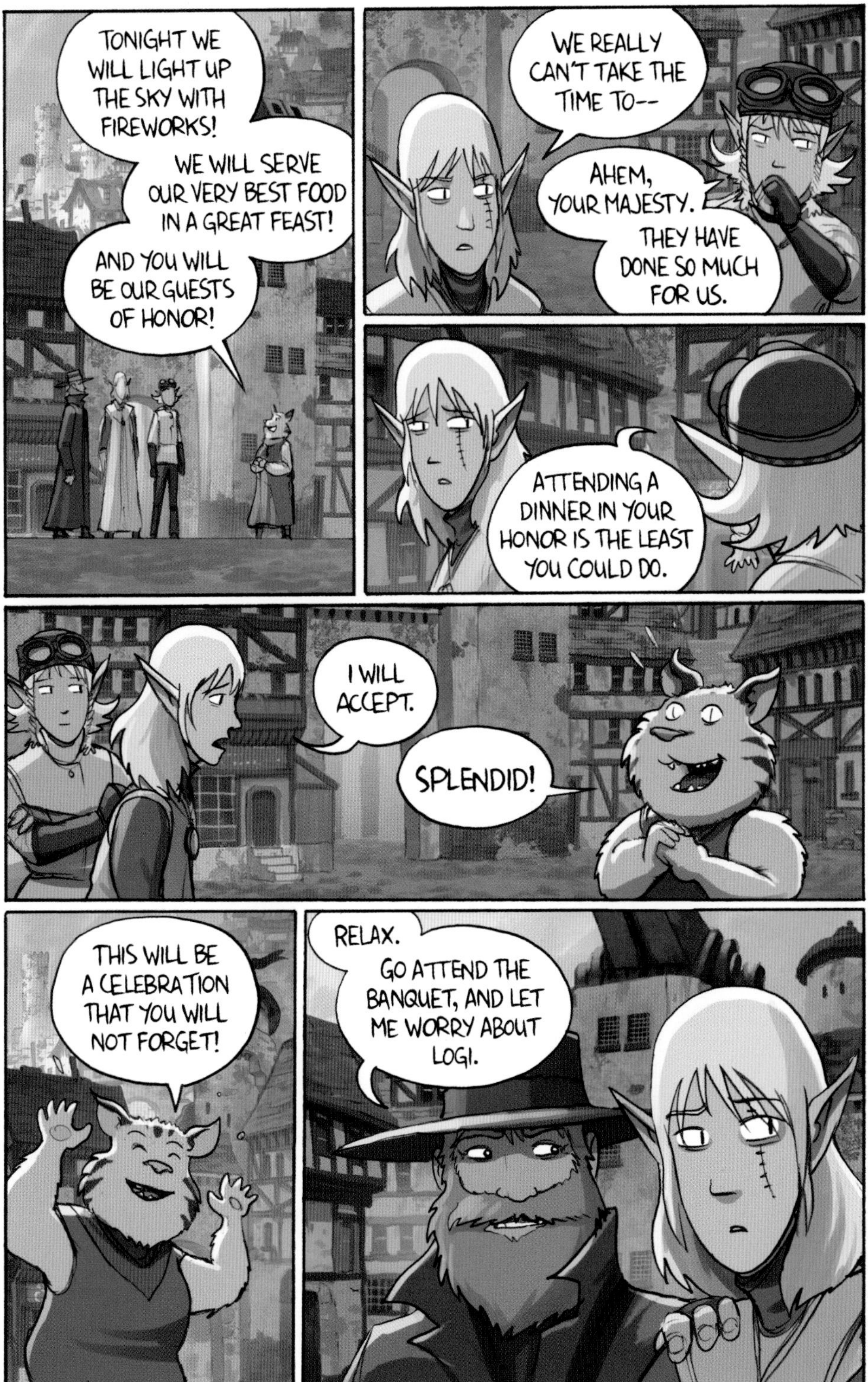
TONIGHT WE WILL LIGHT UP THE SKY WITH FIREWORKS!
WE WILL SERVE OUR VERY BEST FOOD IN A GREAT FEAST!
AND YOU WILL BE OUR GUESTS OF HONOR!
WE REALLY CAN'T TAKE THE TIME TO--
AHEM, YOUR MAJESTY.
THEY HAVE DONE SO MUCH FOR US.
ATTENDING A DINNER IN YOUR HONOR IS THE LEAST YOU COULD DO.
I WILL ACCEPT.
SPLENDID!
THIS WILL BE A CELEBRATION THAT YOU WILL NOT FORGET!
RELAX.
GO ATTEND THE BANQUET, AND LET ME WORRY ABOUT LOGI.

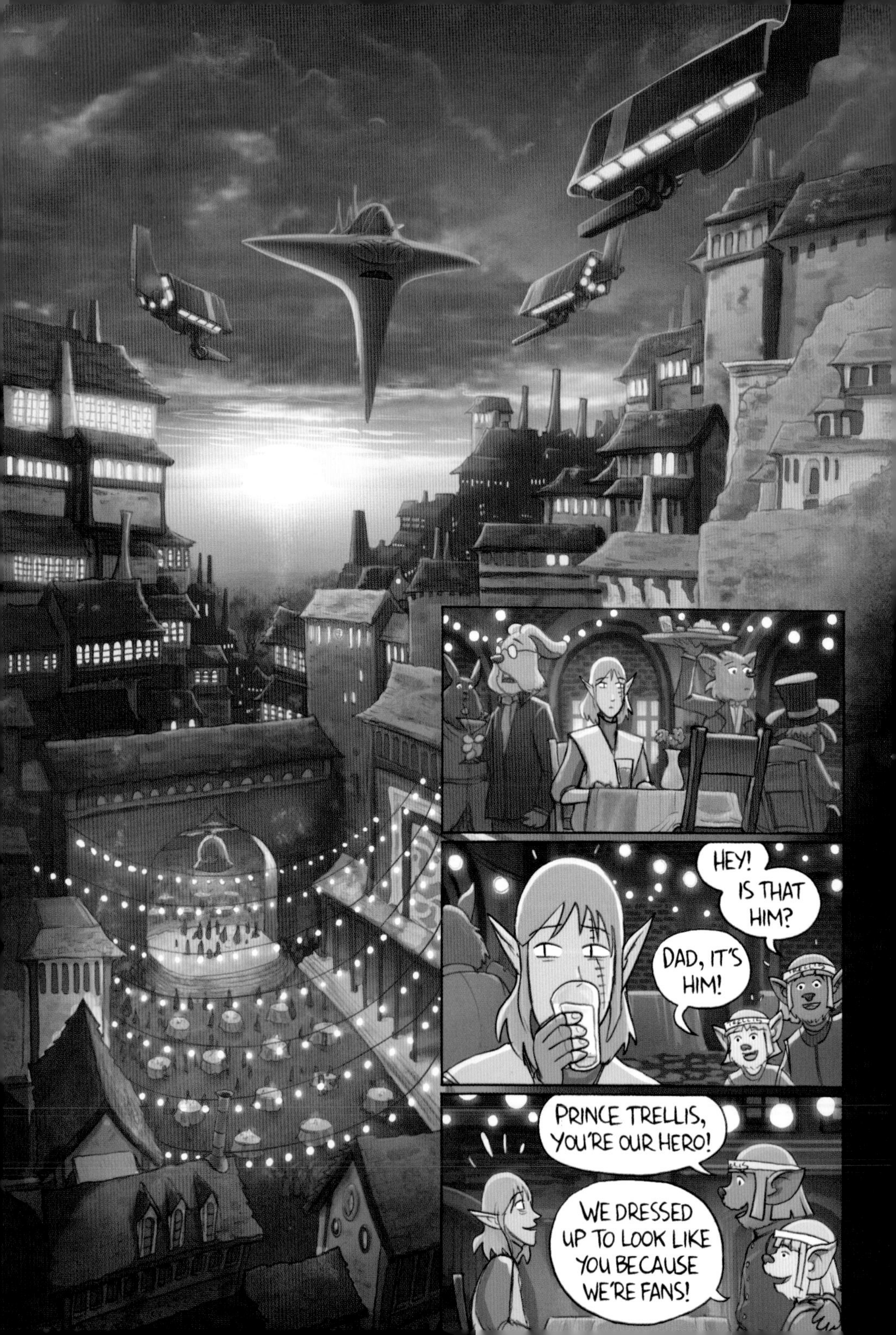
HEY!
IS THAT HIM?
DAD, IT'S HIM!
PRINCE TRELLIS, YOU'RE OUR HERO!
WE DRESSED UP TO LOOK LIKE YOU BECAUSE WE'RE FANS!

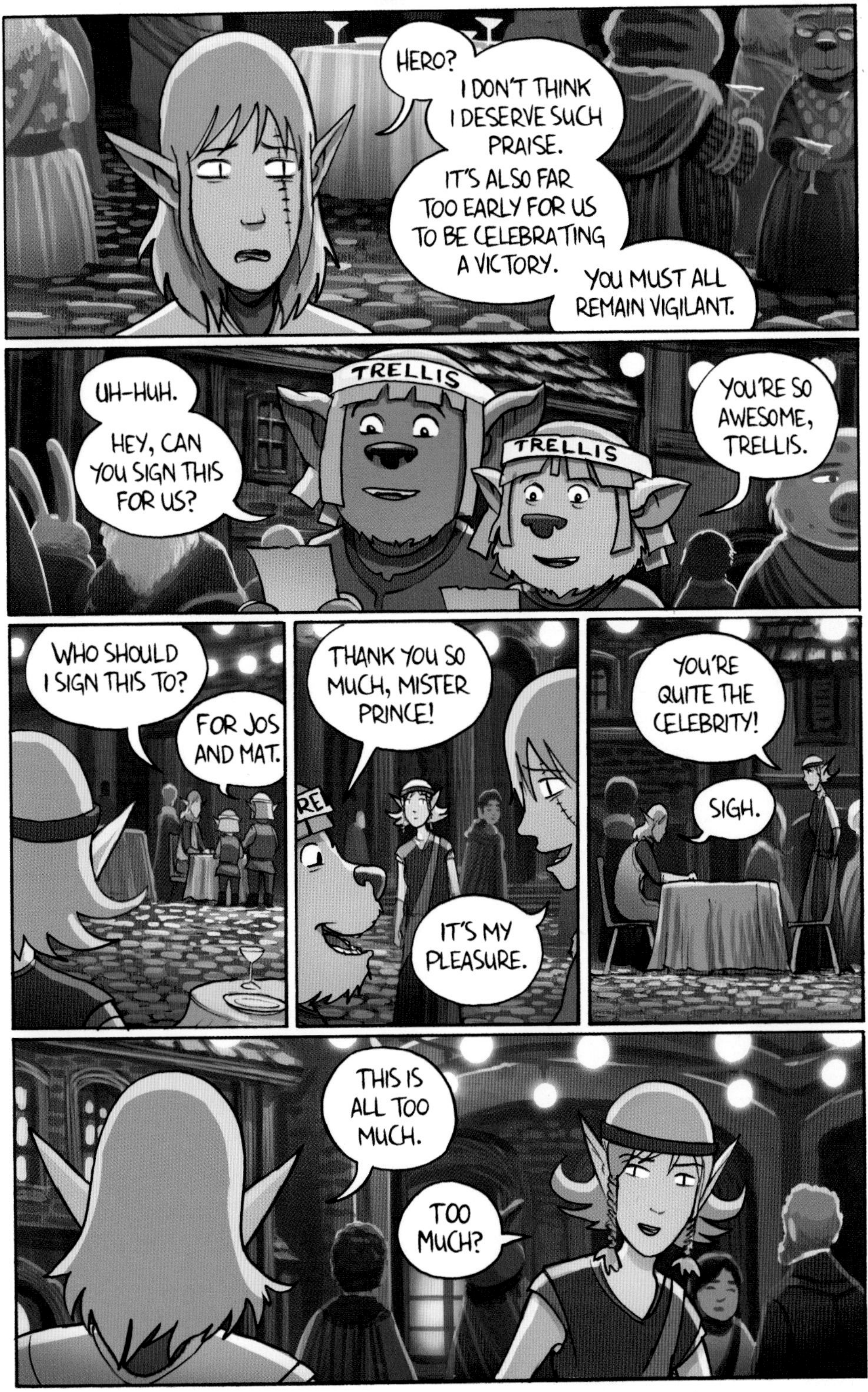
HERO?
I DON'T THINK I DESERVE SUCH PRAISE.
IT'S ALSO FAR TOO EARLY FOR US TO BE CELEBRATING A VICTORY.
YOU MUST ALL REMAIN VIGILANT.
TRELLIS
TRELLIS
UH-HUH.
HEY, CAN YOU SIGN THIS FOR US?
YOU'RE SO AWESOME, TRELLIS.
WHO SHOULD I SIGN THIS TO?
FOR JOS AND MAT.
THANK YOU SO MUCH, MISTER PRINCE!
IT'S MY PLEASURE.
YOU'RE QUITE THE CELEBRITY!
SIGH.
THIS IS ALL TOO MUCH.
TOO MUCH?

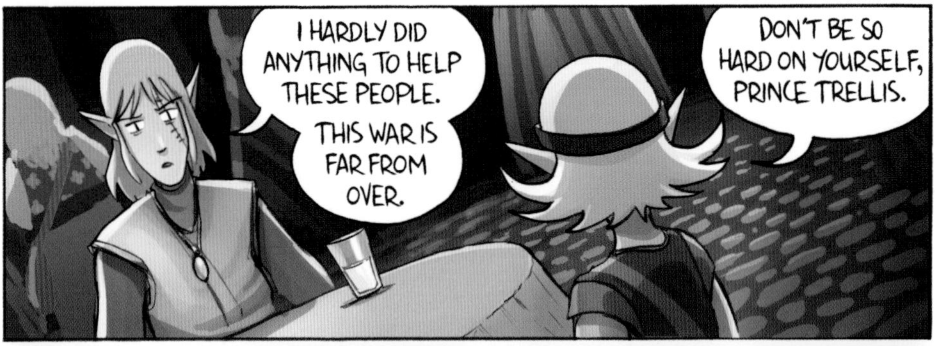

I HARDLY DID ANYTHING TO HELP THESE PEOPLE.
THIS WAR IS FAR FROM OVER.
DON'T BE SO HARD ON YOURSELF, PRINCE TRELLIS.

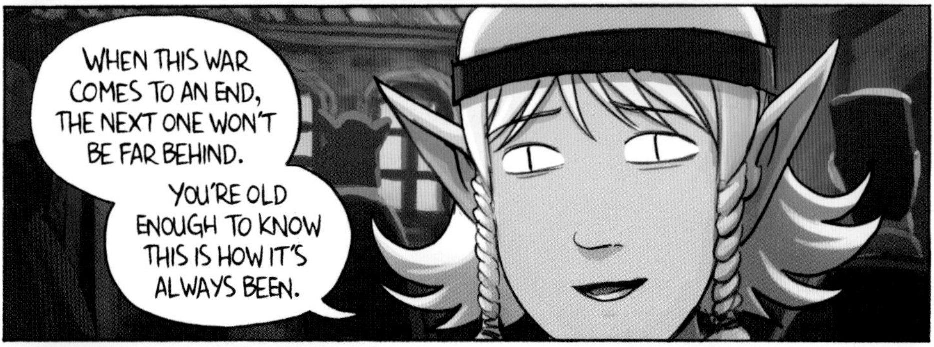

WHEN THIS WAR COMES TO AN END, THE NEXT ONE WON'T BE FAR BEHIND.
YOU'RE OLD ENOUGH TO KNOW THIS IS HOW IT'S ALWAYS BEEN.

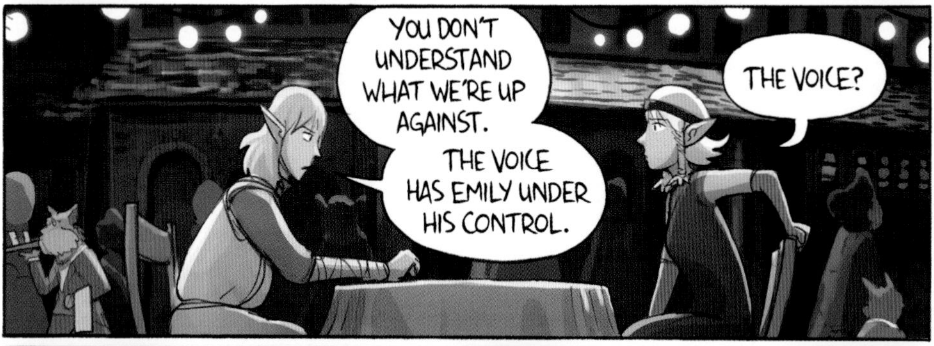

YOU DON'T UNDERSTAND WHAT WE'RE UP AGAINST.
THE VOICE HAS EMILY UNDER HIS CONTROL.
THE VOICE?

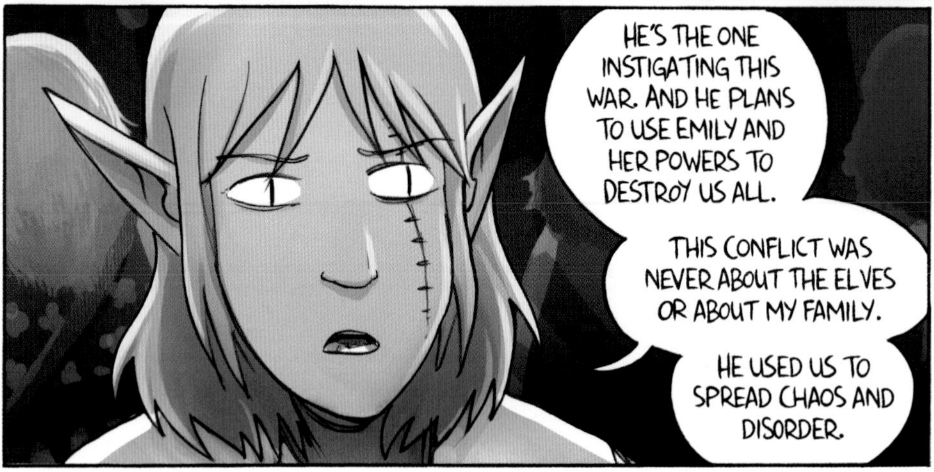

HE'S THE ONE INSTIGATING THIS WAR. AND HE PLANS TO USE EMILY AND HER POWERS TO DESTROY US ALL.
THIS CONFLICT WAS NEVER ABOUT THE ELVES OR ABOUT MY FAMILY.
HE USED US TO SPREAD CHAOS AND DISORDER.

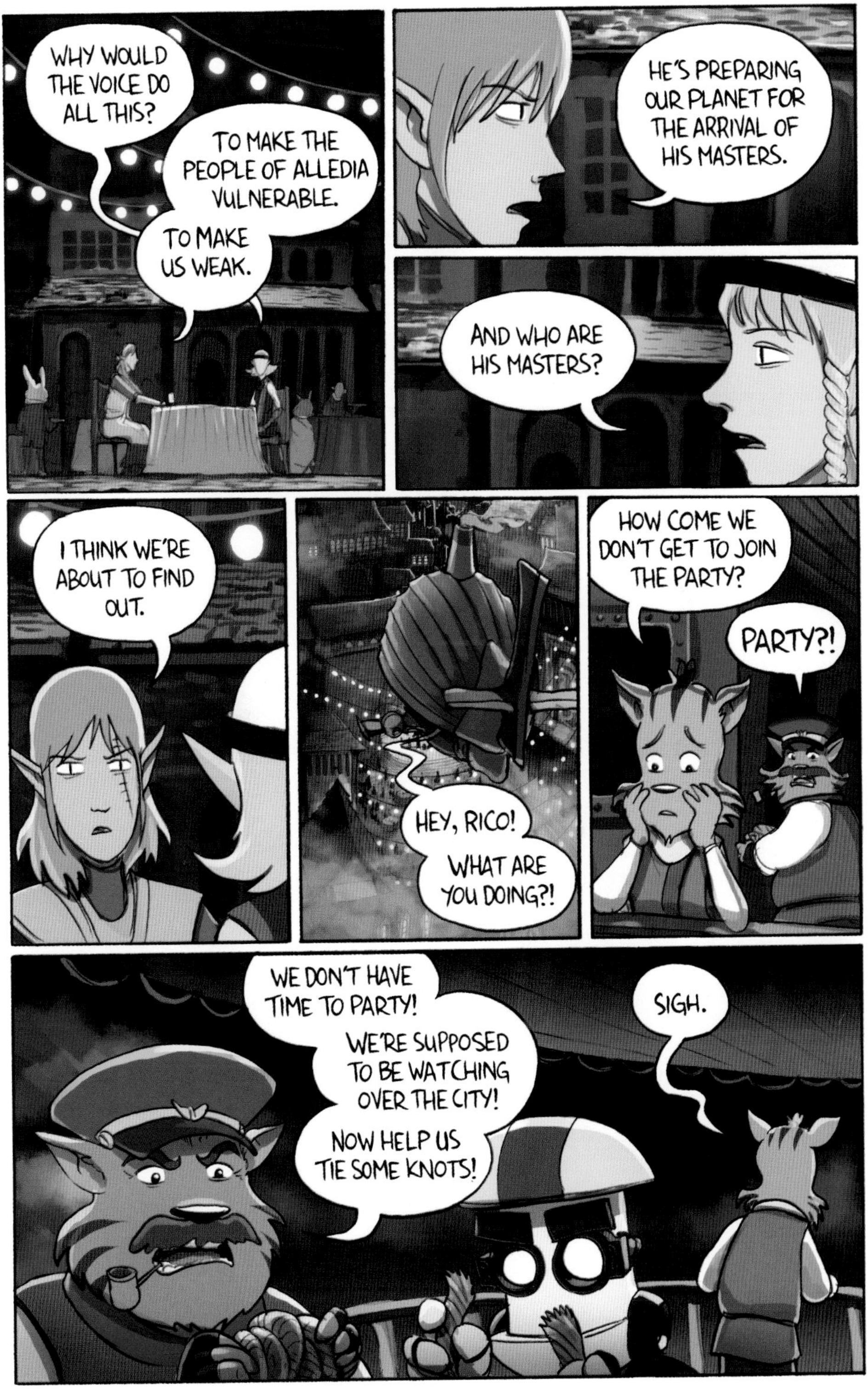
WHY WOULD THE VOICE DO ALL THIS?
TO MAKE THE PEOPLE OF ALLEDIA VULNERABLE.
TO MAKE US WEAK.
HE'S PREPARING OUR PLANET FOR THE ARRIVAL OF HIS MASTERS.
AND WHO ARE HIS MASTERS?
I THINK WE'RE ABOUT TO FIND OUT.
HEY, RICO!
WHAT ARE YOU DOING?!
HOW COME WE DON'T GET TO JOIN THE PARTY?
PARTY?!
WE DON'T HAVE TIME TO PARTY!
WE'RE SUPPOSED TO BE WATCHING OVER THE CITY!
NOW HELP US TIE SOME KNOTS!
SIGH.

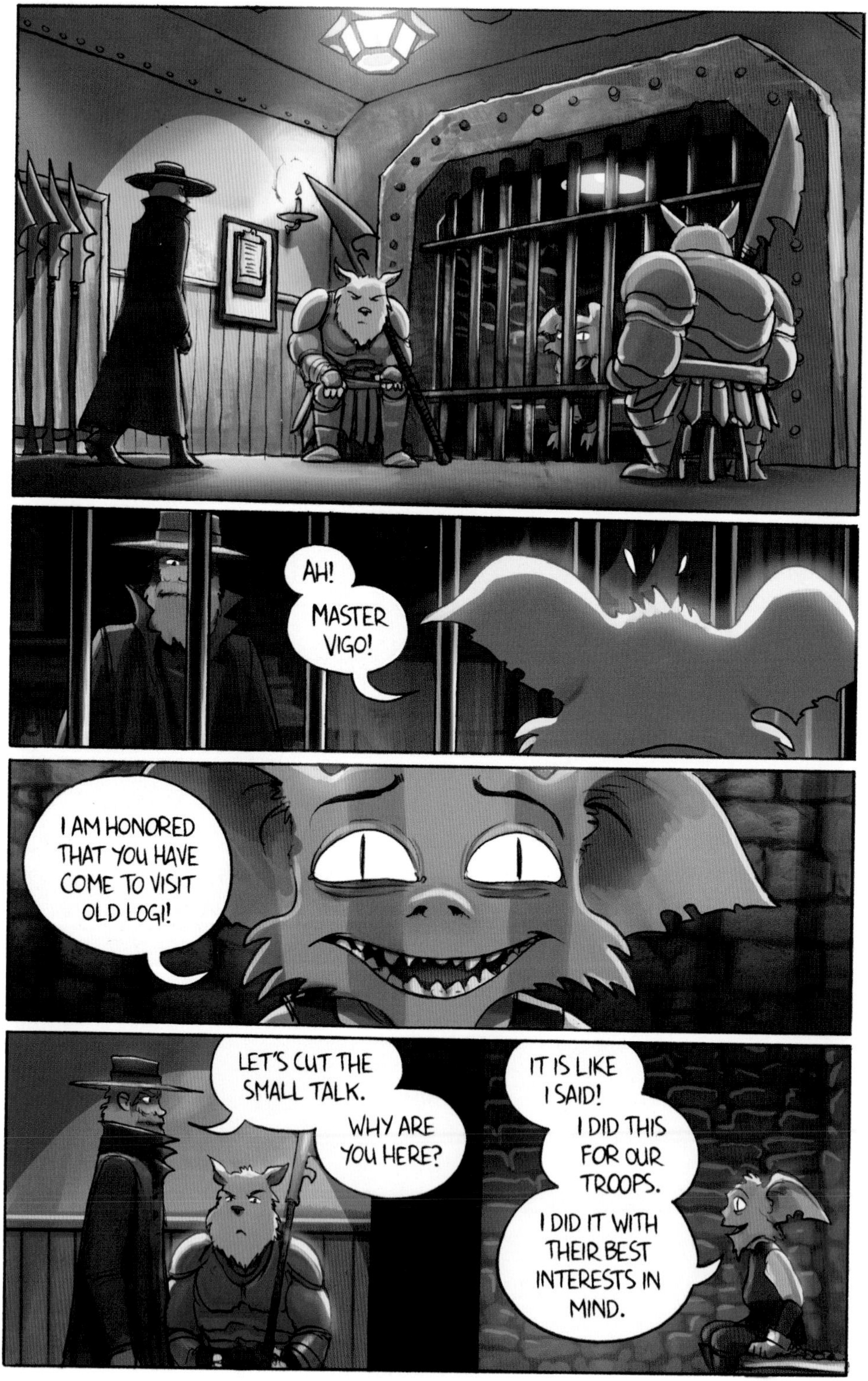
AH!
MASTER VIGO!
I AM HONORED THAT YOU HAVE COME TO VISIT OLD LOGI!
LET'S CUT THE SMALL TALK.
WHY ARE YOU HERE?
IT IS LIKE I SAID!
I DID THIS FOR OUR TROOPS.
I DID IT WITH THEIR BEST INTERESTS IN MIND.

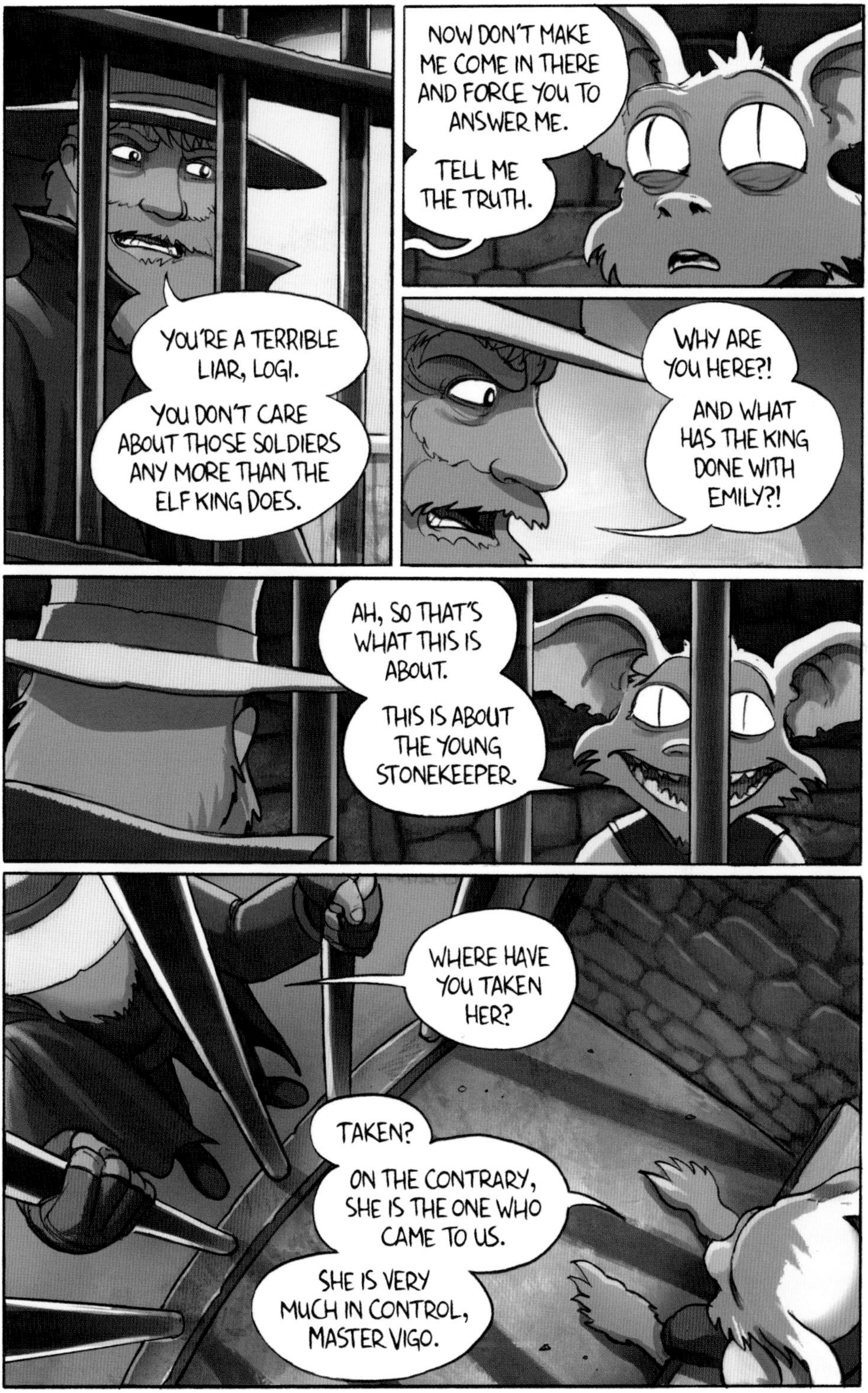
NOW DON'T MAKE ME COME IN THERE AND FORCE YOU TO ANSWER ME.
TELL ME THE TRUTH.
YOU'RE A TERRIBLE LIAR, LOGI.
YOU DON'T CARE ABOUT THOSE SOLDIERS ANY MORE THAN THE ELF KING DOES.
WHY ARE YOU HERE?!
AND WHAT HAS THE KING DONE WITH EMILY?!
AH, SO THAT'S WHAT THIS IS ABOUT.
THIS IS ABOUT THE YOUNG STONEKEEPER.
WHERE HAVE YOU TAKEN HER?
TAKEN?
ON THE CONTRARY, SHE IS THE ONE WHO CAME TO US.
SHE IS VERY MUCH IN CONTROL, MASTER VIGO.

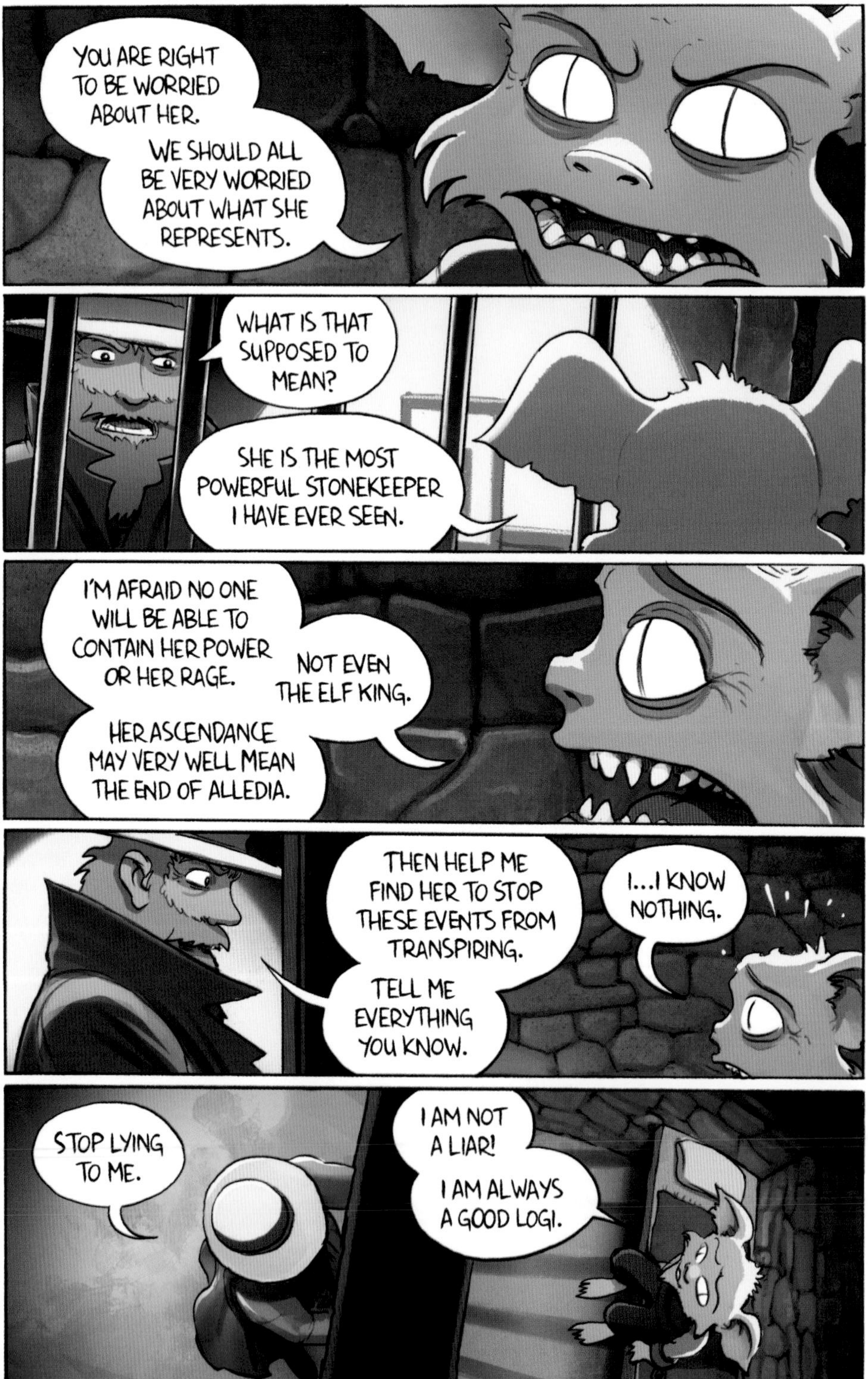
YOU ARE RIGHT TO BE WORRIED ABOUT HER.
WE SHOULD ALL BE VERY WORRIED ABOUT WHAT SHE REPRESENTS.
WHAT IS THAT SUPPOSED TO MEAN?
SHE IS THE MOST POWERFUL STONEKEEPER I HAVE EVER SEEN.
I'M AFRAID NO ONE WILL BE ABLE TO CONTAIN HER POWER OR HER RAGE.
NOT EVEN THE ELF KING.
HER ASCENDANCE MAY VERY WELL MEAN THE END OF ALLEDIA.
THEN HELP ME FIND HER TO STOP THESE EVENTS FROM TRANSPIRING.
TELL ME EVERYTHING YOU KNOW.
I...I KNOW NOTHING.
STOP LYING TO ME.
I AM NOT A LIAR!
I AM ALWAYS A GOOD LOGI.

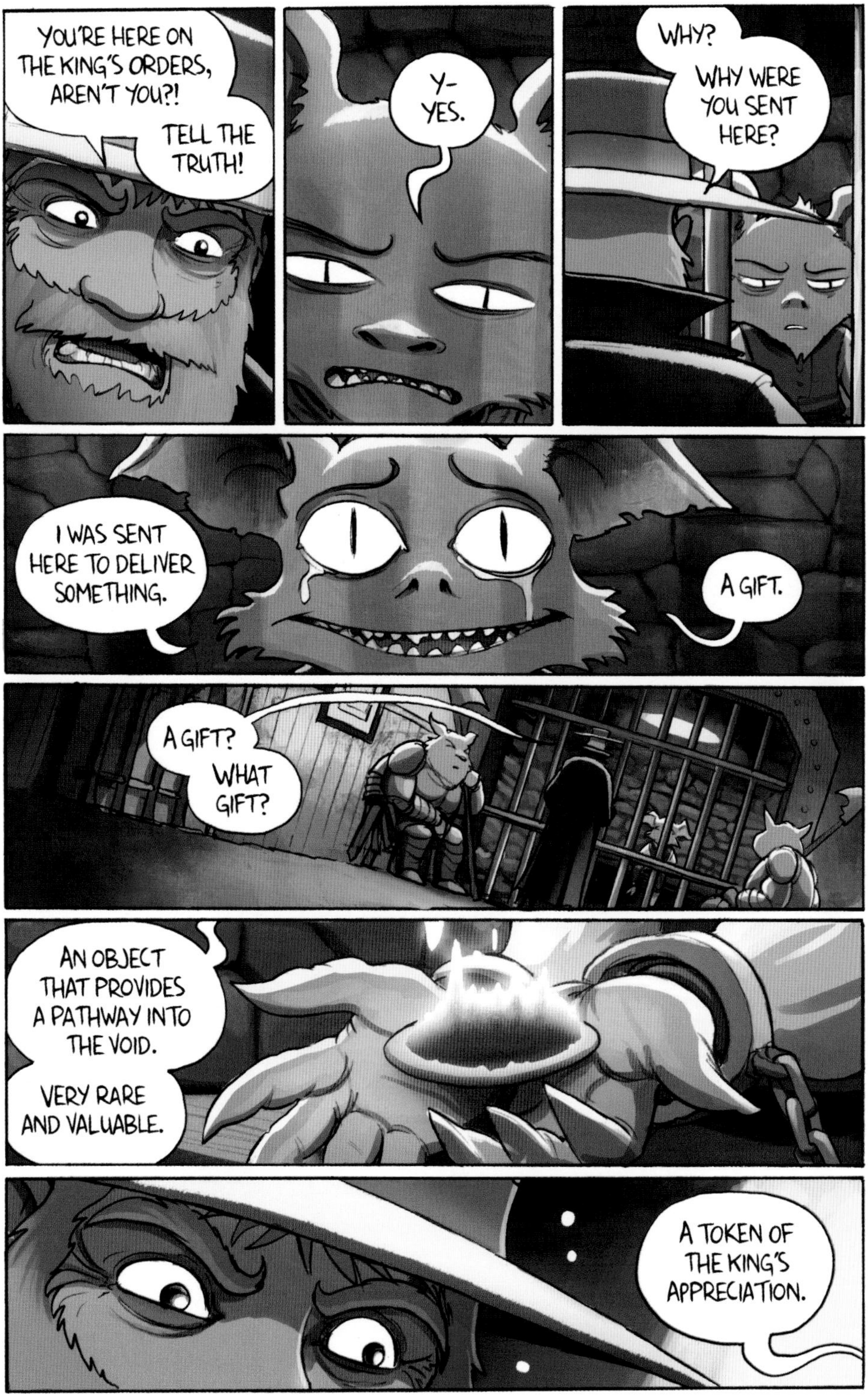
YOU'RE HERE ON THE KING'S ORDERS, AREN'T YOU?!
TELL THE TRUTH!
Y- YES.
WHY?
WHY WERE YOU SENT HERE?
I WAS SENT HERE TO DELIVER SOMETHING.
A GIFT.
A GIFT?
WHAT GIFT?
AN OBJECT THAT PROVIDES A PATHWAY INTO THE VOID.
VERY RARE AND VALUABLE.
A TOKEN OF THE KING'S APPRECIATION.

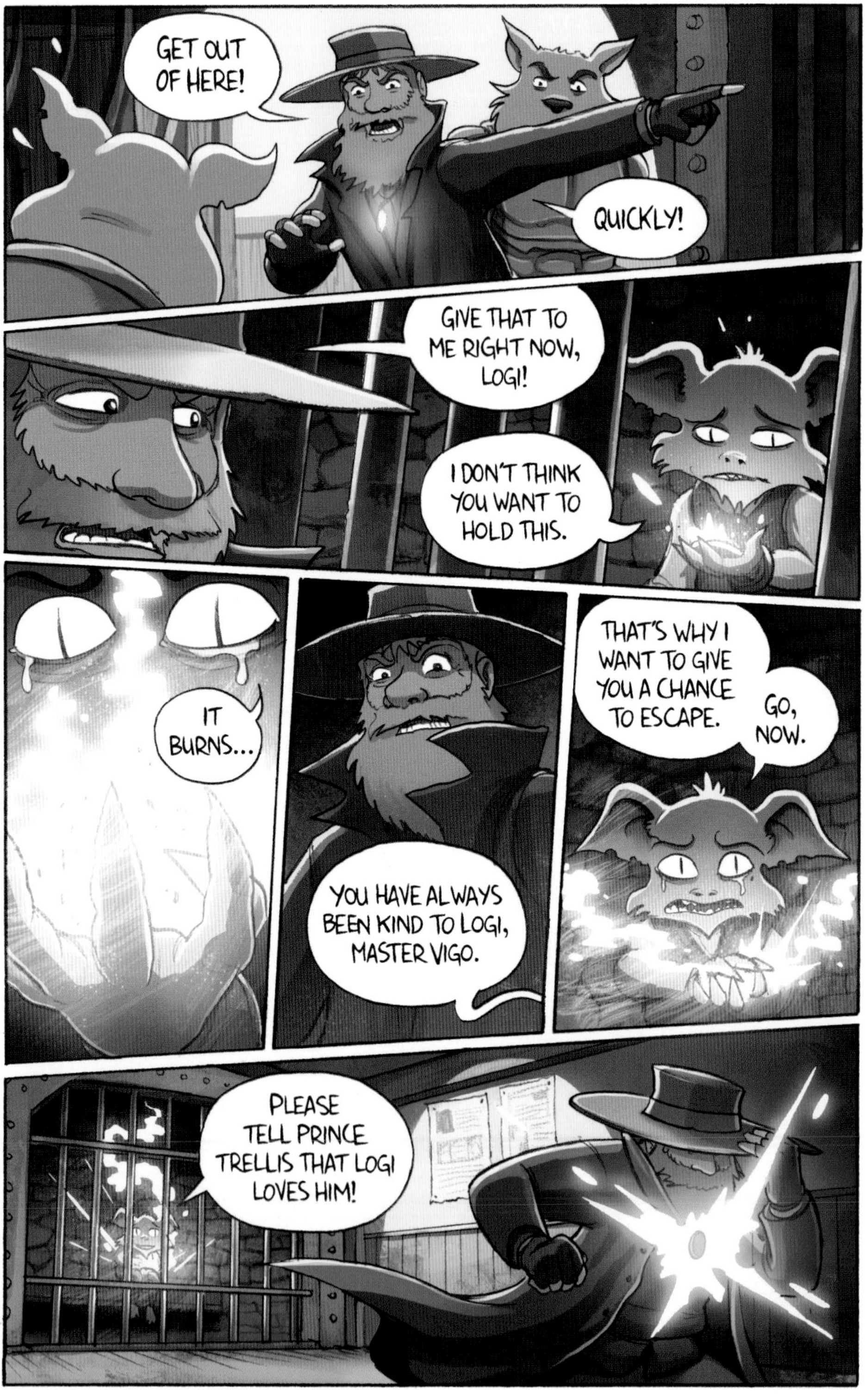
GET OUT OF HERE!
QUICKLY!
GIVE THAT TO ME RIGHT NOW, LOGI!
I DON'T THINK YOU WANT TO HOLD THIS.
IT BURNS...
YOU HAVE ALWAYS BEEN KIND TO LOGI, MASTER VIGO.
THAT'S WHY I WANT TO GIVE YOU A CHANCE TO ESCAPE.
GO, NOW.
PLEASE TELL PRINCE TRELLIS THAT LOGI LOVES HIM!

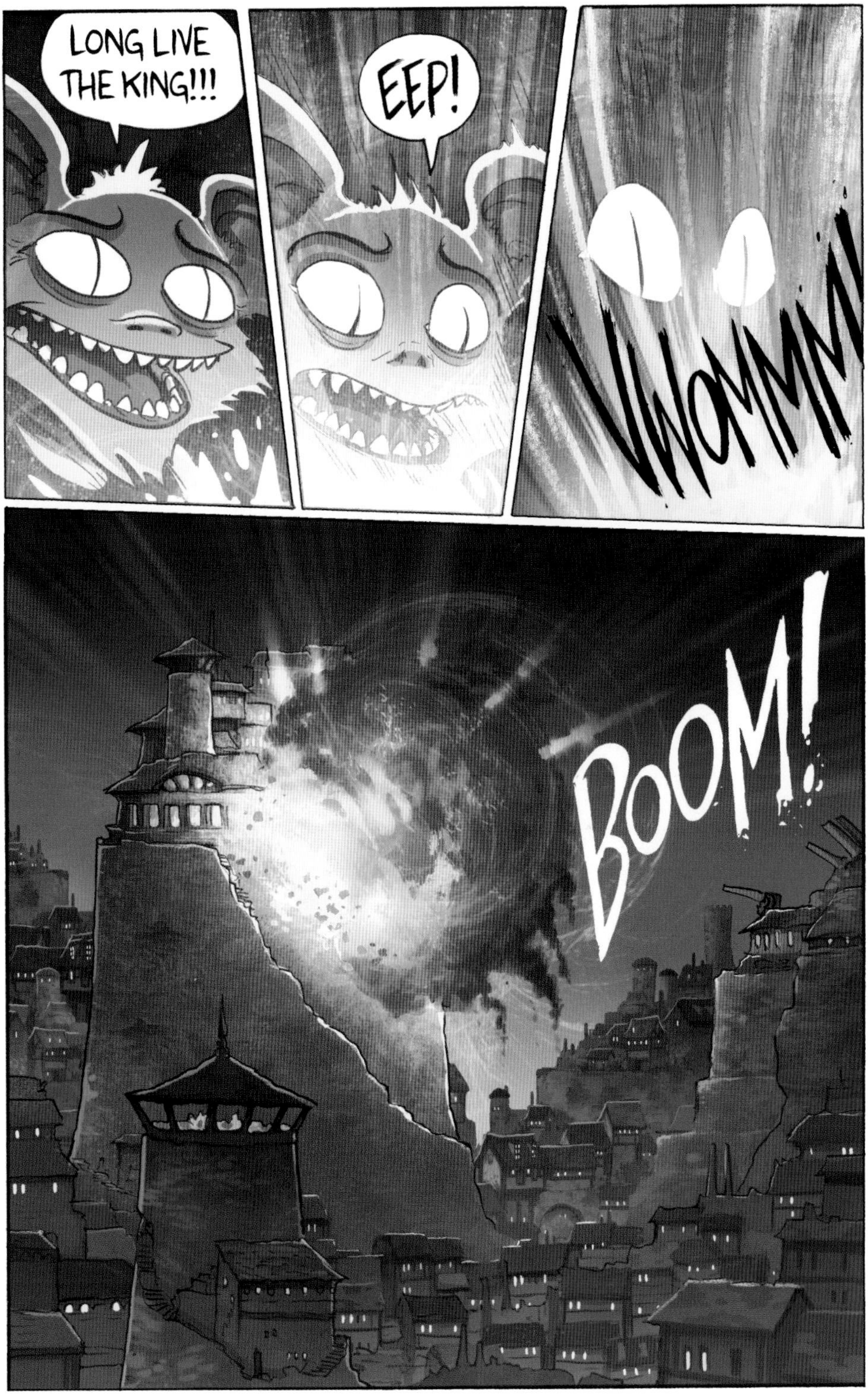
LONG LIVE THE KING!!!
EEP!
VWOMM
BOOM!

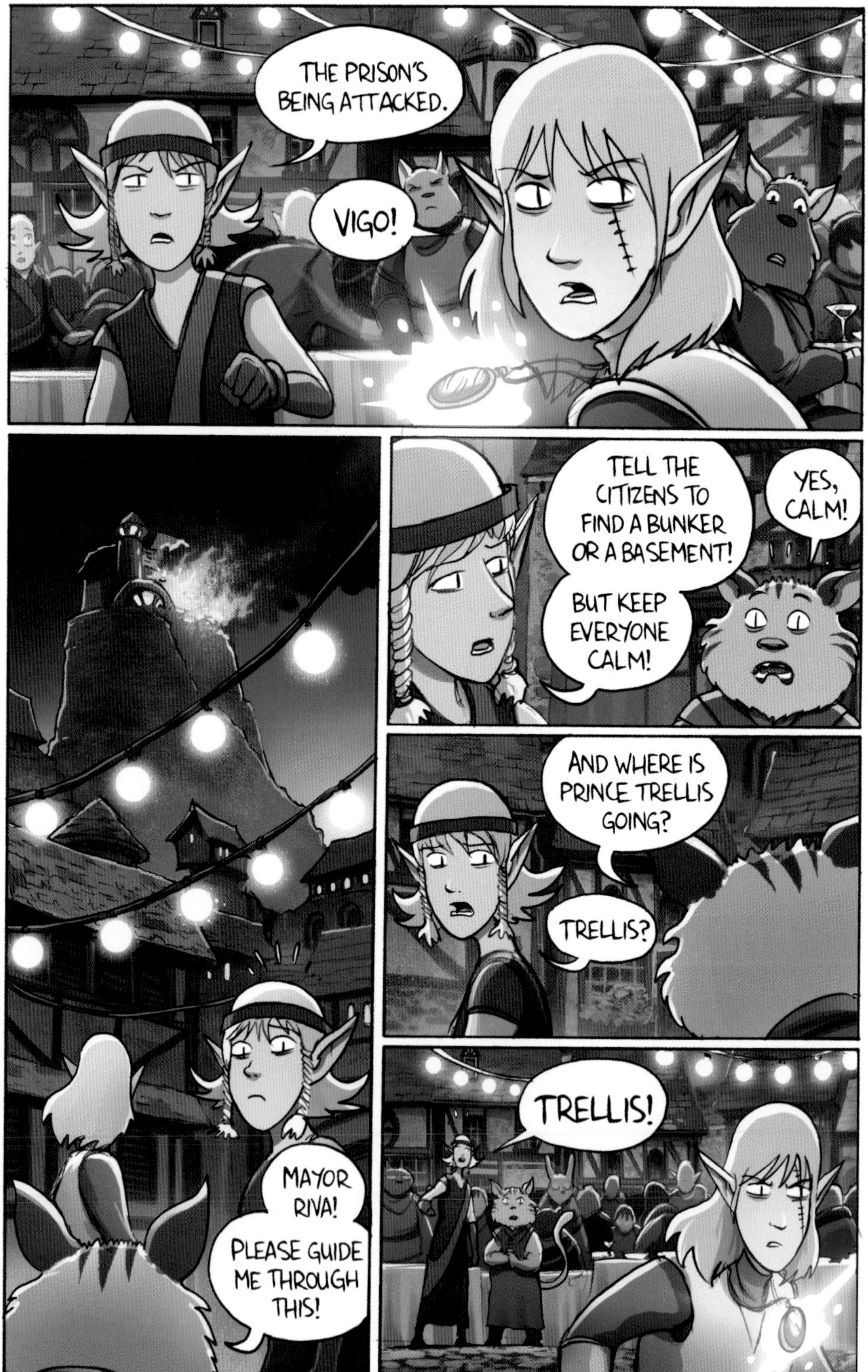
THE PRISON'S BEING ATTACKED.
VIGO!
TELL THE CITIZENS TO FIND A BUNKER OR A BASEMENT!
BUT KEEP EVERYONE CALM!
YES, CALM!
MAYOR RIVA!
PLEASE GUIDE ME THROUGH THIS!
AND WHERE IS PRINCE TRELLIS GOING?
TRELLIS?
TRELLIS!

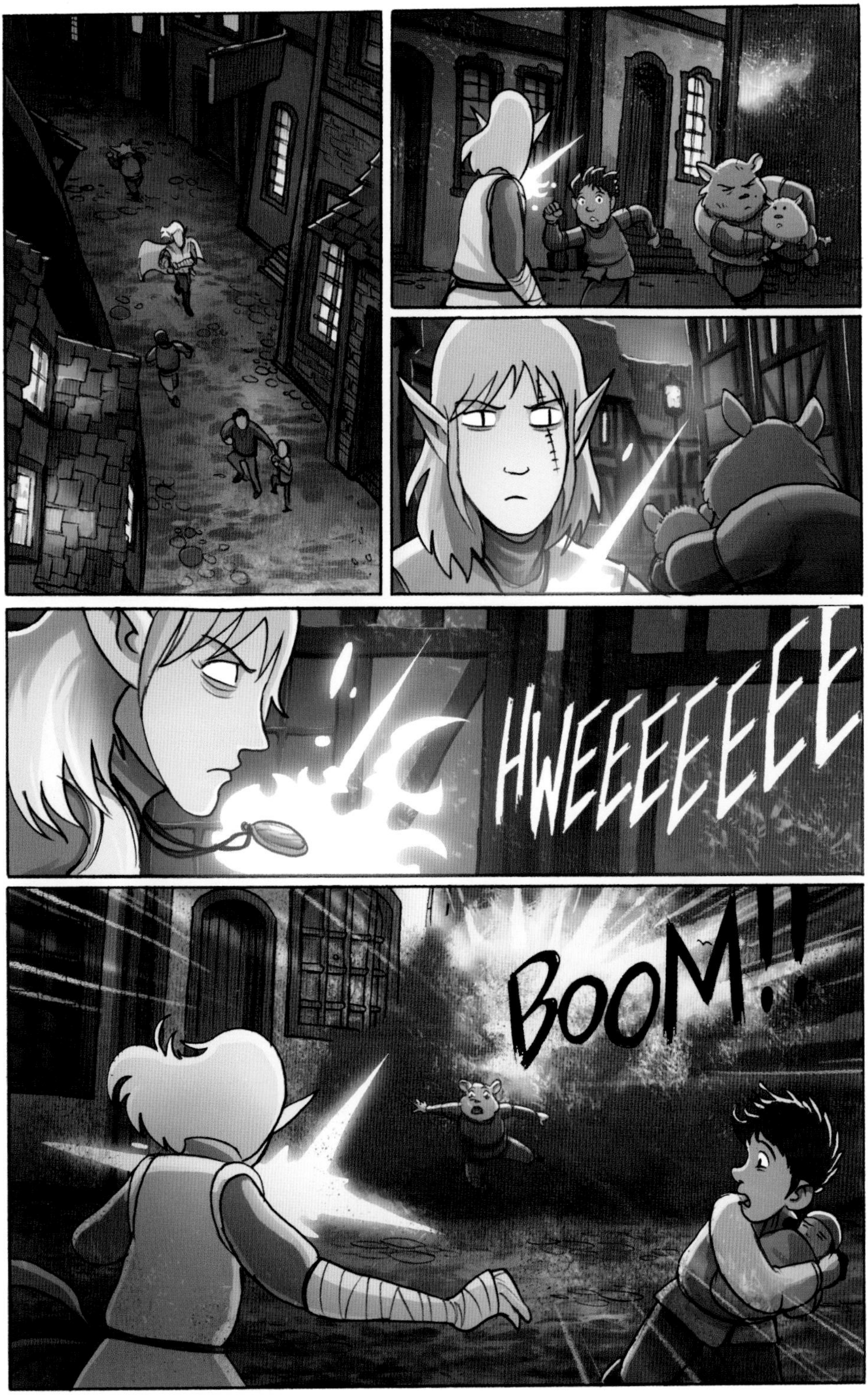
HWEEEEEEE
BOOM!!

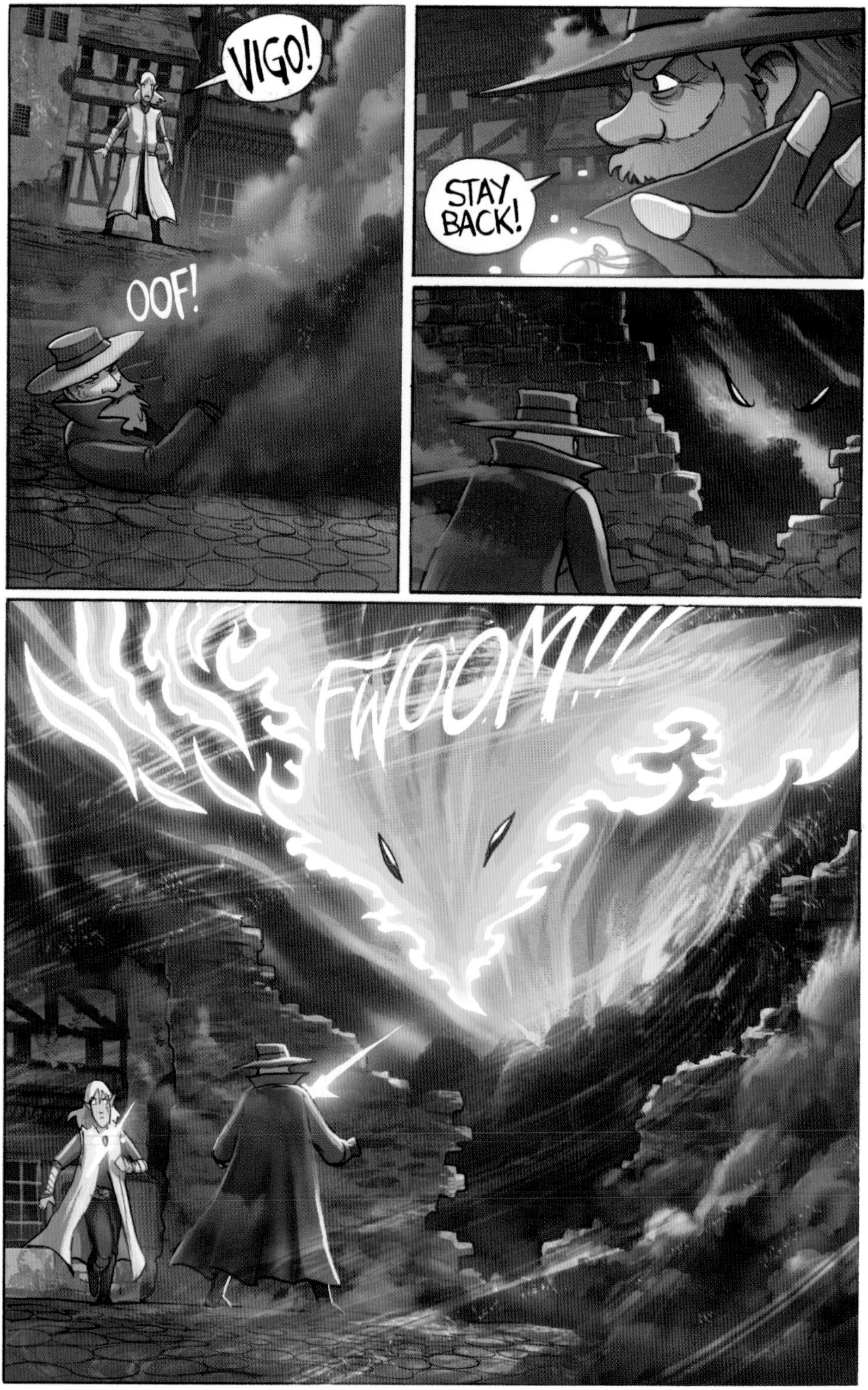
VIGO!
OOF!
STAY BACK!
FWOOM!!!

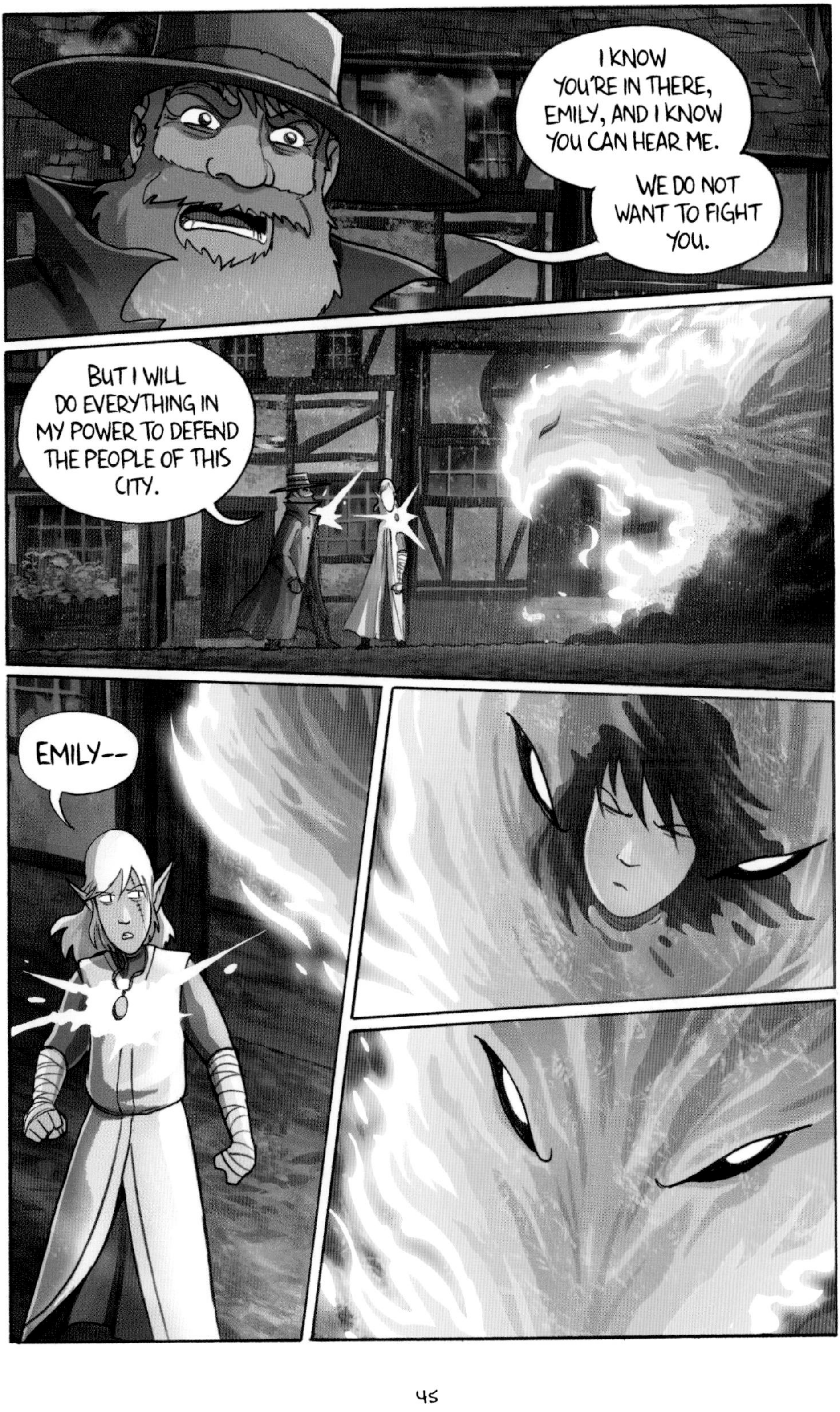
I KNOW YOU'RE IN THERE, EMILY, AND I KNOW YOU CAN HEAR ME.
WE DO NOT WANT TO FIGHT YOU.
BUT I WILL DO EVERYTHING IN MY POWER TO DEFEND THE PEOPLE OF THIS CITY.
EMILY--

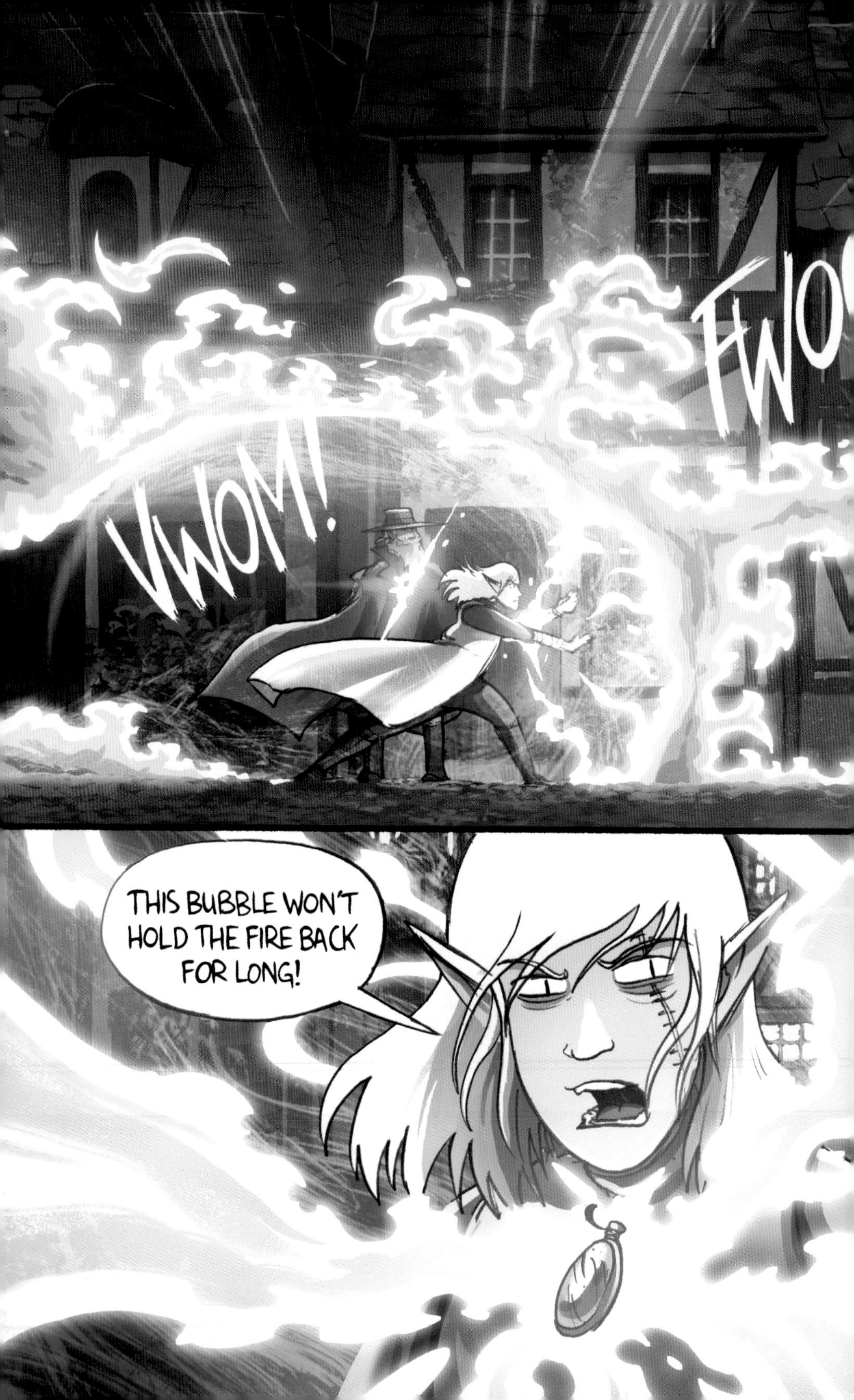
FWO
VWOM!
THIS BUBBLE WON'T HOLD THE FIRE BACK FOR LONG!

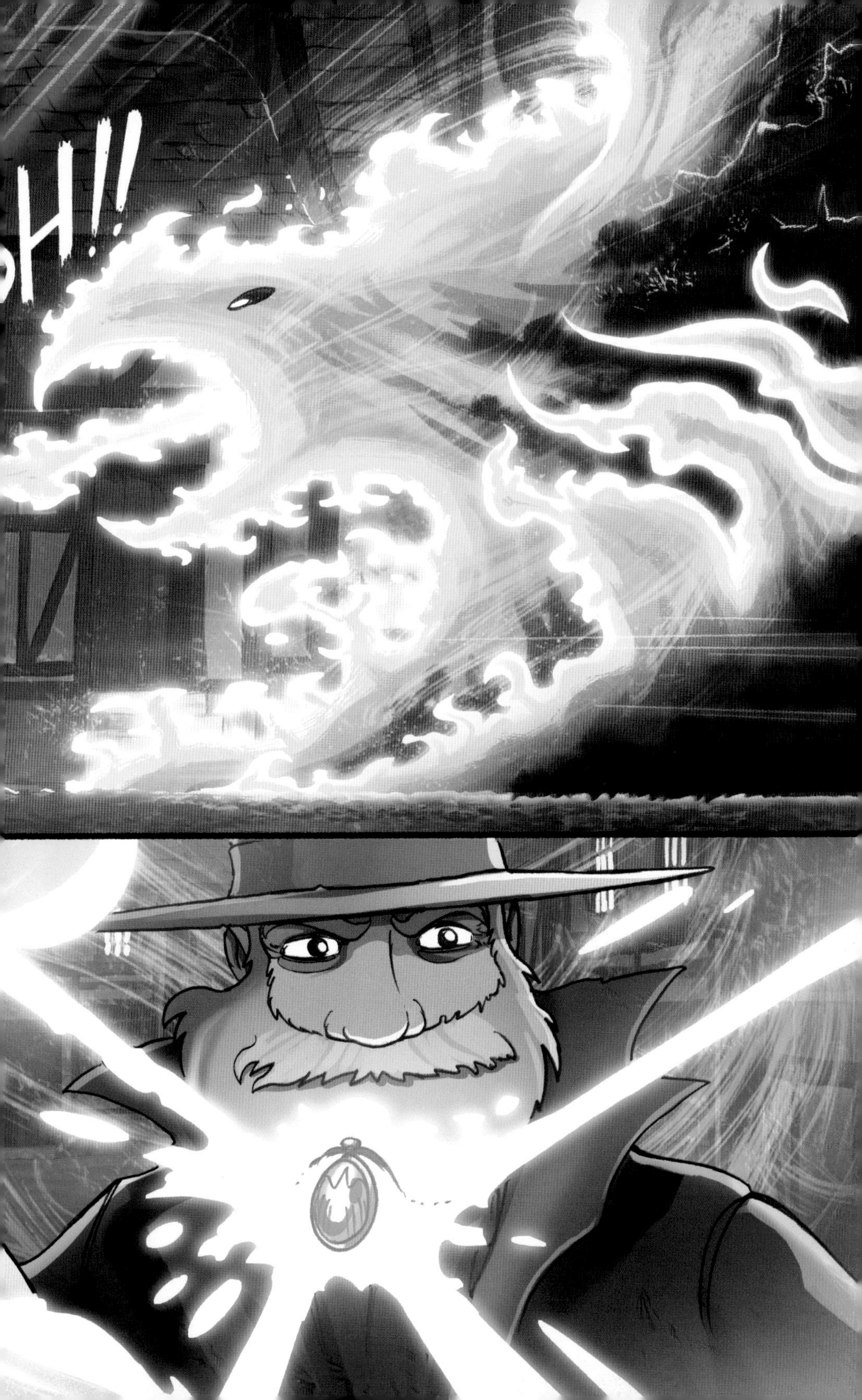
H!!

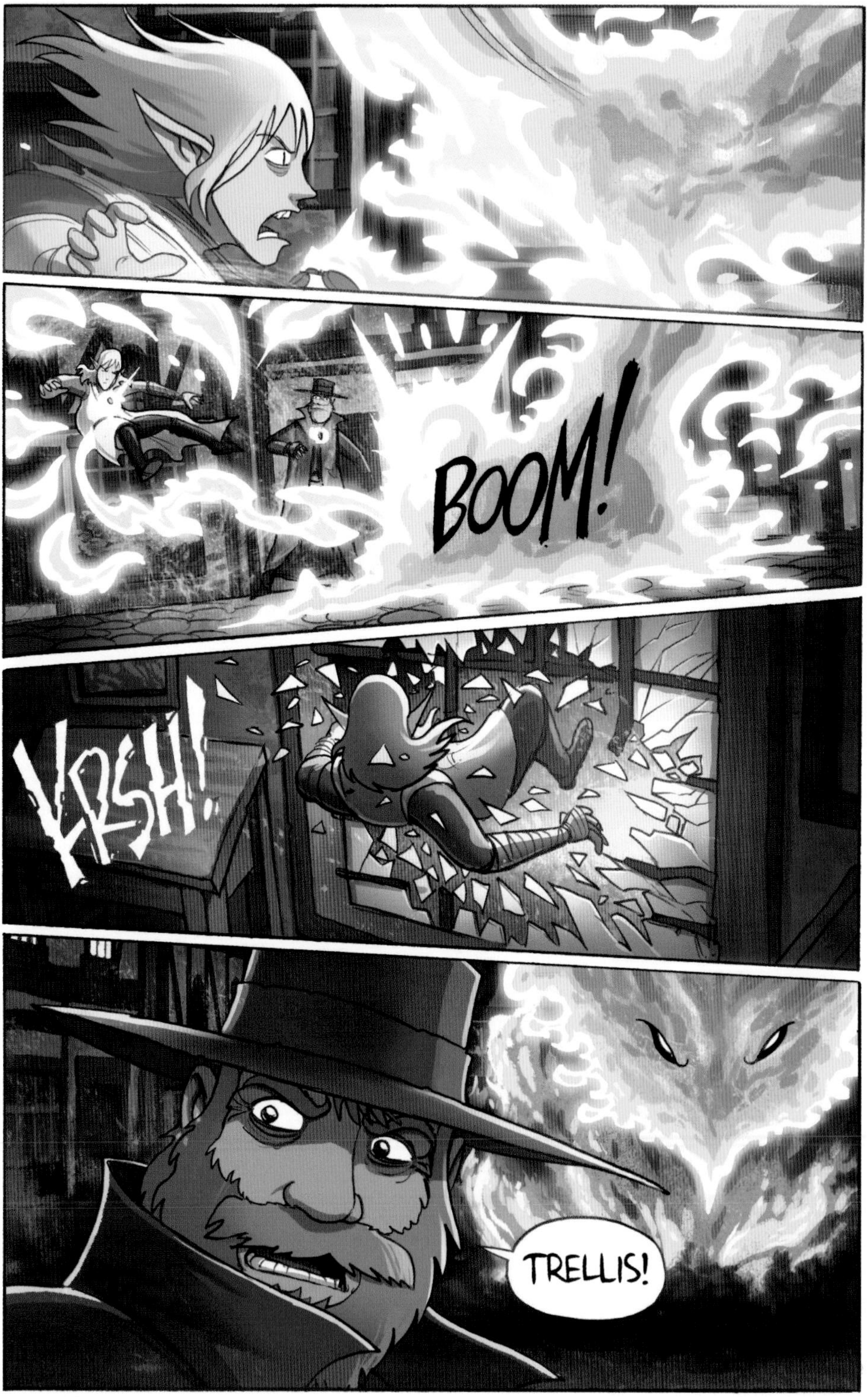
BOOM!
KRSH!
TRELLIS!

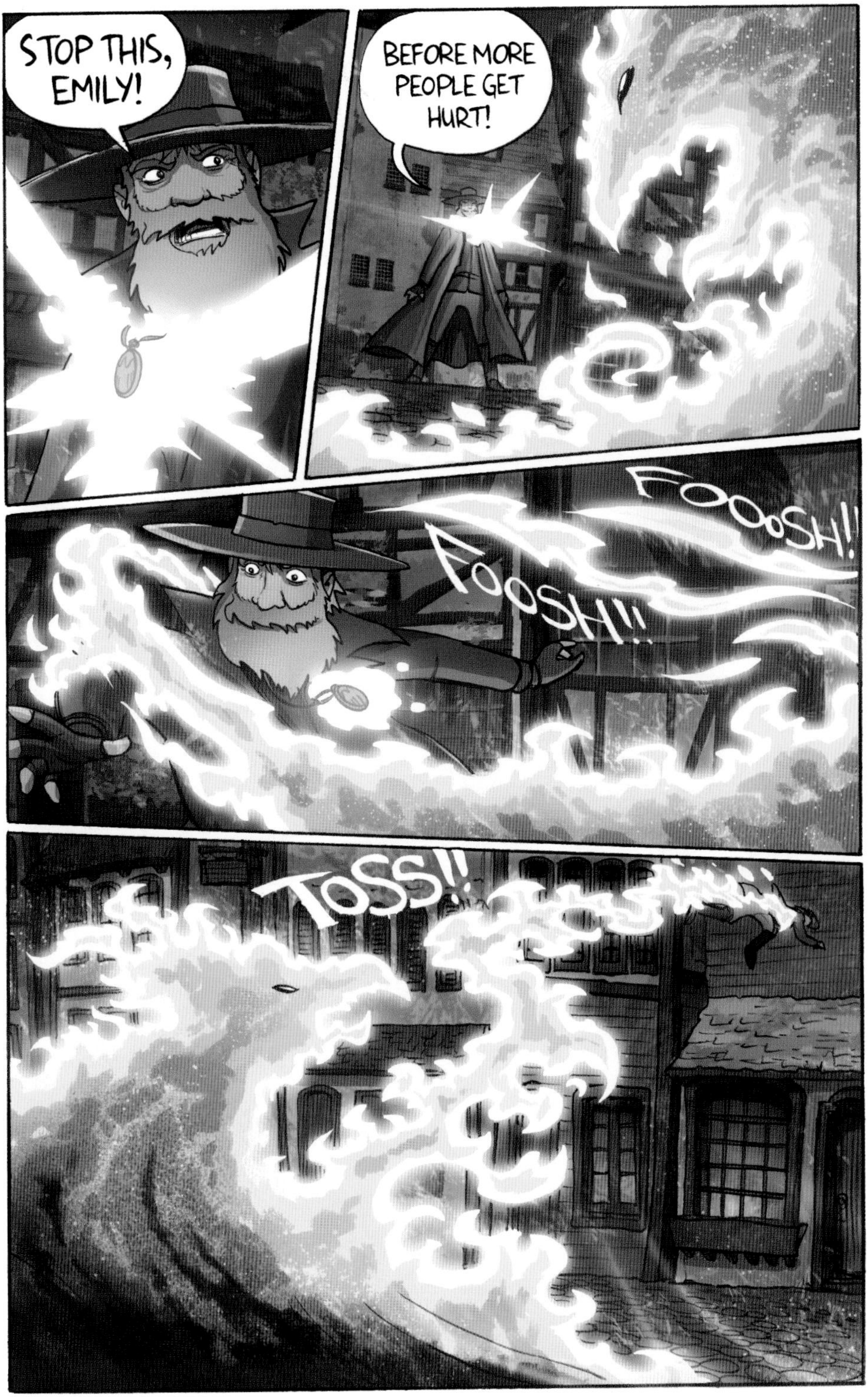
STOP THIS, EMILY!
BEFORE MORE PEOPLE GET HURT!
FOOOSH!!
FOOSH!!
TOSS!!

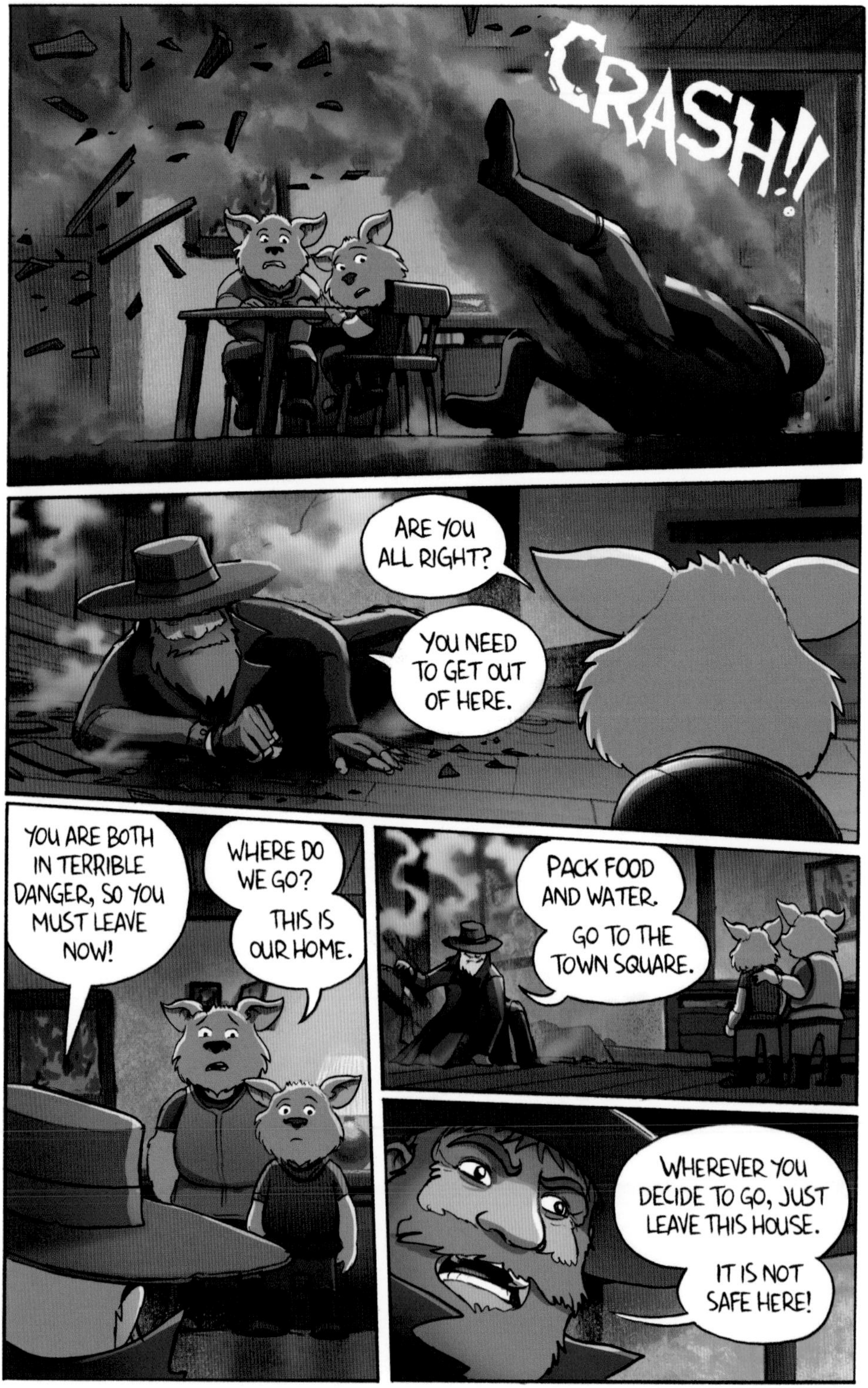
CRASH!!
ARE YOU ALL RIGHT?
YOU NEED TO GET OUT OF HERE.
YOU ARE BOTH IN TERRIBLE DANGER, SO YOU MUST LEAVE NOW!
WHERE DO WE GO?
THIS IS OUR HOME.
PACK FOOD AND WATER.
GO TO THE TOWN SQUARE.
WHEREVER YOU DECIDE TO GO, JUST LEAVE THIS HOUSE.
IT IS NOT SAFE HERE!

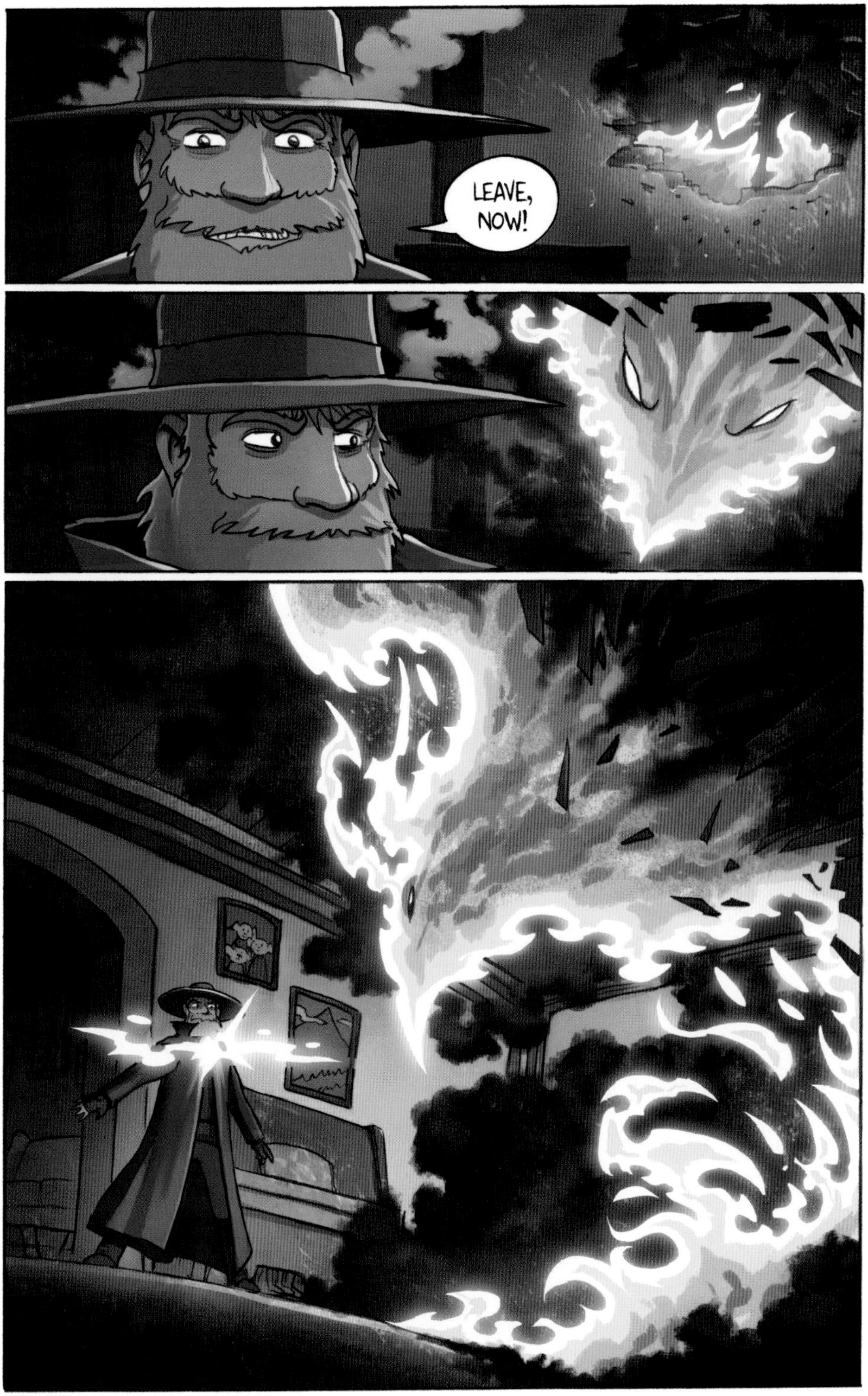
LEAVE, NOW!

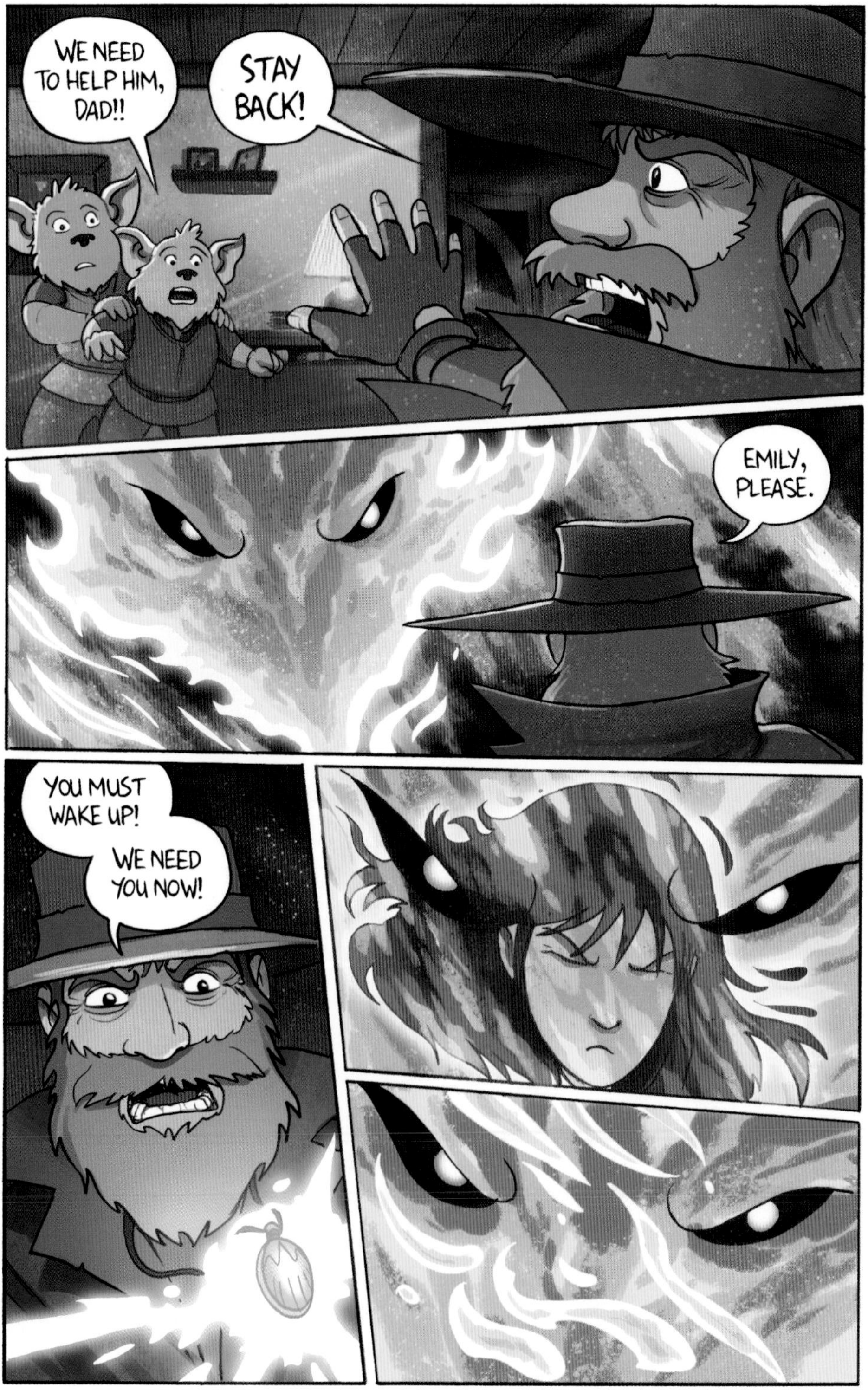
WE NEED TO HELP HIM, DAD!!
STAY BACK!
EMILY, PLEASE.
YOU MUST WAKE UP!
WE NEED YOU NOW!

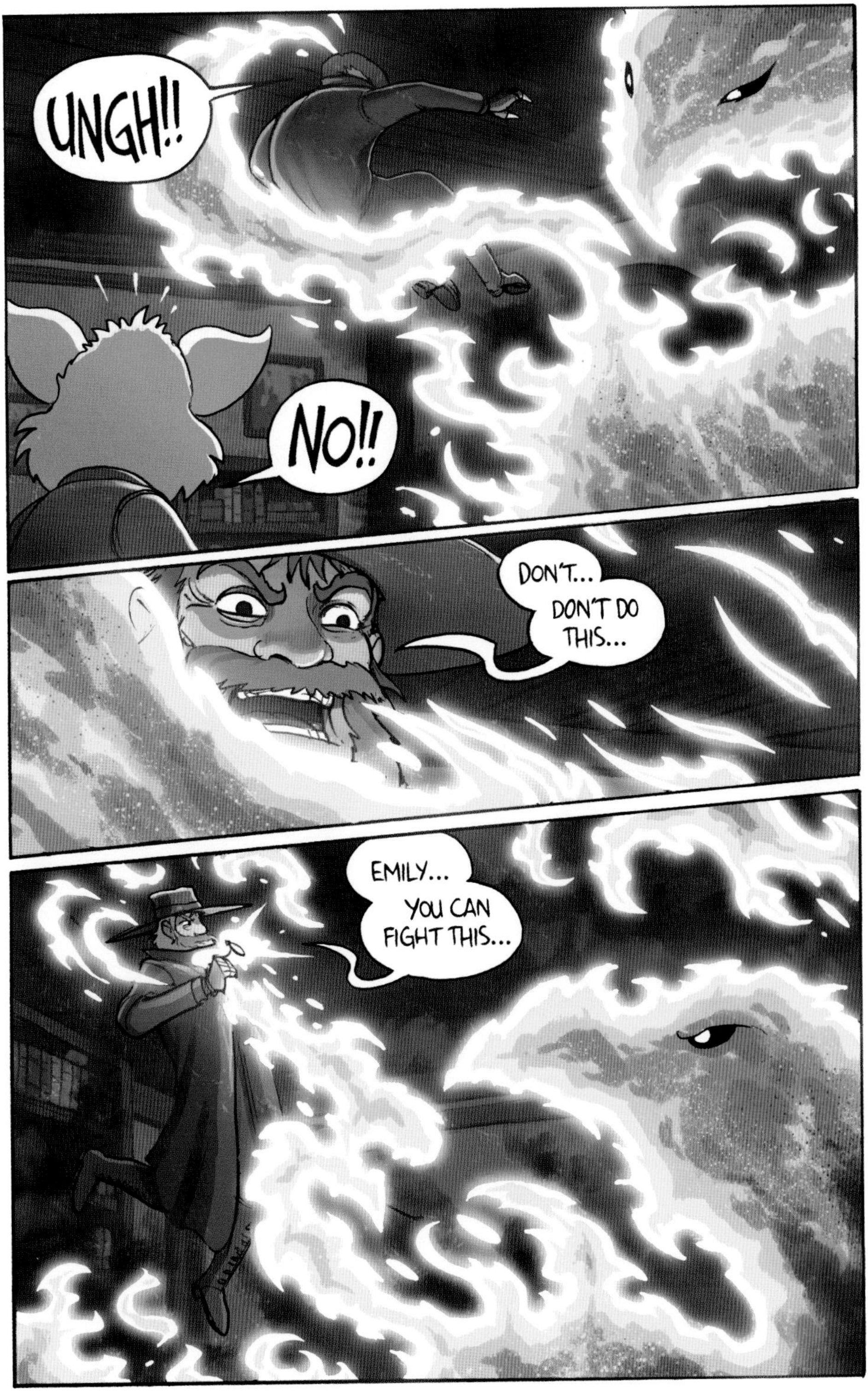
UNGH!!
NO!!
DON'T... DON'T DO THIS...
EMILY... YOU CAN FIGHT THIS...

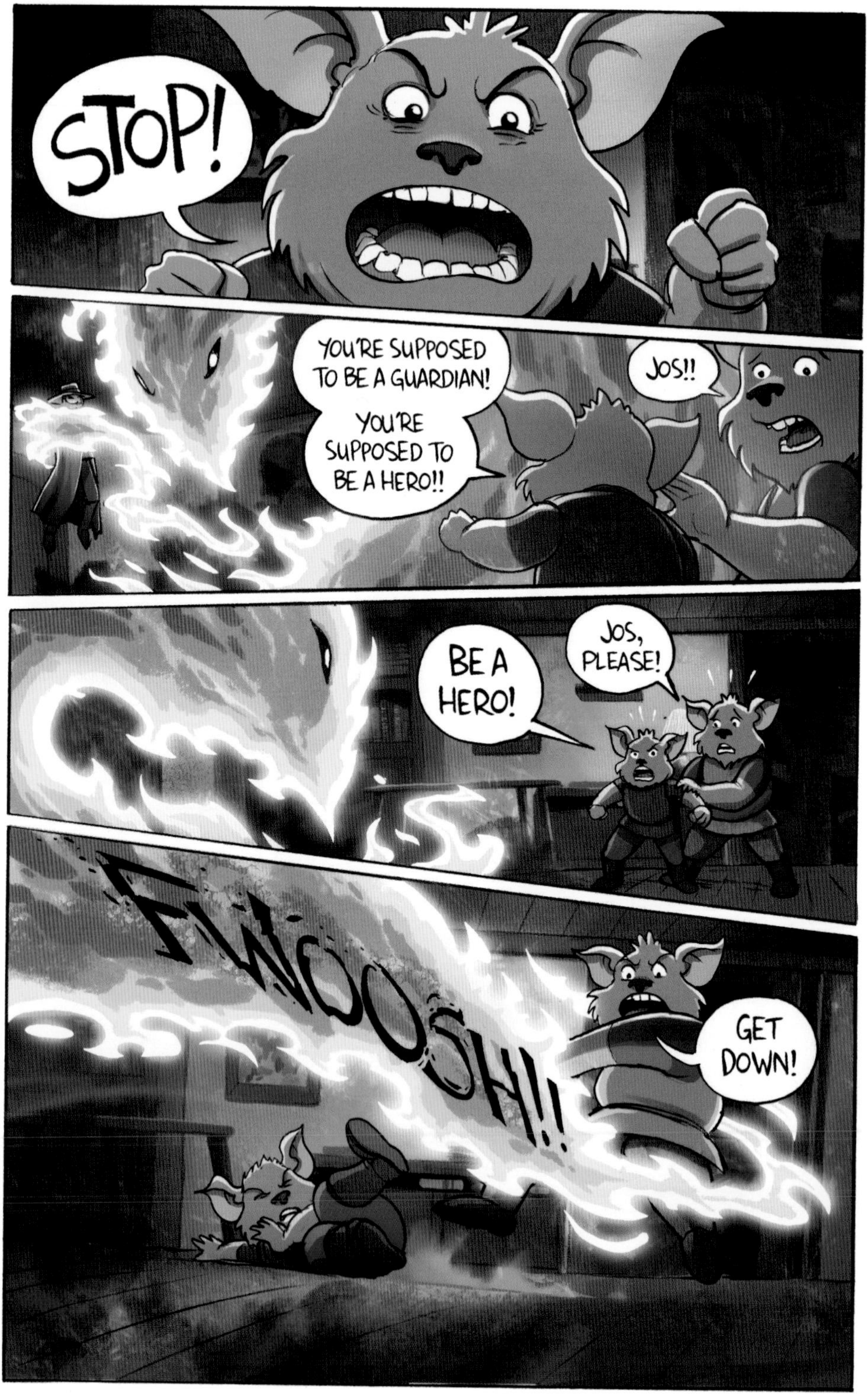
STOP!
YOU'RE SUPPOSED TO BE A GUARDIAN!
YOU'RE SUPPOSED TO BE A HERO!!
JOS!!
BE A HERO!
JOS, PLEASE!
FWOOSH!!
GET DOWN!

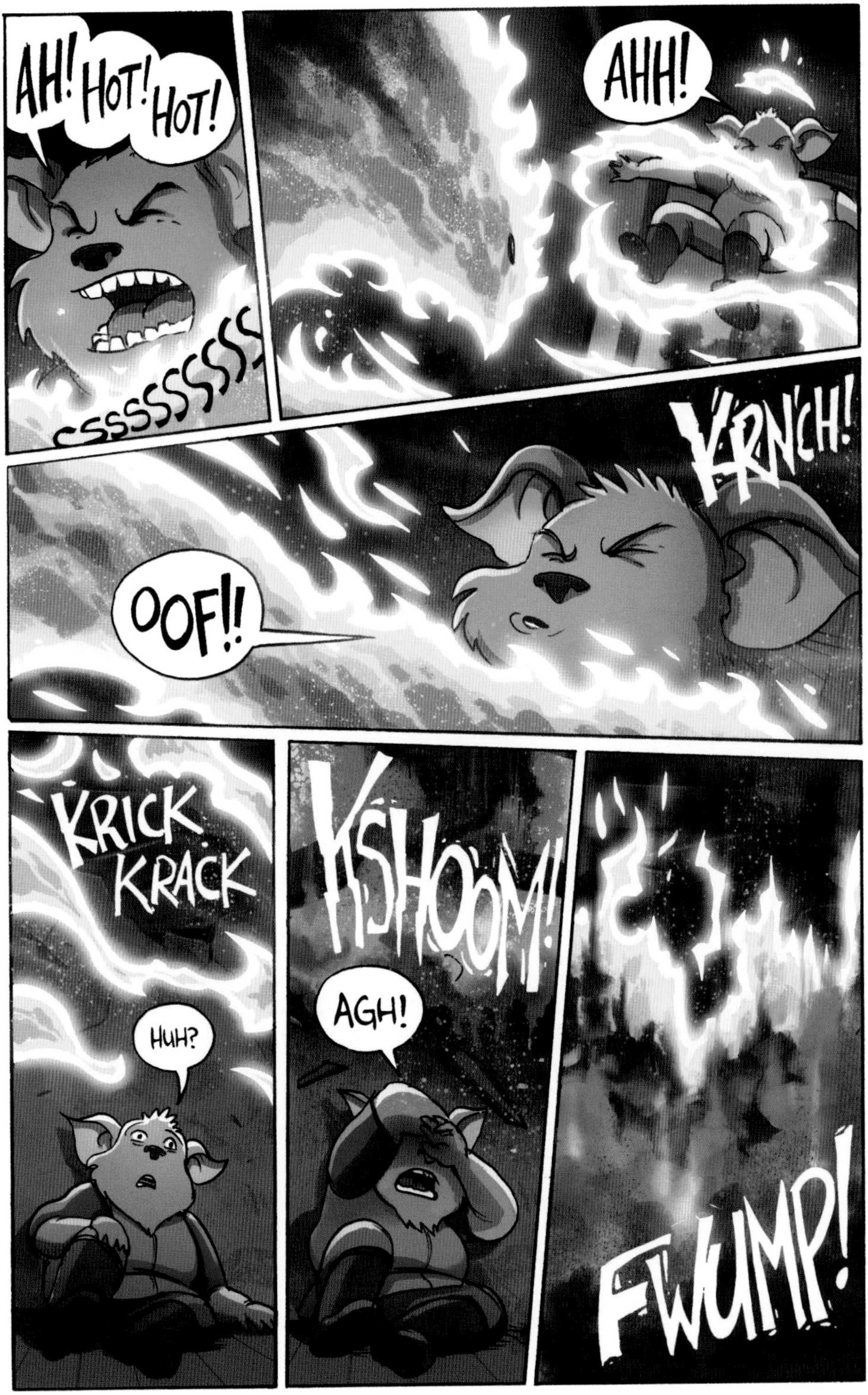
AH! HOT! HOT!
CSSSSSSSSS
AHH!
KRNCH!
OOF!!
KRICK KRACK
HUH?
KSHOOM!
AGH!
FWUMP!

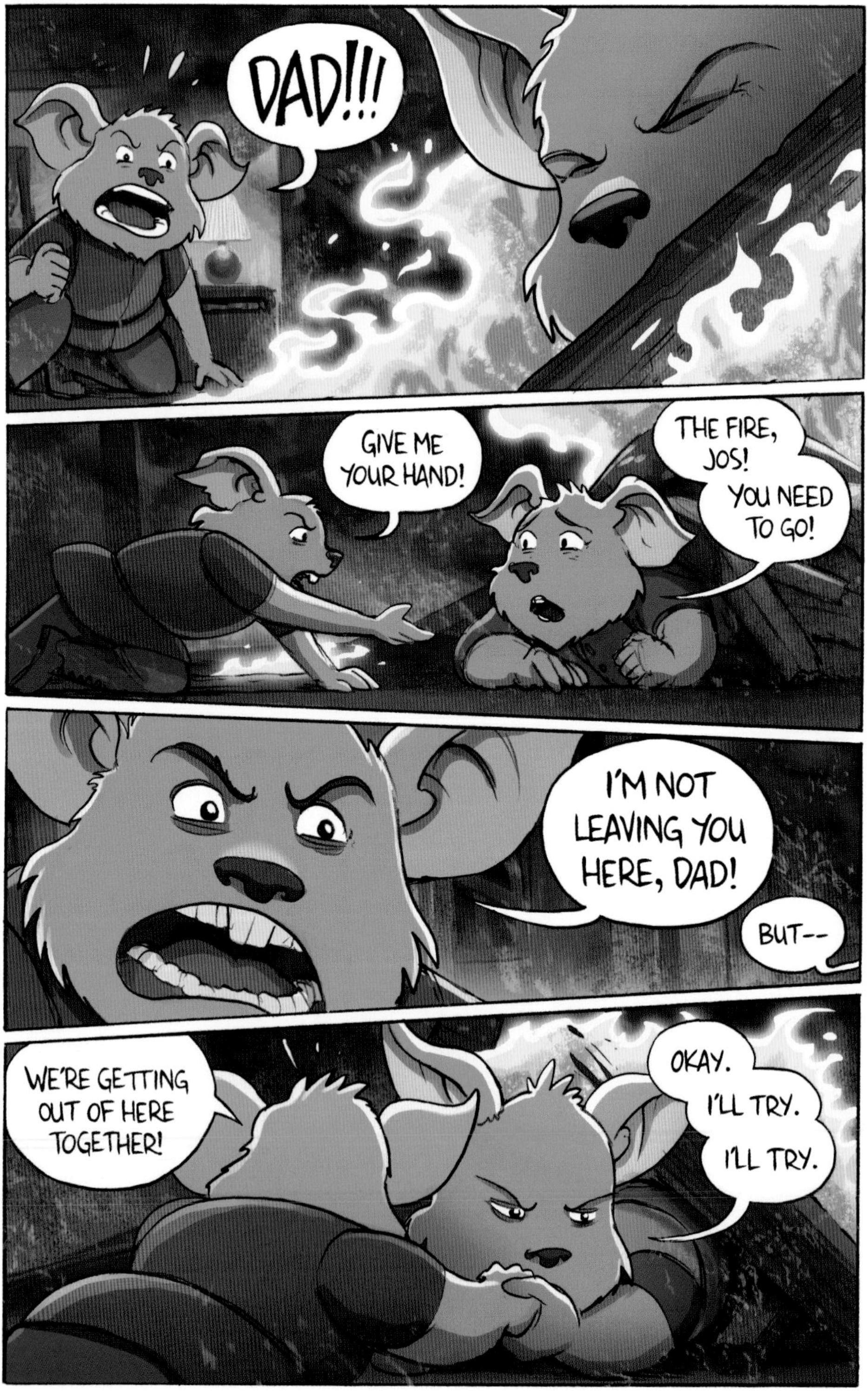
DAD!!!
GIVE ME YOUR HAND!
THE FIRE, JOS!
YOU NEED TO GO!
I'M NOT LEAVING YOU HERE, DAD!
BUT--
WE'RE GETTING OUT OF HERE TOGETHER!
OKAY.
I'LL TRY.
I'LL TRY.

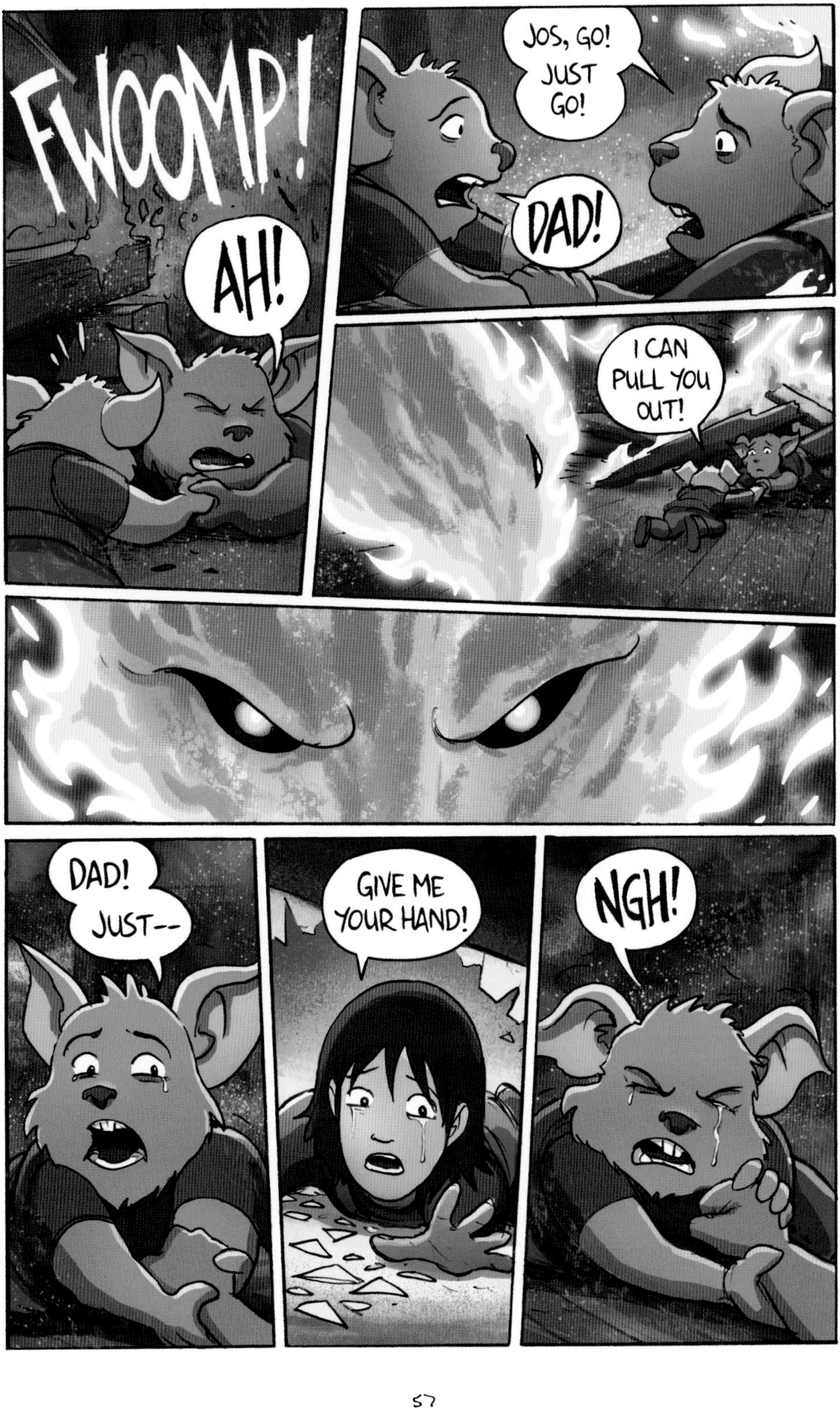
FWOOMP!
AH!
JOS, GO!
JUST GO!
DAD!
I CAN PULL YOU OUT!
DAD!
JUST--
GIVE ME YOUR HAND!
NGH!

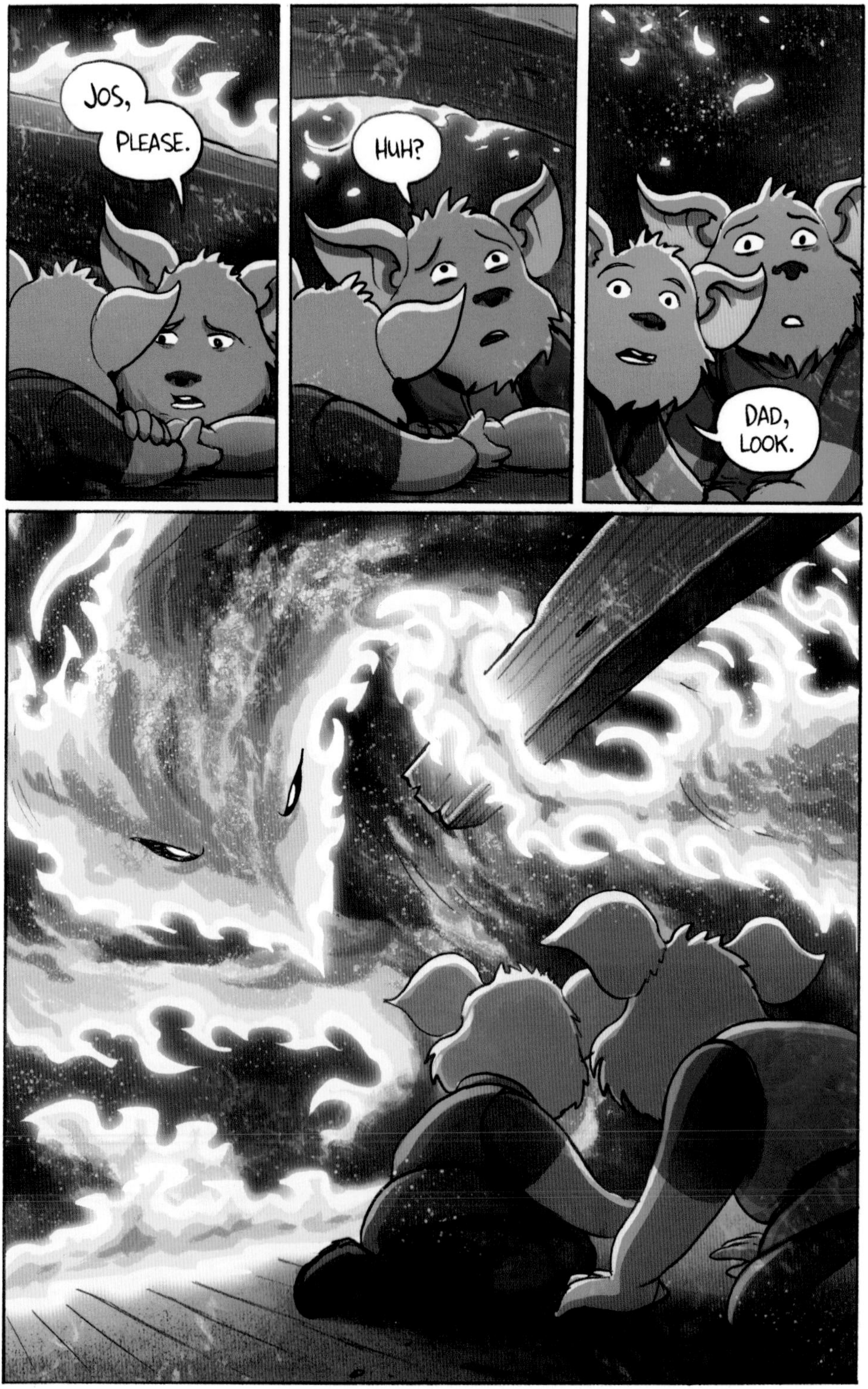
JOS,
PLEASE.
HUH?
DAD,
LOOK.

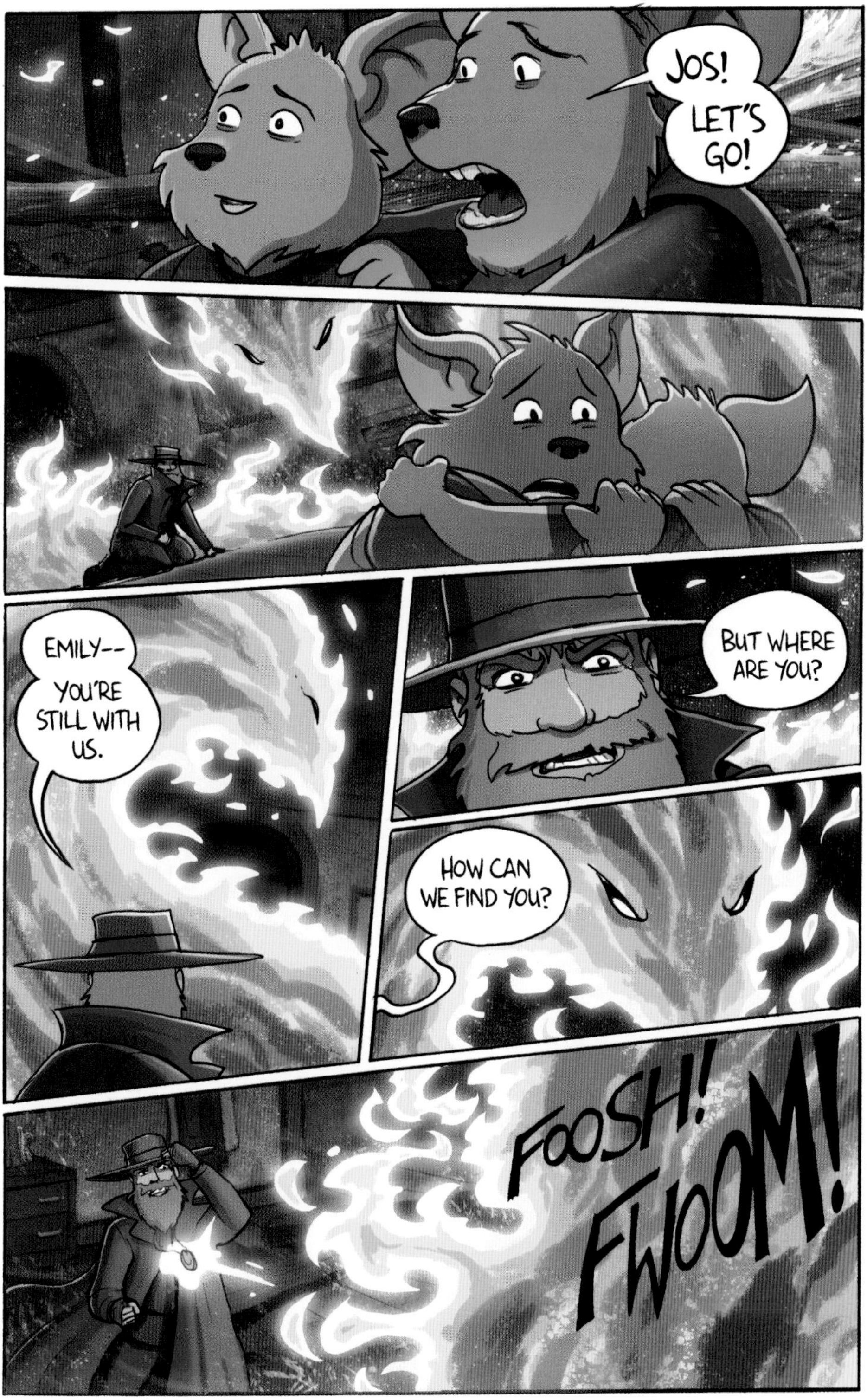
JOS!
LET'S GO!
EMILY--
YOU'RE STILL WITH US.
BUT WHERE ARE YOU?
HOW CAN WE FIND YOU?
FOOSH!
FWOOM!

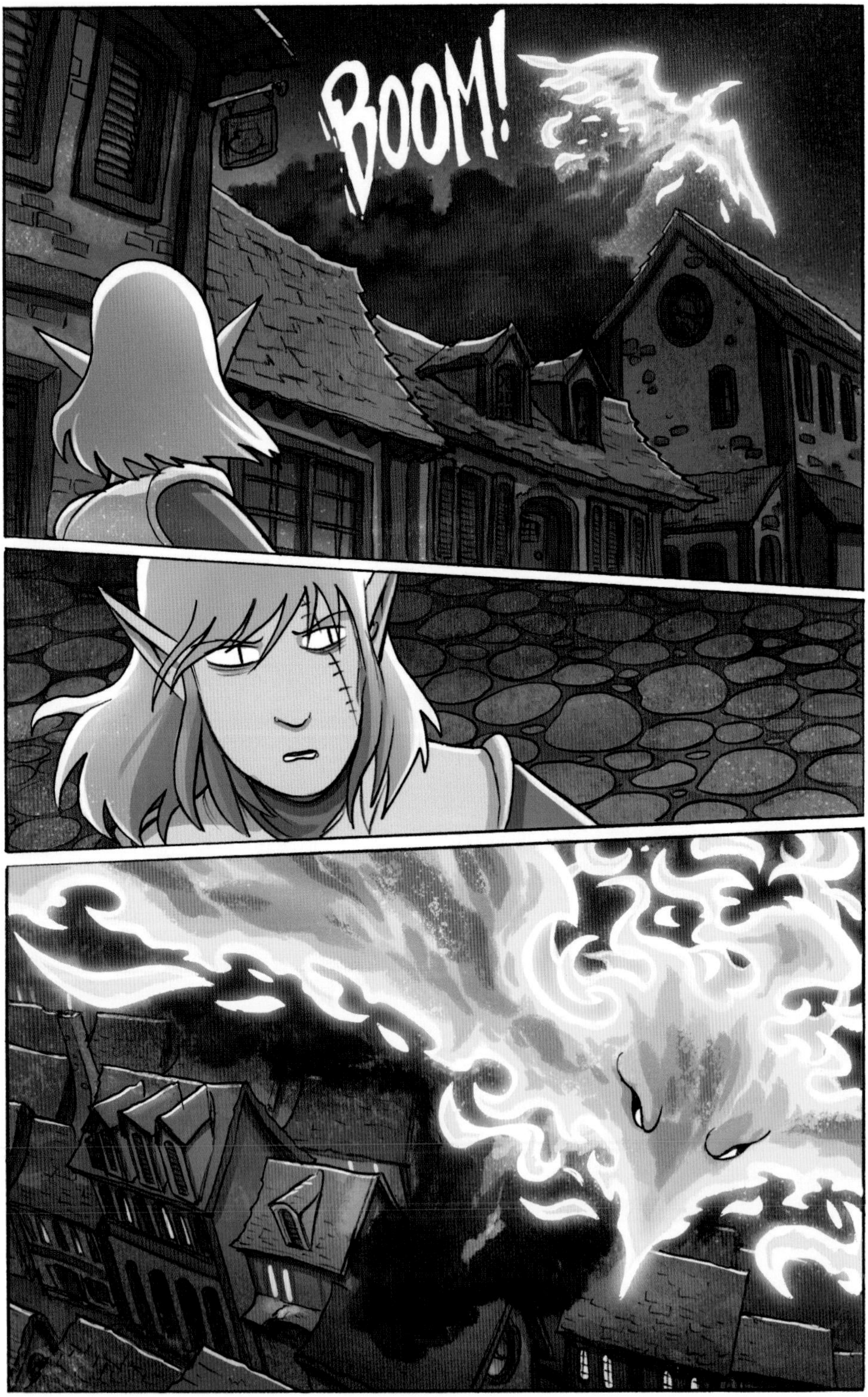
BOOM!

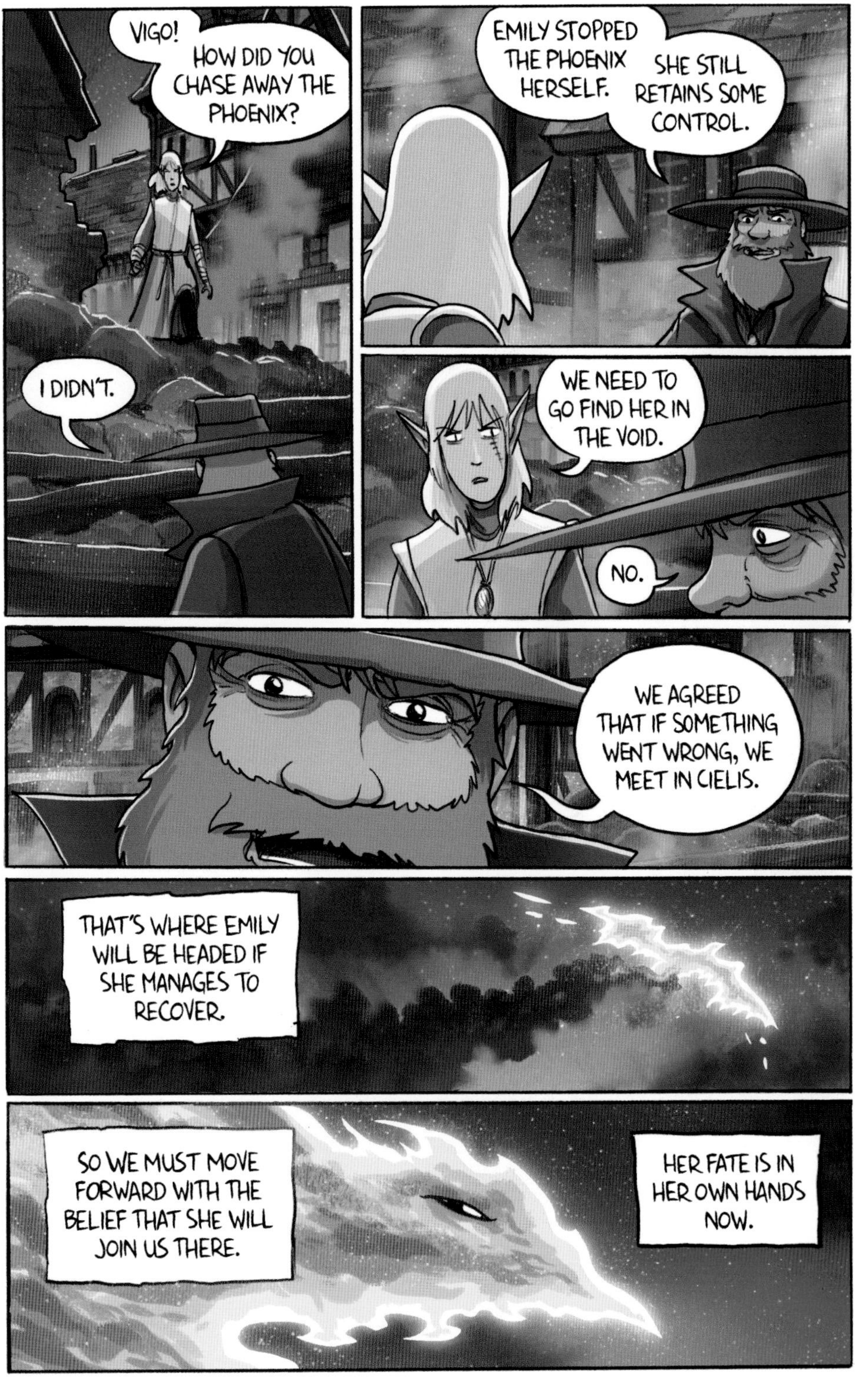
VIGO!
HOW DID YOU CHASE AWAY THE PHOENIX?
EMILY STOPPED THE PHOENIX HERSELF.
SHE STILL RETAINS SOME CONTROL.
I DIDN'T.
WE NEED TO GO FIND HER IN THE VOID.
NO.
WE AGREED THAT IF SOMETHING WENT WRONG, WE MEET IN CIELIS.
THAT'S WHERE EMILY WILL BE HEADED IF SHE MANAGES TO RECOVER.
SO WE MUST MOVE FORWARD WITH THE BELIEF THAT SHE WILL JOIN US THERE.
HER FATE IS IN HER OWN HANDS NOW.

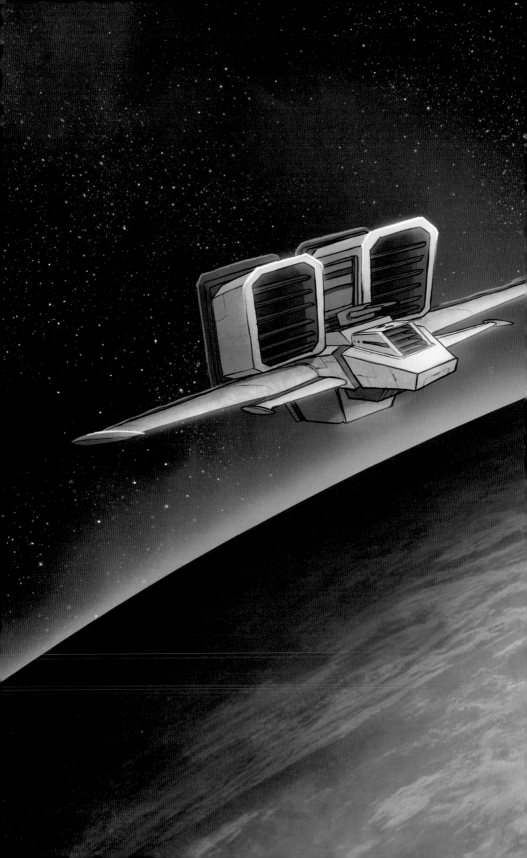

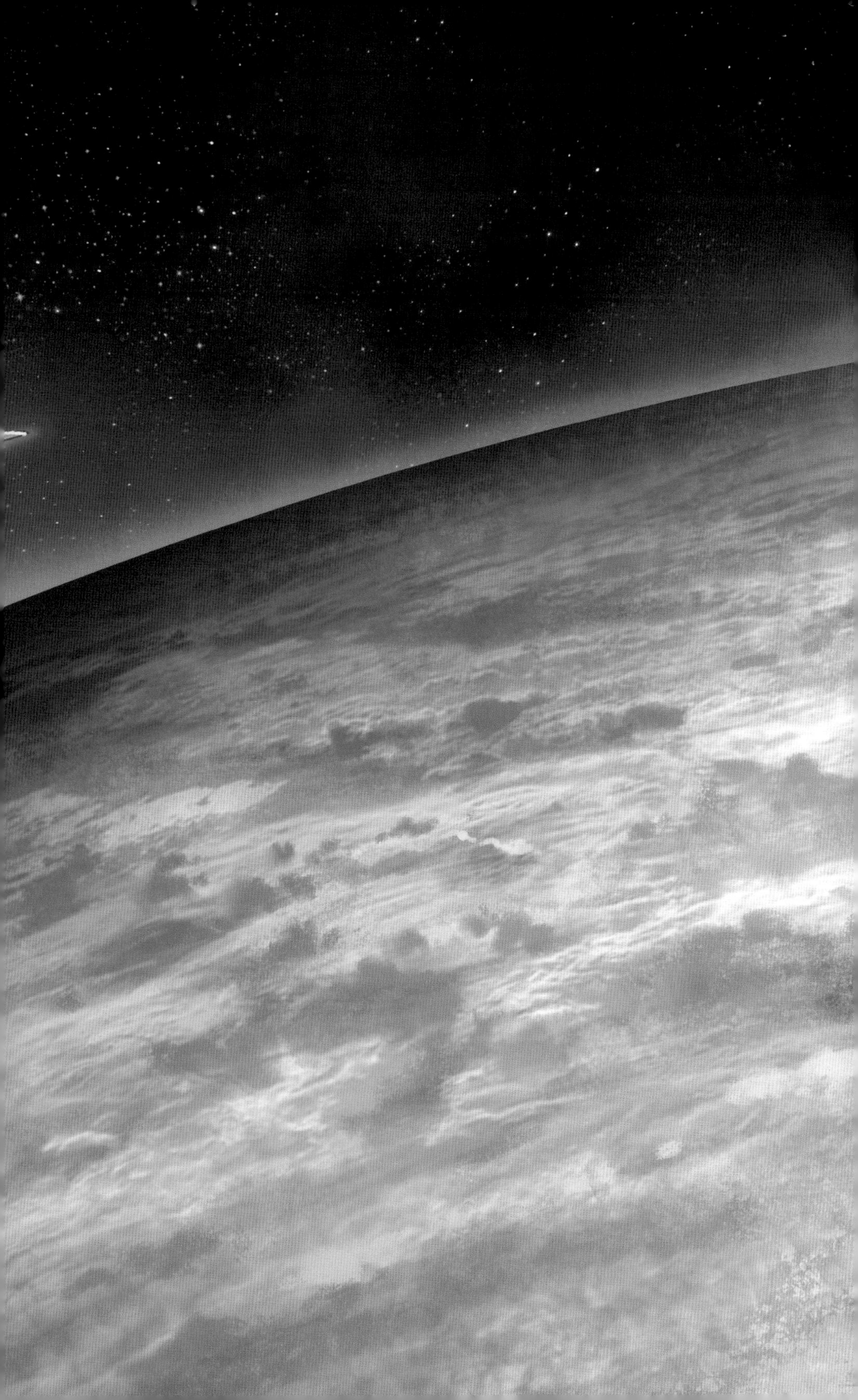

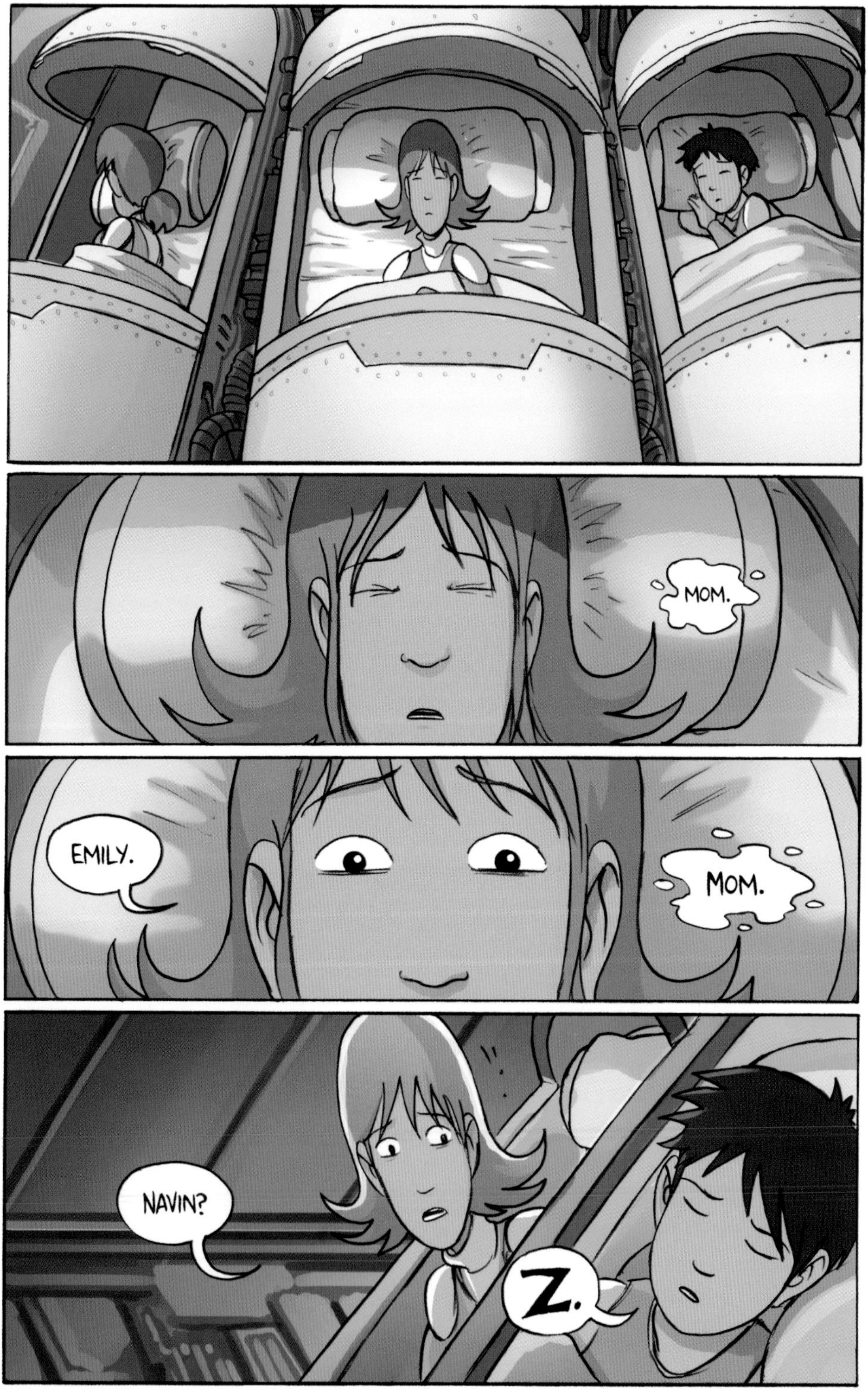
MOM.
EMILY.
MOM.
NAVIN?
Z.

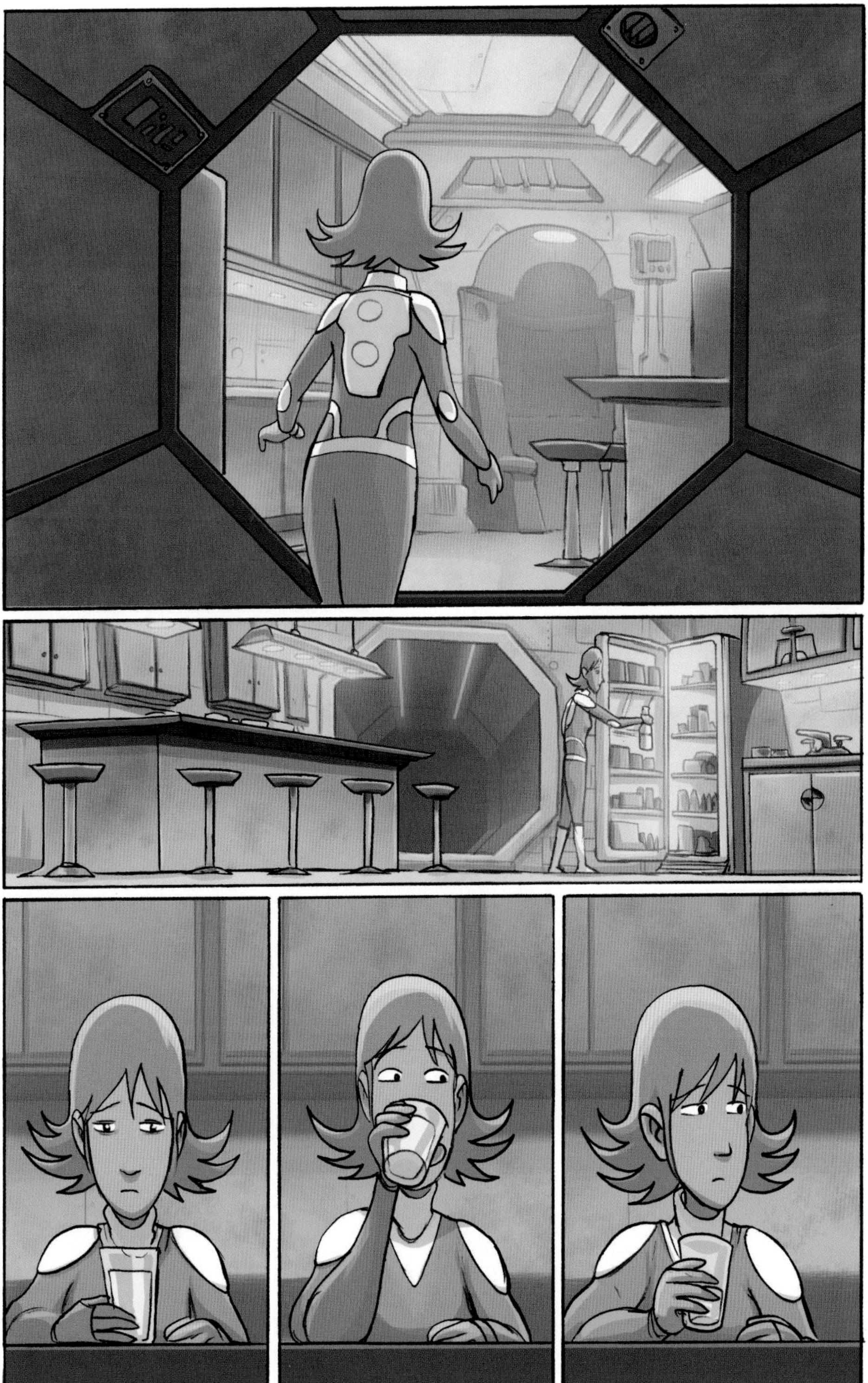

LEON? HAVE YOU BEEN AWAKE ALL THIS TIME?

OH.

IT'S BEEN HARD TO SLEEP.

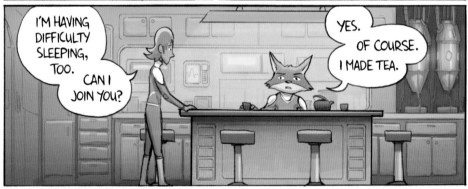
I'M HAVING DIFFICULTY SLEEPING, TOO. CAN I JOIN YOU?

YES. OF COURSE. I MADE TEA.

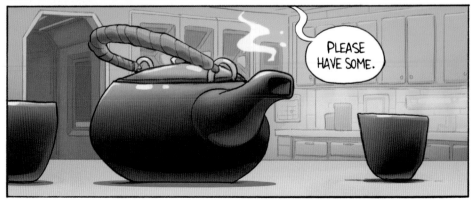
PLEASE HAVE SOME.

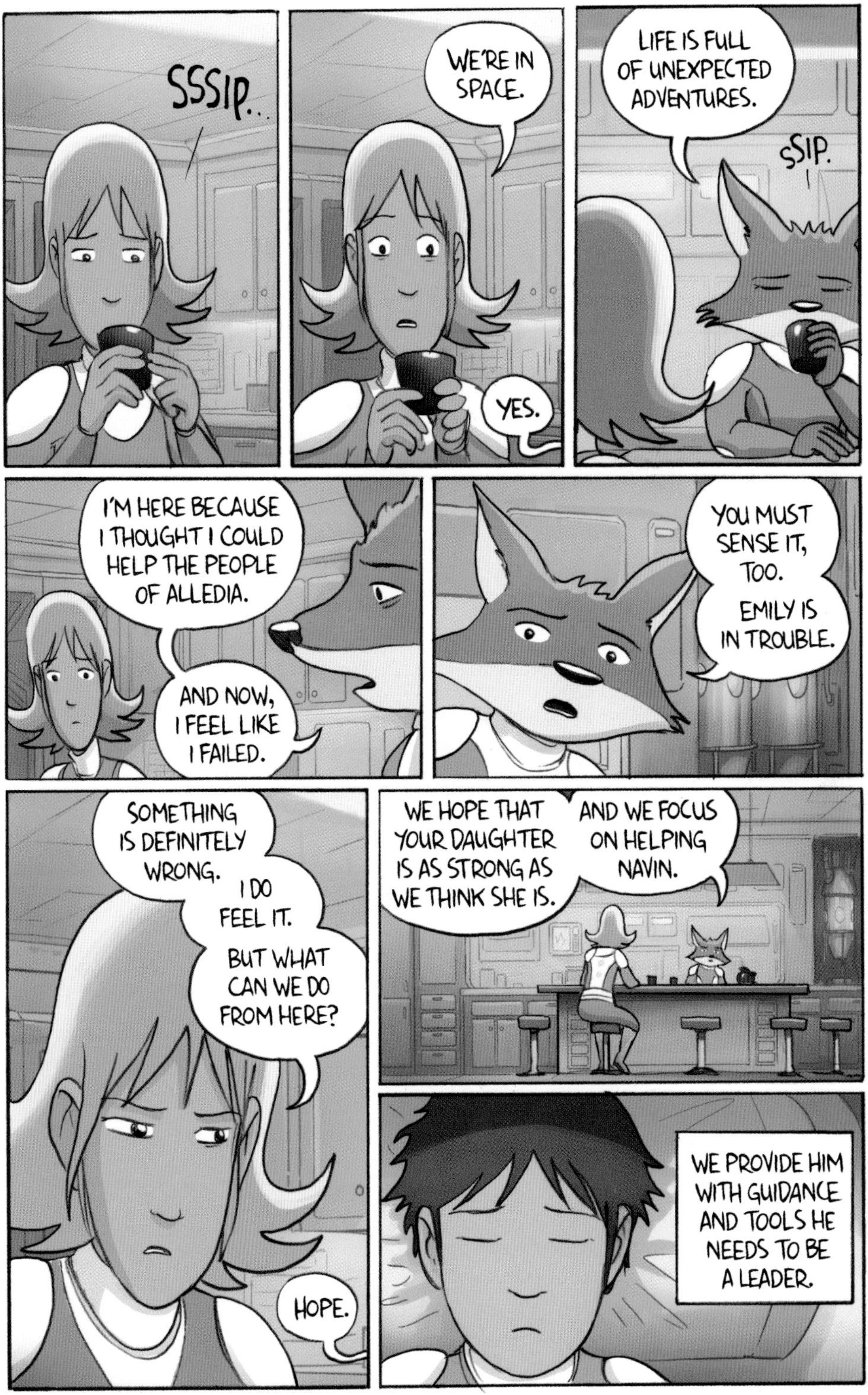
SSSIP...
WE'RE IN SPACE.
YES.
LIFE IS FULL OF UNEXPECTED ADVENTURES.
SSIP.
I'M HERE BECAUSE I THOUGHT I COULD HELP THE PEOPLE OF ALLEDIA.
AND NOW, I FEEL LIKE I FAILED.
YOU MUST SENSE IT, TOO.
EMILY IS IN TROUBLE.
SOMETHING IS DEFINITELY WRONG.
I DO FEEL IT.
BUT WHAT CAN WE DO FROM HERE?
HOPE.
WE HOPE THAT YOUR DAUGHTER IS AS STRONG AS WE THINK SHE IS.
AND WE FOCUS ON HELPING NAVIN.
WE PROVIDE HIM WITH GUIDANCE AND TOOLS HE NEEDS TO BE A LEADER.

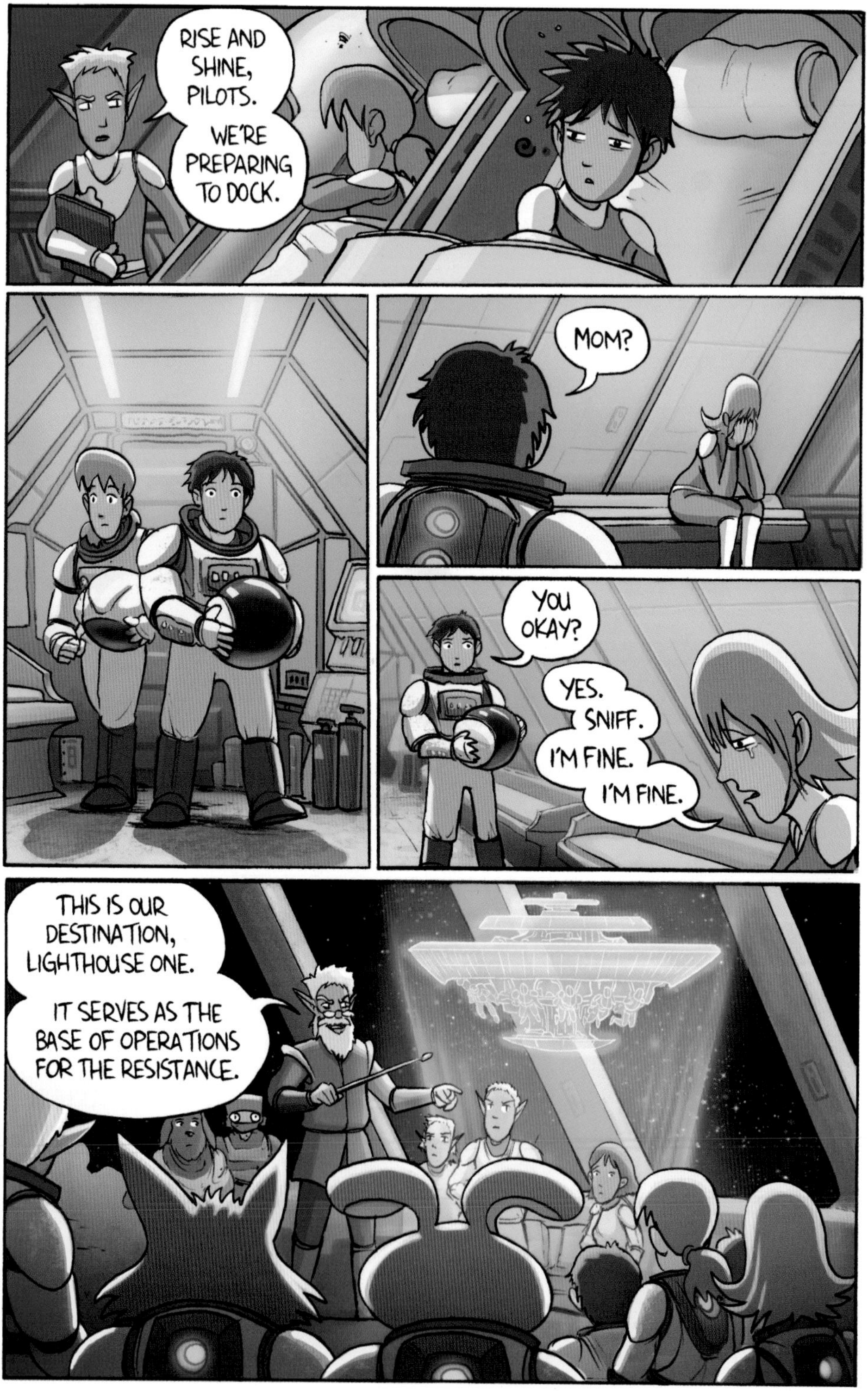
RISE AND SHINE, PILOTS.
WE'RE PREPARING TO DOCK.
MOM?
YOU OKAY?
YES.
SNIFF.
I'M FINE.
I'M FINE.
THIS IS OUR DESTINATION, LIGHTHOUSE ONE.
IT SERVES AS THE BASE OF OPERATIONS FOR THE RESISTANCE.

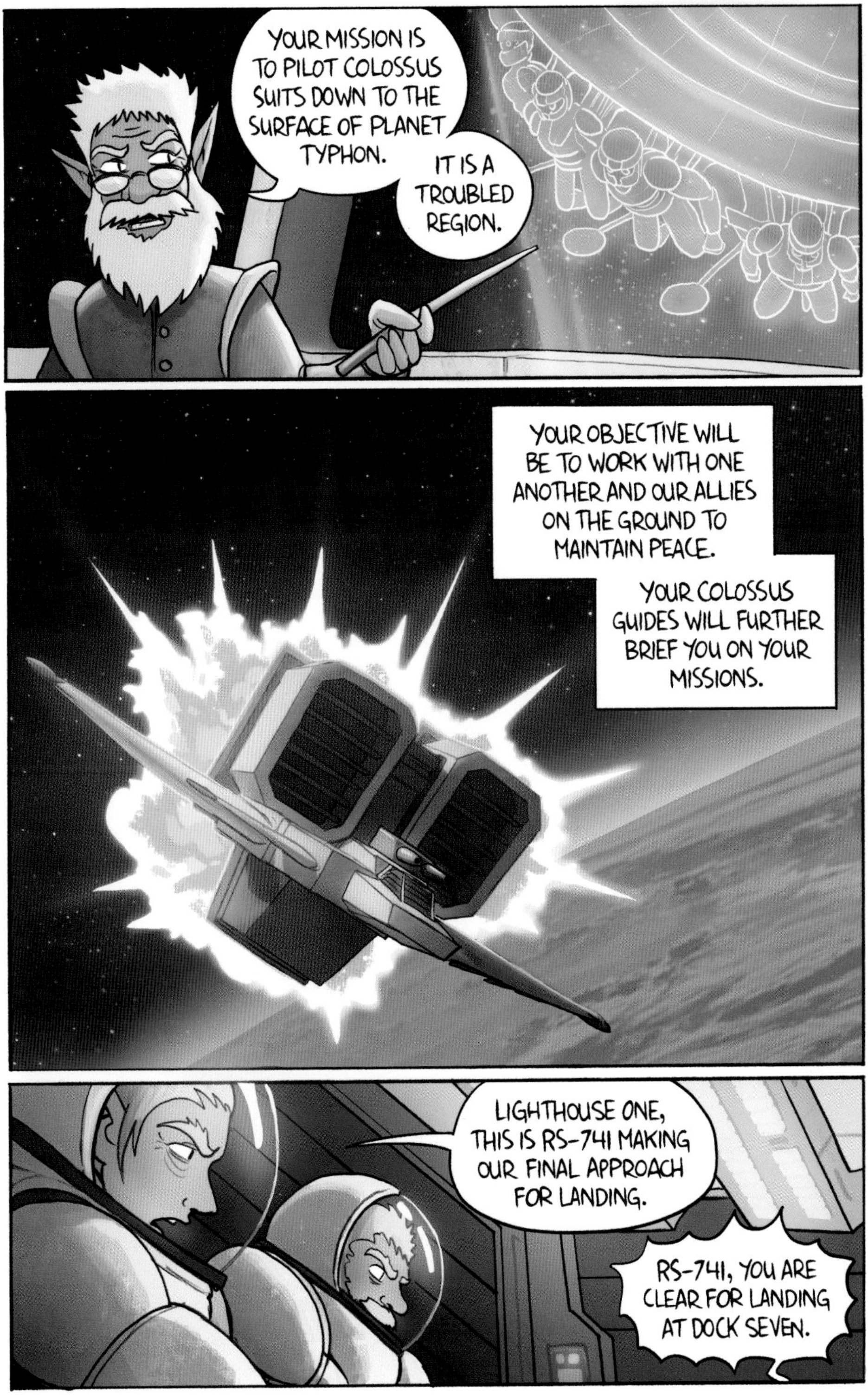
YOUR MISSION IS TO PILOT COLOSSUS SUITS DOWN TO THE SURFACE OF PLANET TYPHON.
IT IS A TROUBLED REGION.
YOUR OBJECTIVE WILL BE TO WORK WITH ONE ANOTHER AND OUR ALLIES ON THE GROUND TO MAINTAIN PEACE.
YOUR COLOSSUS GUIDES WILL FURTHER BRIEF YOU ON YOUR MISSIONS.
LIGHTHOUSE ONE, THIS IS RS-741 MAKING OUR FINAL APPROACH FOR LANDING.
RS-741, YOU ARE CLEAR FOR LANDING AT DOCK SEVEN.

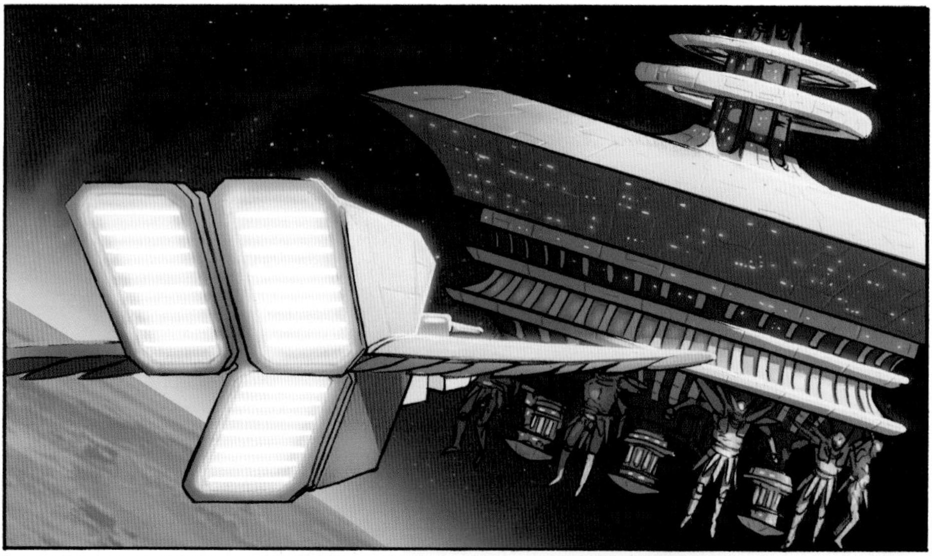

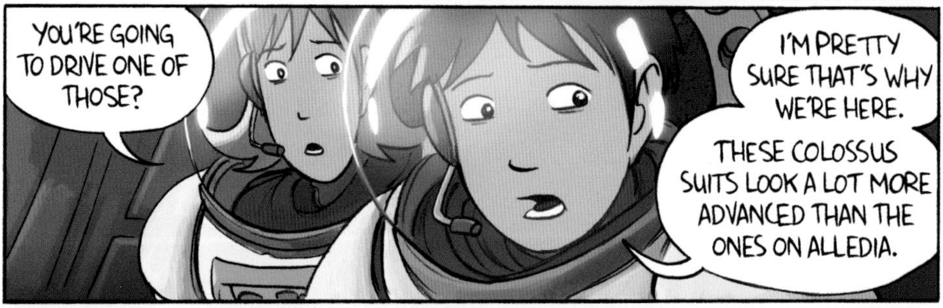
YOU'RE GOING TO DRIVE ONE OF THOSE?
I'M PRETTY SURE THAT'S WHY WE'RE HERE.
THESE COLOSSUS SUITS LOOK A LOT MORE ADVANCED THAN THE ONES ON ALLEDIA.

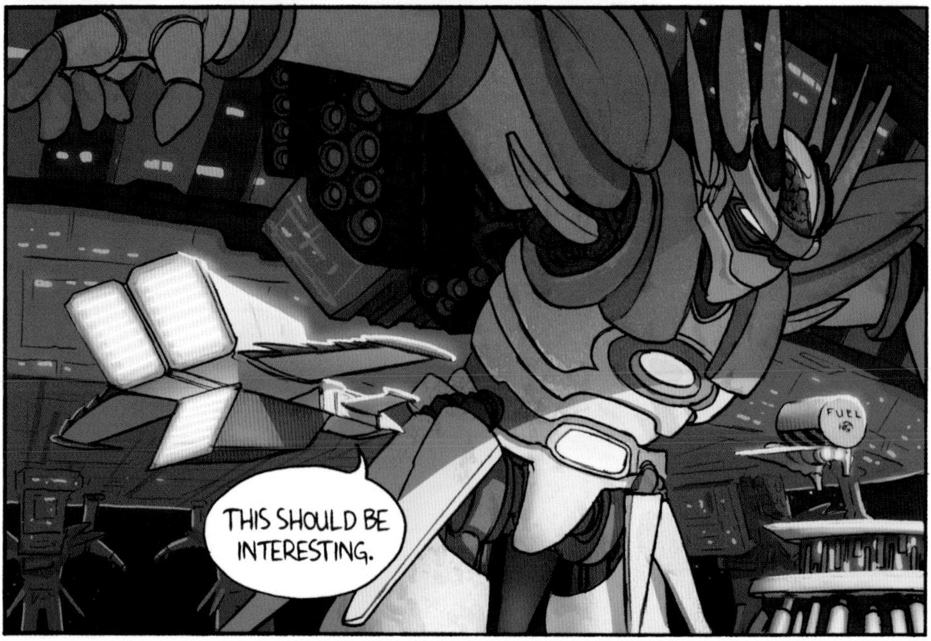
FUEL
THIS SHOULD BE INTERESTING.

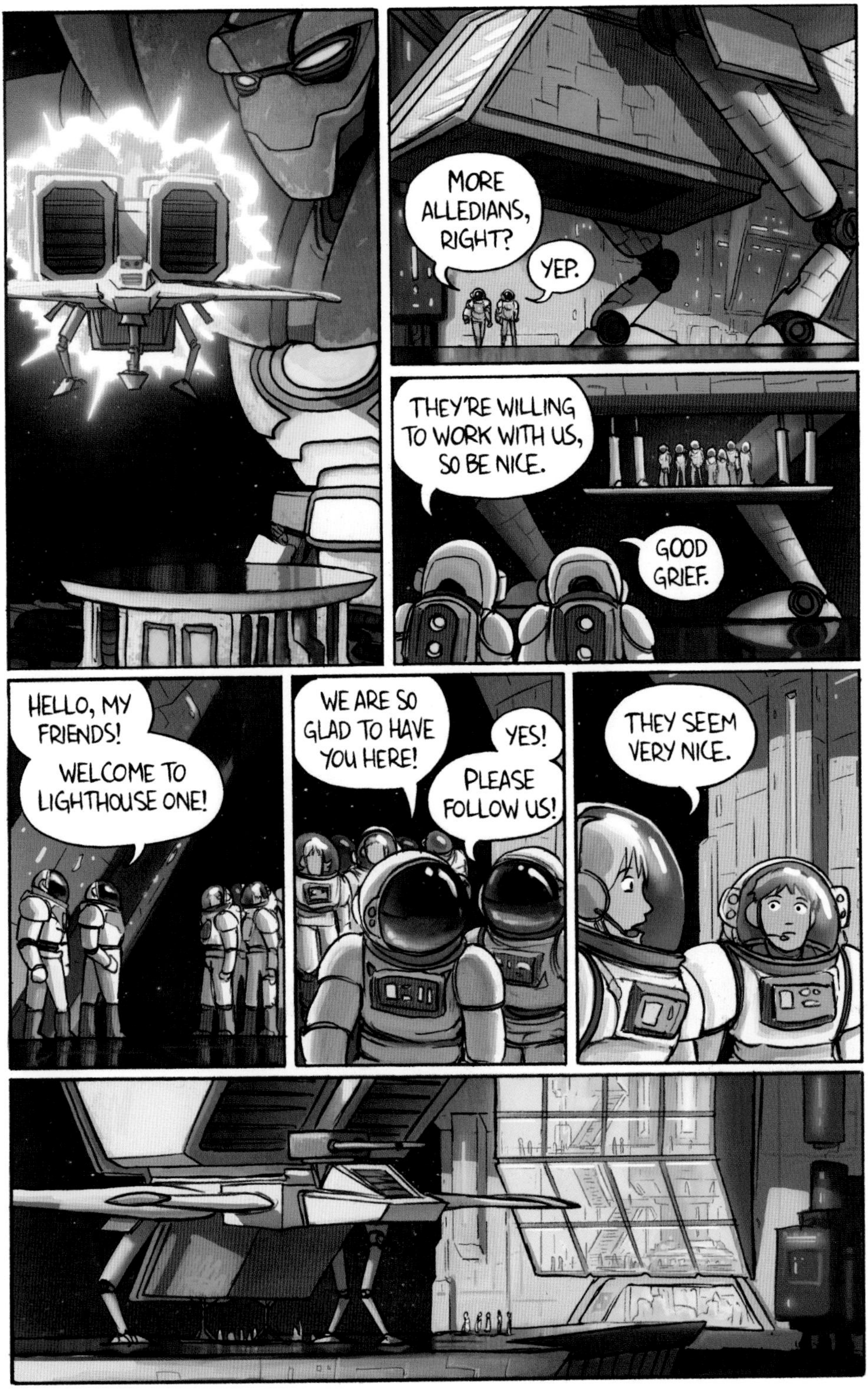
MORE ALLEDIANS, RIGHT?
YEP.
THEY'RE WILLING TO WORK WITH US, SO BE NICE.
GOOD GRIEF.
HELLO, MY FRIENDS!
WELCOME TO LIGHTHOUSE ONE!
WE ARE SO GLAD TO HAVE YOU HERE!
YES!
PLEASE FOLLOW US!
THEY SEEM VERY NICE.

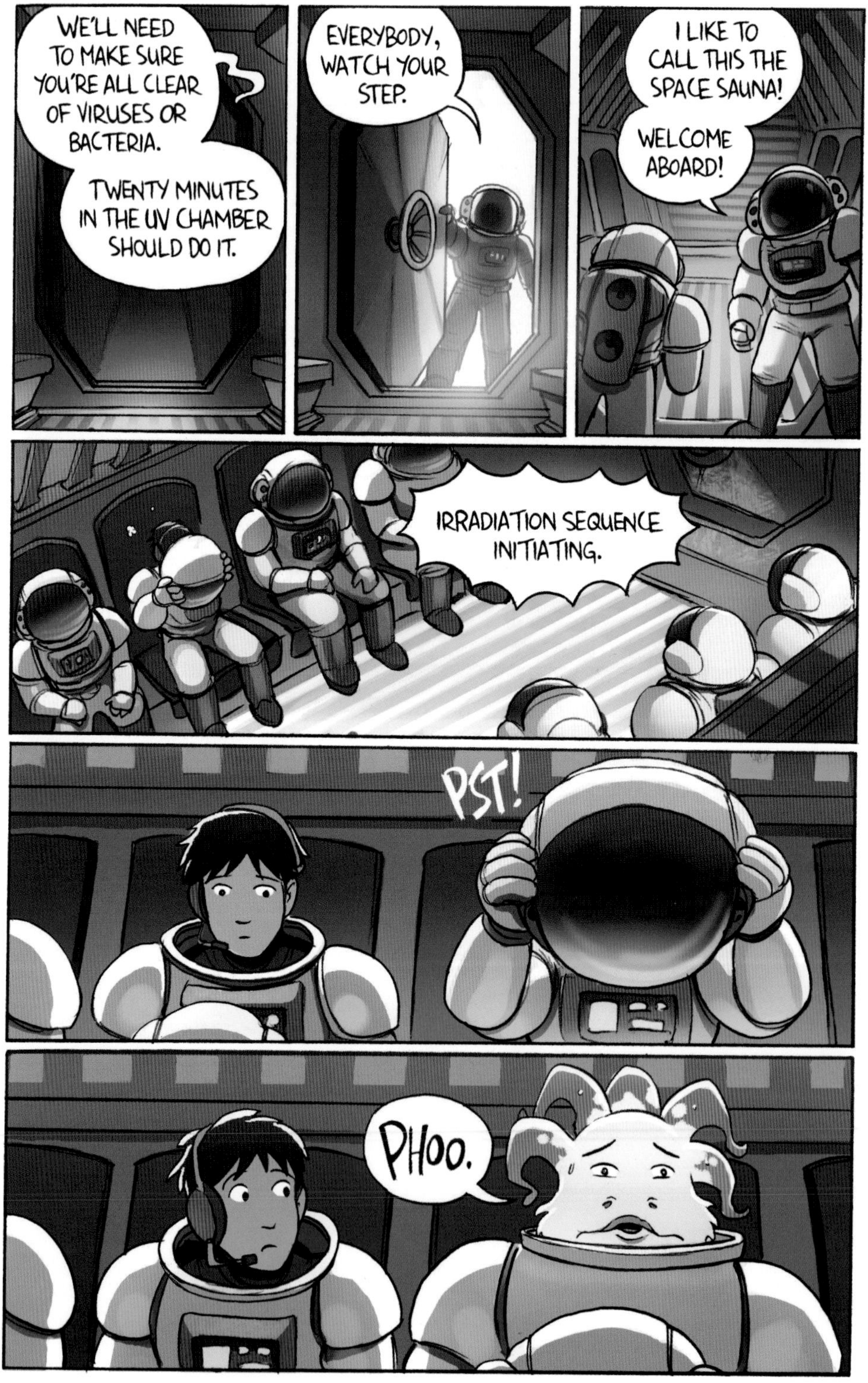
WE'LL NEED TO MAKE SURE YOU'RE ALL CLEAR OF VIRUSES OR BACTERIA.
TWENTY MINUTES IN THE UV CHAMBER SHOULD DO IT.
EVERYBODY, WATCH YOUR STEP.
I LIKE TO CALL THIS THE SPACE SAUNA!
WELCOME ABOARD!
IRRADIATION SEQUENCE INITIATING.
PST!
PHOO.

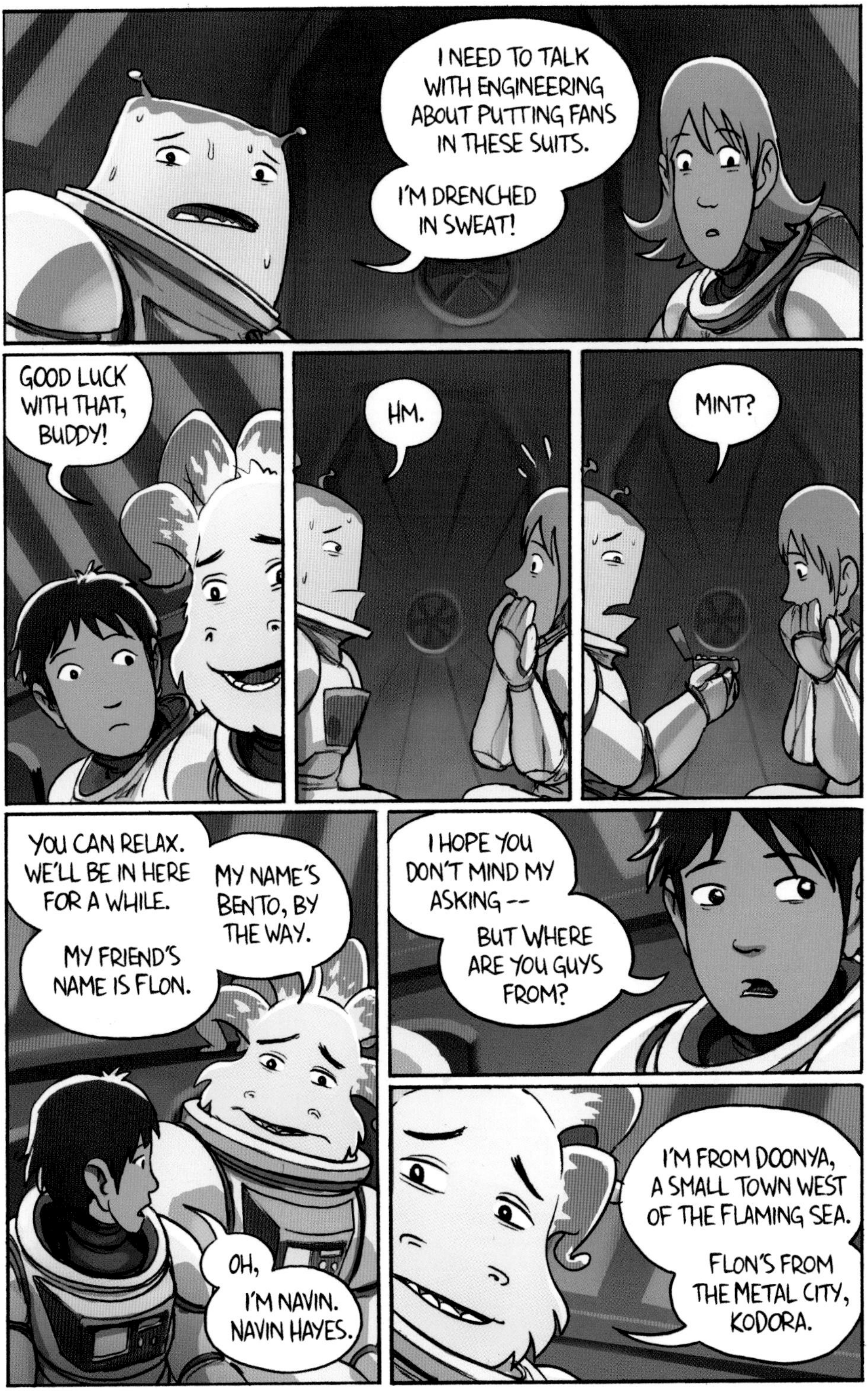
I NEED TO TALK WITH ENGINEERING ABOUT PUTTING FANS IN THESE SUITS.
I'M DRENCHED IN SWEAT!
GOOD LUCK WITH THAT, BUDDY!
HM.
MINT?
YOU CAN RELAX. WE'LL BE IN HERE FOR A WHILE.
MY FRIEND'S NAME IS FLON.
MY NAME'S BENTO, BY THE WAY.
OH,
I'M NAVIN. NAVIN HAYES.
I HOPE YOU DON'T MIND MY ASKING --
BUT WHERE ARE YOU GUYS FROM?
I'M FROM DOONYA, A SMALL TOWN WEST OF THE FLAMING SEA.
FLON'S FROM THE METAL CITY, KODORA.

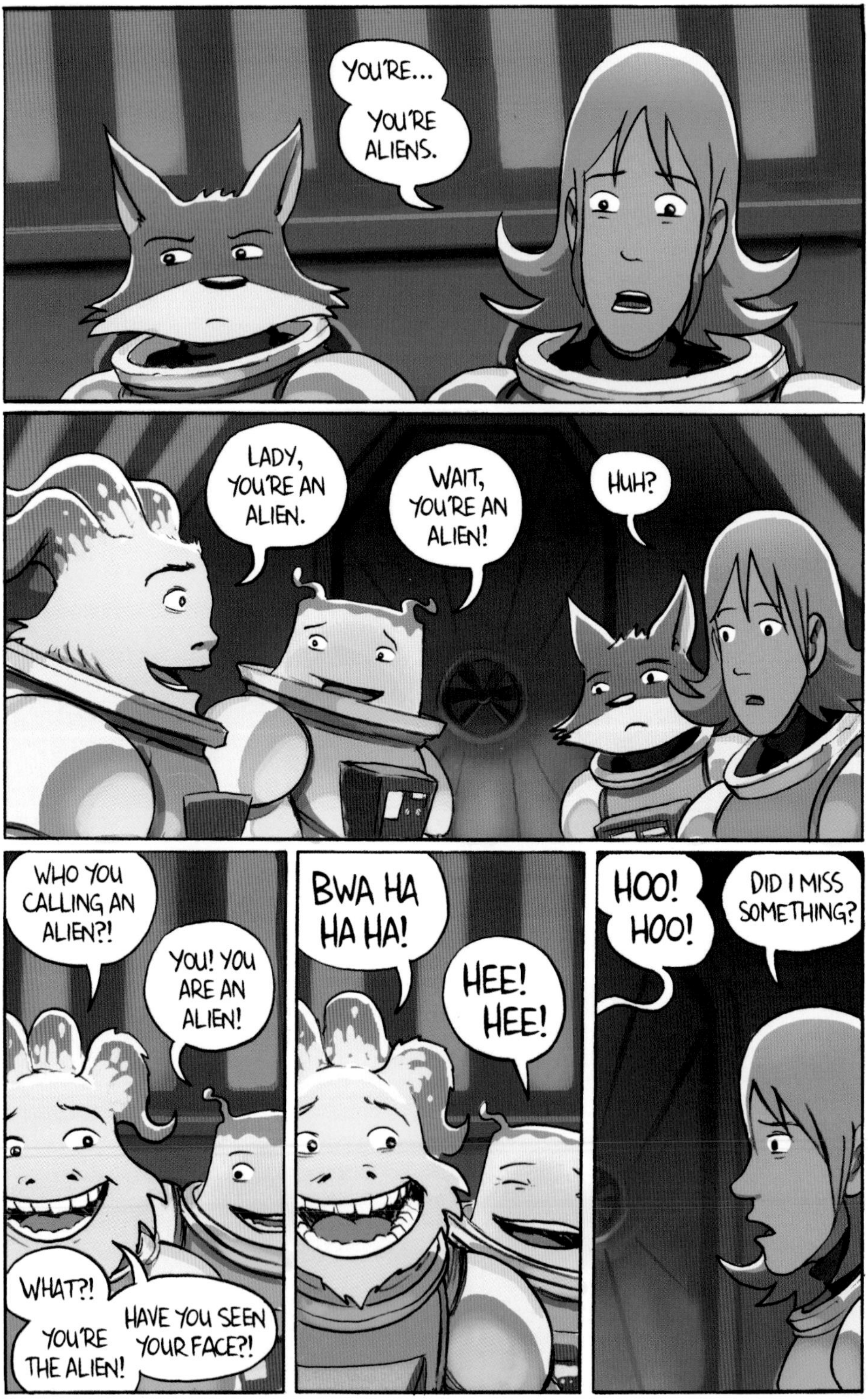
YOU'RE...
YOU'RE ALIENS.
LADY, YOU'RE AN ALIEN.
WAIT, YOU'RE AN ALIEN!
HUH?
WHO YOU CALLING AN ALIEN?!
YOU! YOU ARE AN ALIEN!
WHAT?!
YOU'RE THE ALIEN!
HAVE YOU SEEN YOUR FACE?!
BWA HA HA HA!
HEE! HEE!
HOO! HOO!
DID I MISS SOMETHING?

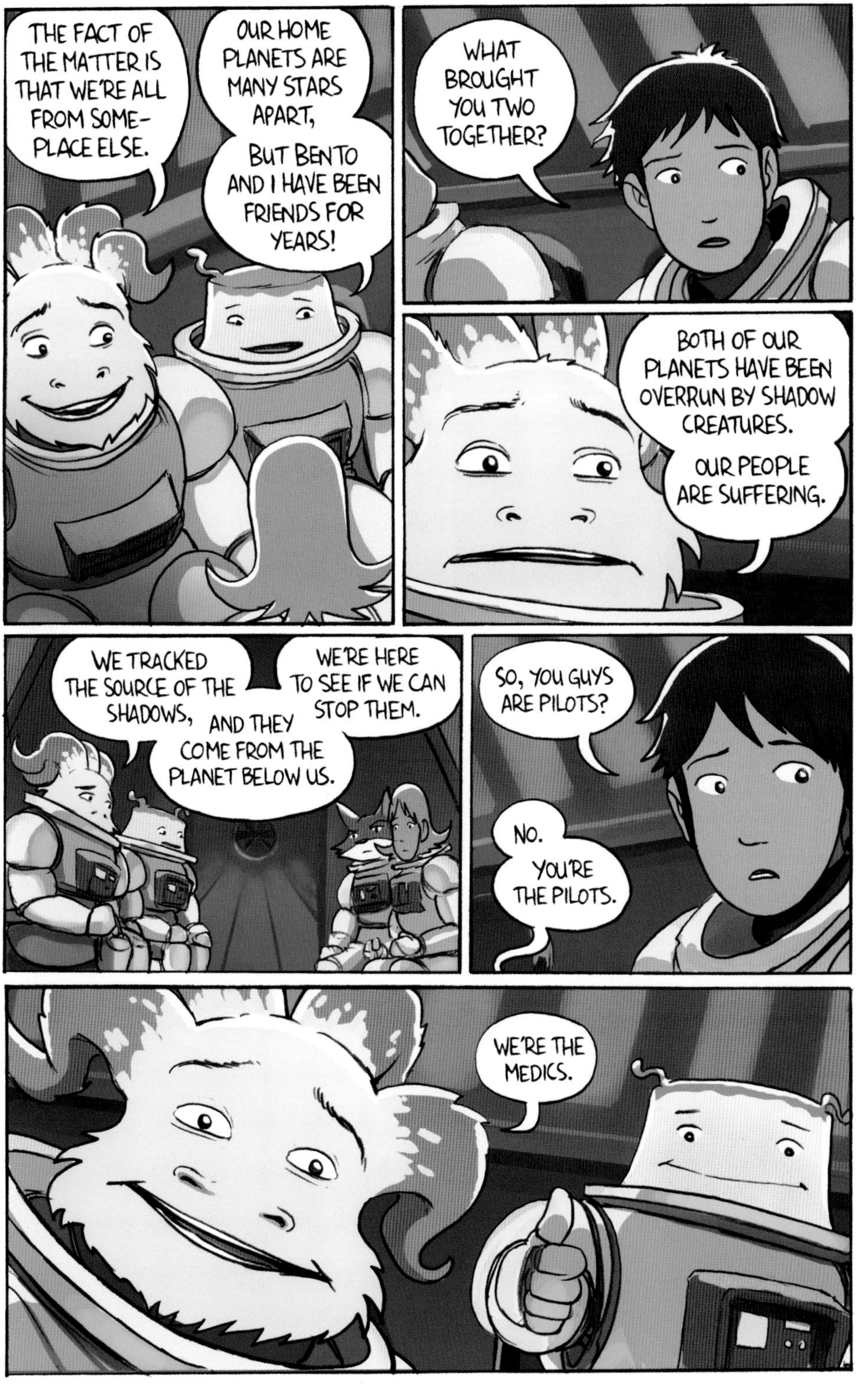
THE FACT OF THE MATTER IS THAT WE'RE ALL FROM SOME-PLACE ELSE.
OUR HOME PLANETS ARE MANY STARS APART,
BUT BENTO AND I HAVE BEEN FRIENDS FOR YEARS!
WHAT BROUGHT YOU TWO TOGETHER?
BOTH OF OUR PLANETS HAVE BEEN OVERRUN BY SHADOW CREATURES.
OUR PEOPLE ARE SUFFERING.
WE TRACKED THE SOURCE OF THE SHADOWS,
AND THEY COME FROM THE PLANET BELOW US.
WE'RE HERE TO SEE IF WE CAN STOP THEM.
SO, YOU GUYS ARE PILOTS?
NO.
YOU'RE THE PILOTS.
WE'RE THE MEDICS.

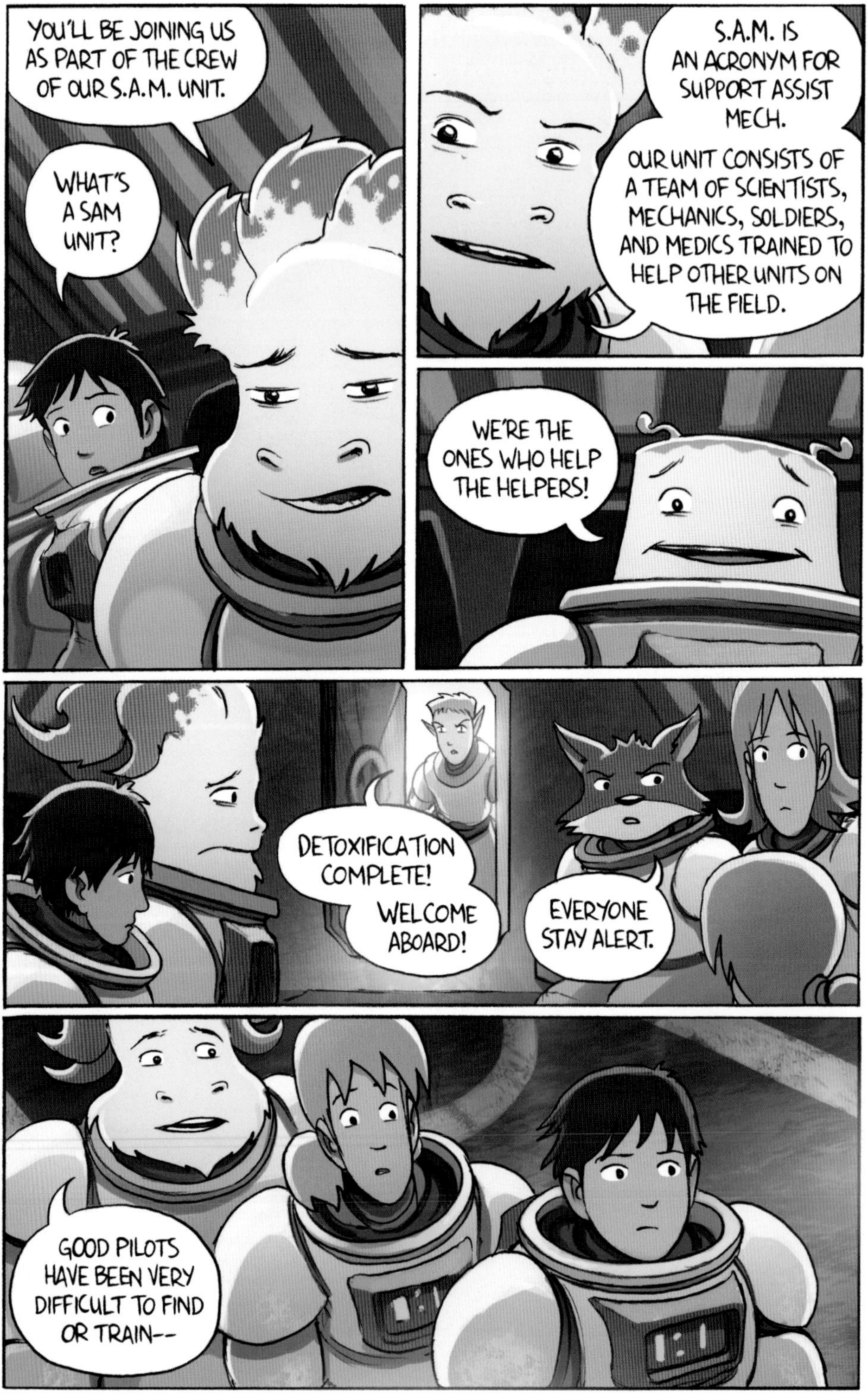
YOU'LL BE JOINING US AS PART OF THE CREW OF OUR S.A.M. UNIT.
WHAT'S A SAM UNIT?
S.A.M. IS AN ACRONYM FOR SUPPORT ASSIST MECH.
OUR UNIT CONSISTS OF A TEAM OF SCIENTISTS, MECHANICS, SOLDIERS, AND MEDICS TRAINED TO HELP OTHER UNITS ON THE FIELD.
WE'RE THE ONES WHO HELP THE HELPERS!
DETOXIFICATION COMPLETE!
WELCOME ABOARD!
EVERYONE STAY ALERT.
GOOD PILOTS HAVE BEEN VERY DIFFICULT TO FIND OR TRAIN--

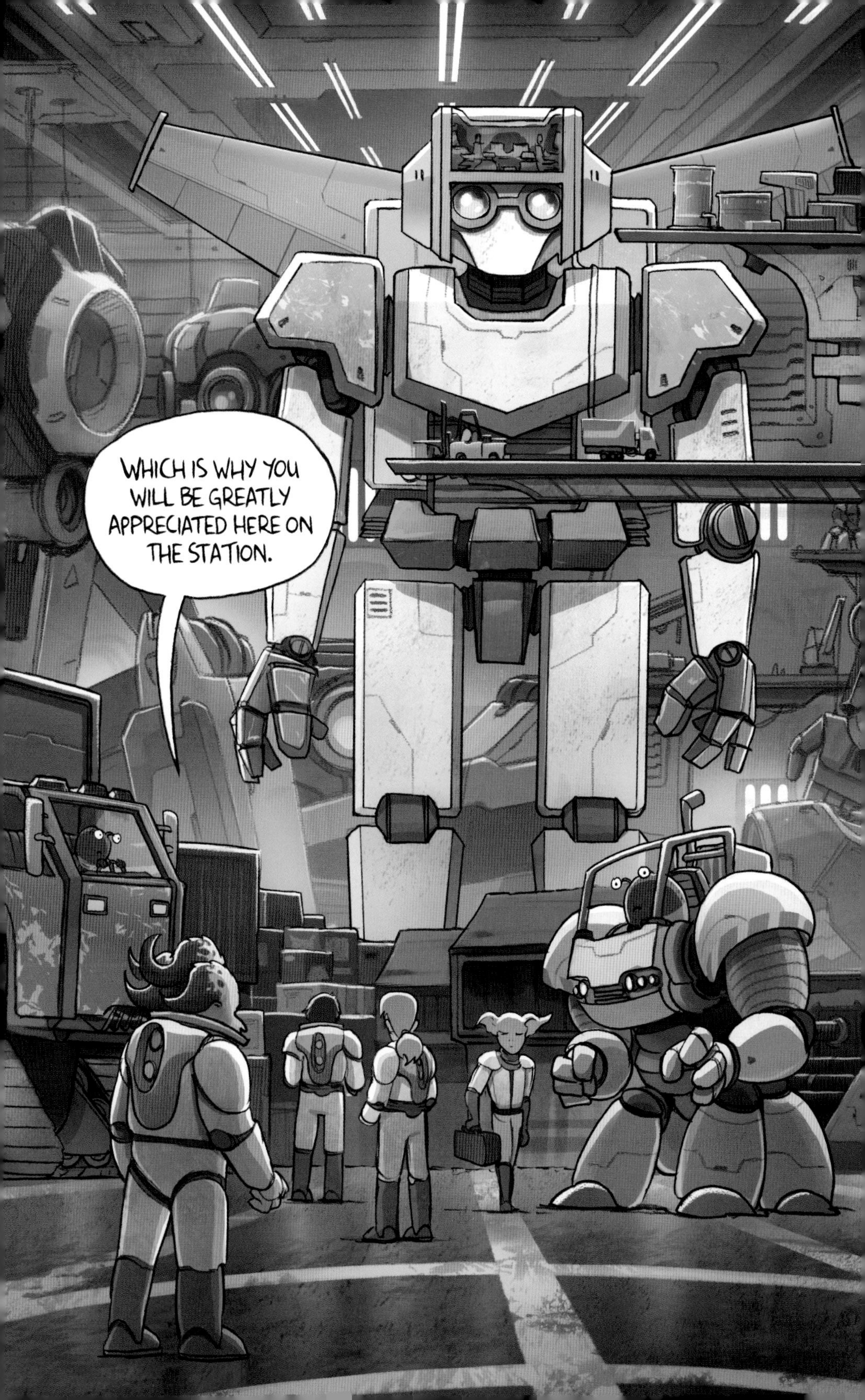
WHICH IS WHY YOU WILL BE GREATLY APPRECIATED HERE ON THE STATION.

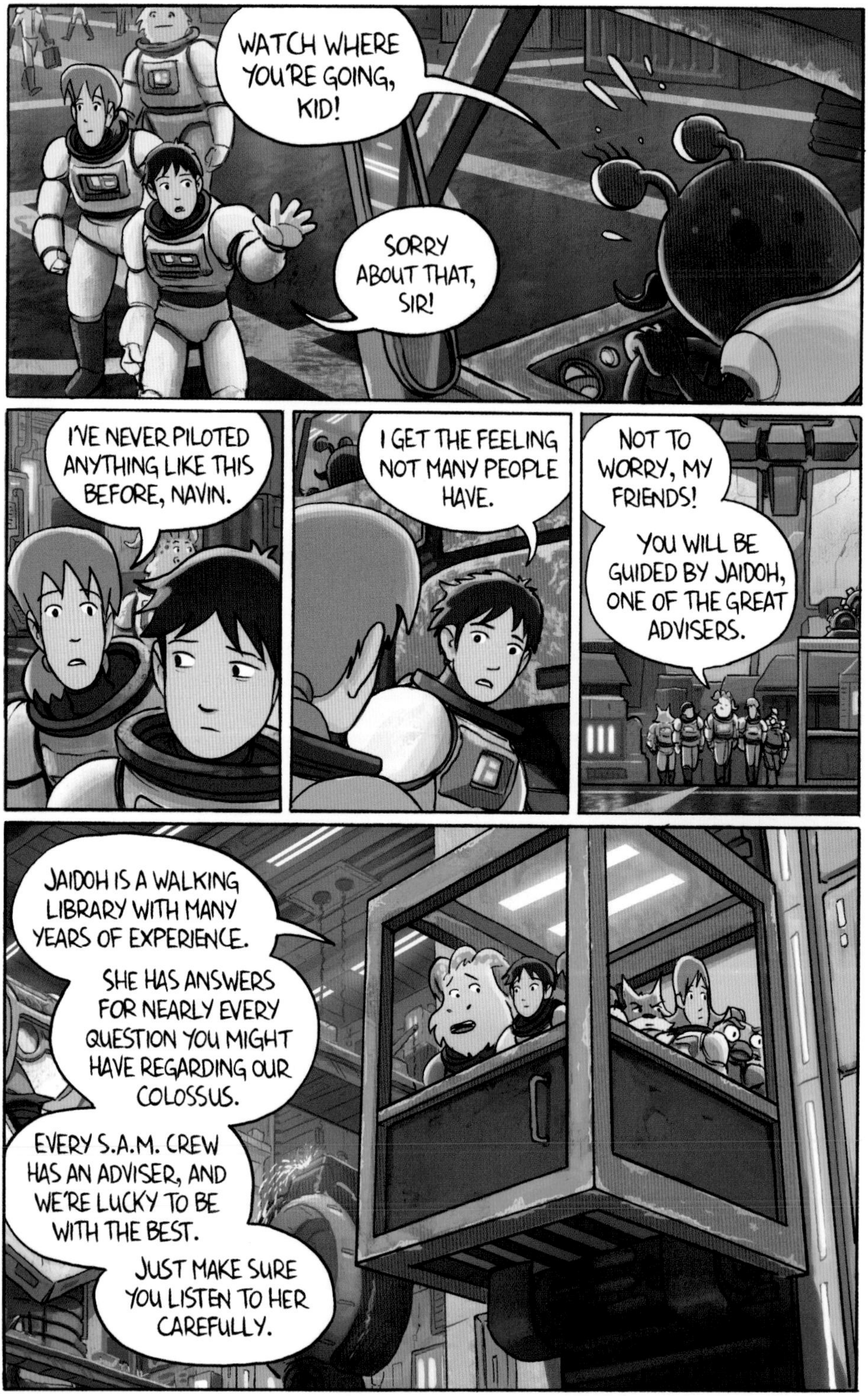
WATCH WHERE YOU'RE GOING, KID!
SORRY ABOUT THAT, SIR!
I'VE NEVER PILOTED ANYTHING LIKE THIS BEFORE, NAVIN.
I GET THE FEELING NOT MANY PEOPLE HAVE.
NOT TO WORRY, MY FRIENDS!
YOU WILL BE GUIDED BY JAIDOH, ONE OF THE GREAT ADVISERS.
JAIDOH IS A WALKING LIBRARY WITH MANY YEARS OF EXPERIENCE.
SHE HAS ANSWERS FOR NEARLY EVERY QUESTION YOU MIGHT HAVE REGARDING OUR COLOSSUS.
EVERY S.A.M. CREW HAS AN ADVISER, AND WE'RE LUCKY TO BE WITH THE BEST.
JUST MAKE SURE YOU LISTEN TO HER CAREFULLY.

YOU HAVE EIGHT HANDS, MORRISON!
HOW IS IT POSSIBLE FOR YOU TO BE SO SLOW?!
WE RELY ON YOUR SKILL AND SPEED TO KEEP US ALIVE ON THE FIELD!
UM--
YUP.
NOW GET BACK IN THE ENGINE ROOM AND STOP LETTING US ALL DOWN!
YOU'RE SO MUCH BETTER THAN THIS!
YOU'RE RIGHT, BOSS.
I GOT THIS.
OH!
YOU MUST BE OUR NEW PILOTS!
S.A.M CREW

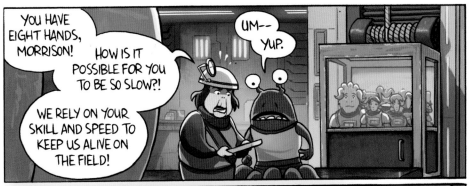

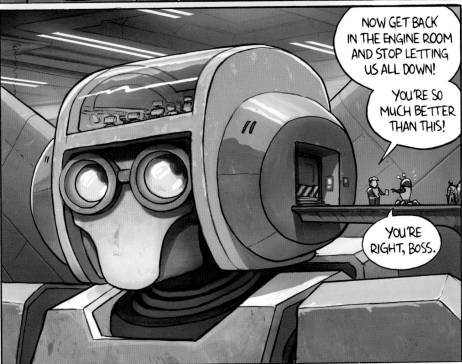

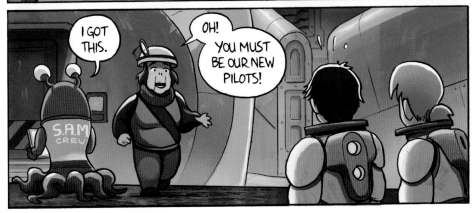

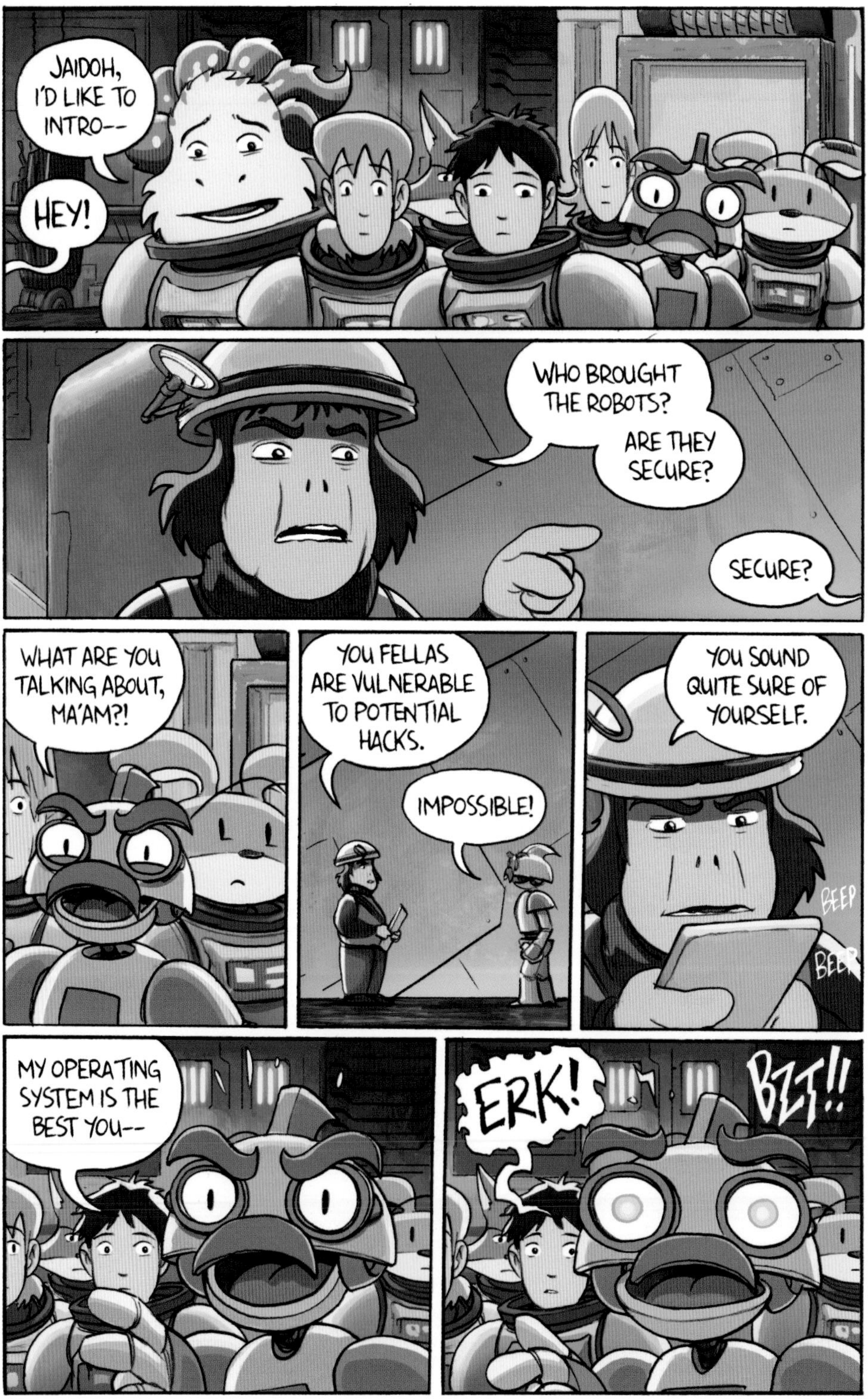
JAIDOH, I'D LIKE TO INTRO--
HEY!
WHO BROUGHT THE ROBOTS?
ARE THEY SECURE?
SECURE?
WHAT ARE YOU TALKING ABOUT, MA'AM?!
YOU FELLAS ARE VULNERABLE TO POTENTIAL HACKS.
IMPOSSIBLE!
YOU SOUND QUITE SURE OF YOURSELF.
BEEP
MY OPERATING SYSTEM IS THE BEST YOU--
ERK!
BZT!!

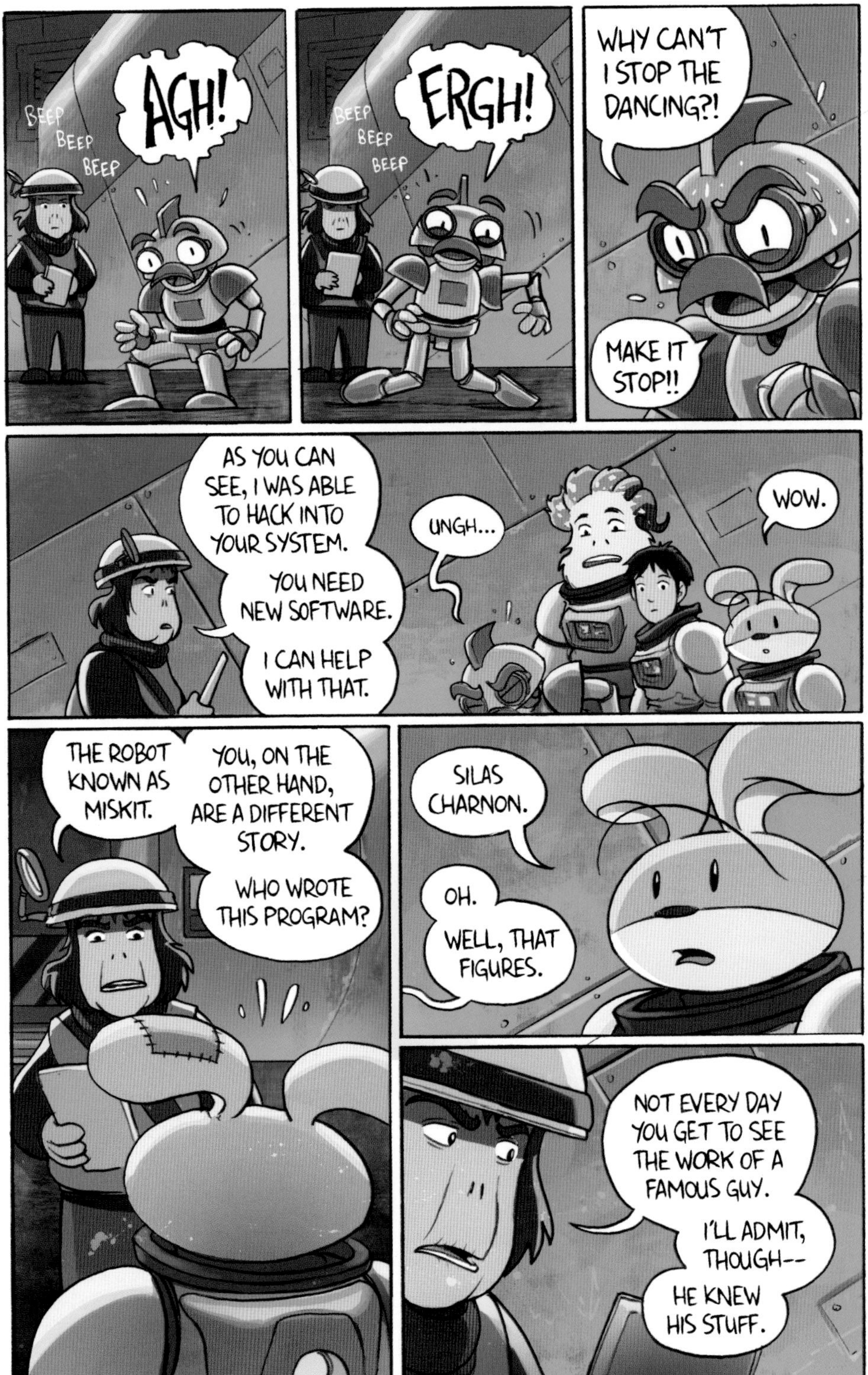
BEEP BEEP BEEP
AGH!
BEEP BEEP BEEP
ERGH!
WHY CAN'T I STOP THE DANCING?!
MAKE IT STOP!!
AS YOU CAN SEE, I WAS ABLE TO HACK INTO YOUR SYSTEM.
YOU NEED NEW SOFTWARE.
I CAN HELP WITH THAT.
UNGH...
WOW.
THE ROBOT KNOWN AS MISKIT.
YOU, ON THE OTHER HAND, ARE A DIFFERENT STORY.
WHO WROTE THIS PROGRAM?
SILAS CHARNON.
OH.
WELL, THAT FIGURES.
NOT EVERY DAY YOU GET TO SEE THE WORK OF A FAMOUS GUY.
I'LL ADMIT, THOUGH--
HE KNEW HIS STUFF.

I DIDN'T REALIZE ROBOTS COULD BE TAKEN OVER LIKE THAT.

IT'S NOT JUST ROBOTS, KID. YOU'VE SEEN THE SHADOWS?

THOSE THINGS CAN TAKE OVER ANY LIVING THING!

IN FACT, ROBOTS ARE JUST ABOUT THE ONLY THINGS THAT ARE IMMUNE.

I'M TERRIBLY EMBARRASSED.

I PROMISE IT WILL NOT OCCUR AGAIN.

WHAT HAPPENS IF SOMEONE TAKEN OVER BY SHADOWS TAKES OVER A ROBOT?

NOW YOU'RE ASKING THE QUESTIONS THAT KEEP ME UP AT NIGHT.

WE JUST HAVE TO WORK TO STAY AHEAD OF THEM.

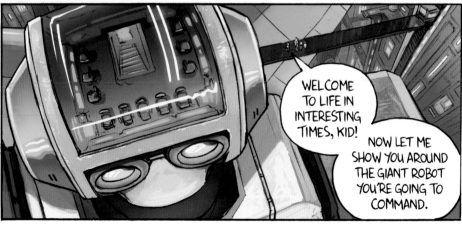

WELCOME TO LIFE IN INTERESTING TIMES, KID!

NOW LET ME SHOW YOU AROUND THE GIANT ROBOT YOU'RE GOING TO COMMAND.

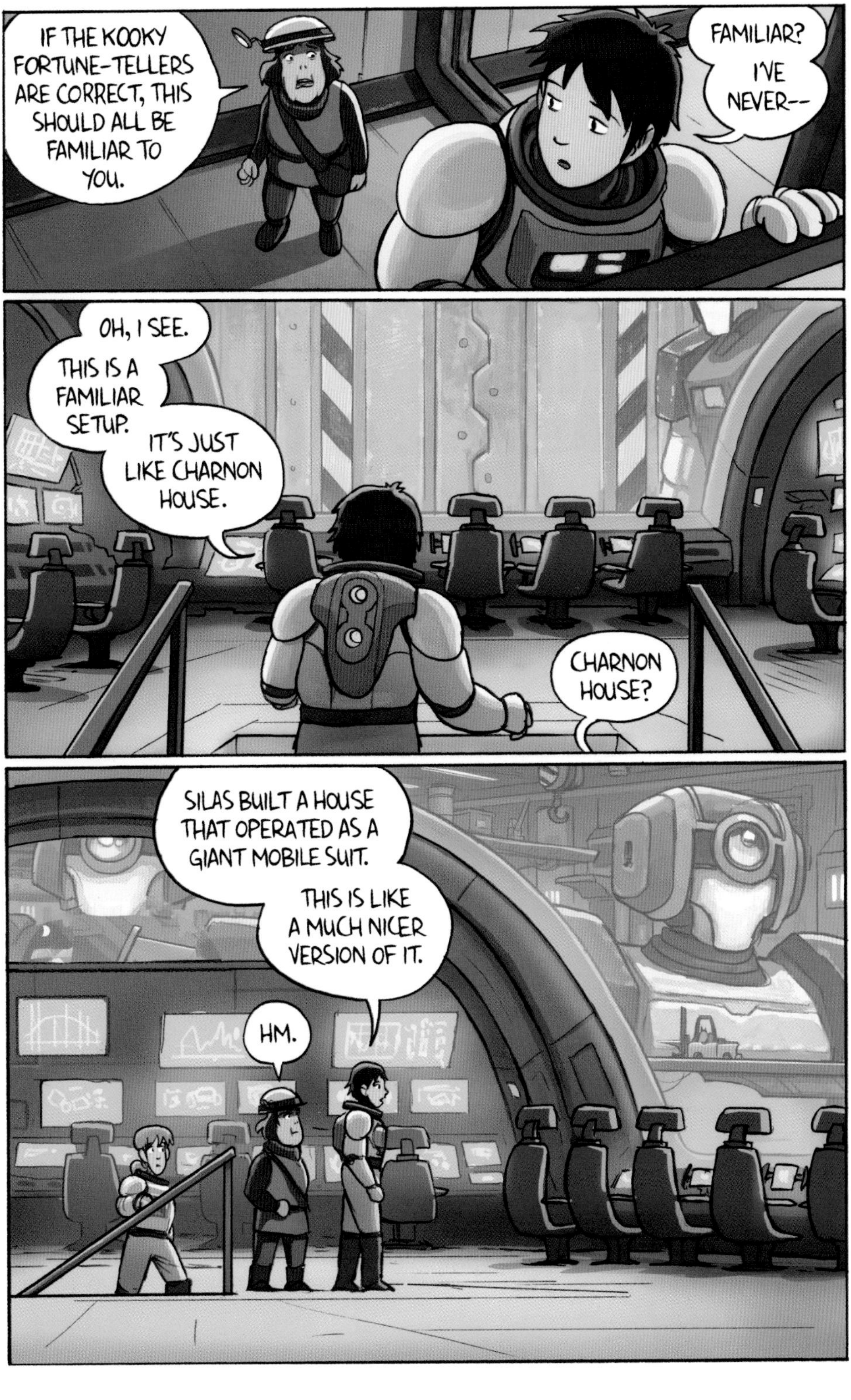
IF THE KOOKY FORTUNE-TELLERS ARE CORRECT, THIS SHOULD ALL BE FAMILIAR TO YOU.
FAMILIAR?
I'VE NEVER--
OH, I SEE.
THIS IS A FAMILIAR SETUP.
IT'S JUST LIKE CHARNON HOUSE.
CHARNON HOUSE?
SILAS BUILT A HOUSE THAT OPERATED AS A GIANT MOBILE SUIT.
THIS IS LIKE A MUCH NICER VERSION OF IT.
HM.

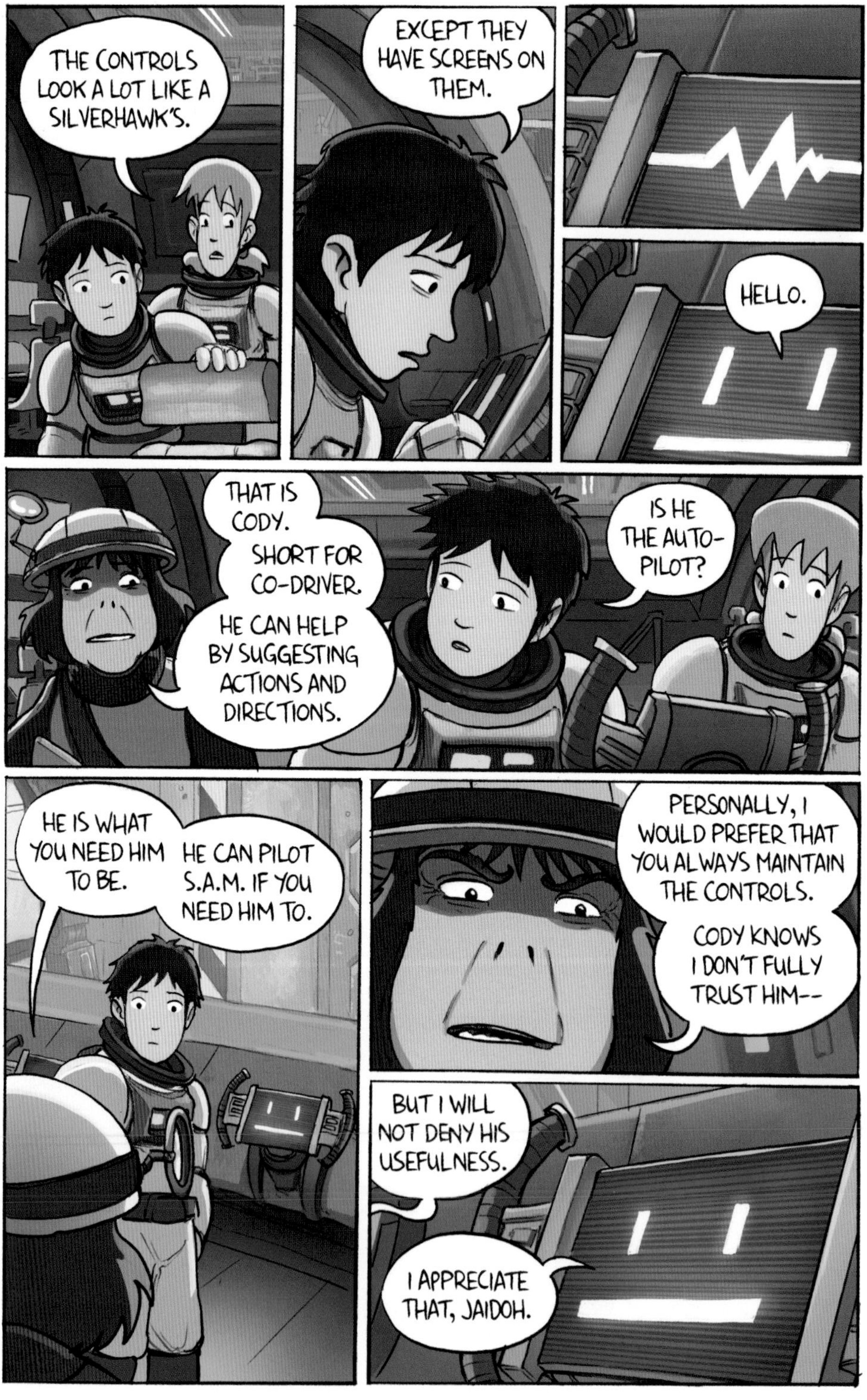
THE CONTROLS LOOK A LOT LIKE A SILVERHAWK'S.
EXCEPT THEY HAVE SCREENS ON THEM.
HELLO.
THAT IS CODY.
SHORT FOR CO-DRIVER.
HE CAN HELP BY SUGGESTING ACTIONS AND DIRECTIONS.
IS HE THE AUTO-PILOT?
HE IS WHAT YOU NEED HIM TO BE.
HE CAN PILOT S.A.M. IF YOU NEED HIM TO.
PERSONALLY, I WOULD PREFER THAT YOU ALWAYS MAINTAIN THE CONTROLS.
CODY KNOWS I DON'T FULLY TRUST HIM--
BUT I WILL NOT DENY HIS USEFULNESS.
I APPRECIATE THAT, JAIDOH.

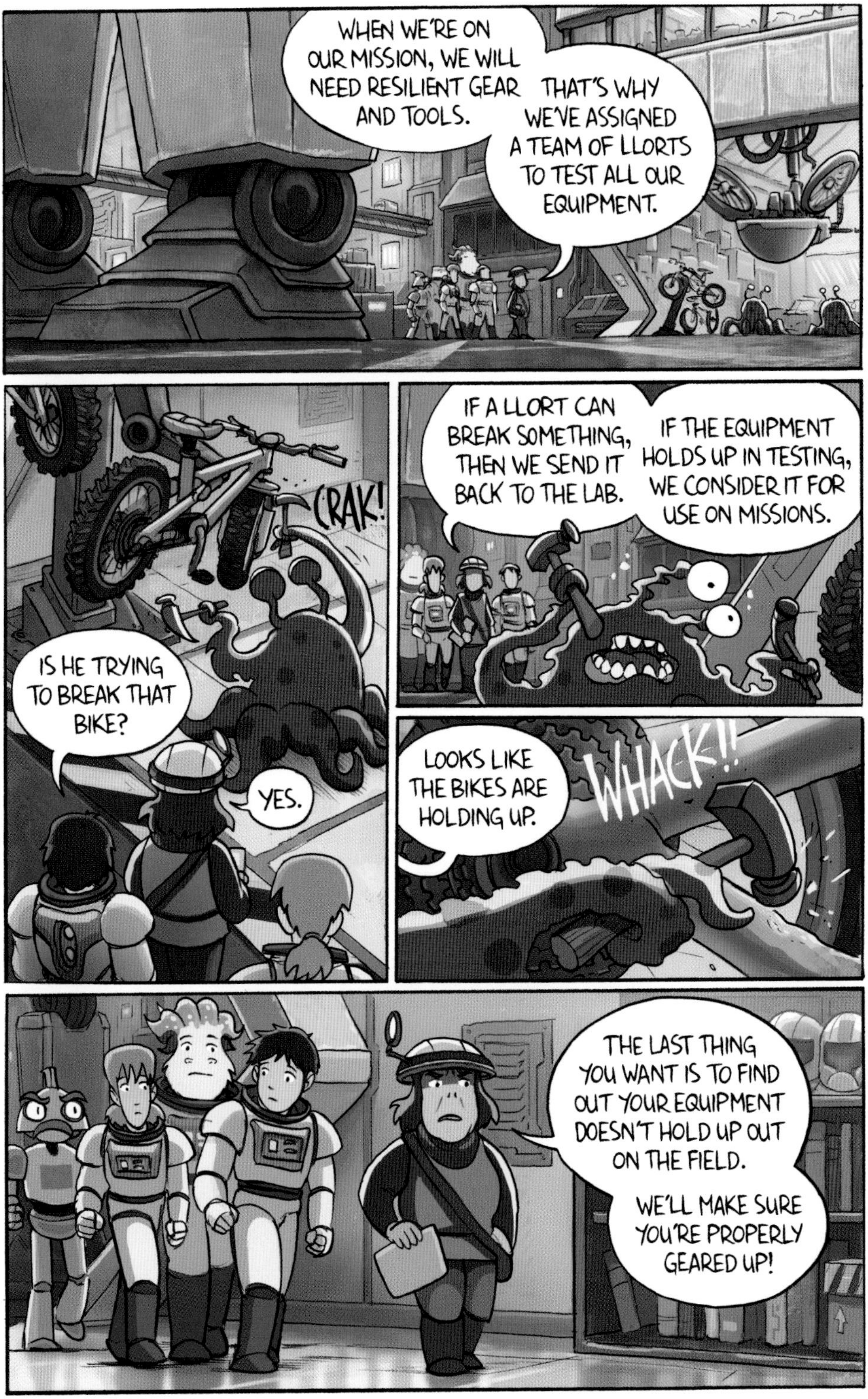
WHEN WE'RE ON OUR MISSION, WE WILL NEED RESILIENT GEAR AND TOOLS.
THAT'S WHY WE'VE ASSIGNED A TEAM OF LLORTS TO TEST ALL OUR EQUIPMENT.
CRAK!
IS HE TRYING TO BREAK THAT BIKE?
YES.
IF A LLORT CAN BREAK SOMETHING, THEN WE SEND IT BACK TO THE LAB.
IF THE EQUIPMENT HOLDS UP IN TESTING, WE CONSIDER IT FOR USE ON MISSIONS.
LOOKS LIKE THE BIKES ARE HOLDING UP.
WHACK!!
THE LAST THING YOU WANT IS TO FIND OUT YOUR EQUIPMENT DOESN'T HOLD UP OUT ON THE FIELD.
WE'LL MAKE SURE YOU'RE PROPERLY GEARED UP!

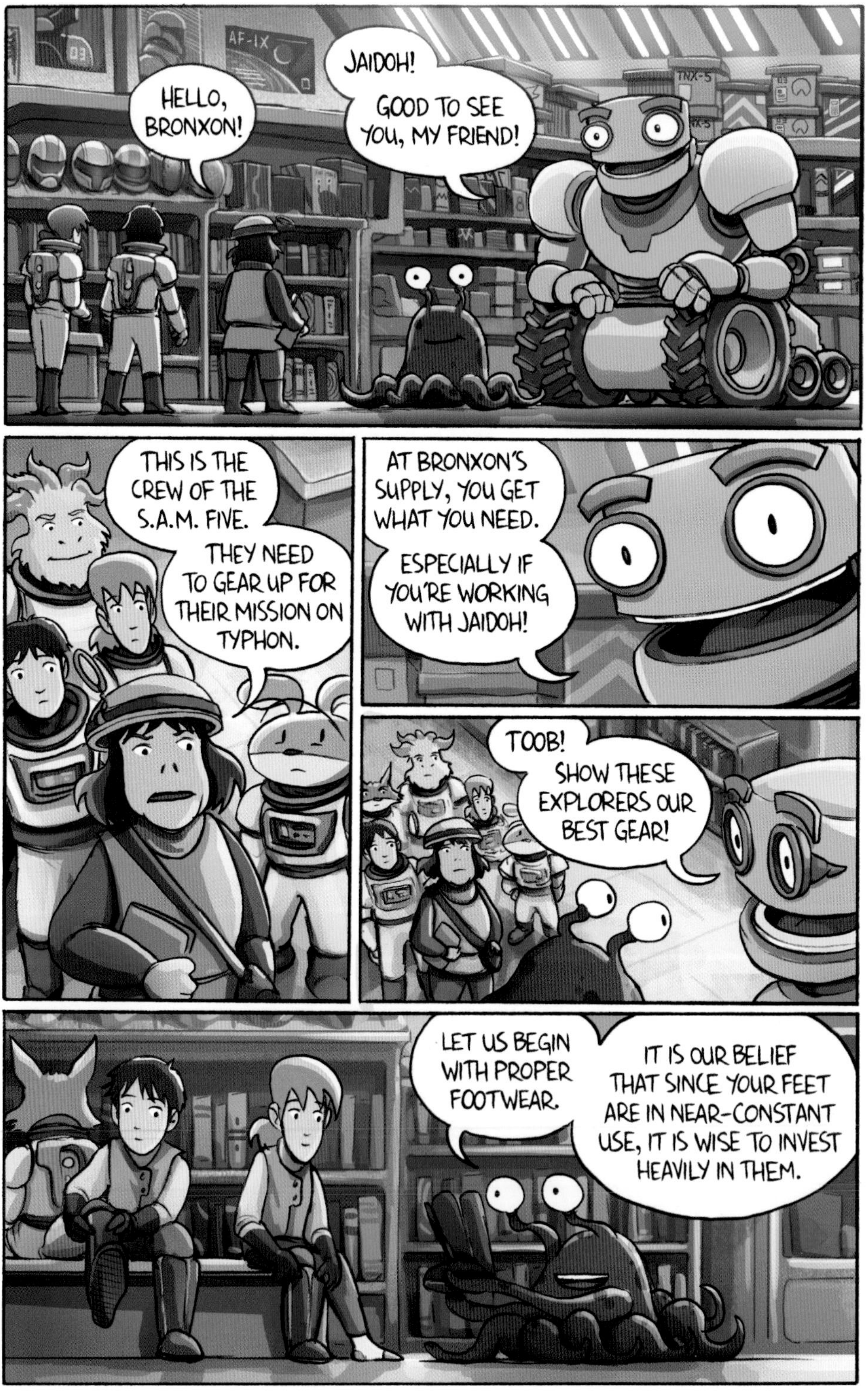
AF-IX
HELLO, BRONXON!
JAIDOH!
GOOD TO SEE YOU, MY FRIEND!
THIS IS THE CREW OF THE S.A.M. FIVE.
THEY NEED TO GEAR UP FOR THEIR MISSION ON TYPHON.
AT BRONXON'S SUPPLY, YOU GET WHAT YOU NEED.
ESPECIALLY IF YOU'RE WORKING WITH JAIDOH!
TOOB!
SHOW THESE EXPLORERS OUR BEST GEAR!
LET US BEGIN WITH PROPER FOOTWEAR.
IT IS OUR BELIEF THAT SINCE YOUR FEET ARE IN NEAR-CONSTANT USE, IT IS WISE TO INVEST HEAVILY IN THEM.

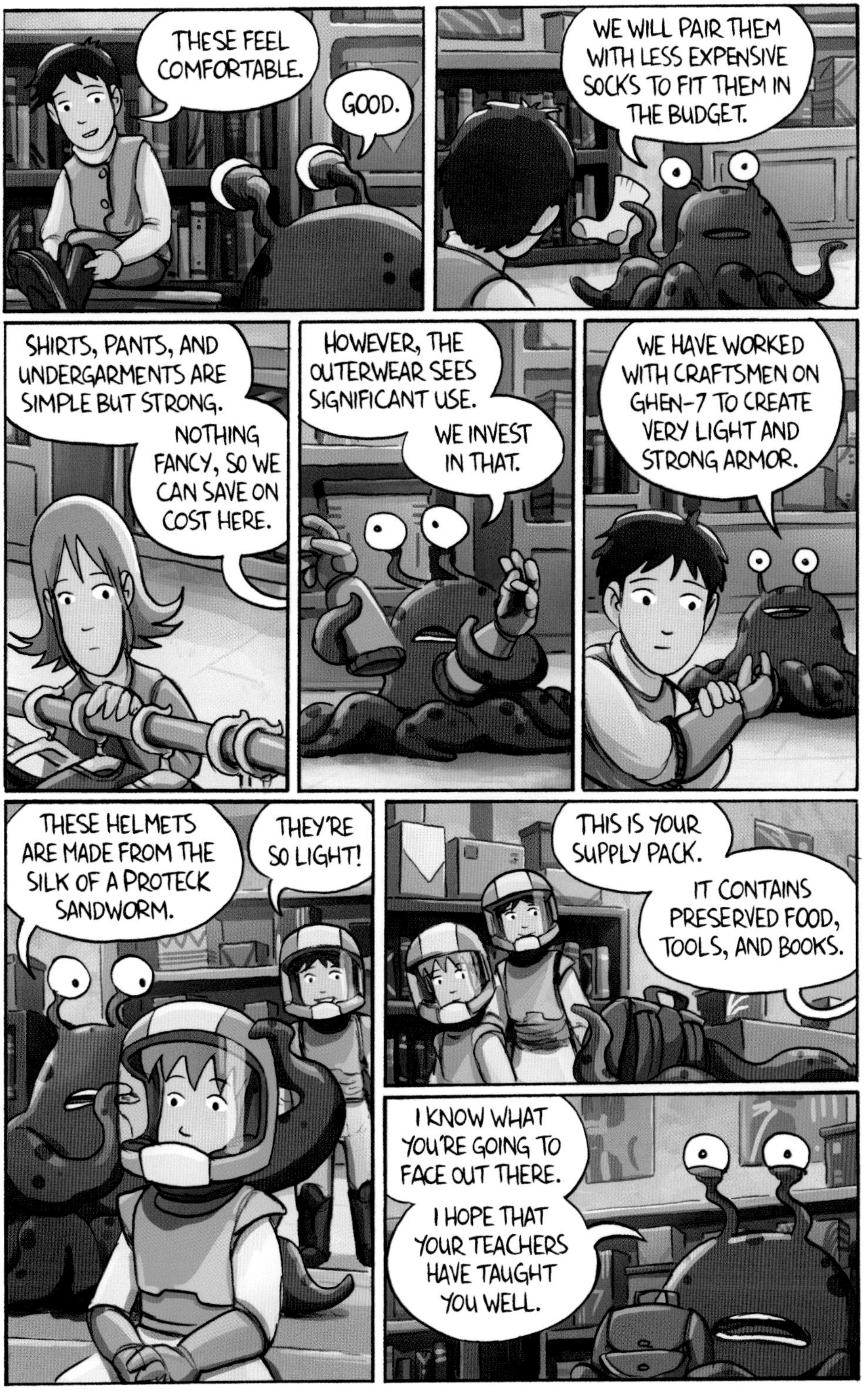
THESE FEEL COMFORTABLE.
GOOD.
WE WILL PAIR THEM WITH LESS EXPENSIVE SOCKS TO FIT THEM IN THE BUDGET.
SHIRTS, PANTS, AND UNDERGARMENTS ARE SIMPLE BUT STRONG.
NOTHING FANCY, SO WE CAN SAVE ON COST HERE.
HOWEVER, THE OUTERWEAR SEES SIGNIFICANT USE.
WE INVEST IN THAT.
WE HAVE WORKED WITH CRAFTSMEN ON GHEN-7 TO CREATE VERY LIGHT AND STRONG ARMOR.
THESE HELMETS ARE MADE FROM THE SILK OF A PROTECK SANDWORM.
THEY'RE SO LIGHT!
THIS IS YOUR SUPPLY PACK.
IT CONTAINS PRESERVED FOOD, TOOLS, AND BOOKS.
I KNOW WHAT YOU'RE GOING TO FACE OUT THERE.
I HOPE THAT YOUR TEACHERS HAVE TAUGHT YOU WELL.

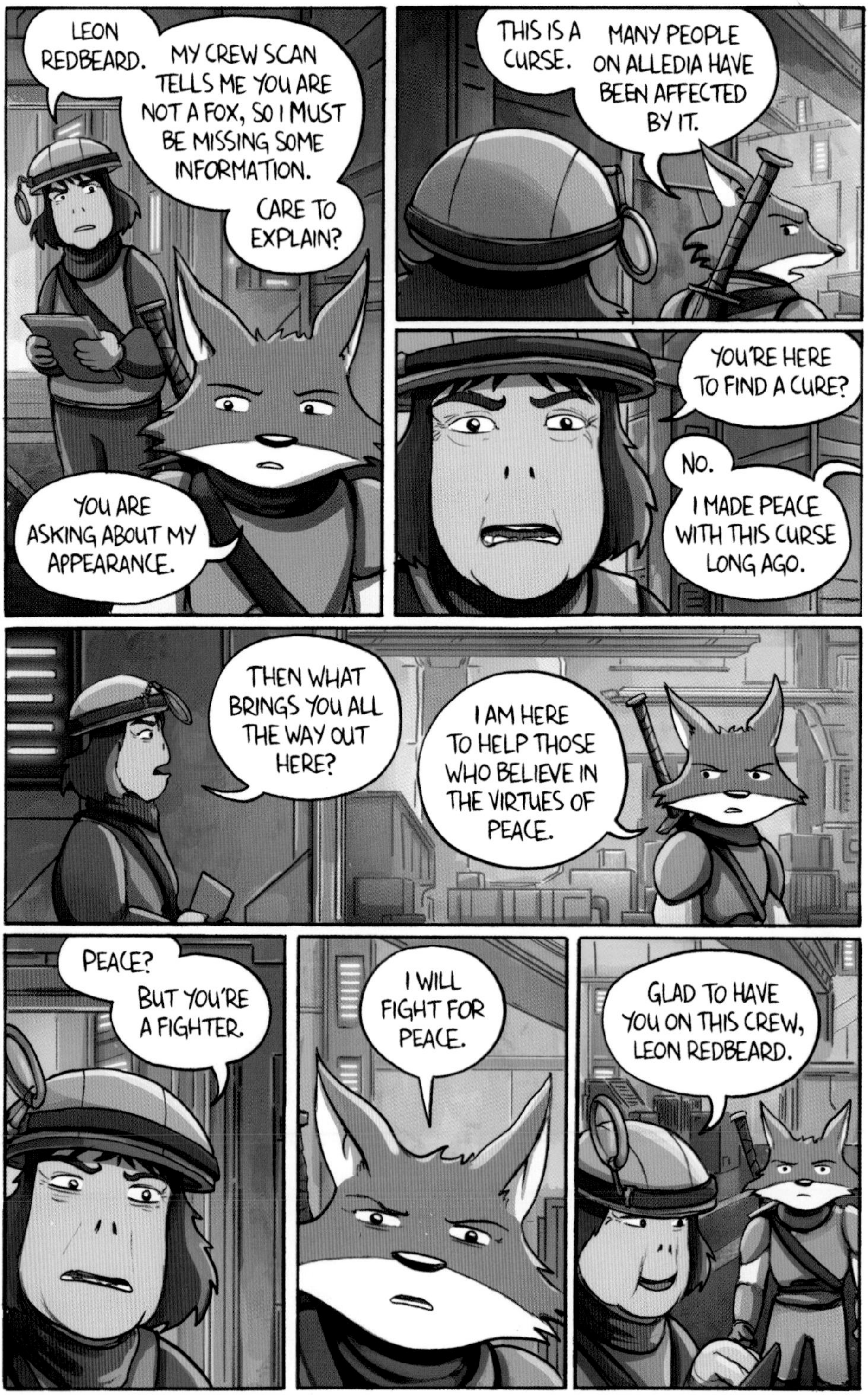
LEON REDBEARD.
MY CREW SCAN TELLS ME YOU ARE NOT A FOX, SO I MUST BE MISSING SOME INFORMATION.
CARE TO EXPLAIN?
YOU ARE ASKING ABOUT MY APPEARANCE.
THIS IS A CURSE.
MANY PEOPLE ON ALLEDIA HAVE BEEN AFFECTED BY IT.
YOU'RE HERE TO FIND A CURE?
NO.
I MADE PEACE WITH THIS CURSE LONG AGO.
THEN WHAT BRINGS YOU ALL THE WAY OUT HERE?
I AM HERE TO HELP THOSE WHO BELIEVE IN THE VIRTUES OF PEACE.
PEACE?
BUT YOU'RE A FIGHTER.
I WILL FIGHT FOR PEACE.
GLAD TO HAVE YOU ON THIS CREW, LEON REDBEARD.

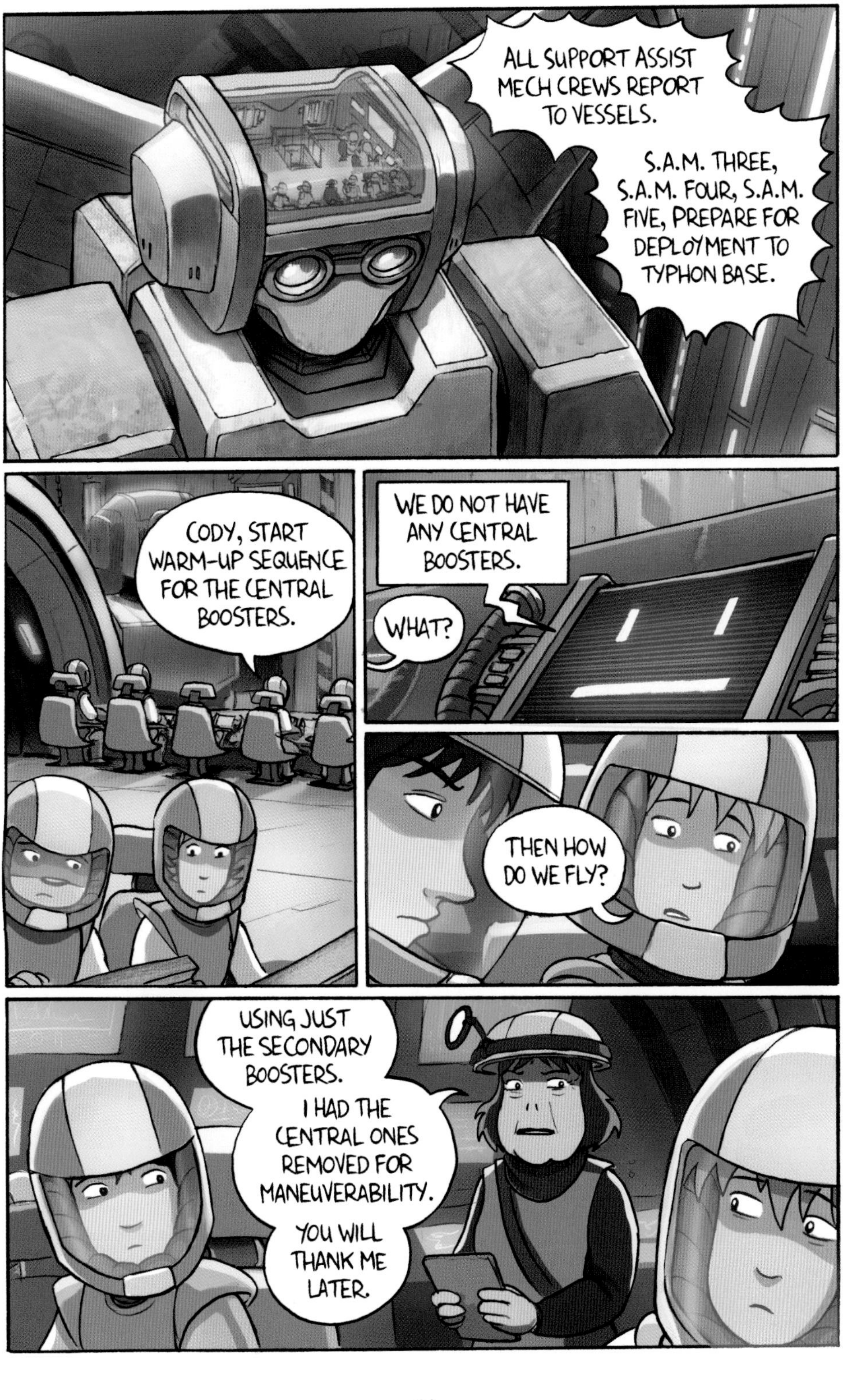
ALL SUPPORT ASSIST MECH CREWS REPORT TO VESSELS.
S.A.M. THREE, S.A.M. FOUR, S.A.M. FIVE, PREPARE FOR DEPLOYMENT TO TYPHON BASE.
CODY, START WARM-UP SEQUENCE FOR THE CENTRAL BOOSTERS.
WE DO NOT HAVE ANY CENTRAL BOOSTERS.
WHAT?
THEN HOW DO WE FLY?
USING JUST THE SECONDARY BOOSTERS.
I HAD THE CENTRAL ONES REMOVED FOR MANEUVERABILITY.
YOU WILL THANK ME LATER.

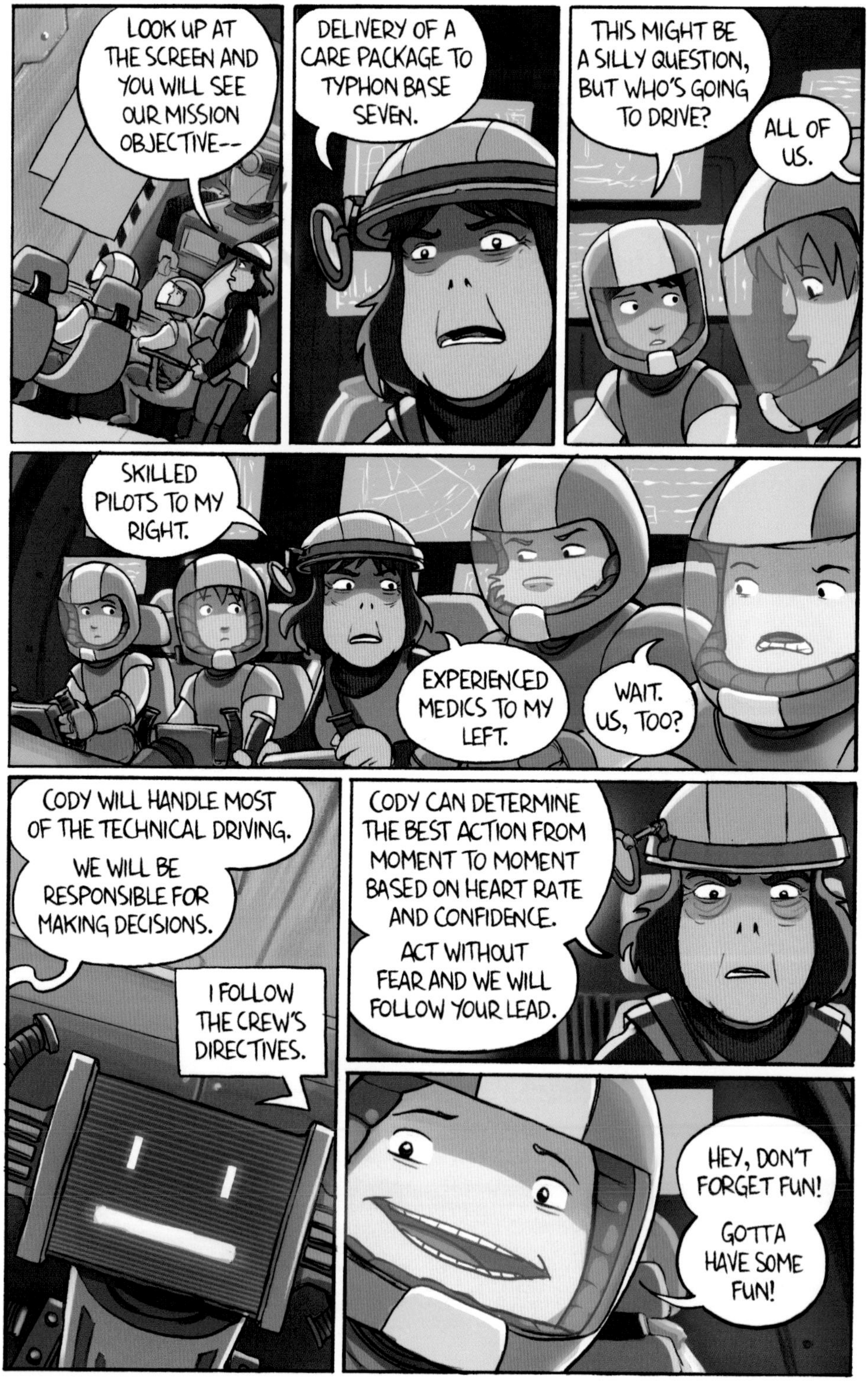
LOOK UP AT THE SCREEN AND YOU WILL SEE OUR MISSION OBJECTIVE--
DELIVERY OF A CARE PACKAGE TO TYPHON BASE SEVEN.
THIS MIGHT BE A SILLY QUESTION, BUT WHO'S GOING TO DRIVE?
ALL OF US.
SKILLED PILOTS TO MY RIGHT.
EXPERIENCED MEDICS TO MY LEFT.
WAIT. US, TOO?
CODY WILL HANDLE MOST OF THE TECHNICAL DRIVING.
WE WILL BE RESPONSIBLE FOR MAKING DECISIONS.
I FOLLOW THE CREW'S DIRECTIVES.
CODY CAN DETERMINE THE BEST ACTION FROM MOMENT TO MOMENT BASED ON HEART RATE AND CONFIDENCE.
ACT WITHOUT FEAR AND WE WILL FOLLOW YOUR LEAD.
HEY, DON'T FORGET FUN!
GOTTA HAVE SOME FUN!

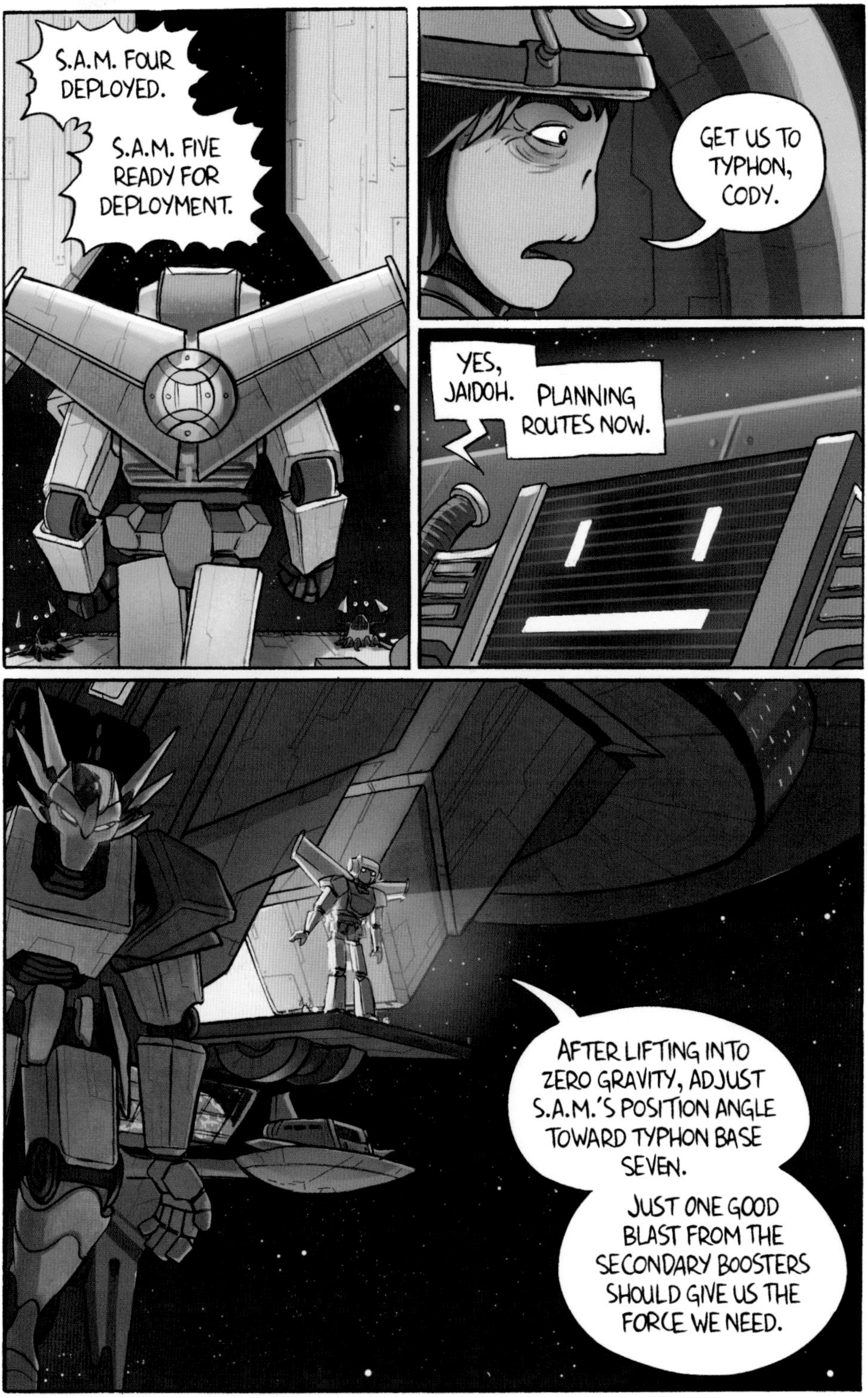
S.A.M. FOUR DEPLOYED.
S.A.M. FIVE READY FOR DEPLOYMENT.
GET US TO TYPHON, CODY.
YES, JAIDOH.
PLANNING ROUTES NOW.
AFTER LIFTING INTO ZERO GRAVITY, ADJUST S.A.M.'S POSITION ANGLE TOWARD TYPHON BASE SEVEN.
JUST ONE GOOD BLAST FROM THE SECONDARY BOOSTERS SHOULD GIVE US THE FORCE WE NEED.

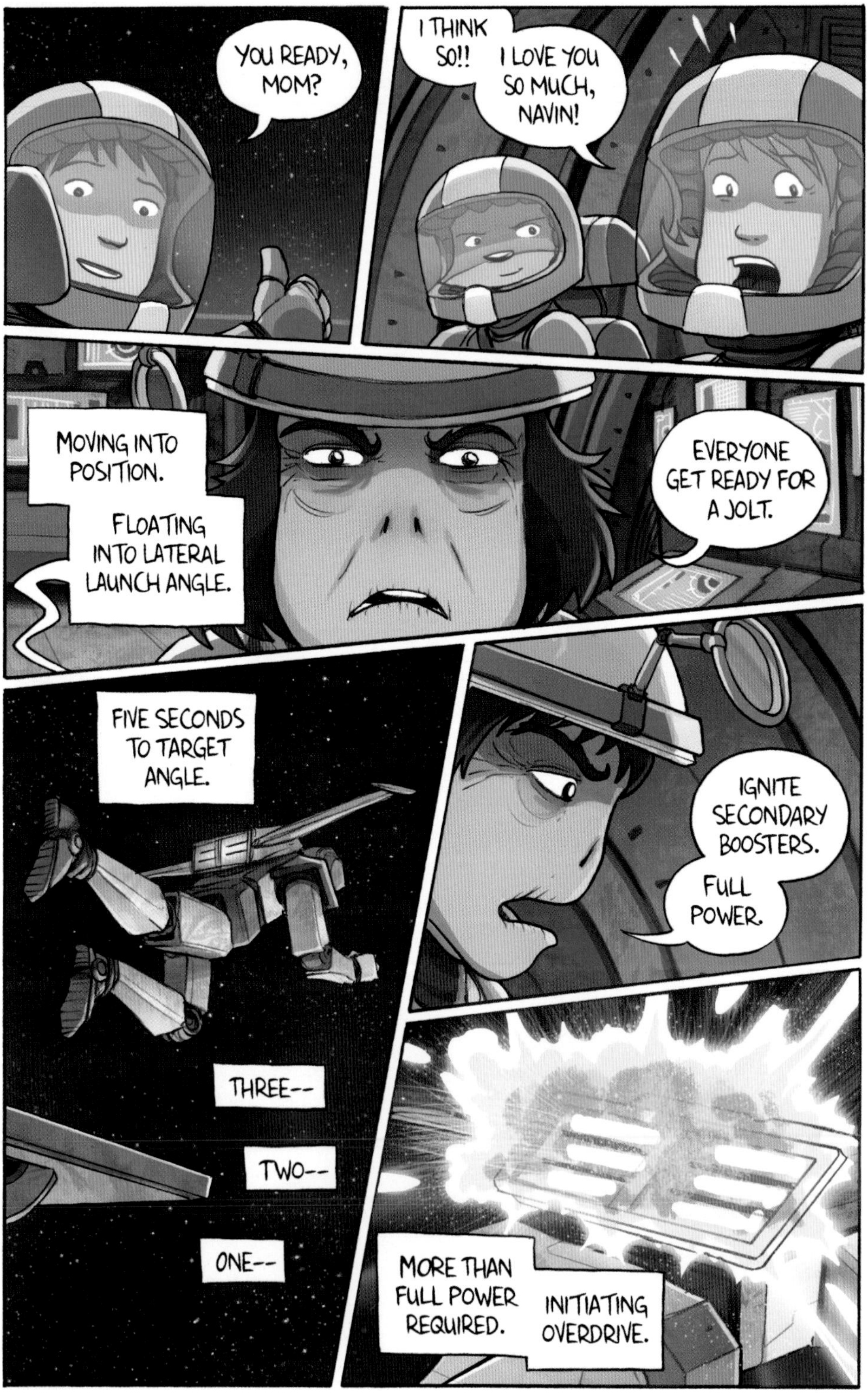
YOU READY, MOM?
I THINK SO!!
I LOVE YOU SO MUCH, NAVIN!
MOVING INTO POSITION.
FLOATING INTO LATERAL LAUNCH ANGLE.
EVERYONE GET READY FOR A JOLT.
FIVE SECONDS TO TARGET ANGLE.
IGNITE SECONDARY BOOSTERS.
FULL POWER.
THREE--
TWO--
ONE--
MORE THAN FULL POWER REQUIRED.
INITIATING OVERDRIVE.

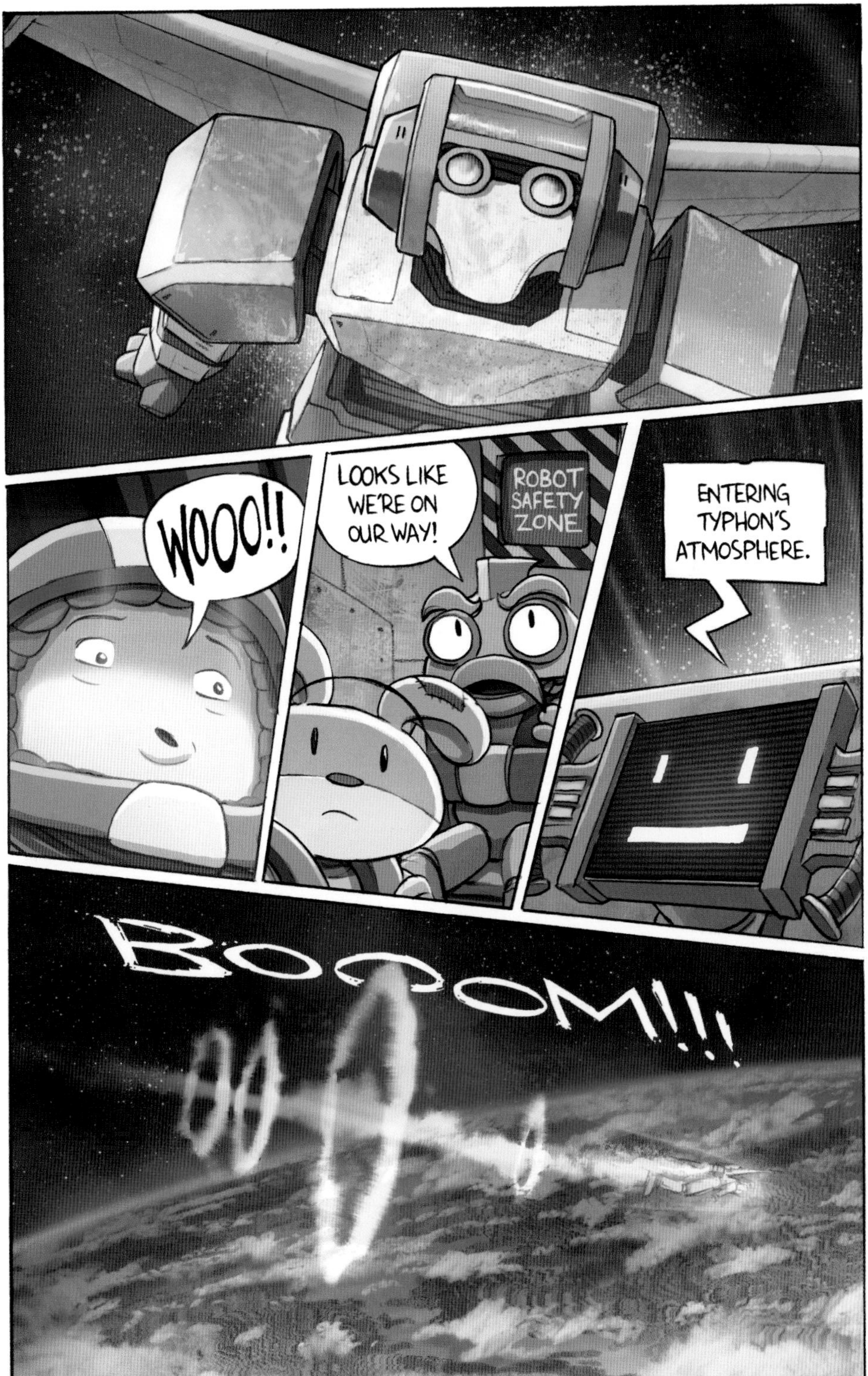
WOOO!!
LOOKS LIKE WE'RE ON OUR WAY!
ROBOT SAFETY ZONE
ENTERING TYPHON'S ATMOSPHERE.
BOOOM!!!

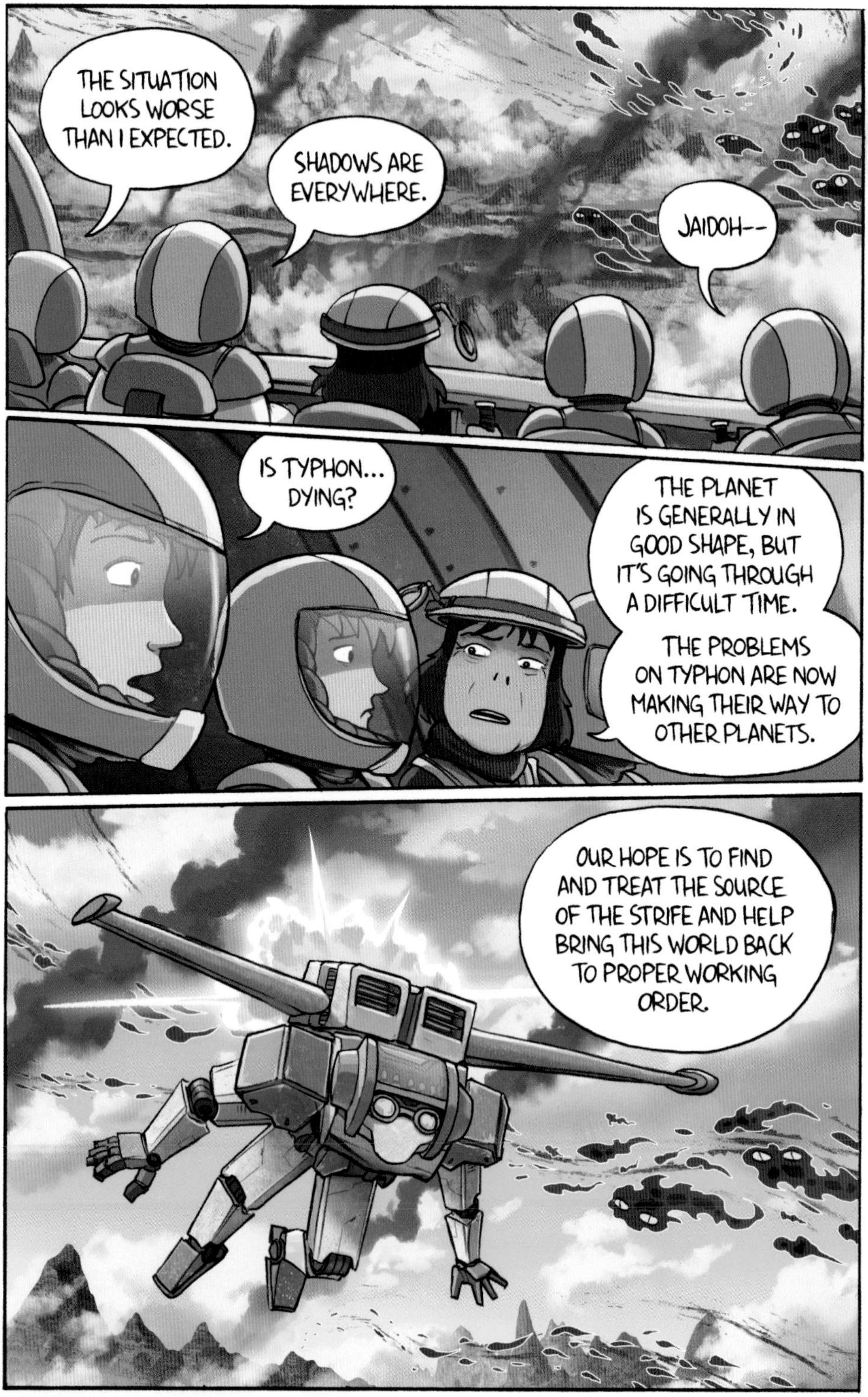
THE SITUATION LOOKS WORSE THAN I EXPECTED.
SHADOWS ARE EVERYWHERE.
JAIDOH--
IS TYPHON... DYING?
THE PLANET IS GENERALLY IN GOOD SHAPE, BUT IT'S GOING THROUGH A DIFFICULT TIME.
THE PROBLEMS ON TYPHON ARE NOW MAKING THEIR WAY TO OTHER PLANETS.
OUR HOPE IS TO FIND AND TREAT THE SOURCE OF THE STRIFE AND HELP BRING THIS WORLD BACK TO PROPER WORKING ORDER.

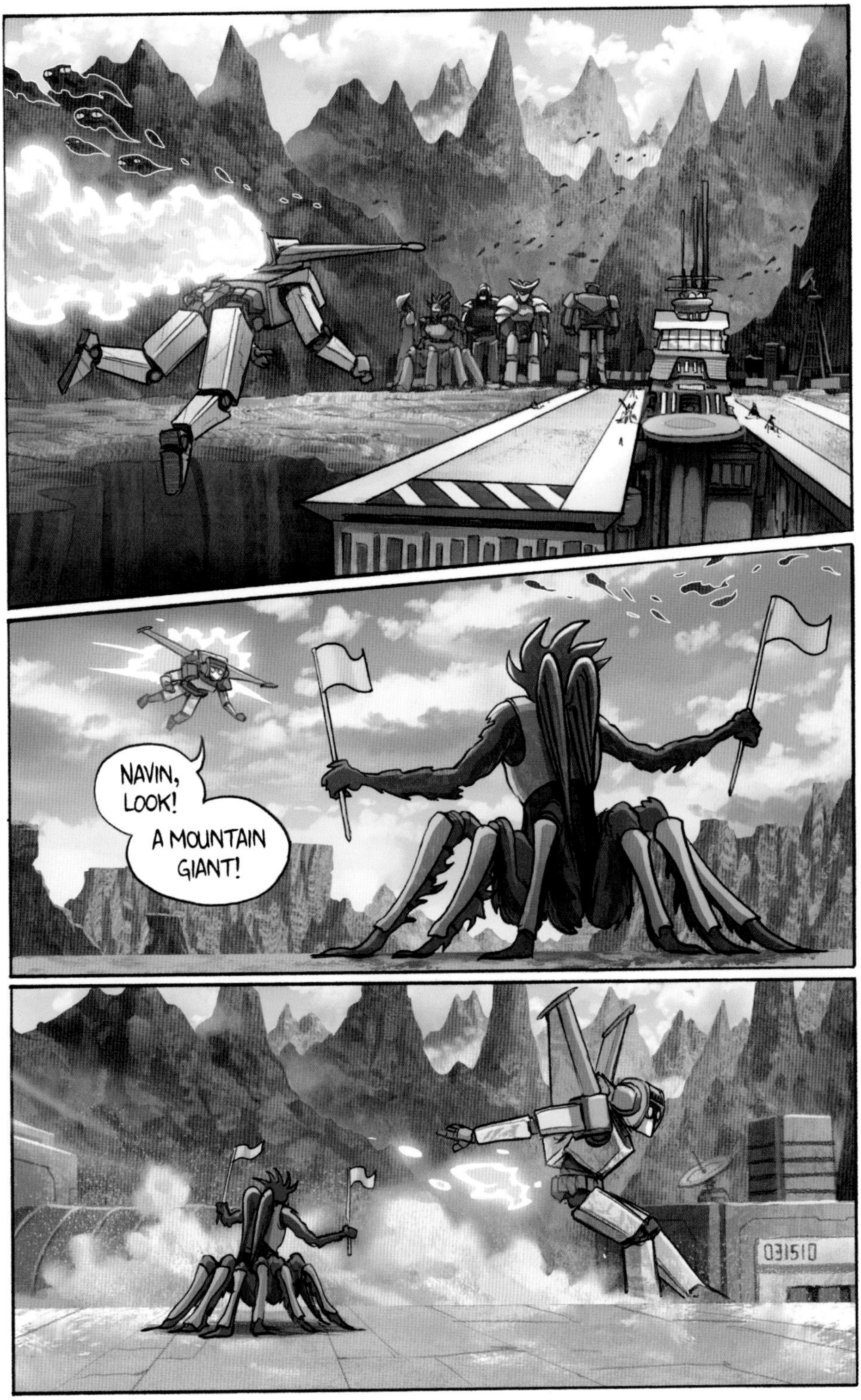
NAVIN, LOOK!
A MOUNTAIN GIANT!
031510

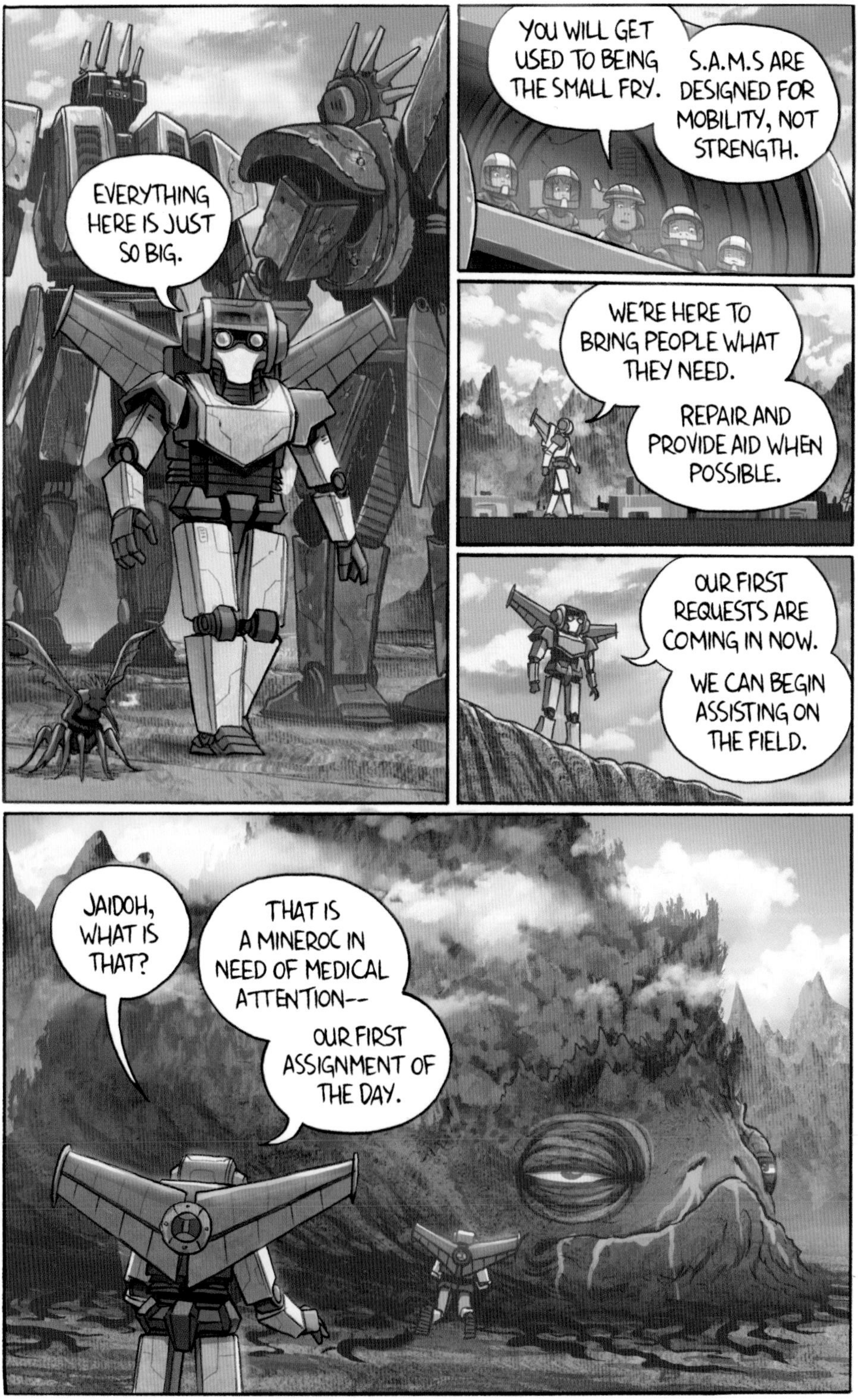
EVERYTHING HERE IS JUST SO BIG.
YOU WILL GET USED TO BEING THE SMALL FRY.
S.A.M.S ARE DESIGNED FOR MOBILITY, NOT STRENGTH.
WE'RE HERE TO BRING PEOPLE WHAT THEY NEED.
REPAIR AND PROVIDE AID WHEN POSSIBLE.
OUR FIRST REQUESTS ARE COMING IN NOW.
WE CAN BEGIN ASSISTING ON THE FIELD.
JAIDOH, WHAT IS THAT?
THAT IS A MINEROC IN NEED OF MEDICAL ATTENTION--
OUR FIRST ASSIGNMENT OF THE DAY.

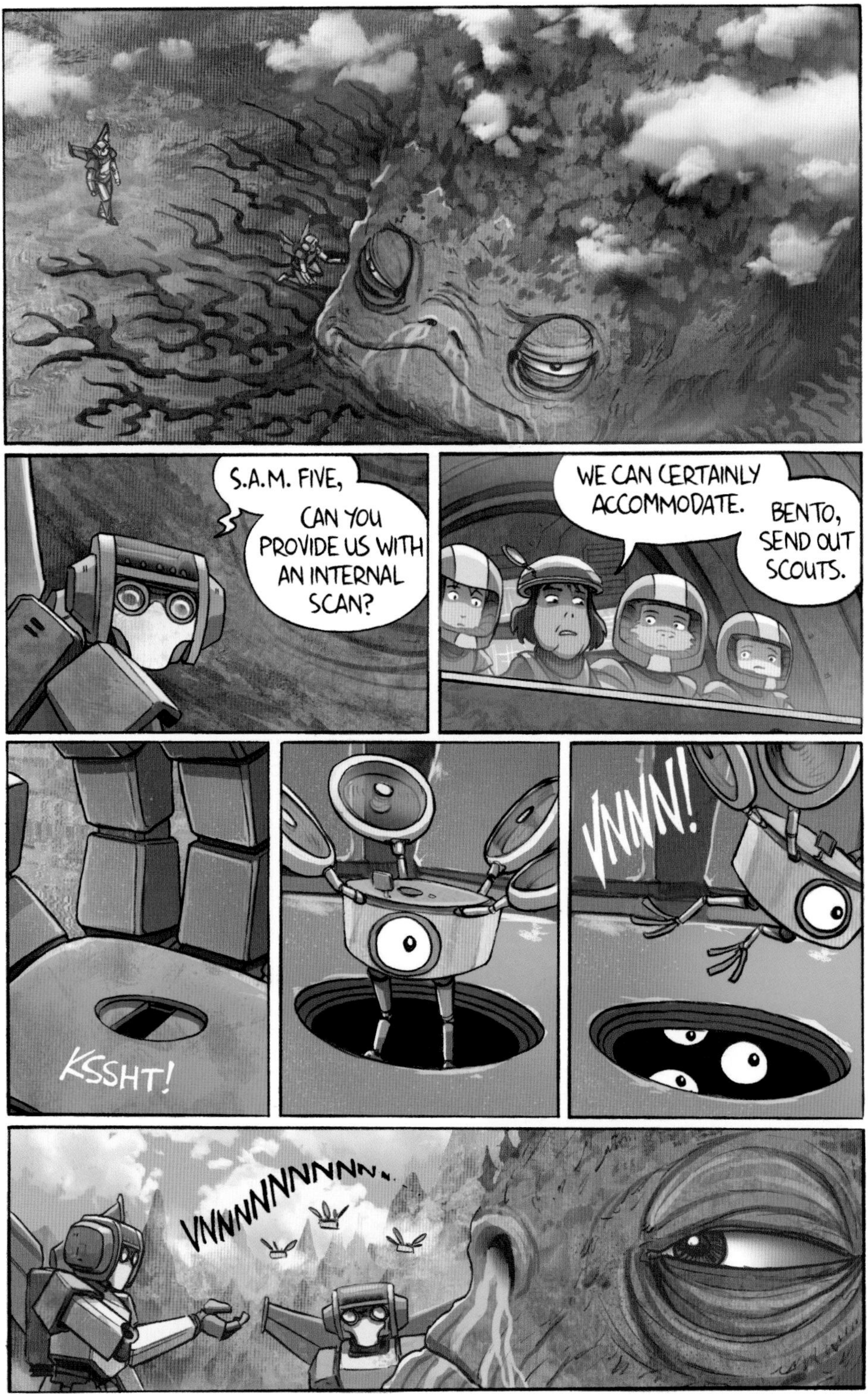
S.A.M. FIVE,
CAN YOU PROVIDE US WITH AN INTERNAL SCAN?
WE CAN CERTAINLY ACCOMMODATE.
BENTO, SEND OUT SCOUTS.
KSSHT!
VNNN!
VNNNNNNNNN...

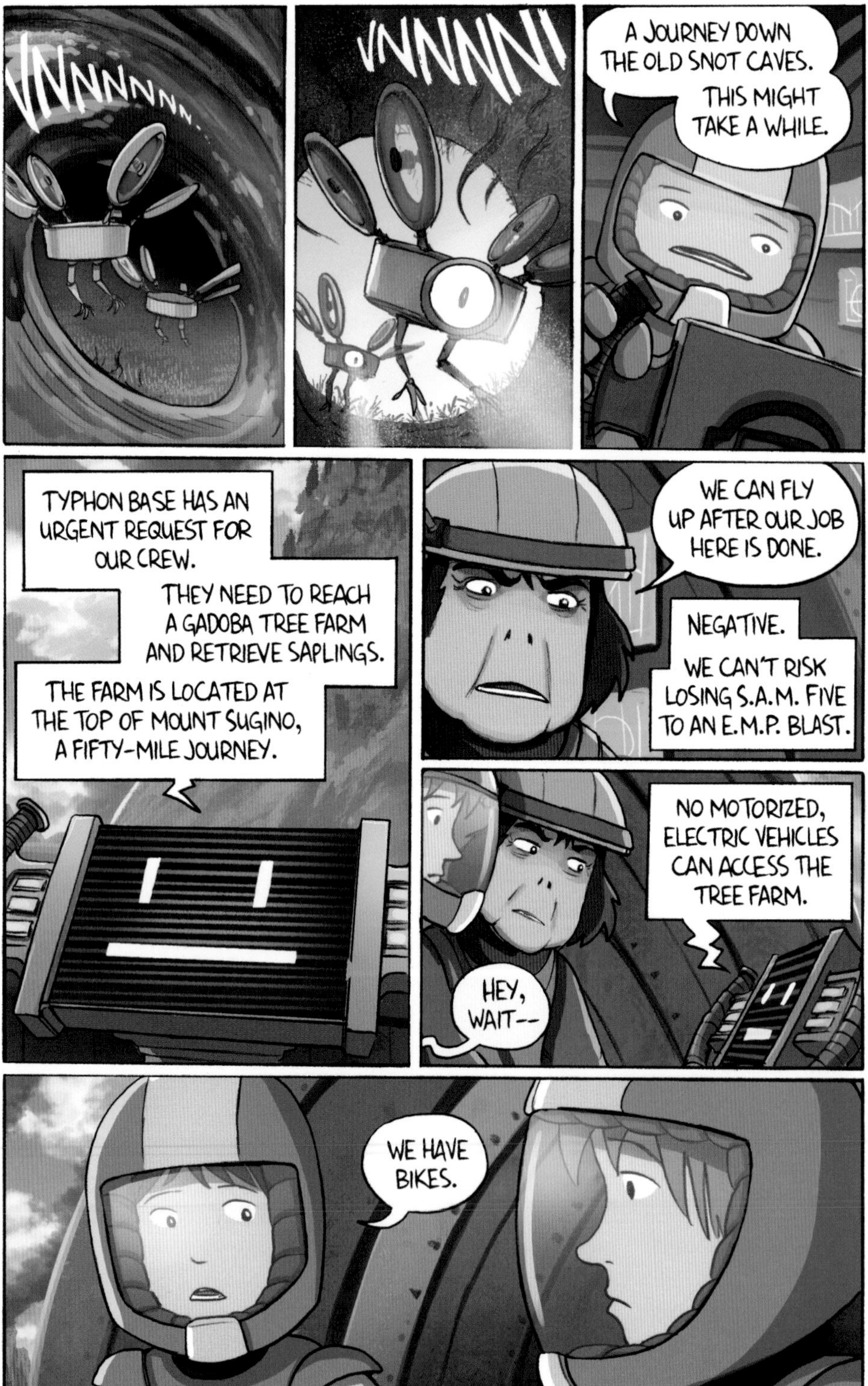
VNNNNNN...
VNNNNI
A JOURNEY DOWN THE OLD SNOT CAVES.
THIS MIGHT TAKE A WHILE.
TYPHON BASE HAS AN URGENT REQUEST FOR OUR CREW.
THEY NEED TO REACH A GADOBA TREE FARM AND RETRIEVE SAPLINGS.
THE FARM IS LOCATED AT THE TOP OF MOUNT SUGINO, A FIFTY-MILE JOURNEY.
WE CAN FLY UP AFTER OUR JOB HERE IS DONE.
NEGATIVE.
WE CAN'T RISK LOSING S.A.M. FIVE TO AN E.M.P. BLAST.
NO MOTORIZED, ELECTRIC VEHICLES CAN ACCESS THE TREE FARM.
HEY, WAIT--
WE HAVE BIKES.

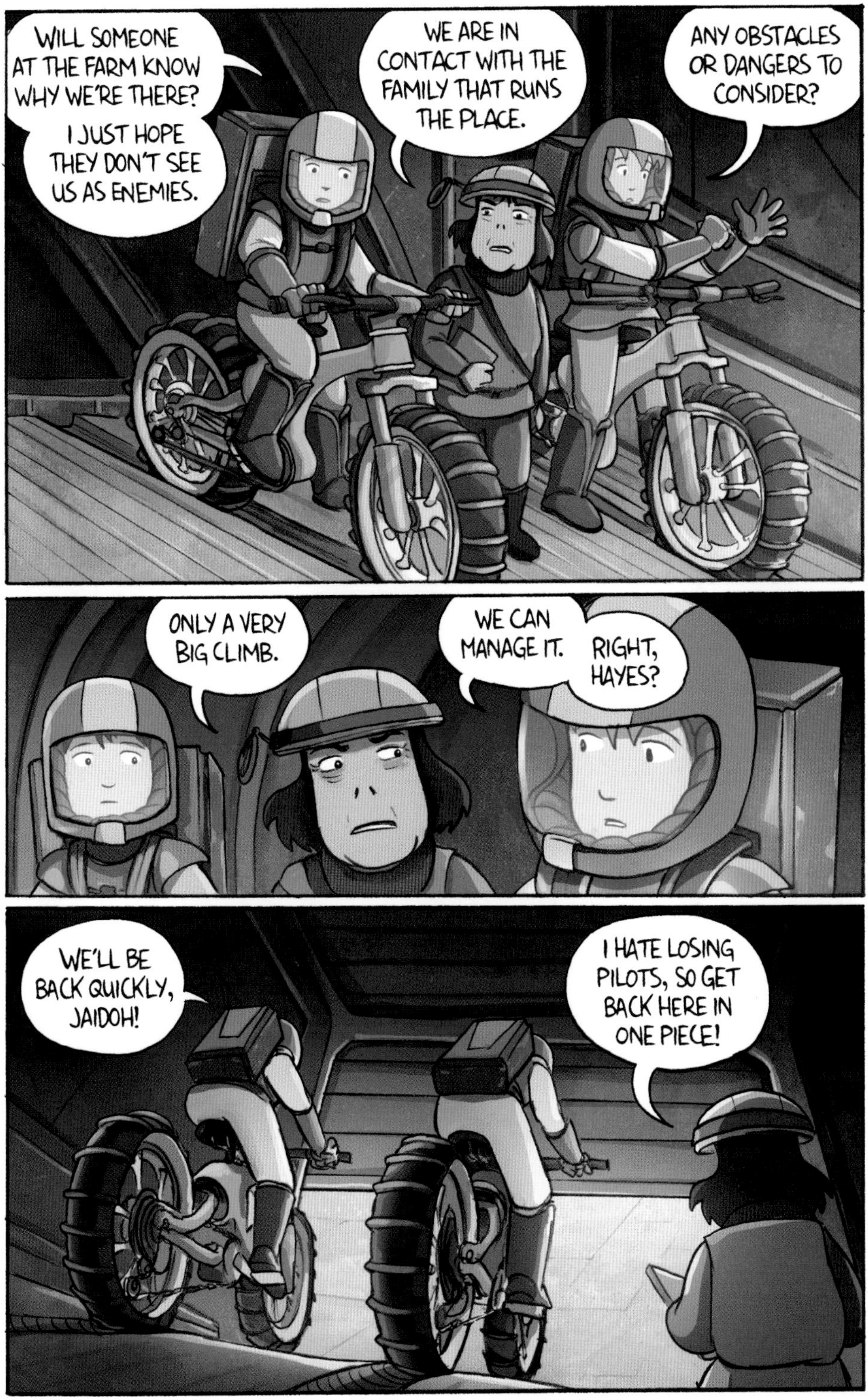

WILL SOMEONE AT THE FARM KNOW WHY WE'RE THERE?
I JUST HOPE THEY DON'T SEE US AS ENEMIES.
WE ARE IN CONTACT WITH THE FAMILY THAT RUNS THE PLACE.
ANY OBSTACLES OR DANGERS TO CONSIDER?
ONLY A VERY BIG CLIMB.
WE CAN MANAGE IT.
RIGHT, HAYES?
WE'LL BE BACK QUICKLY, JAIDOH!
I HATE LOSING PILOTS, SO GET BACK HERE IN ONE PIECE!

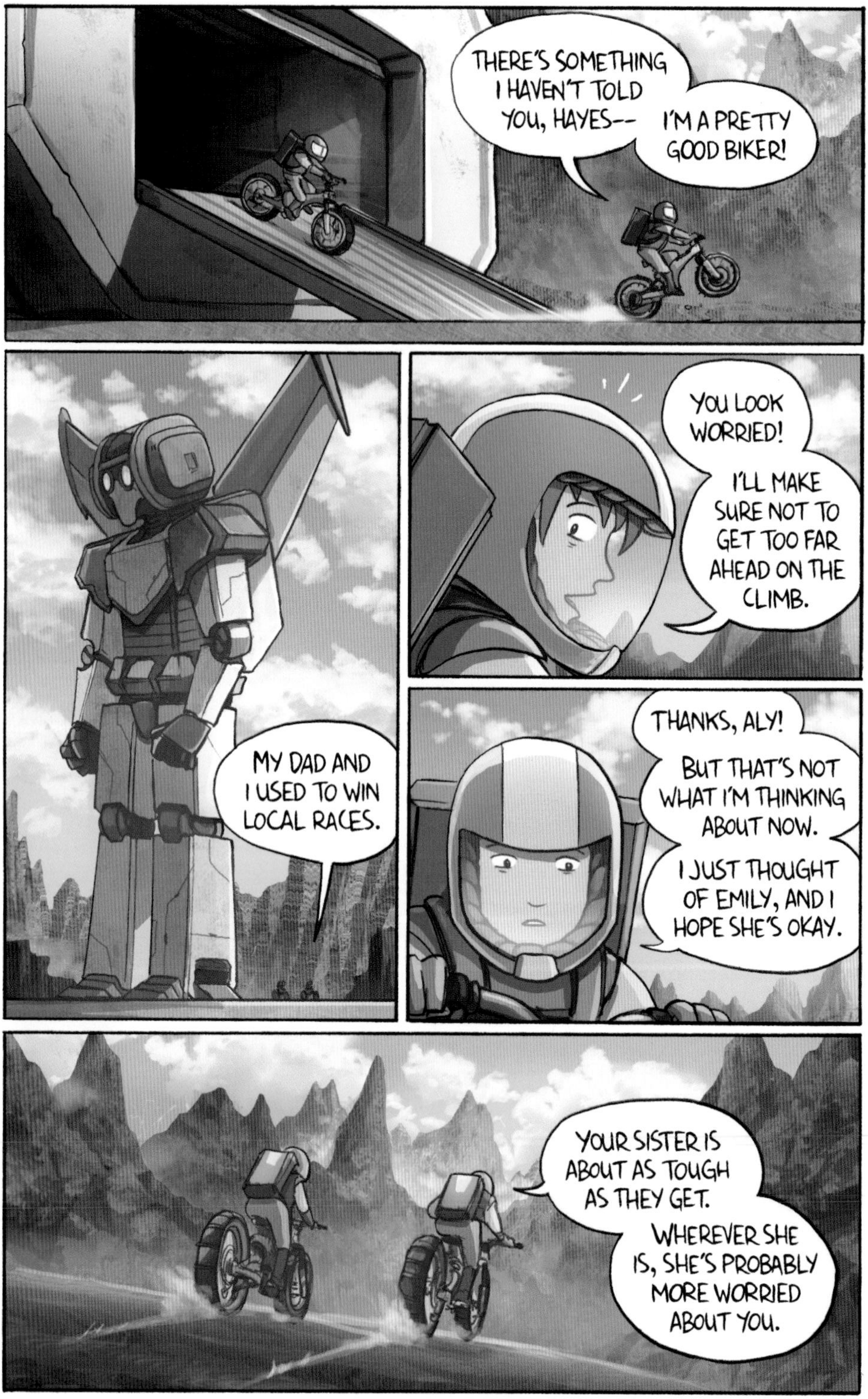
THERE'S SOMETHING I HAVEN'T TOLD YOU, HAYES--
I'M A PRETTY GOOD BIKER!
MY DAD AND I USED TO WIN LOCAL RACES.
YOU LOOK WORRIED!
I'LL MAKE SURE NOT TO GET TOO FAR AHEAD ON THE CLIMB.
THANKS, ALY!
BUT THAT'S NOT WHAT I'M THINKING ABOUT NOW.
I JUST THOUGHT OF EMILY, AND I HOPE SHE'S OKAY.
YOUR SISTER IS ABOUT AS TOUGH AS THEY GET.
WHEREVER SHE IS, SHE'S PROBABLY MORE WORRIED ABOUT YOU.

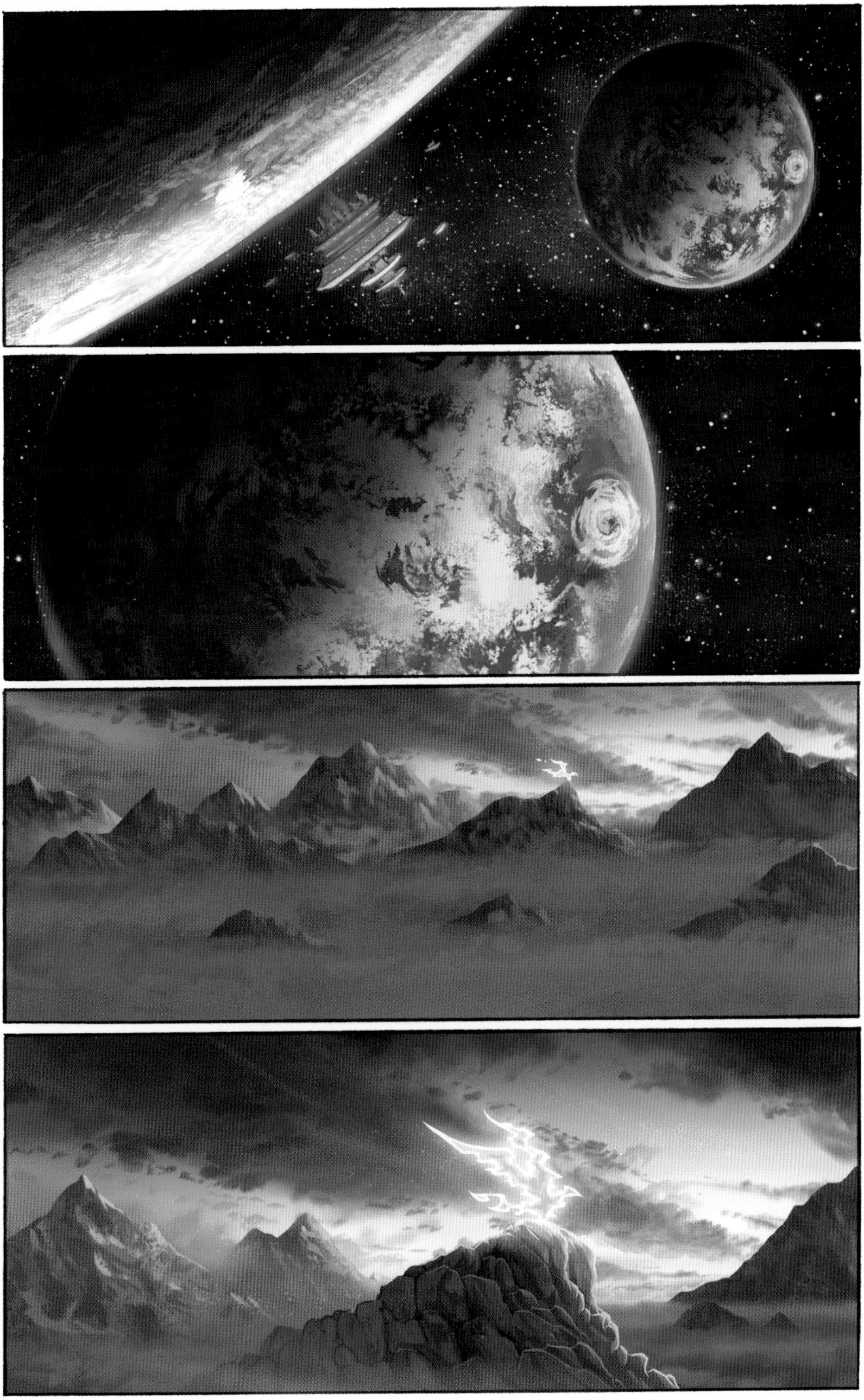

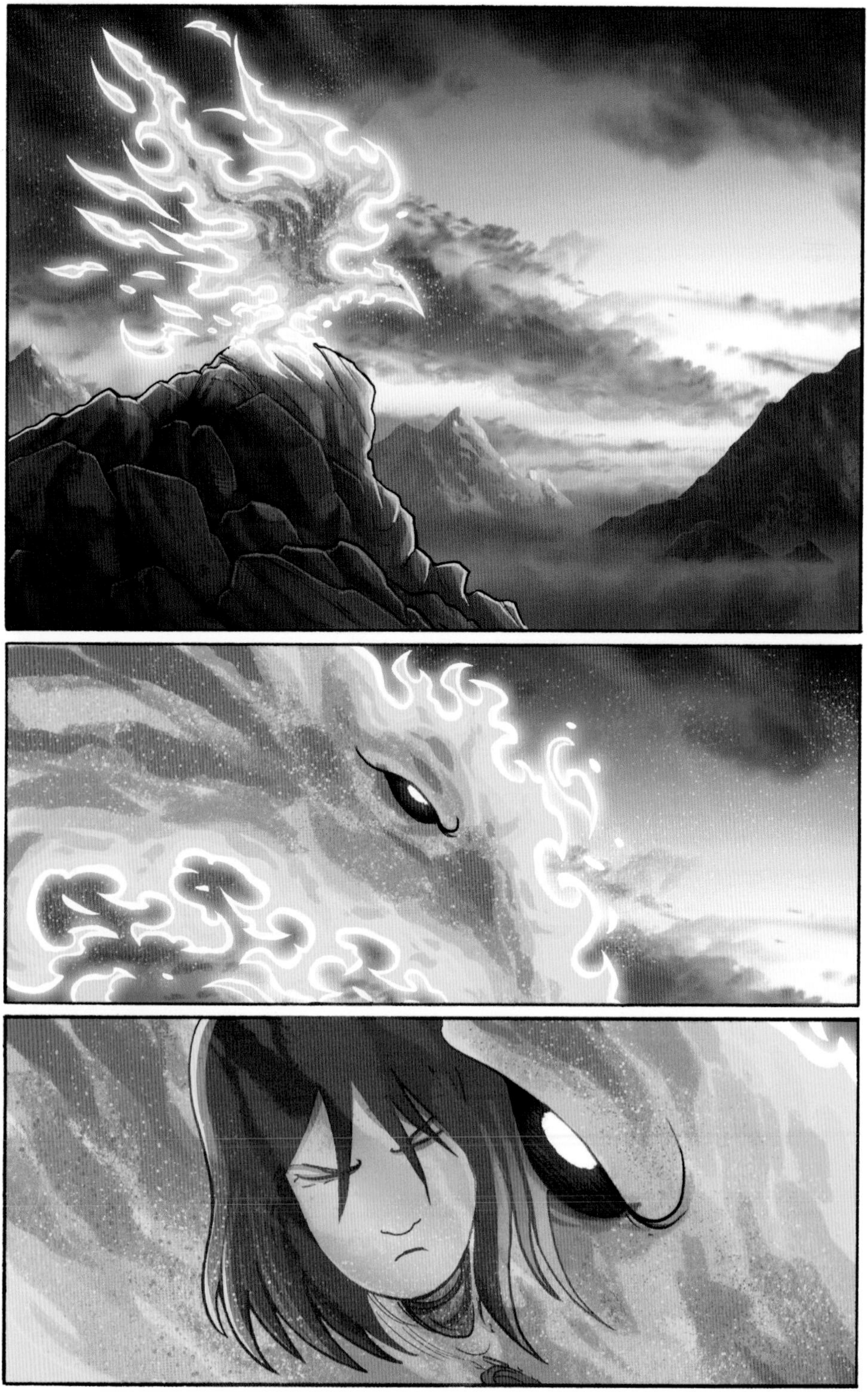

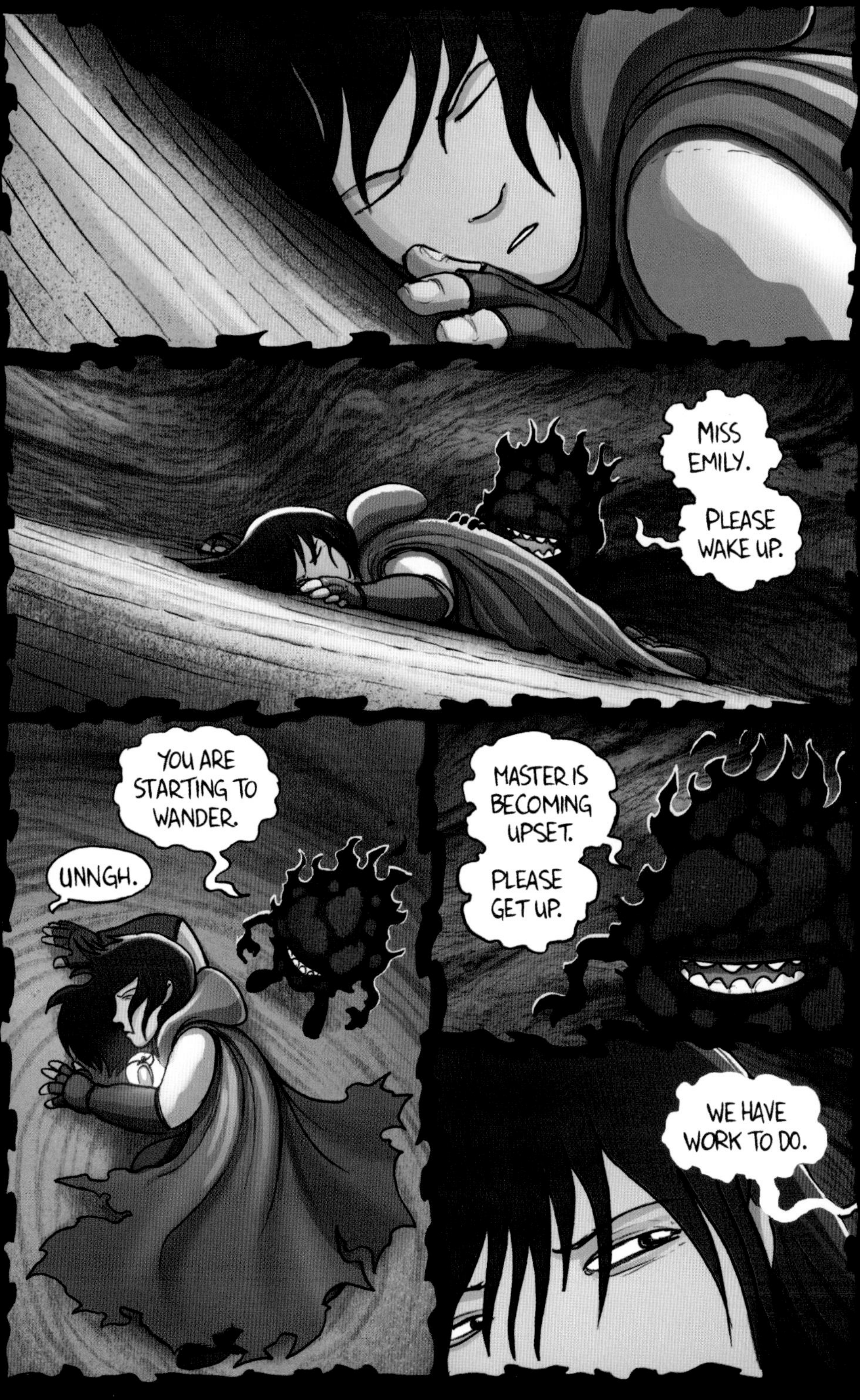
MISS EMILY.
PLEASE WAKE UP.
YOU ARE STARTING TO WANDER.
UNNGH.
MASTER IS BECOMING UPSET.
PLEASE GET UP.
WE HAVE WORK TO DO.

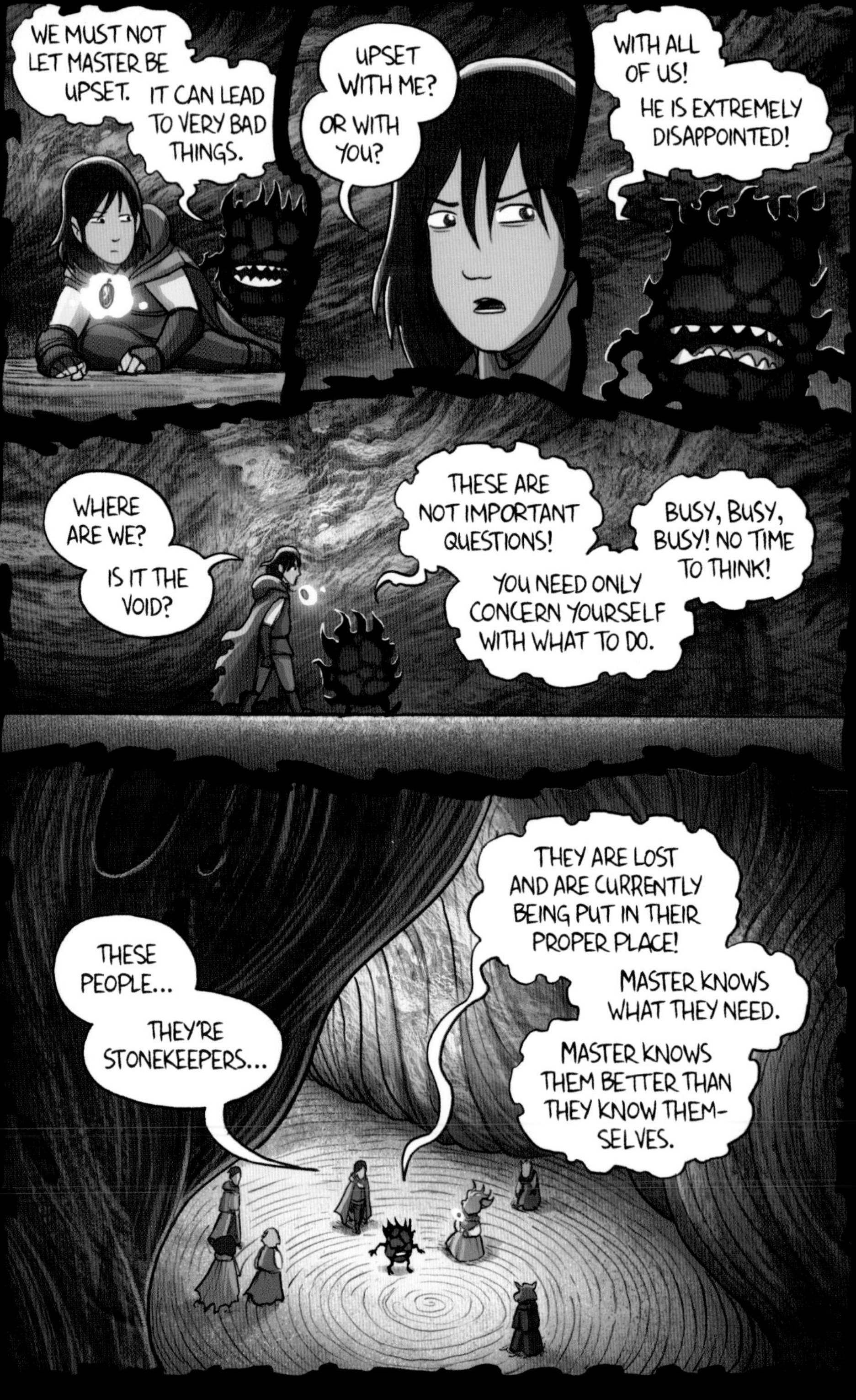
WE MUST NOT LET MASTER BE UPSET.
IT CAN LEAD TO VERY BAD THINGS.
UPSET WITH ME? OR WITH YOU?
WITH ALL OF US!
HE IS EXTREMELY DISAPPOINTED!
WHERE ARE WE?
IS IT THE VOID?
THESE ARE NOT IMPORTANT QUESTIONS!
YOU NEED ONLY CONCERN YOURSELF WITH WHAT TO DO.
BUSY, BUSY, BUSY! NO TIME TO THINK!
THESE PEOPLE...
THEY'RE STONEKEEPERS...
THEY ARE LOST AND ARE CURRENTLY BEING PUT IN THEIR PROPER PLACE!
MASTER KNOWS WHAT THEY NEED.
MASTER KNOWS THEM BETTER THAN THEY KNOW THEM-SELVES.

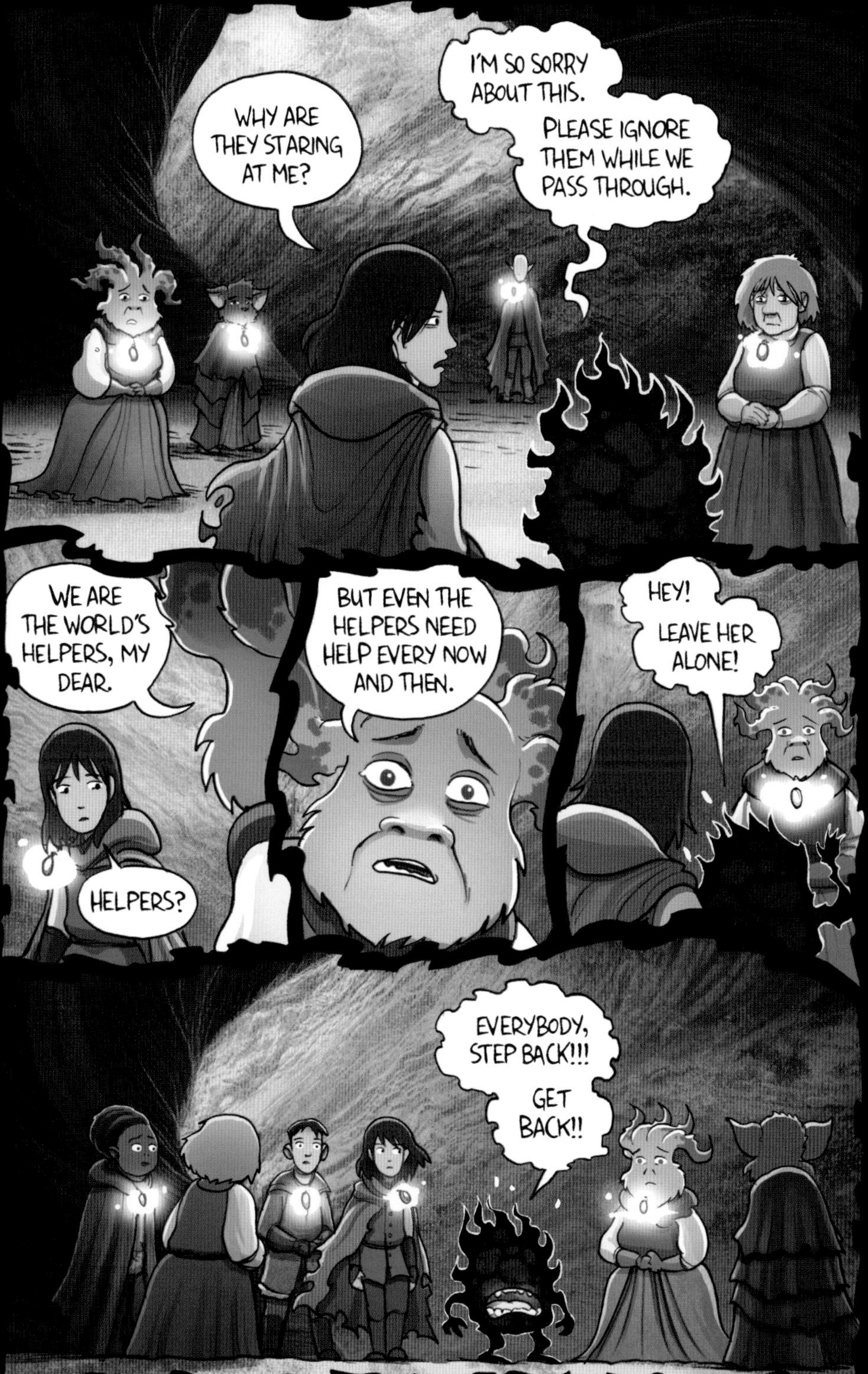
WHY ARE THEY STARING AT ME?
I'M SO SORRY ABOUT THIS.
PLEASE IGNORE THEM WHILE WE PASS THROUGH.
WE ARE THE WORLD'S HELPERS, MY DEAR.
HELPERS?
BUT EVEN THE HELPERS NEED HELP EVERY NOW AND THEN.
HEY!
LEAVE HER ALONE!
EVERYBODY, STEP BACK!!!
GET BACK!!

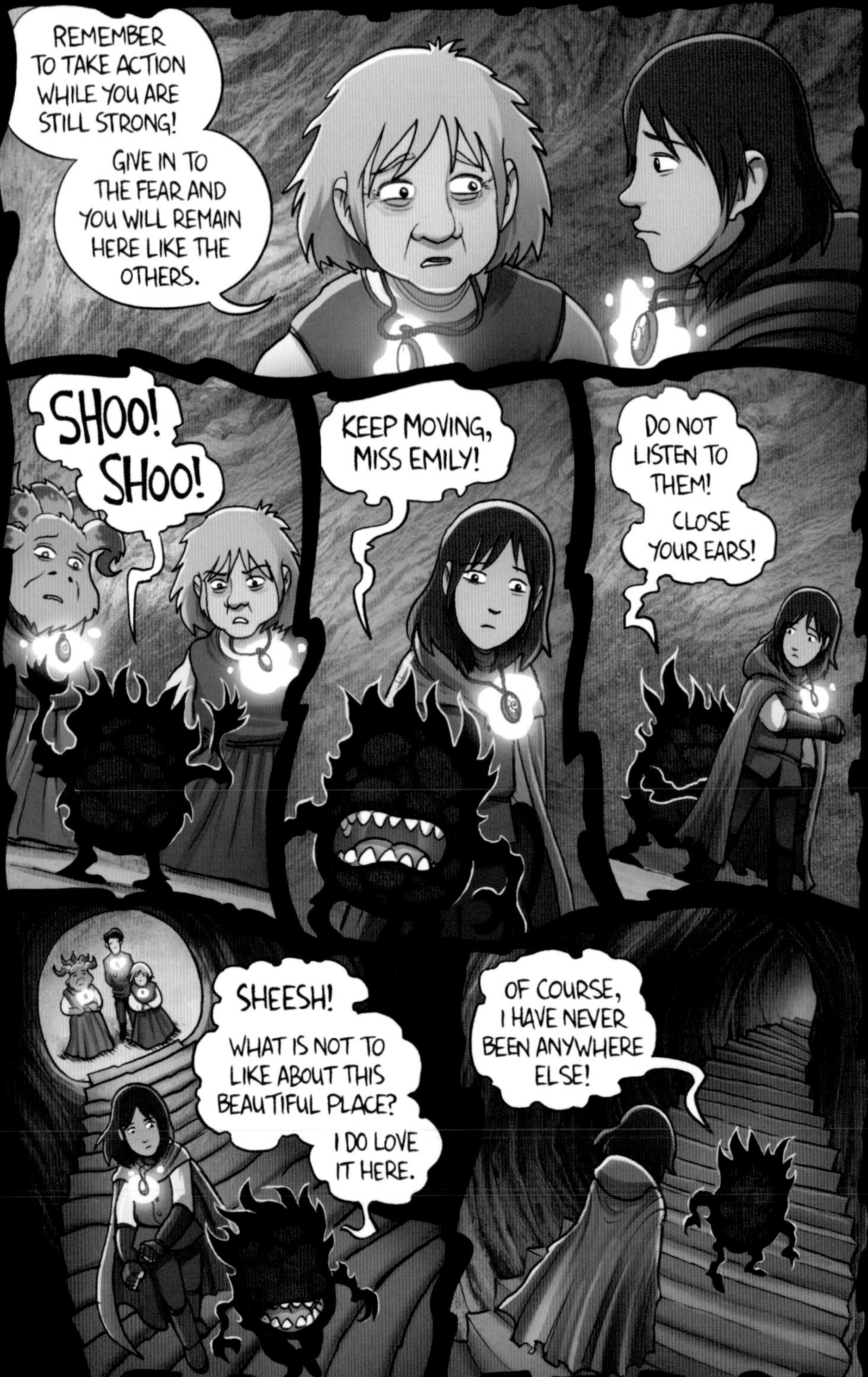

REMEMBER TO TAKE ACTION WHILE YOU ARE STILL STRONG!
GIVE IN TO THE FEAR AND YOU WILL REMAIN HERE LIKE THE OTHERS.
SHOO! SHOO!
KEEP MOVING, MISS EMILY!
DO NOT LISTEN TO THEM!
CLOSE YOUR EARS!
SHEESH!
WHAT IS NOT TO LIKE ABOUT THIS BEAUTIFUL PLACE?
I DO LOVE IT HERE.
OF COURSE, I HAVE NEVER BEEN ANYWHERE ELSE!

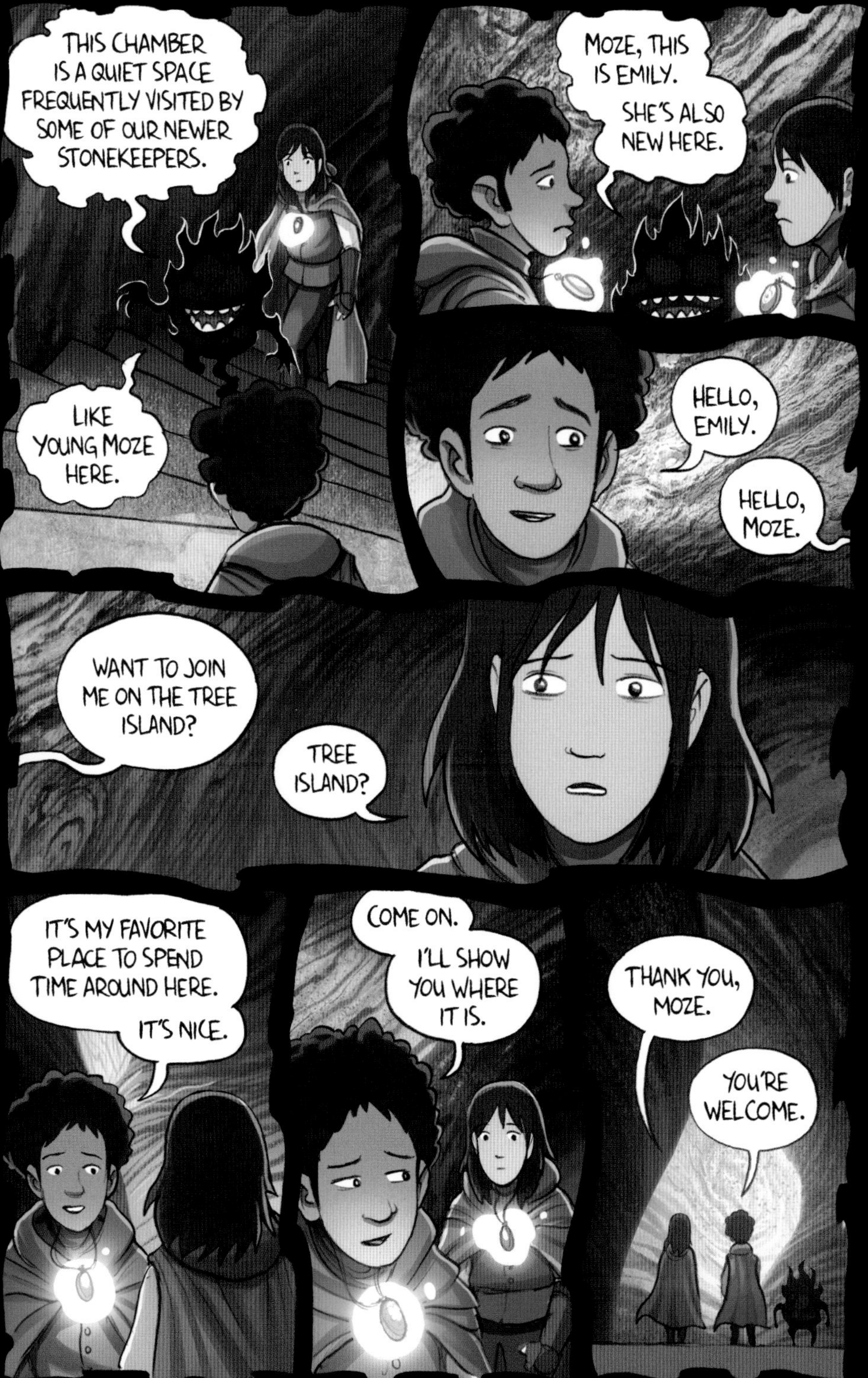
THIS CHAMBER IS A QUIET SPACE FREQUENTLY VISITED BY SOME OF OUR NEWER STONEKEEPERS.
LIKE YOUNG MOZE HERE.
MOZE, THIS IS EMILY.
SHE'S ALSO NEW HERE.
HELLO, EMILY.
HELLO, MOZE.
WANT TO JOIN ME ON THE TREE ISLAND?
TREE ISLAND?
IT'S MY FAVORITE PLACE TO SPEND TIME AROUND HERE.
IT'S NICE.
COME ON.
I'LL SHOW YOU WHERE IT IS.
THANK YOU, MOZE.
YOU'RE WELCOME.

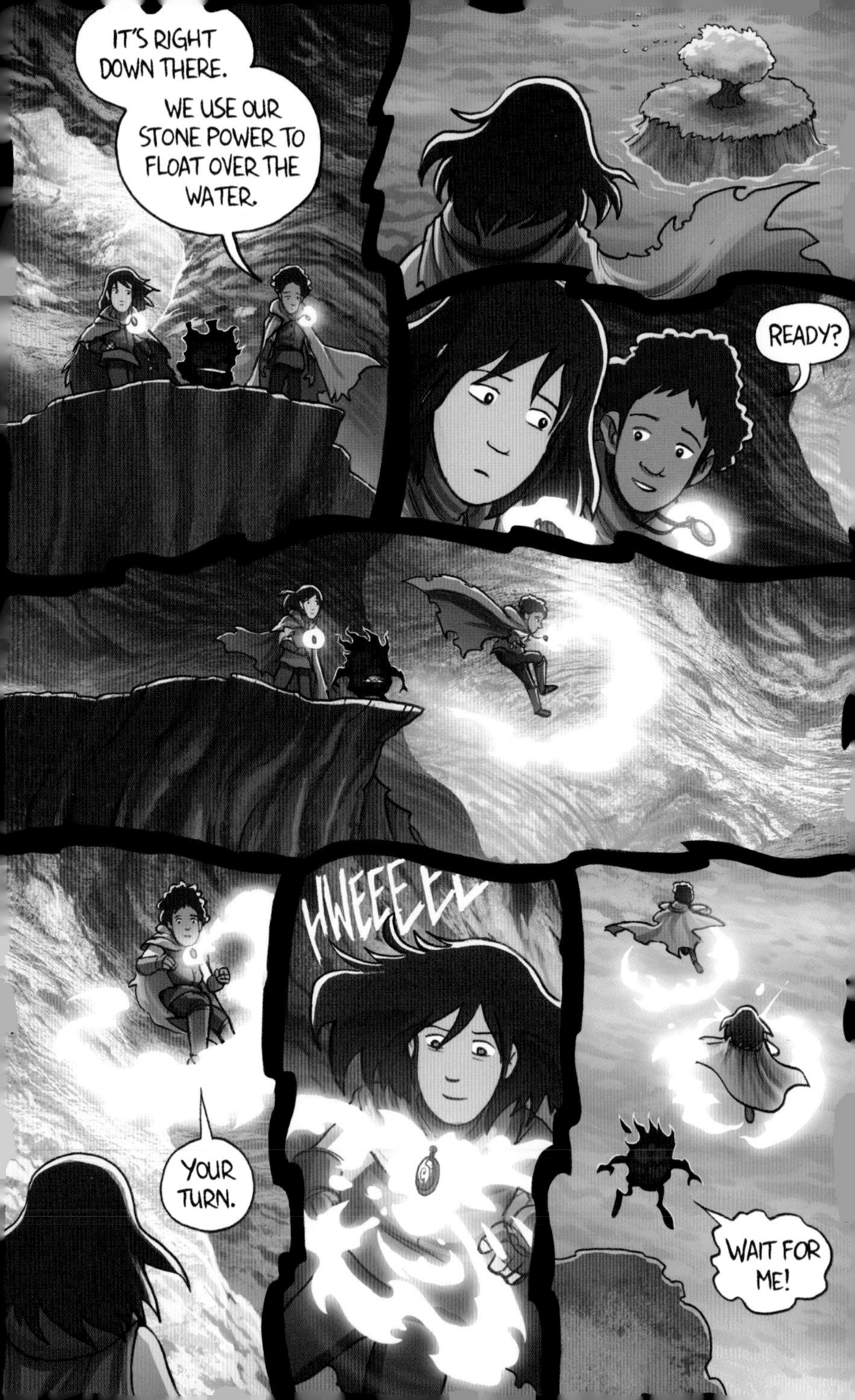
IT'S RIGHT DOWN THERE.
WE USE OUR STONE POWER TO FLOAT OVER THE WATER.
READY?
YOUR TURN.
HWEEEEE
WAIT FOR ME!

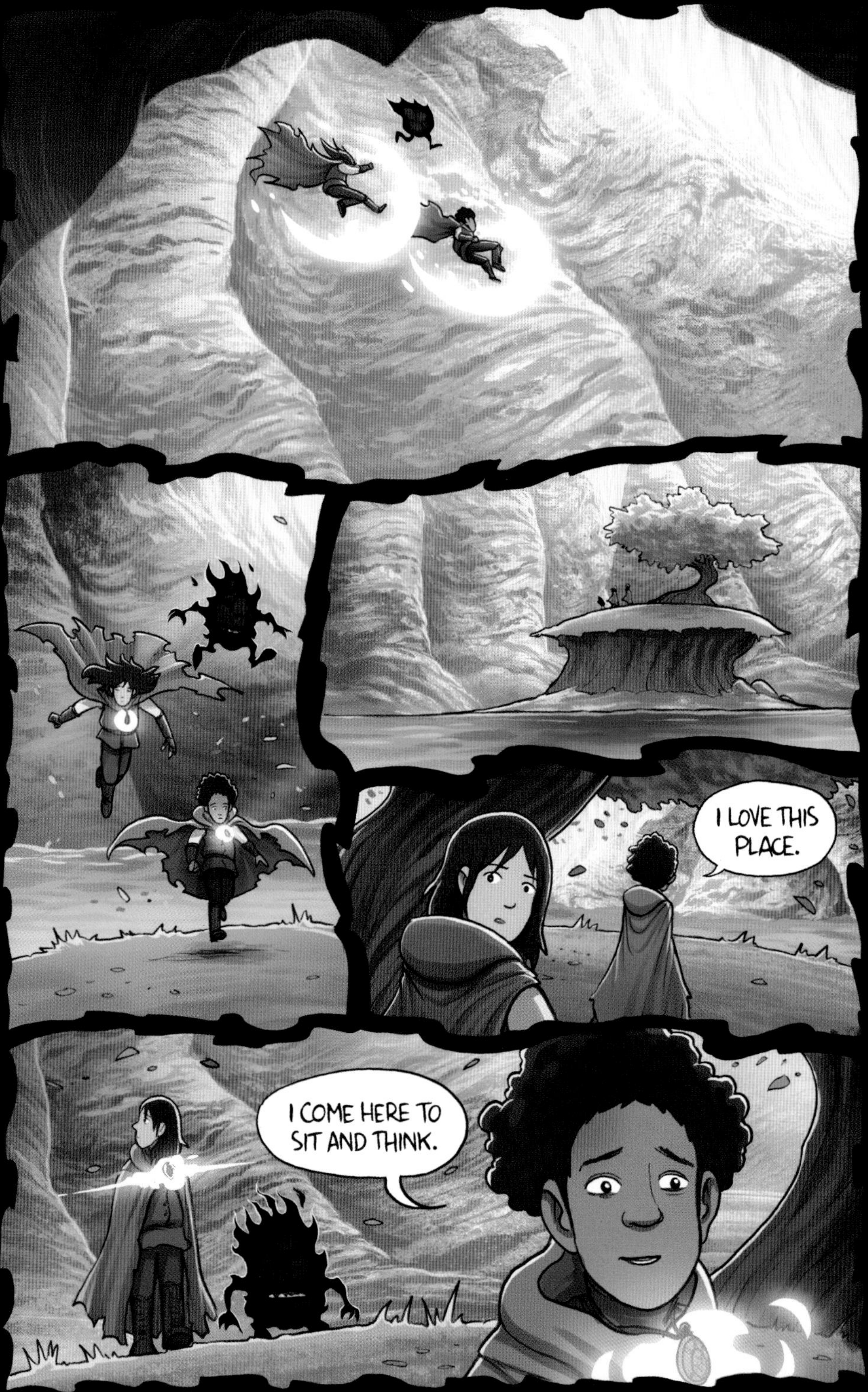
I LOVE THIS PLACE.
I COME HERE TO SIT AND THINK.

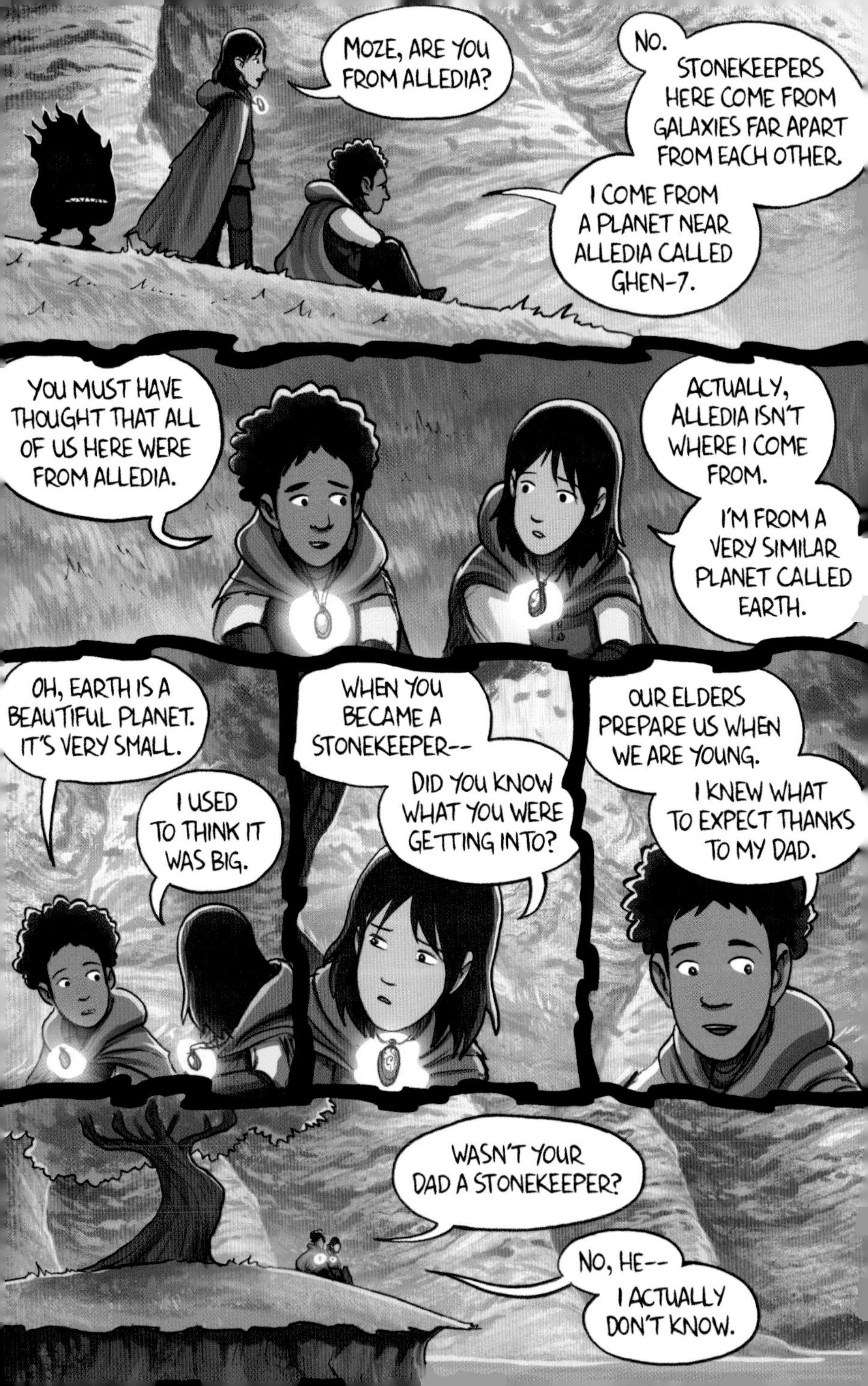
MOZE, ARE YOU FROM ALLEDIA?
NO.
STONEKEEPERS HERE COME FROM GALAXIES FAR APART FROM EACH OTHER.
I COME FROM A PLANET NEAR ALLEDIA CALLED GHEN-7.
YOU MUST HAVE THOUGHT THAT ALL OF US HERE WERE FROM ALLEDIA.
ACTUALLY, ALLEDIA ISN'T WHERE I COME FROM.
I'M FROM A VERY SIMILAR PLANET CALLED EARTH.
OH, EARTH IS A BEAUTIFUL PLANET. IT'S VERY SMALL.
I USED TO THINK IT WAS BIG.
WHEN YOU BECAME A STONEKEEPER--
DID YOU KNOW WHAT YOU WERE GETTING INTO?
OUR ELDERS PREPARE US WHEN WE ARE YOUNG.
I KNEW WHAT TO EXPECT THANKS TO MY DAD.
WASN'T YOUR DAD A STONEKEEPER?
NO, HE--
I ACTUALLY DON'T KNOW.

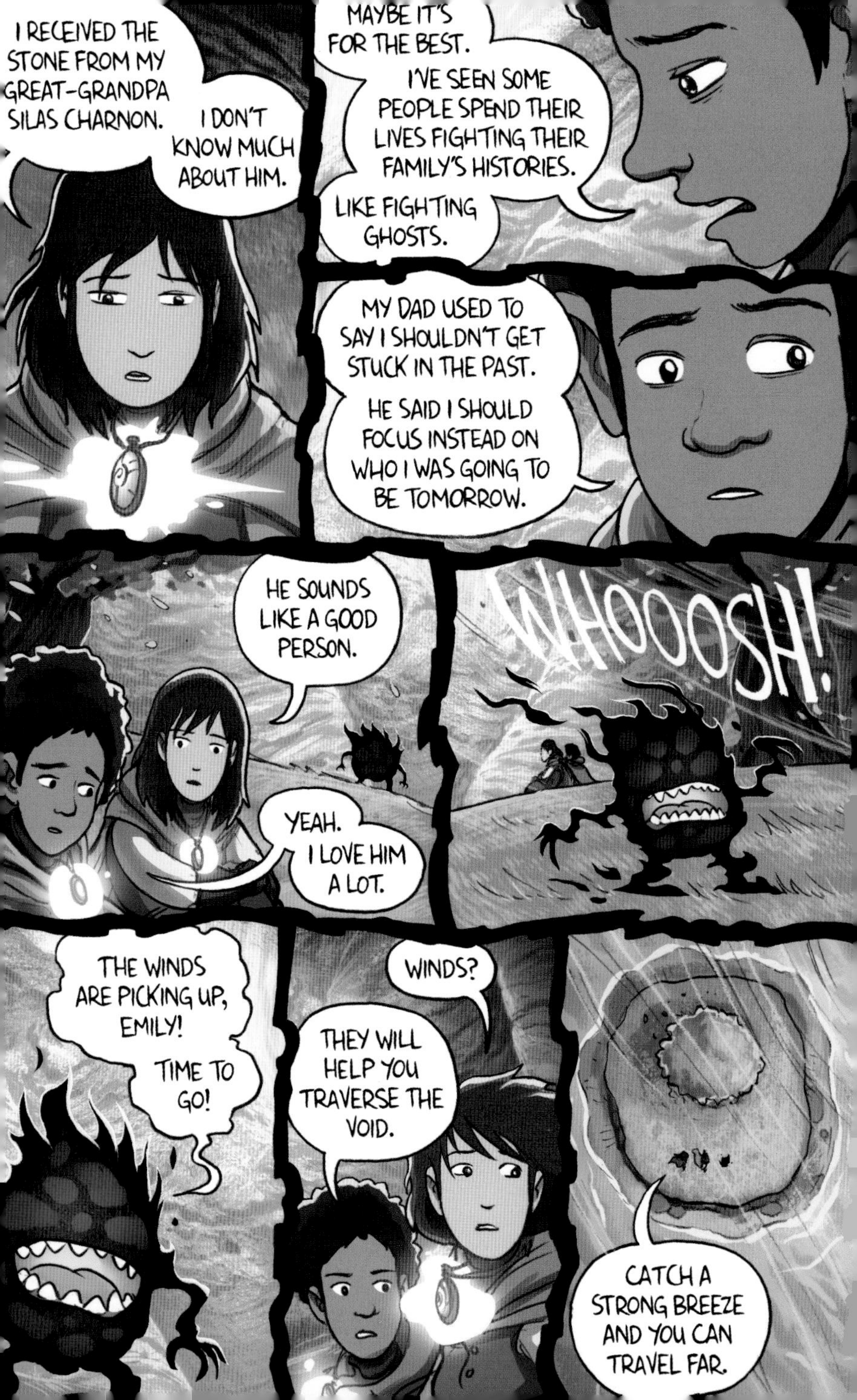
I RECEIVED THE STONE FROM MY GREAT-GRANDPA SILAS CHARNON.
I DON'T KNOW MUCH ABOUT HIM.
MAYBE IT'S FOR THE BEST.
I'VE SEEN SOME PEOPLE SPEND THEIR LIVES FIGHTING THEIR FAMILY'S HISTORIES.
LIKE FIGHTING GHOSTS.
MY DAD USED TO SAY I SHOULDN'T GET STUCK IN THE PAST.
HE SAID I SHOULD FOCUS INSTEAD ON WHO I WAS GOING TO BE TOMORROW.
HE SOUNDS LIKE A GOOD PERSON.
YEAH. I LOVE HIM A LOT.
WHOOOSH!
THE WINDS ARE PICKING UP, EMILY!
TIME TO GO!
WINDS?
THEY WILL HELP YOU TRAVERSE THE VOID.
CATCH A STRONG BREEZE AND YOU CAN TRAVEL FAR.

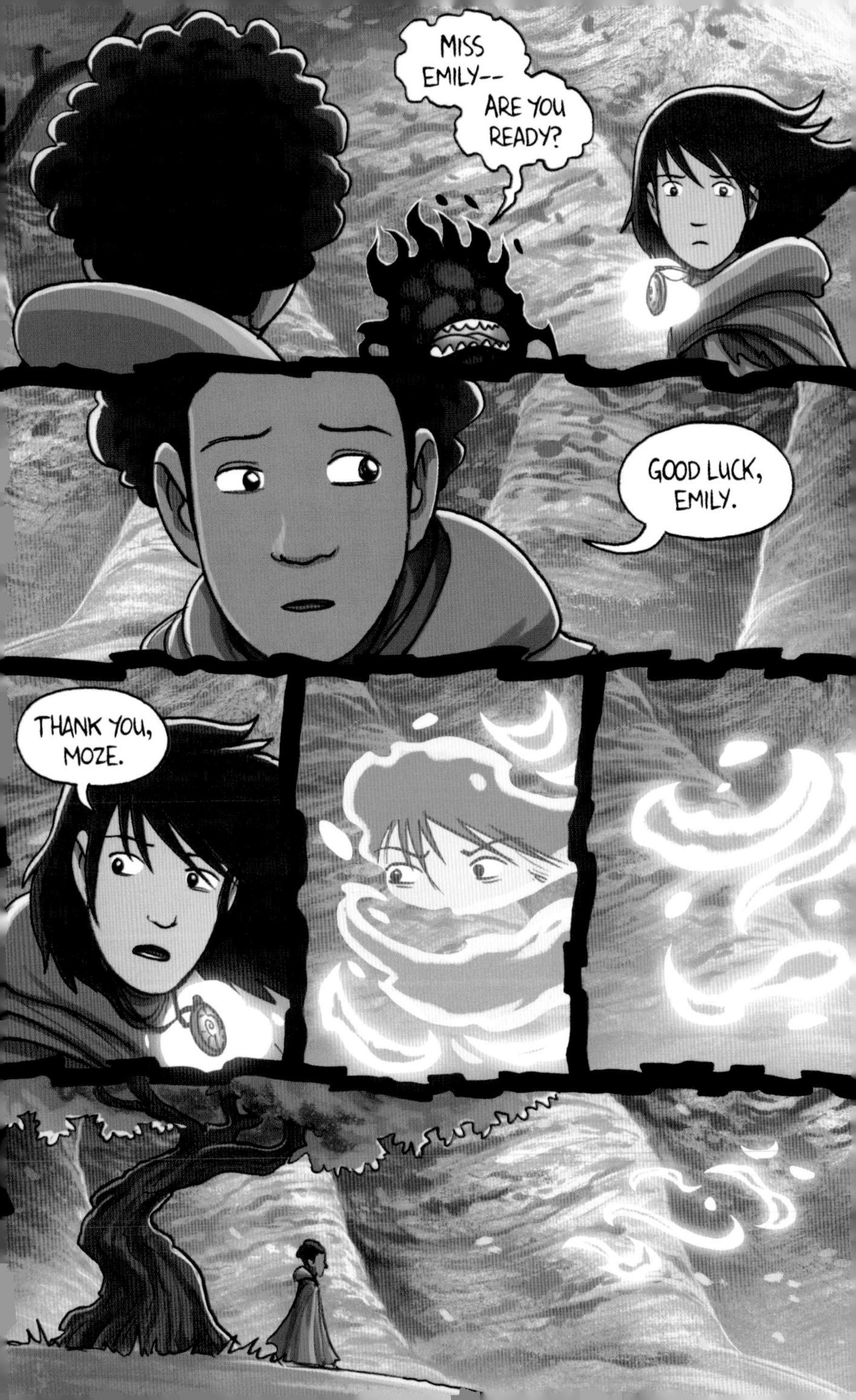
MISS EMILY-- ARE YOU READY?
GOOD LUCK, EMILY.
THANK YOU, MOZE.

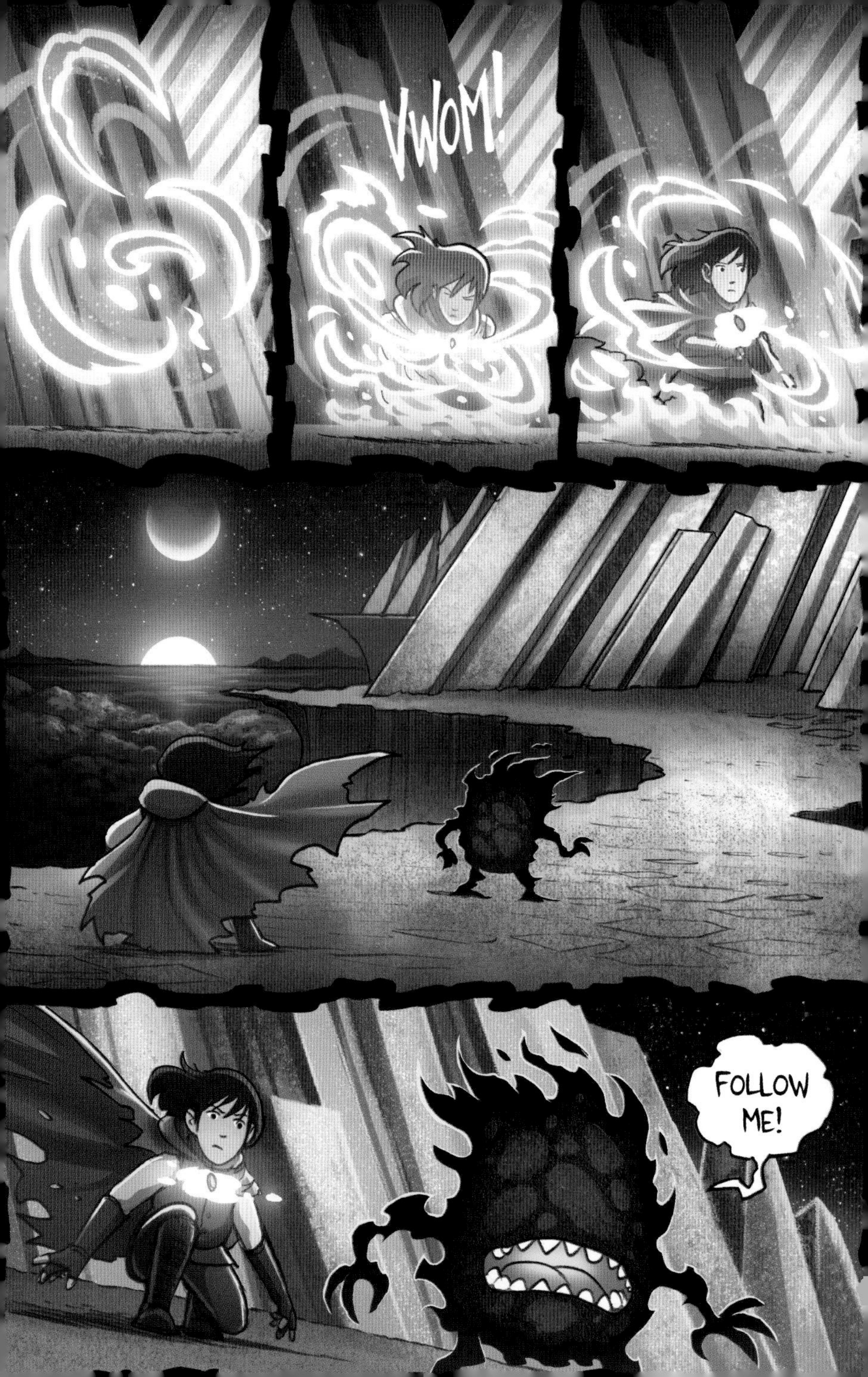
VWOM!
FOLLOW ME!

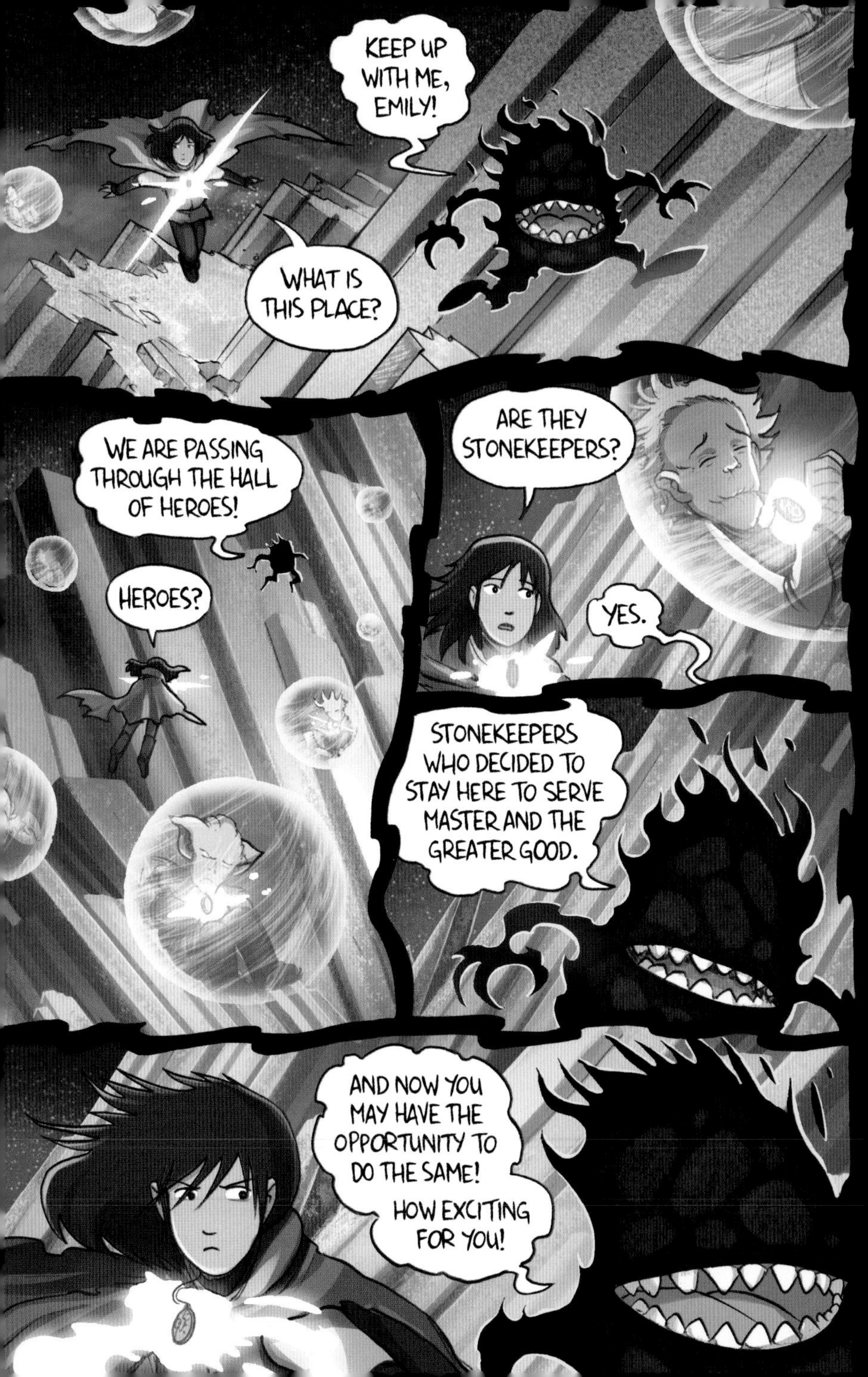
KEEP UP WITH ME, EMILY!
WHAT IS THIS PLACE?
WE ARE PASSING THROUGH THE HALL OF HEROES!
HEROES?
ARE THEY STONEKEEPERS?
YES.
STONEKEEPERS WHO DECIDED TO STAY HERE TO SERVE MASTER AND THE GREATER GOOD.
AND NOW YOU MAY HAVE THE OPPORTUNITY TO DO THE SAME!
HOW EXCITING FOR YOU!

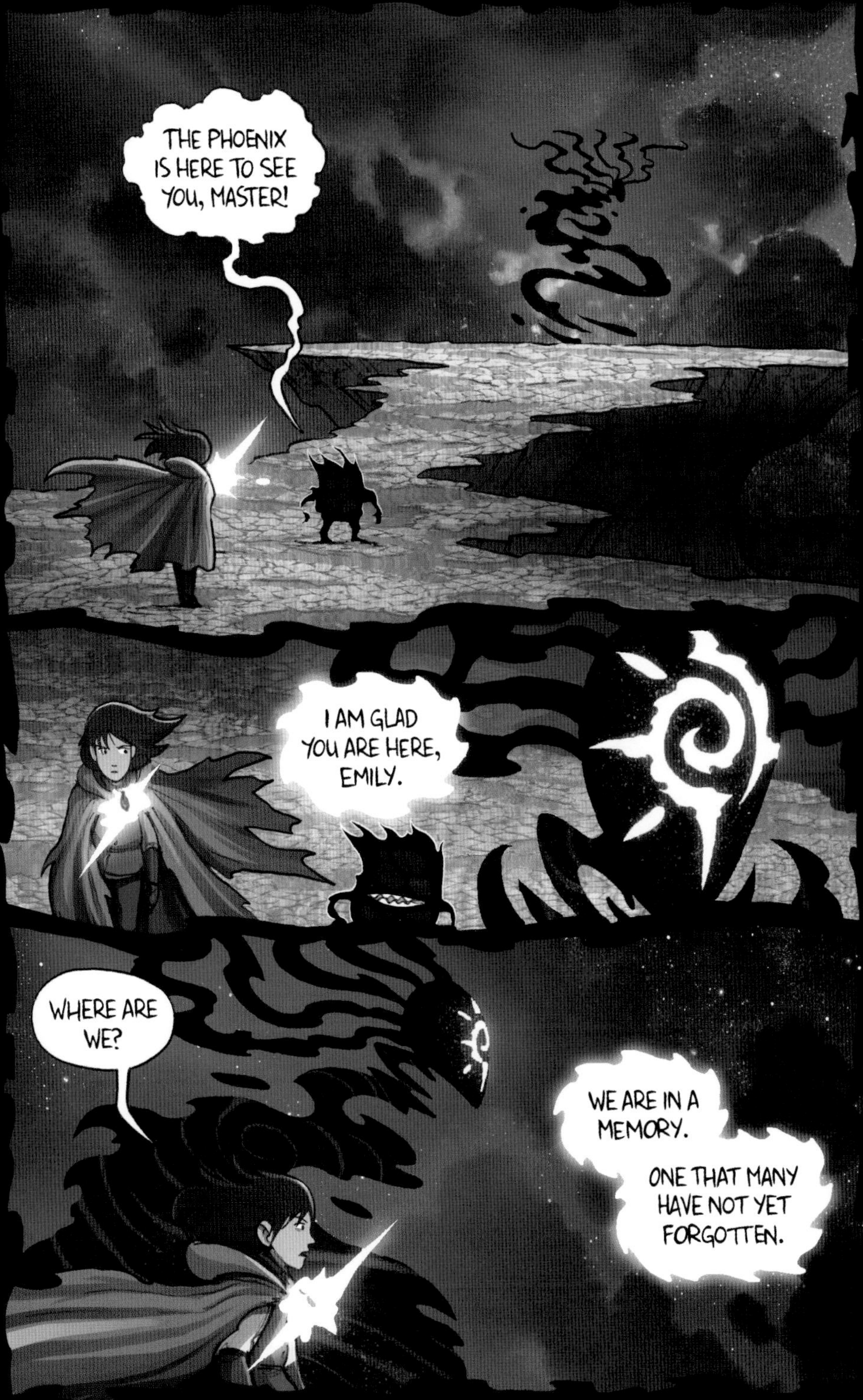
THE PHOENIX IS HERE TO SEE YOU, MASTER!
I AM GLAD YOU ARE HERE, EMILY.
WHERE ARE WE?
WE ARE IN A MEMORY.
ONE THAT MANY HAVE NOT YET FORGOTTEN.

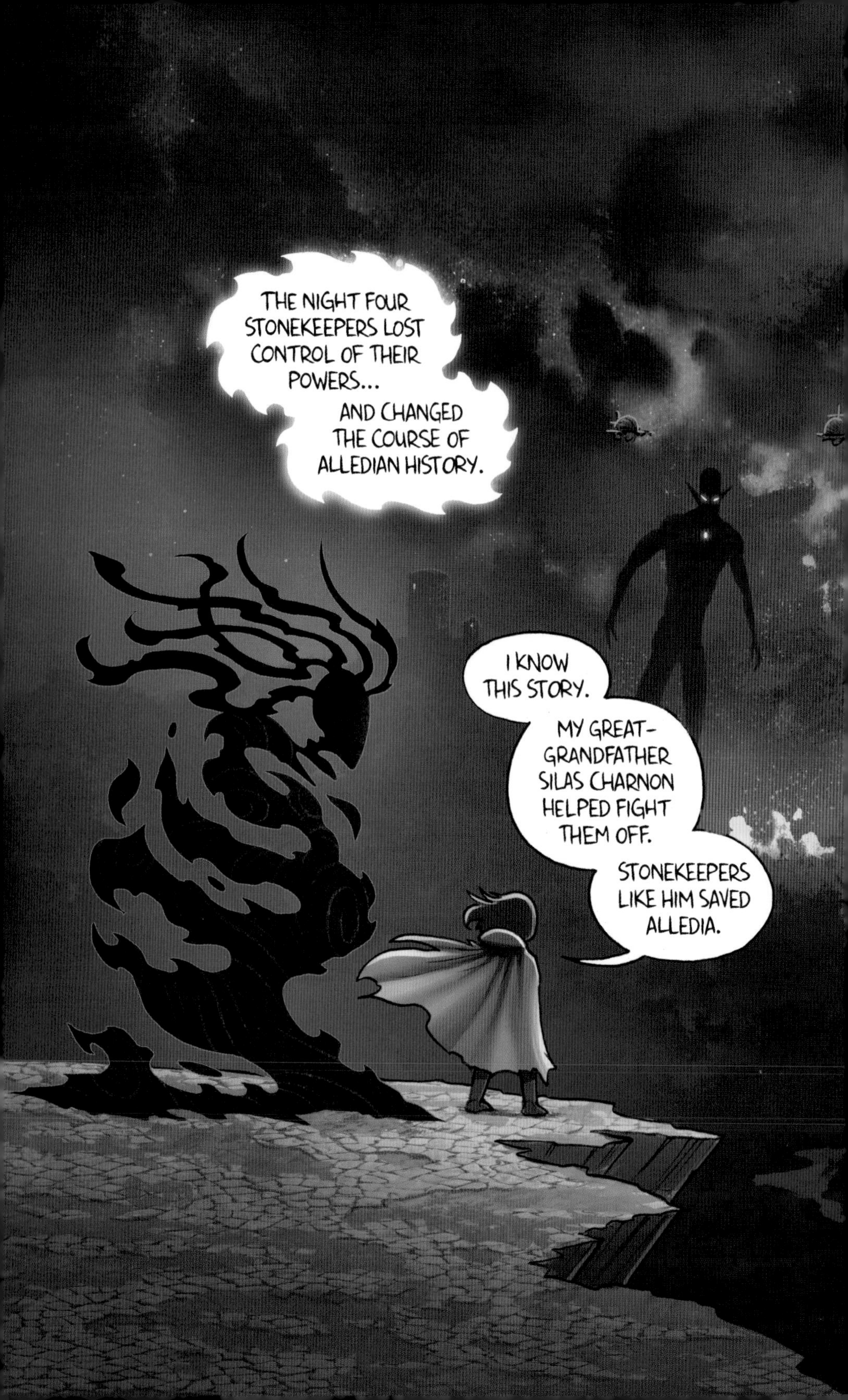
THE NIGHT FOUR STONEKEEPERS LOST CONTROL OF THEIR POWERS...
AND CHANGED THE COURSE OF ALLEDIAN HISTORY.
I KNOW THIS STORY.
MY GREAT-GRANDFATHER SILAS CHARNON HELPED FIGHT THEM OFF.
STONEKEEPERS LIKE HIM SAVED ALLEDIA.

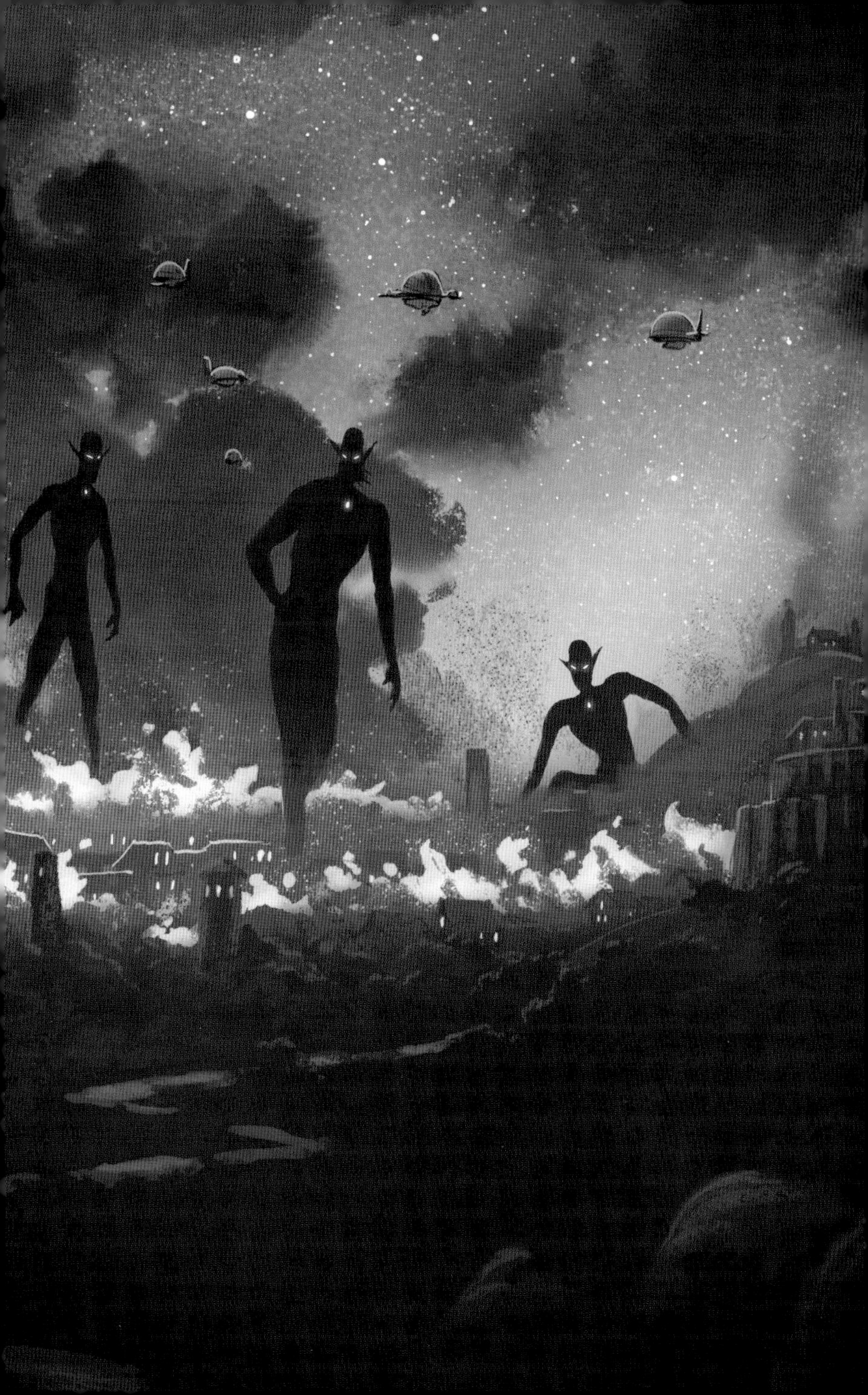

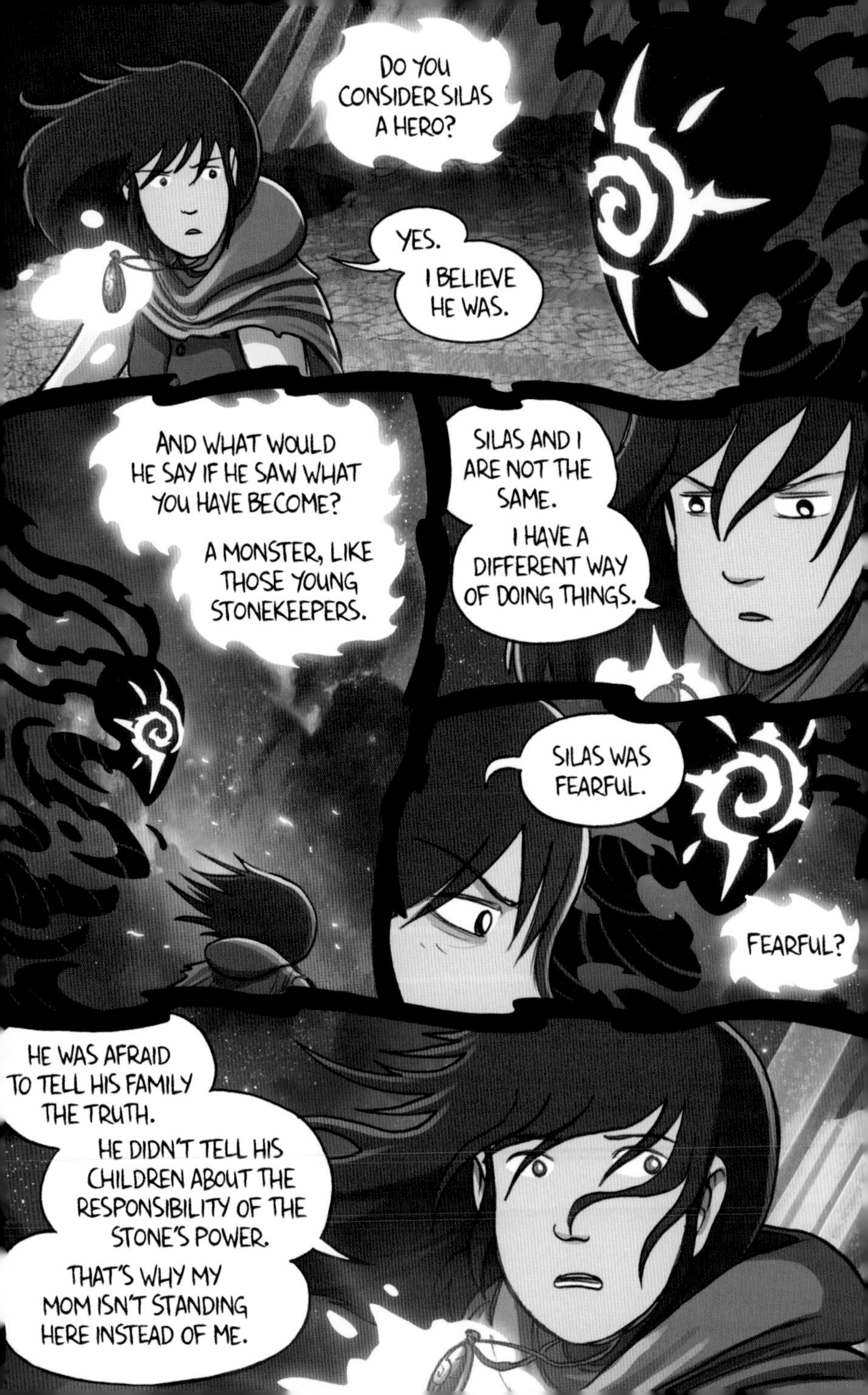
DO YOU CONSIDER SILAS A HERO?
YES.
I BELIEVE HE WAS.
AND WHAT WOULD HE SAY IF HE SAW WHAT YOU HAVE BECOME?
A MONSTER, LIKE THOSE YOUNG STONEKEEPERS.
SILAS AND I ARE NOT THE SAME.
I HAVE A DIFFERENT WAY OF DOING THINGS.
SILAS WAS FEARFUL.
FEARFUL?
HE WAS AFRAID TO TELL HIS FAMILY THE TRUTH.
HE DIDN'T TELL HIS CHILDREN ABOUT THE RESPONSIBILITY OF THE STONE'S POWER.
THAT'S WHY MY MOM ISN'T STANDING HERE INSTEAD OF ME.

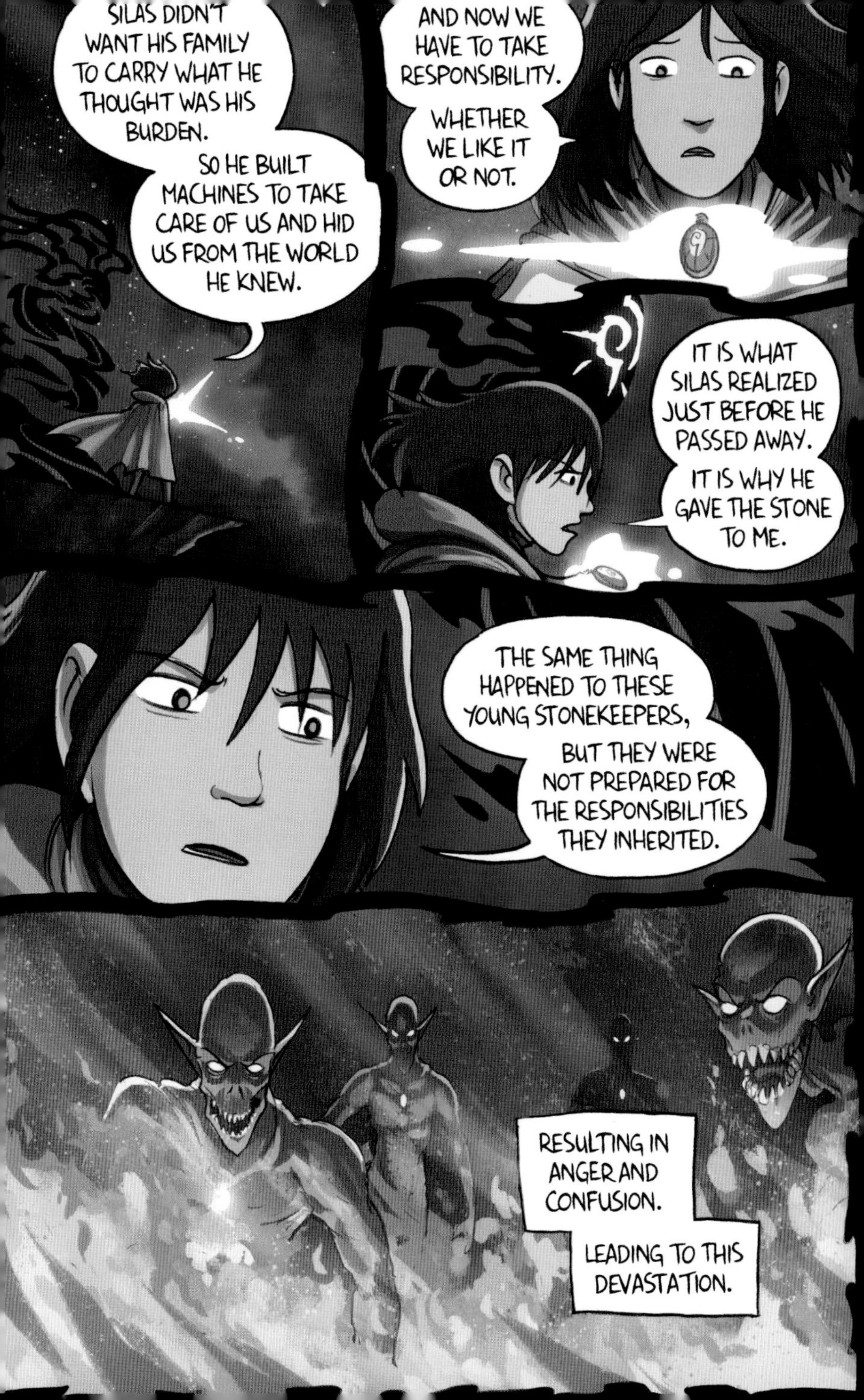
SILAS DIDN'T WANT HIS FAMILY TO CARRY WHAT HE THOUGHT WAS HIS BURDEN.
SO HE BUILT MACHINES TO TAKE CARE OF US AND HID US FROM THE WORLD HE KNEW.
AND NOW WE HAVE TO TAKE RESPONSIBILITY.
WHETHER WE LIKE IT OR NOT.
IT IS WHAT SILAS REALIZED JUST BEFORE HE PASSED AWAY.
IT IS WHY HE GAVE THE STONE TO ME.
THE SAME THING HAPPENED TO THESE YOUNG STONEKEEPERS,
BUT THEY WERE NOT PREPARED FOR THE RESPONSIBILITIES THEY INHERITED.
RESULTING IN ANGER AND CONFUSION.
LEADING TO THIS DEVASTATION.

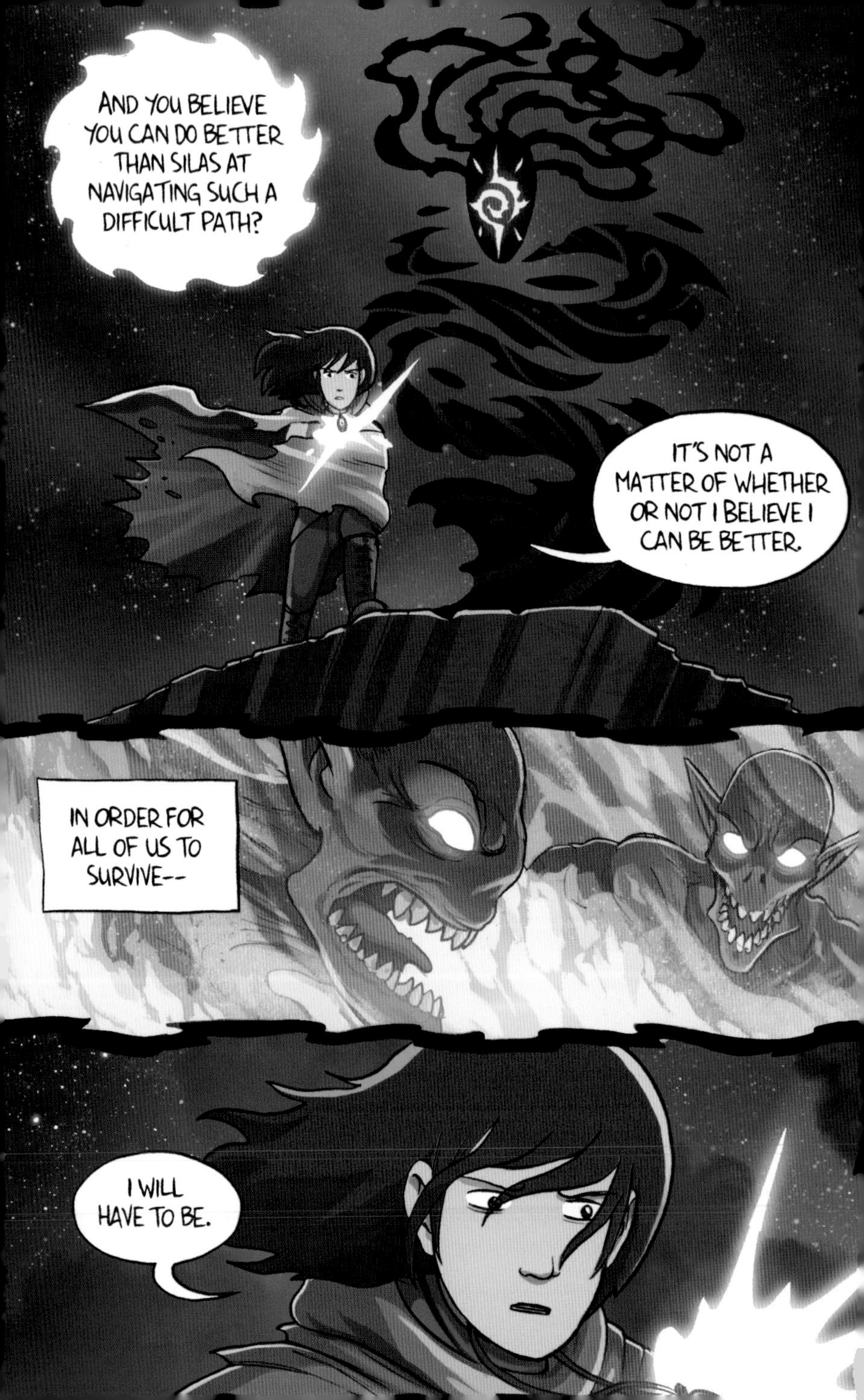
AND YOU BELIEVE YOU CAN DO BETTER THAN SILAS AT NAVIGATING SUCH A DIFFICULT PATH?
IT'S NOT A MATTER OF WHETHER OR NOT I BELIEVE I CAN BE BETTER.
IN ORDER FOR ALL OF US TO SURVIVE--
I WILL HAVE TO BE.

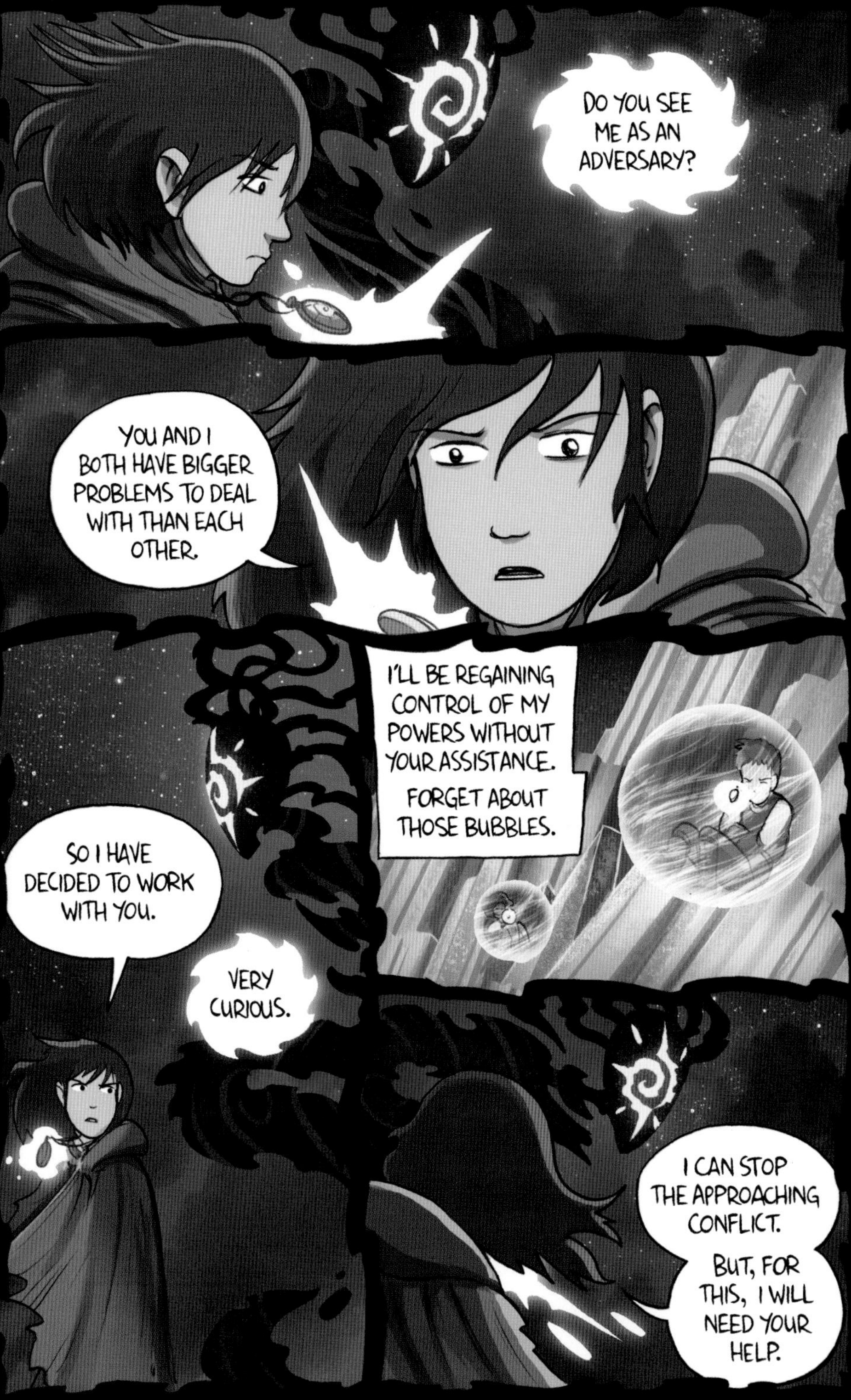
DO YOU SEE ME AS AN ADVERSARY?
YOU AND I BOTH HAVE BIGGER PROBLEMS TO DEAL WITH THAN EACH OTHER.
I'LL BE REGAINING CONTROL OF MY POWERS WITHOUT YOUR ASSISTANCE.
FORGET ABOUT THOSE BUBBLES.
SO I HAVE DECIDED TO WORK WITH YOU.
VERY CURIOUS.
I CAN STOP THE APPROACHING CONFLICT.
BUT, FOR THIS, I WILL NEED YOUR HELP.

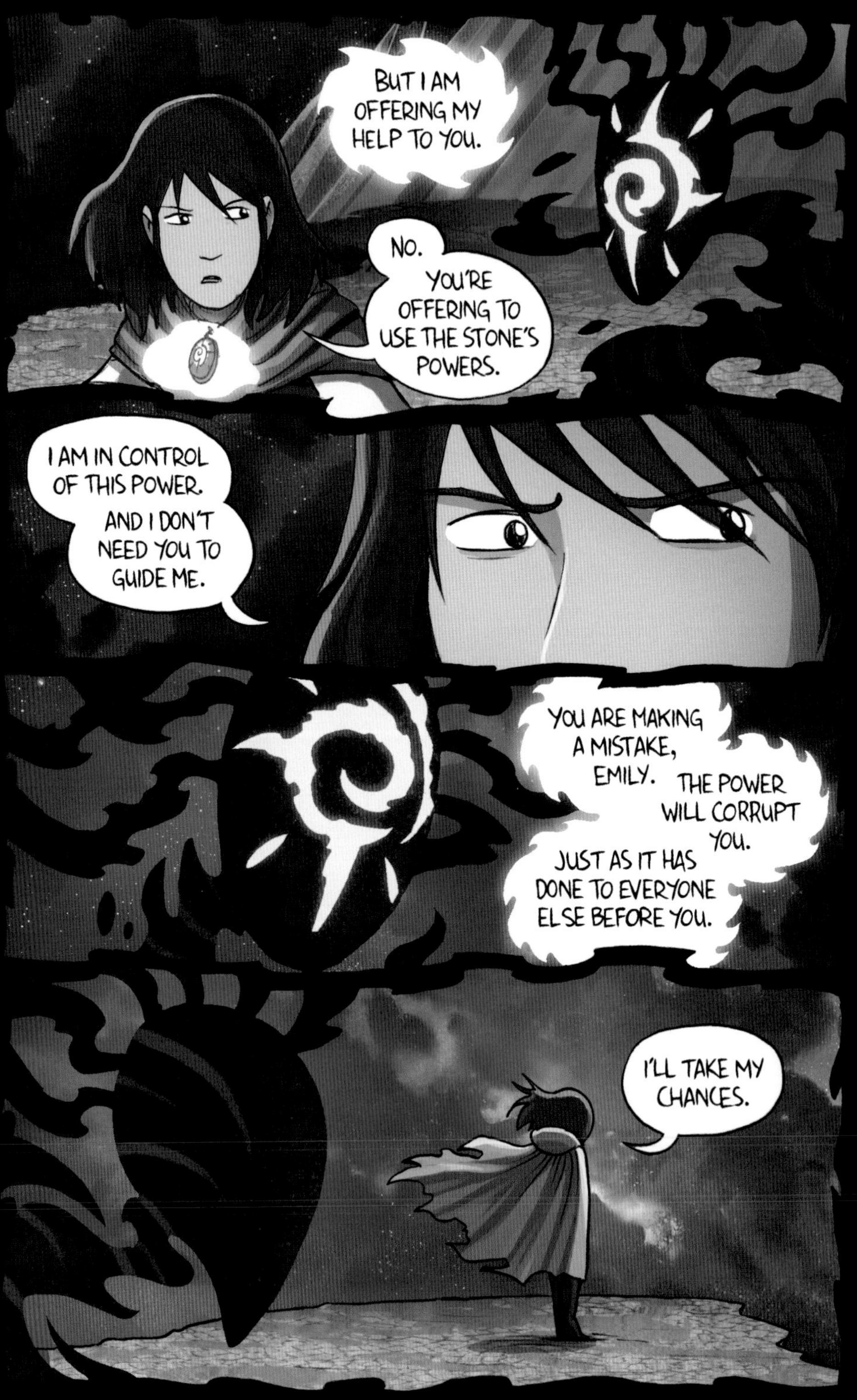
BUT I AM OFFERING MY HELP TO YOU.
NO.
YOU'RE OFFERING TO USE THE STONE'S POWERS.
I AM IN CONTROL OF THIS POWER.
AND I DON'T NEED YOU TO GUIDE ME.
YOU ARE MAKING A MISTAKE, EMILY.
THE POWER WILL CORRUPT YOU.
JUST AS IT HAS DONE TO EVERYONE ELSE BEFORE YOU.
I'LL TAKE MY CHANCES.

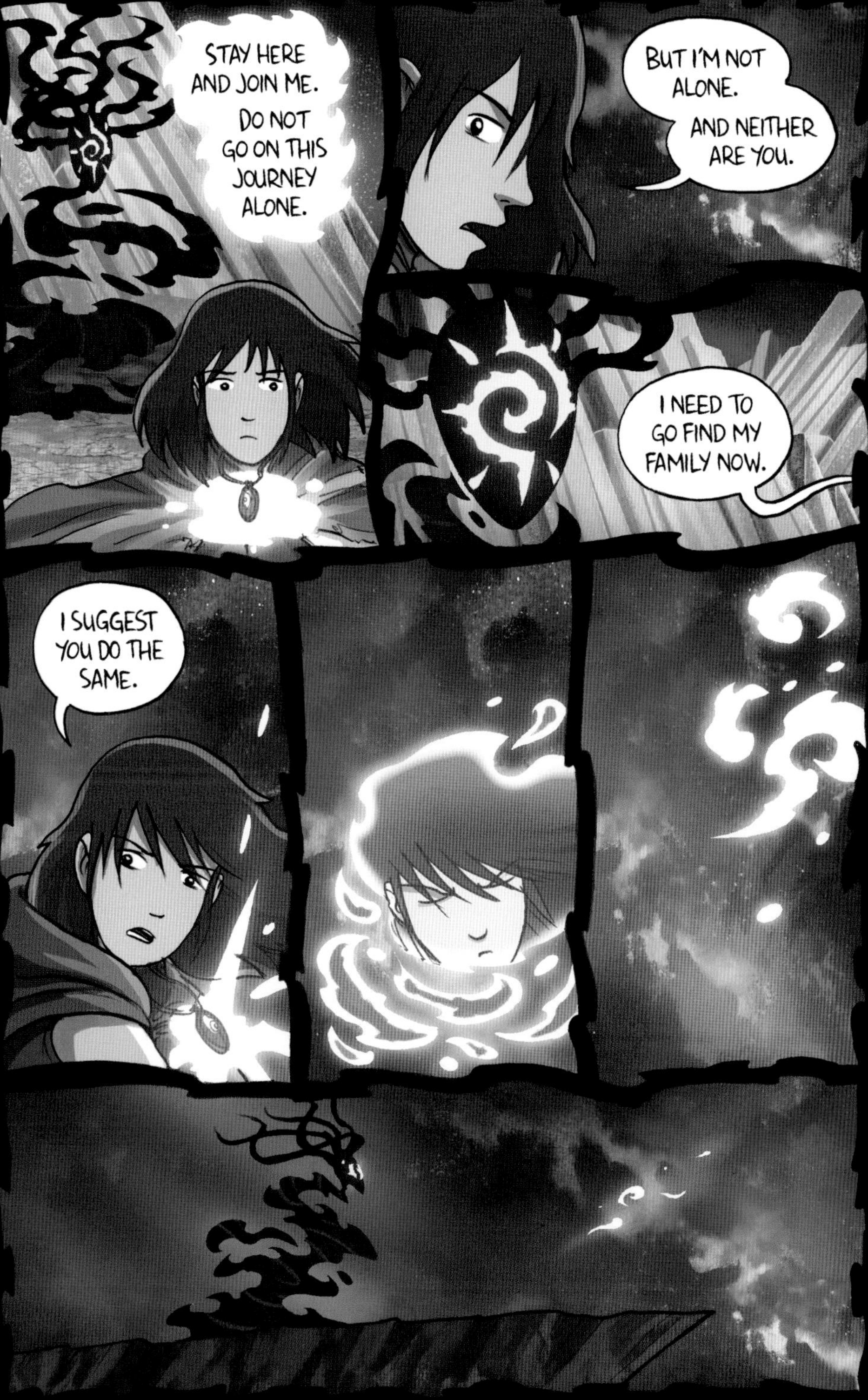
STAY HERE AND JOIN ME.
DO NOT GO ON THIS JOURNEY ALONE.
BUT I'M NOT ALONE.
AND NEITHER ARE YOU.
I NEED TO GO FIND MY FAMILY NOW.
I SUGGEST YOU DO THE SAME.

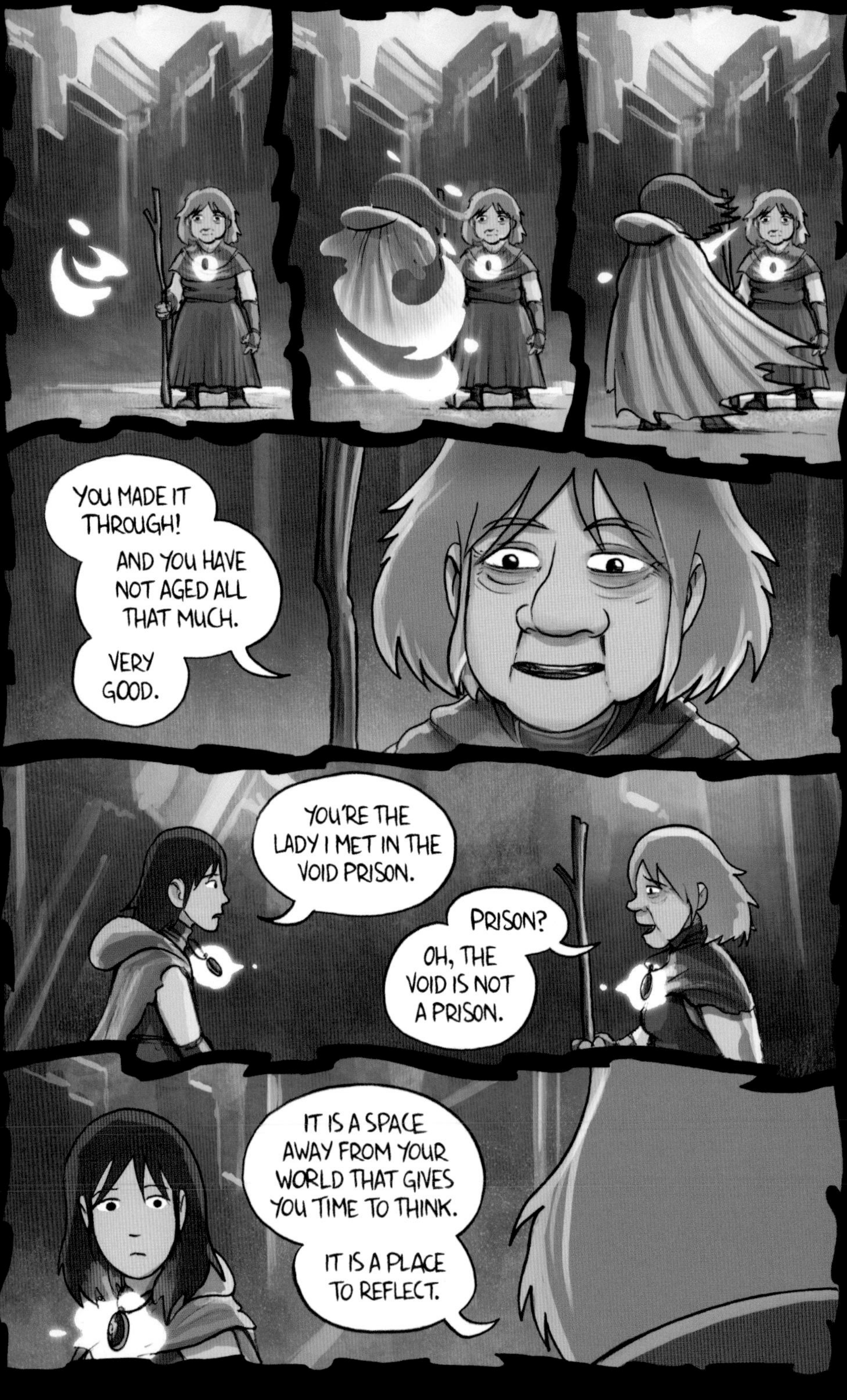
YOU MADE IT THROUGH!
AND YOU HAVE NOT AGED ALL THAT MUCH.
VERY GOOD.
YOU'RE THE LADY I MET IN THE VOID PRISON.
PRISON?
OH, THE VOID IS NOT A PRISON.
IT IS A SPACE AWAY FROM YOUR WORLD THAT GIVES YOU TIME TO THINK.
IT IS A PLACE TO REFLECT.

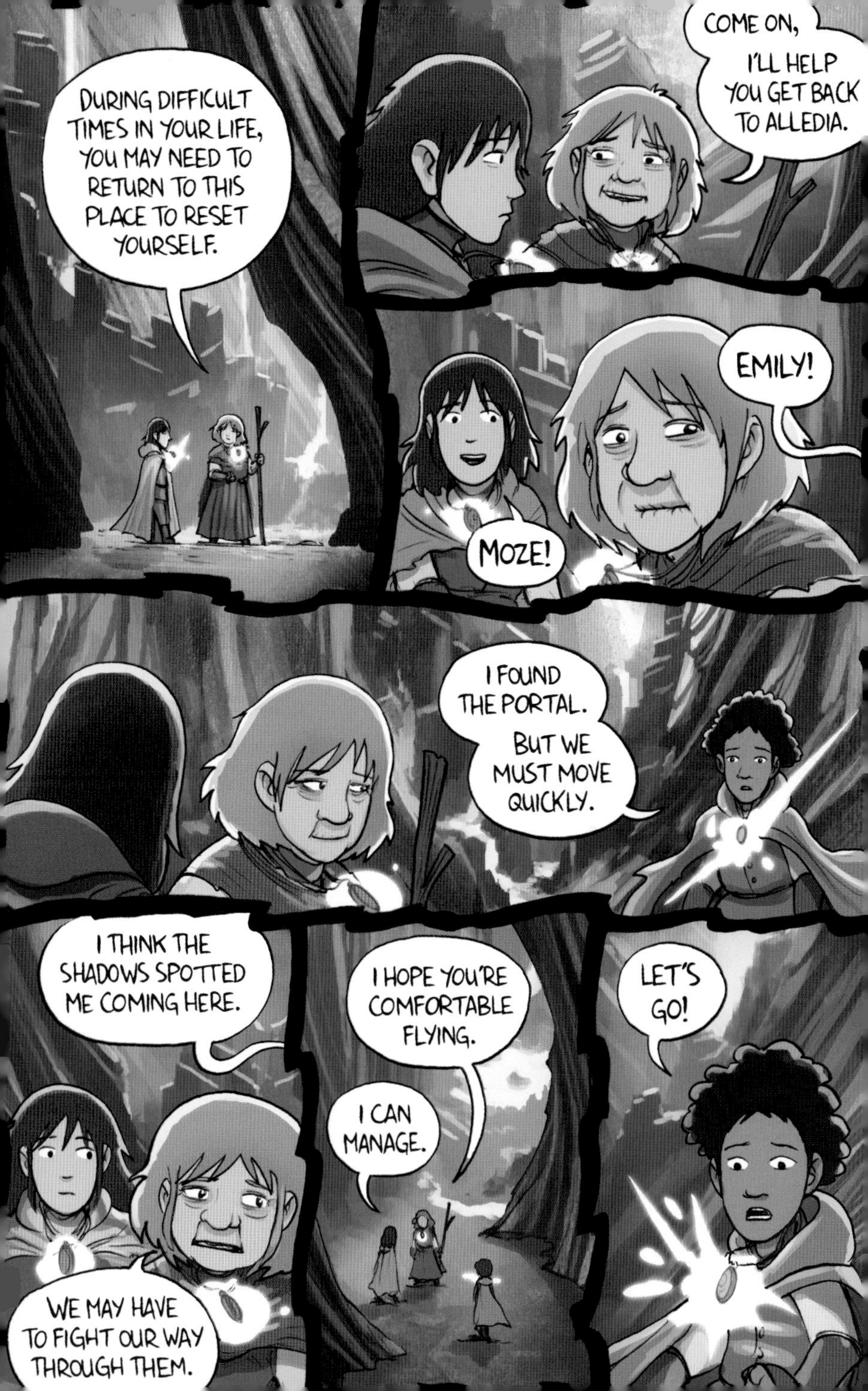
DURING DIFFICULT TIMES IN YOUR LIFE, YOU MAY NEED TO RETURN TO THIS PLACE TO RESET YOURSELF.
COME ON,
I'LL HELP YOU GET BACK TO ALLEDIA.
EMILY!
MOZE!
I FOUND THE PORTAL.
BUT WE MUST MOVE QUICKLY.
I THINK THE SHADOWS SPOTTED ME COMING HERE.
WE MAY HAVE TO FIGHT OUR WAY THROUGH THEM.
I HOPE YOU'RE COMFORTABLE FLYING.
I CAN MANAGE.
LET'S GO!

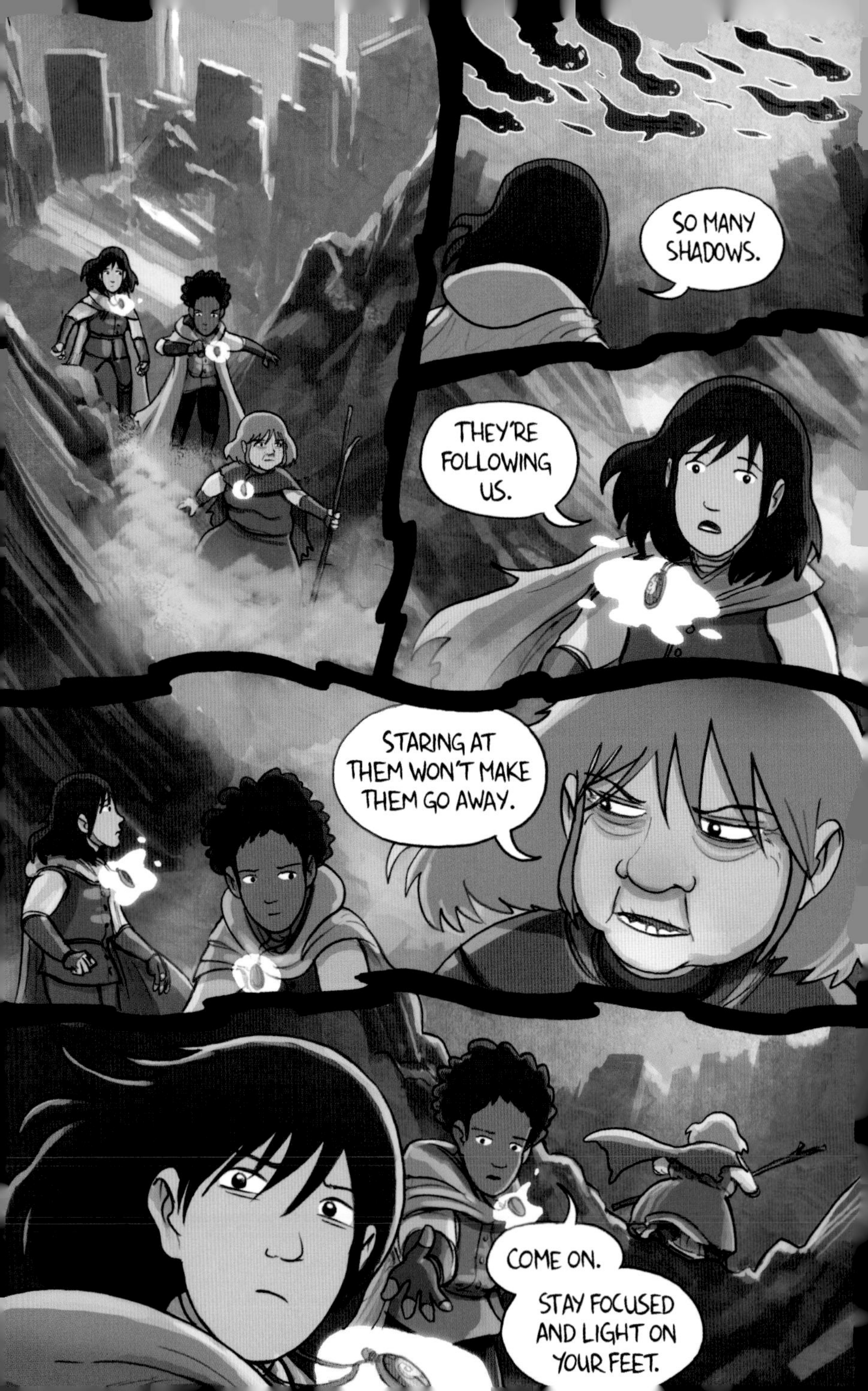
SO MANY SHADOWS.
THEY'RE FOLLOWING US.
STARING AT THEM WON'T MAKE THEM GO AWAY.
COME ON.
STAY FOCUSED AND LIGHT ON YOUR FEET.

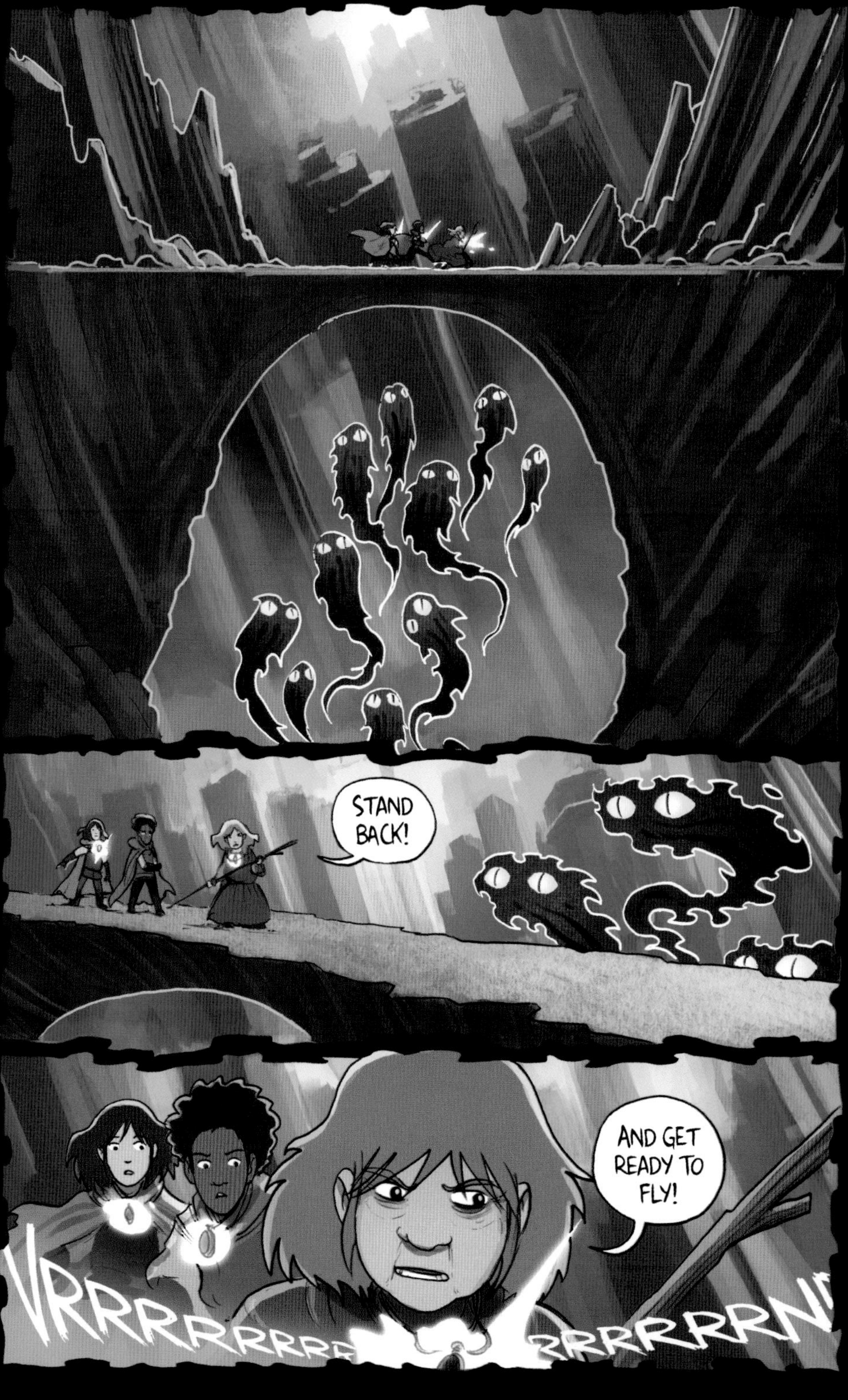
STAND BACK!
AND GET READY TO FLY!
VRRRRRRRRRRRRRRRRN

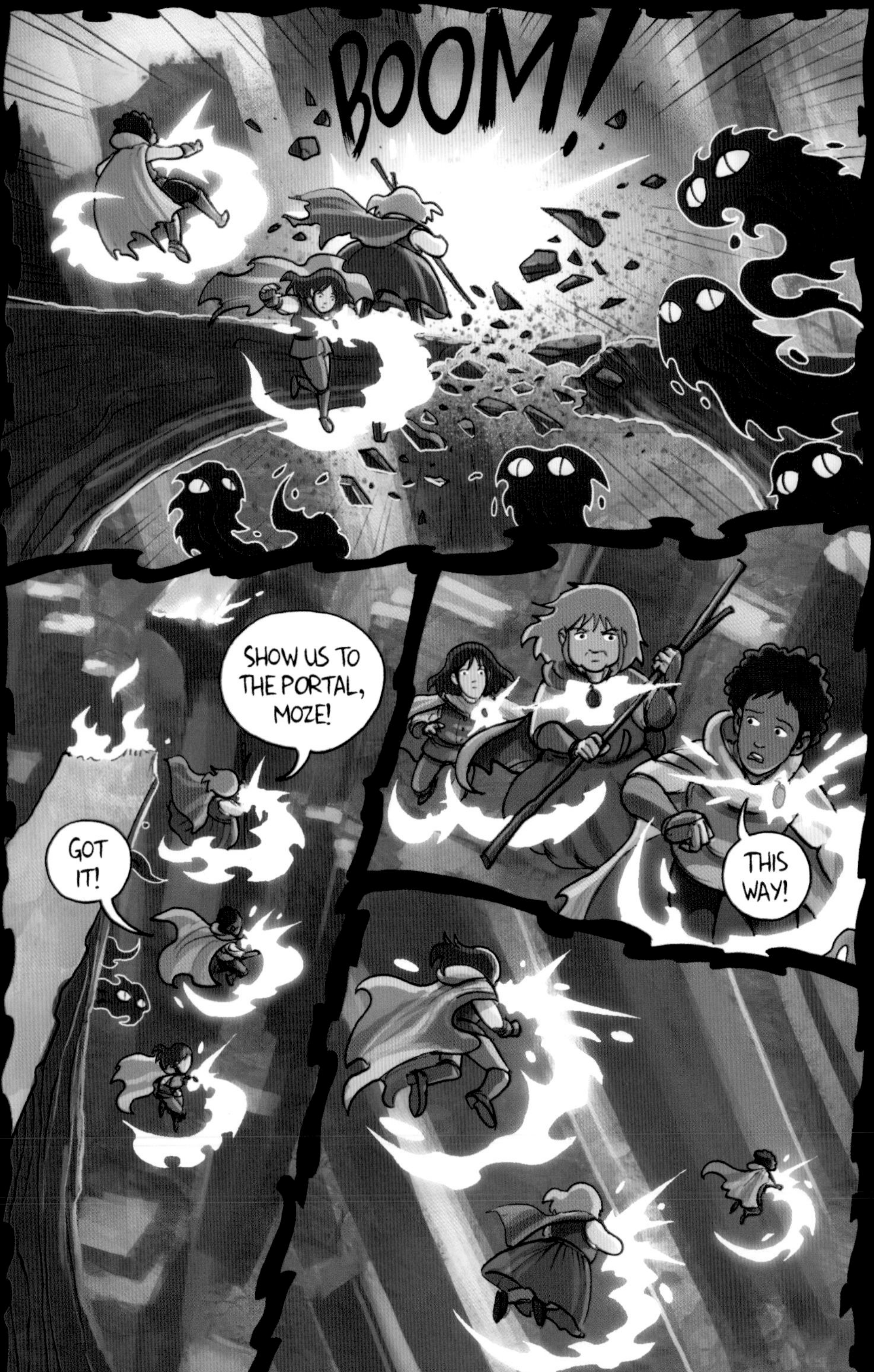
BOOM!
SHOW US TO THE PORTAL, MOZE!
GOT IT!
THIS WAY!

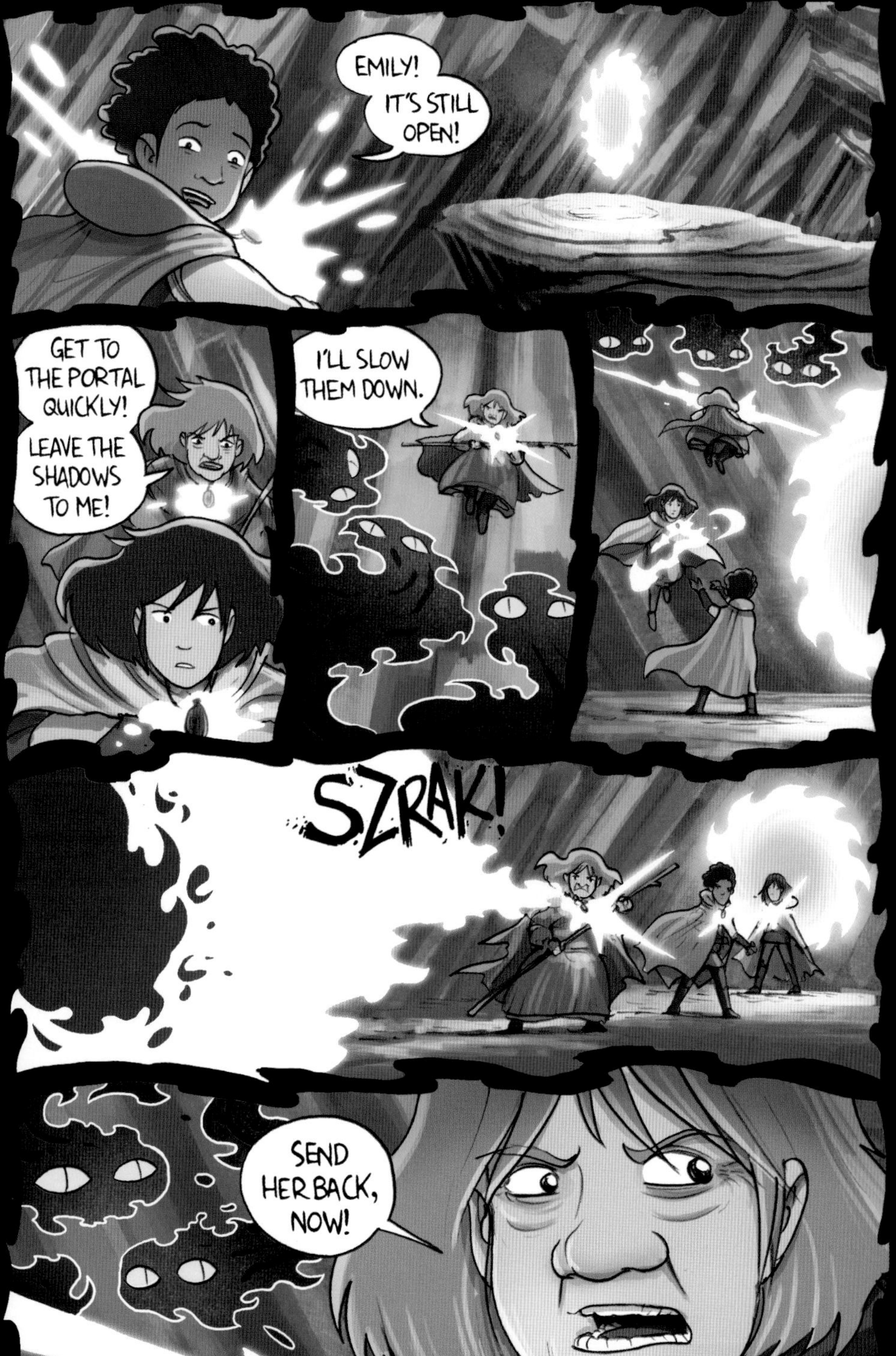
EMILY!
IT'S STILL OPEN!
GET TO THE PORTAL QUICKLY!
LEAVE THE SHADOWS TO ME!
I'LL SLOW THEM DOWN.
SZRAK!
SEND HER BACK, NOW!

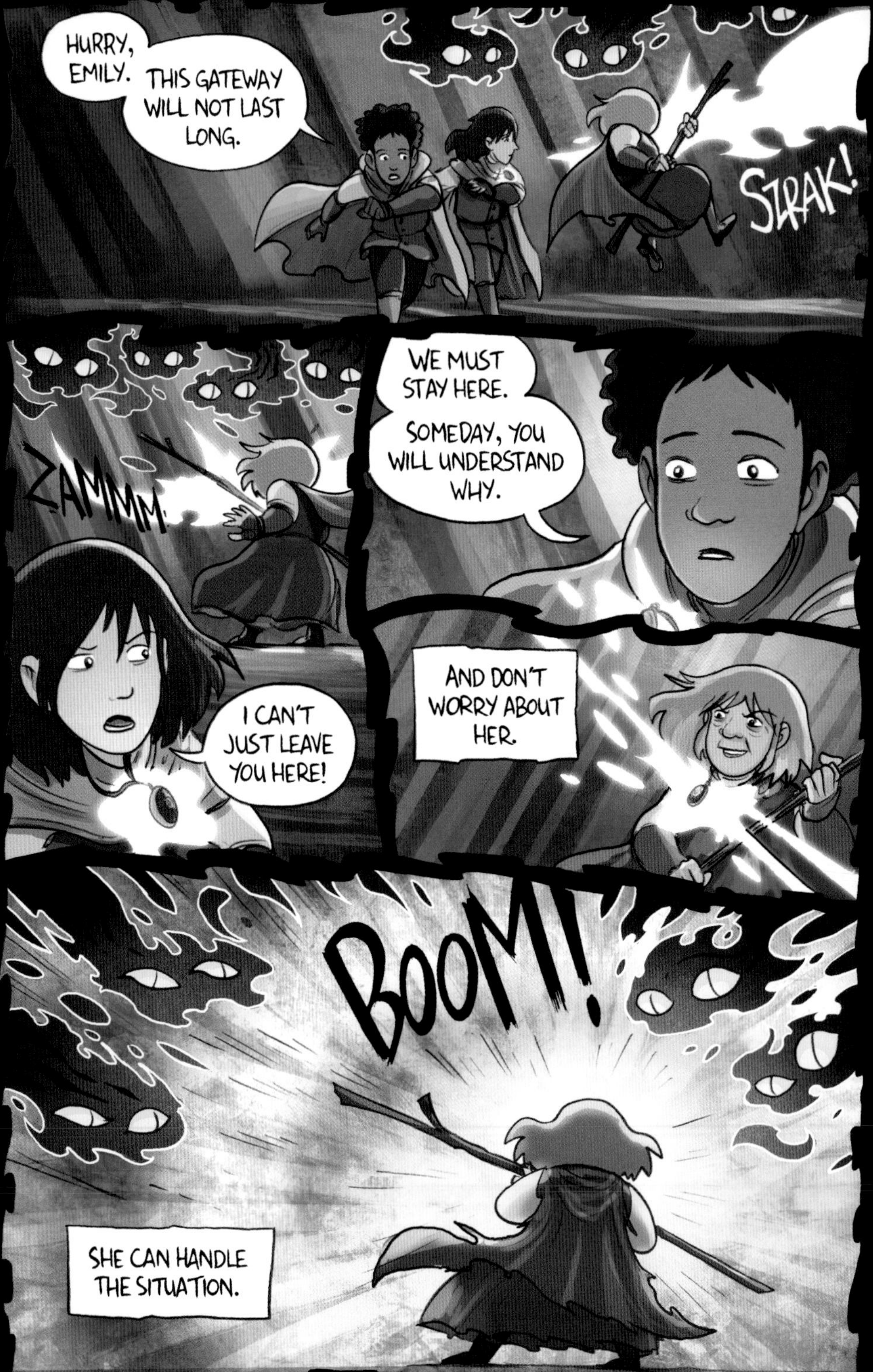
HURRY, EMILY.
THIS GATEWAY WILL NOT LAST LONG.
SZRAK!
ZAMMM
WE MUST STAY HERE.
SOMEDAY, YOU WILL UNDERSTAND WHY.
I CAN'T JUST LEAVE YOU HERE!
AND DON'T WORRY ABOUT HER.
BOOM!
SHE CAN HANDLE THE SITUATION.

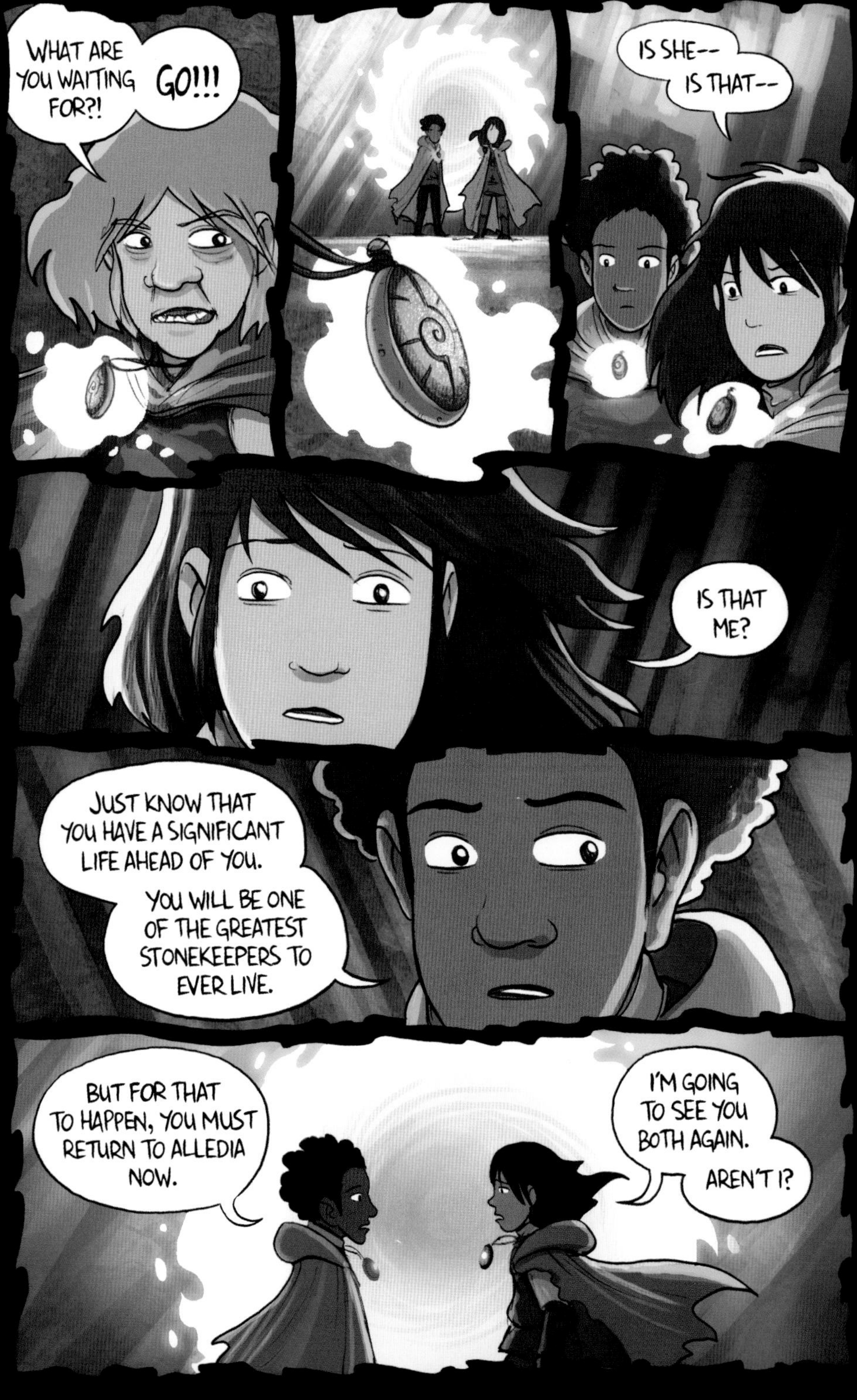
WHAT ARE YOU WAITING FOR?!
GO!!!
IS SHE--
IS THAT--
IS THAT ME?
JUST KNOW THAT YOU HAVE A SIGNIFICANT LIFE AHEAD OF YOU.
YOU WILL BE ONE OF THE GREATEST STONEKEEPERS TO EVER LIVE.
BUT FOR THAT TO HAPPEN, YOU MUST RETURN TO ALLEDIA NOW.
I'M GOING TO SEE YOU BOTH AGAIN.
AREN'T I?

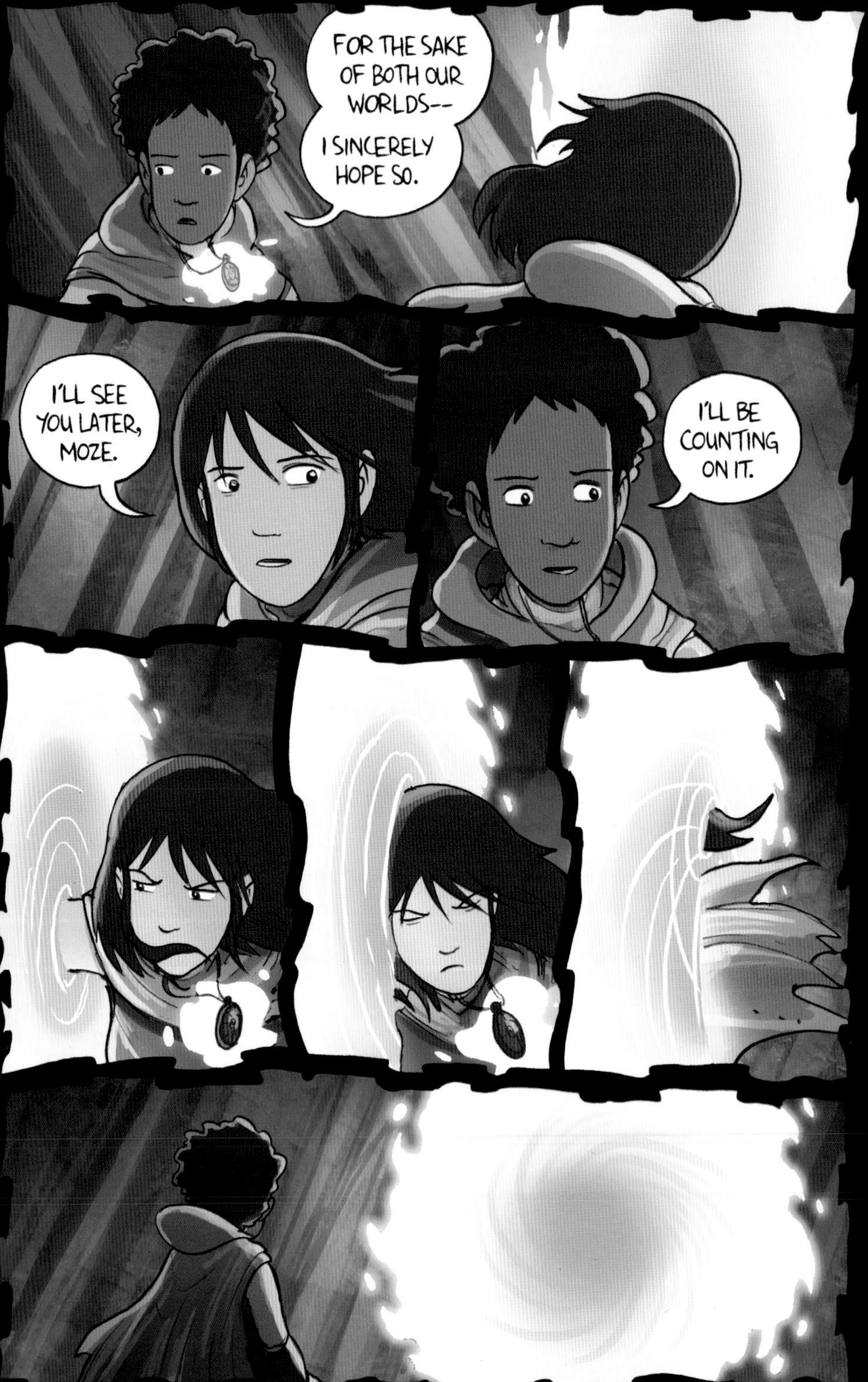
FOR THE SAKE OF BOTH OUR WORLDS--
I SINCERELY HOPE SO.
I'LL SEE YOU LATER, MOZE.
I'LL BE COUNTING ON IT.

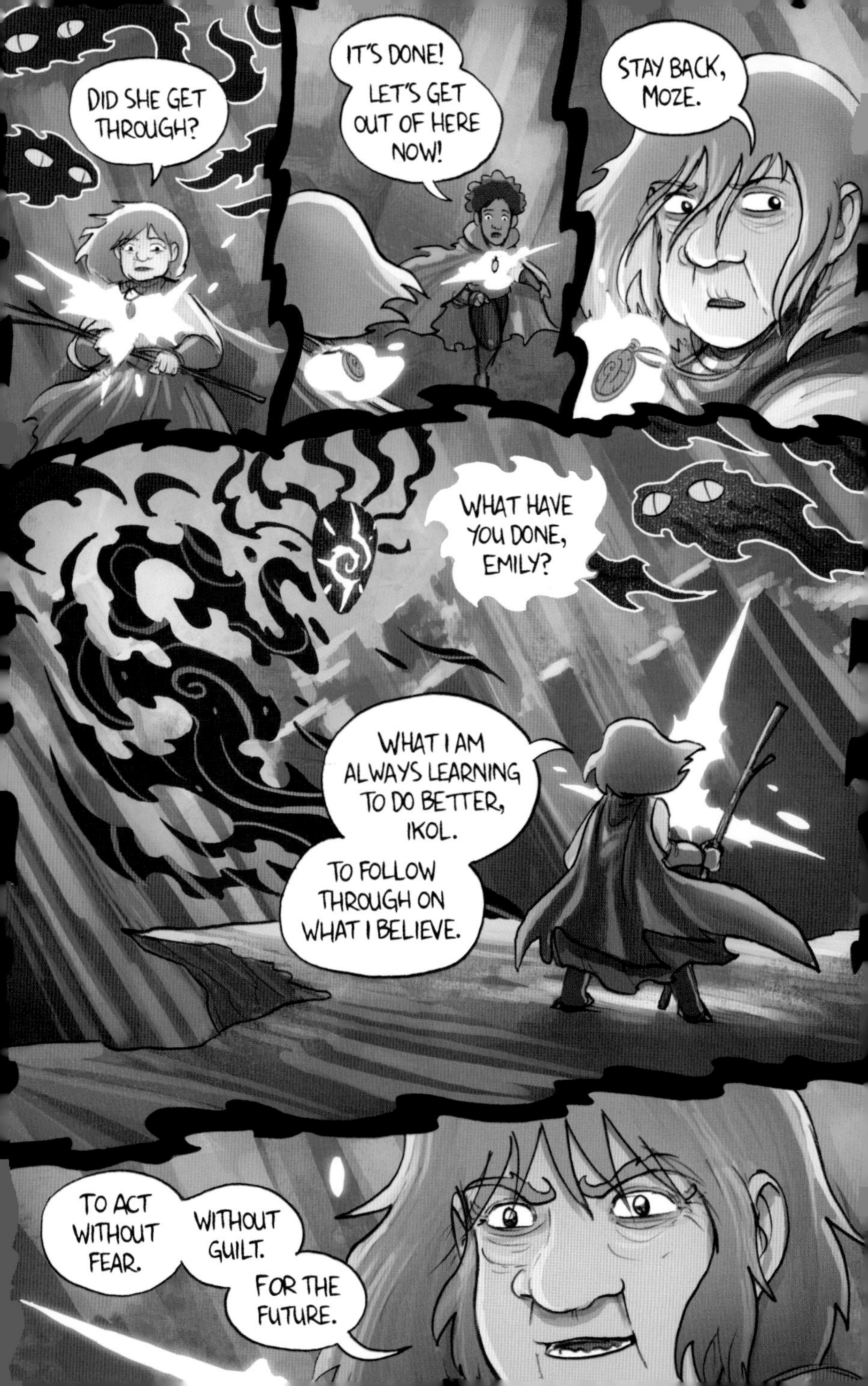
DID SHE GET THROUGH?
IT'S DONE!
LET'S GET OUT OF HERE NOW!
STAY BACK, MOZE.
WHAT HAVE YOU DONE, EMILY?
WHAT I AM ALWAYS LEARNING TO DO BETTER, IKOL.
TO FOLLOW THROUGH ON WHAT I BELIEVE.
TO ACT WITHOUT FEAR.
WITHOUT GUILT.
FOR THE FUTURE.

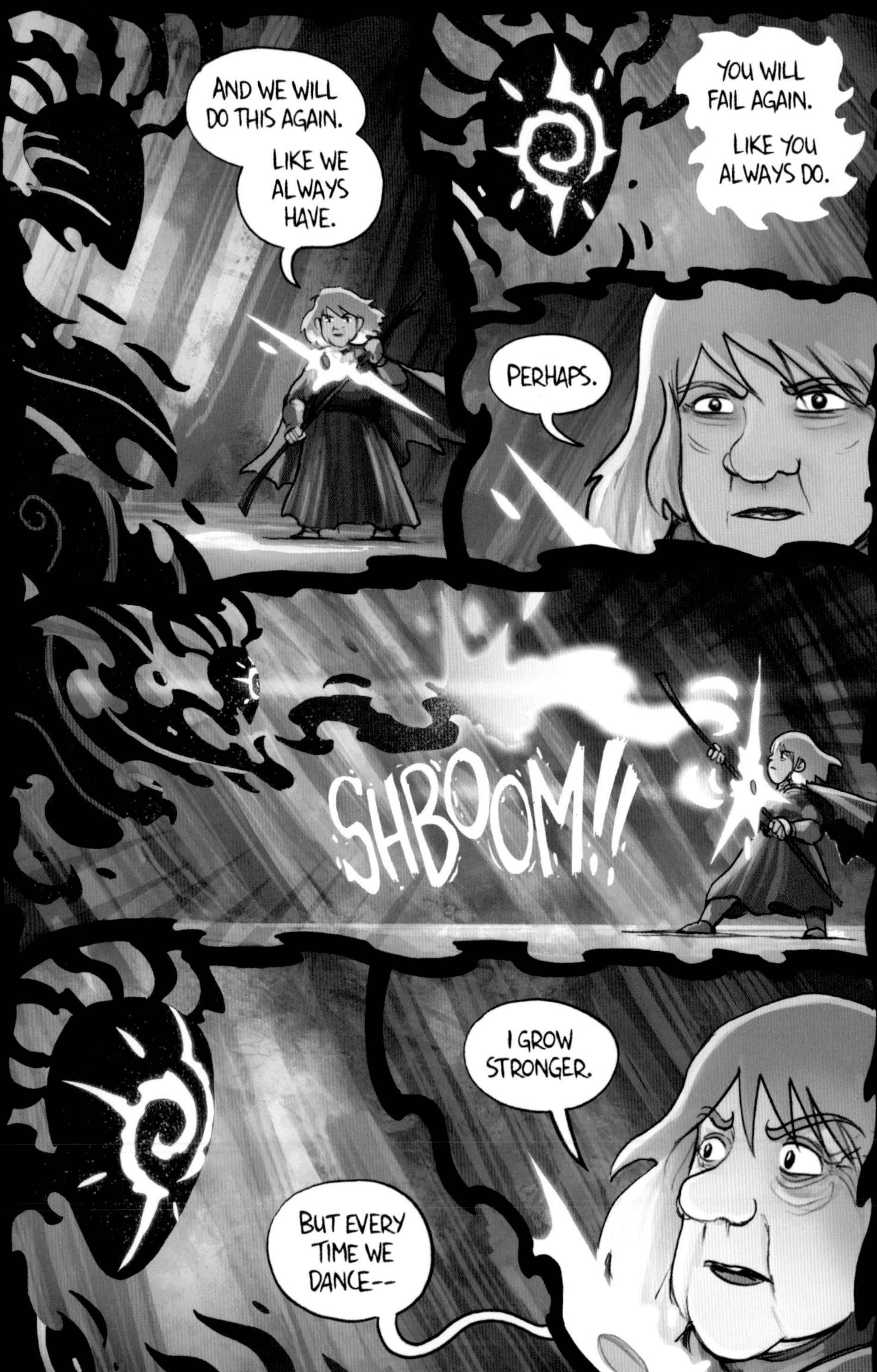
AND WE WILL DO THIS AGAIN.
LIKE WE ALWAYS HAVE.
YOU WILL FAIL AGAIN.
LIKE YOU ALWAYS DO.
PERHAPS.
SHBOOM!!
I GROW STRONGER.
BUT EVERY TIME WE DANCE--

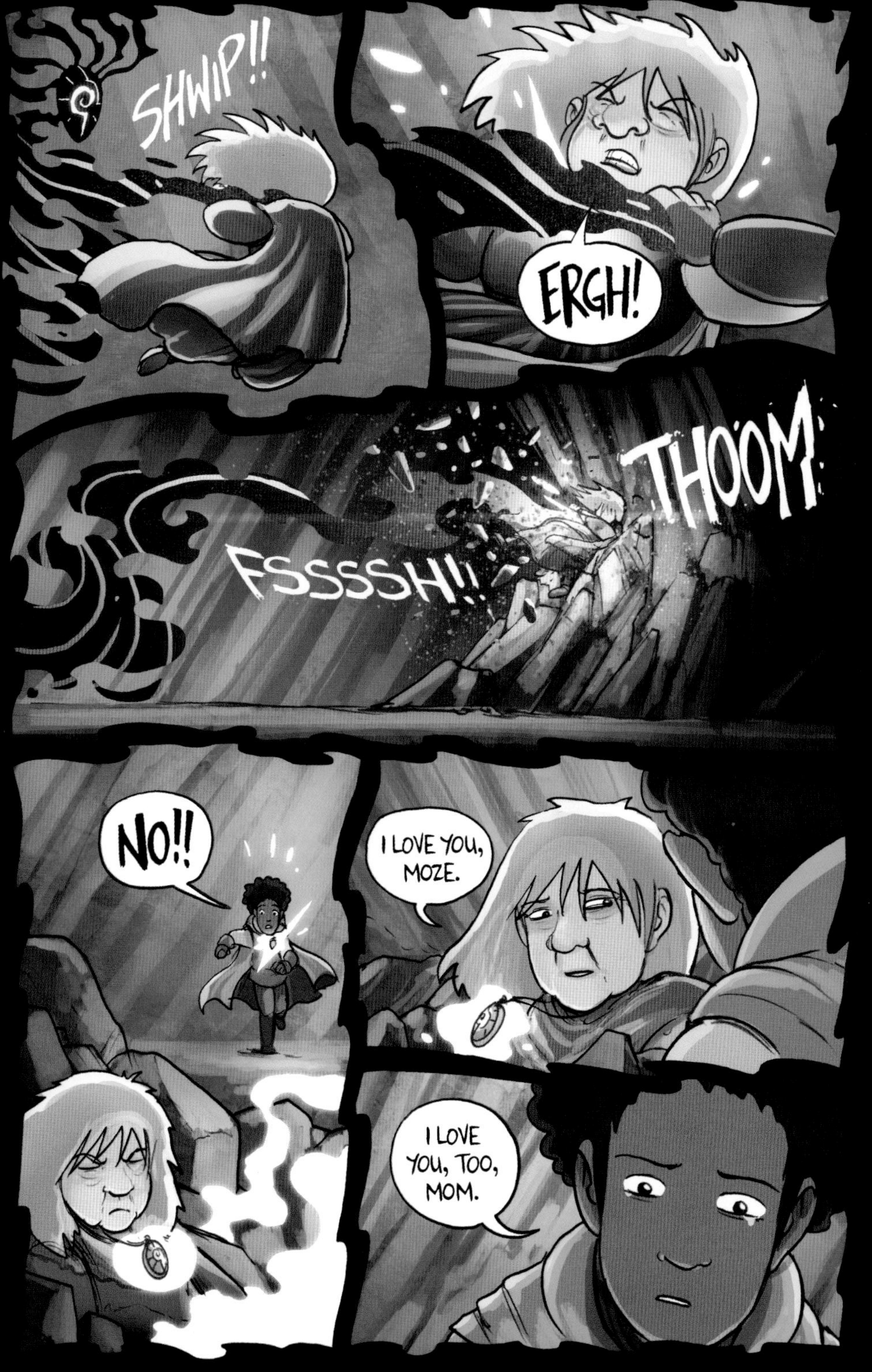
SHWIP!!
ERGH!
FSSSSH!!
THOOM!
NO!!
I LOVE YOU, MOZE.
I LOVE YOU, TOO, MOM.

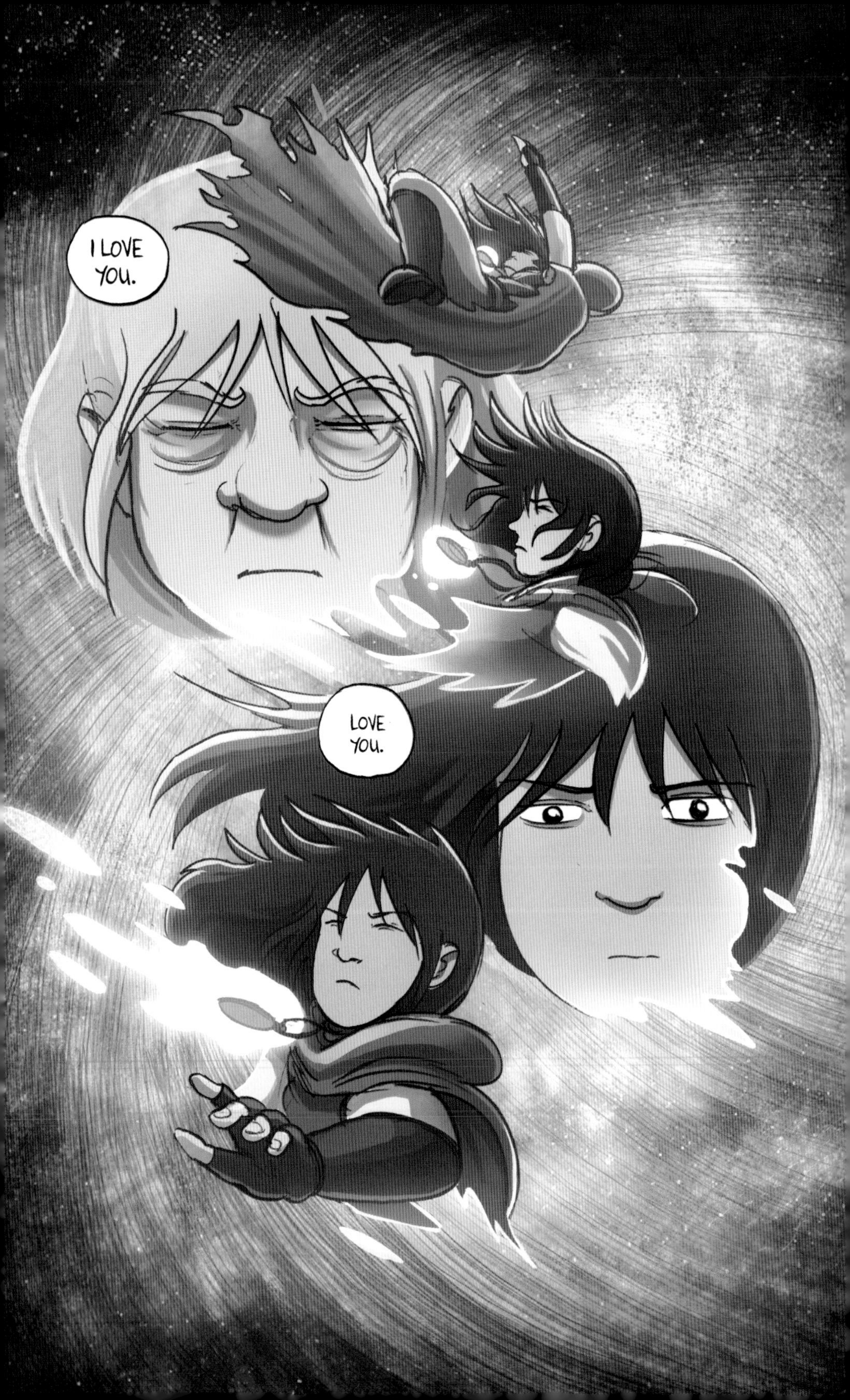
I LOVE YOU.
LOVE YOU.

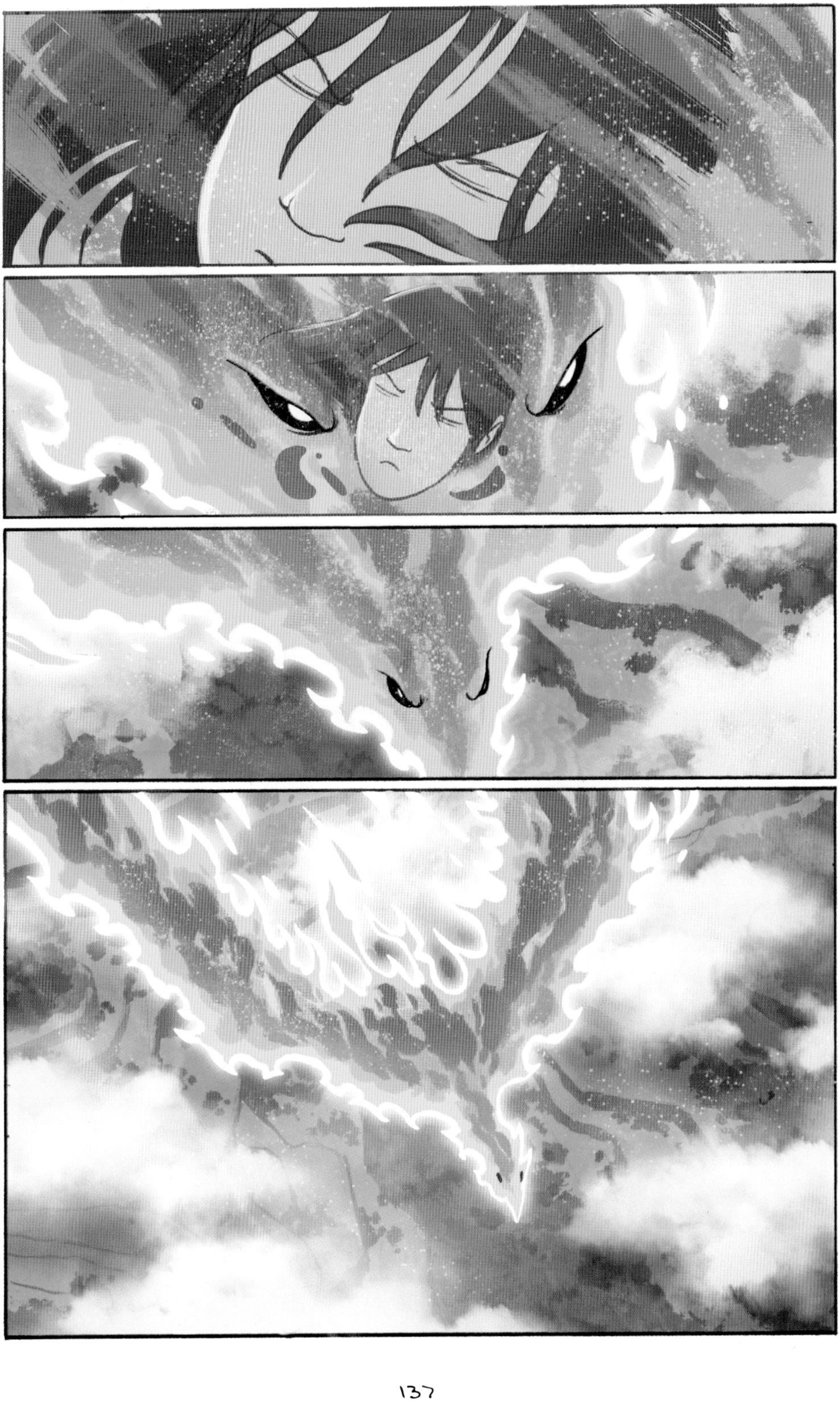

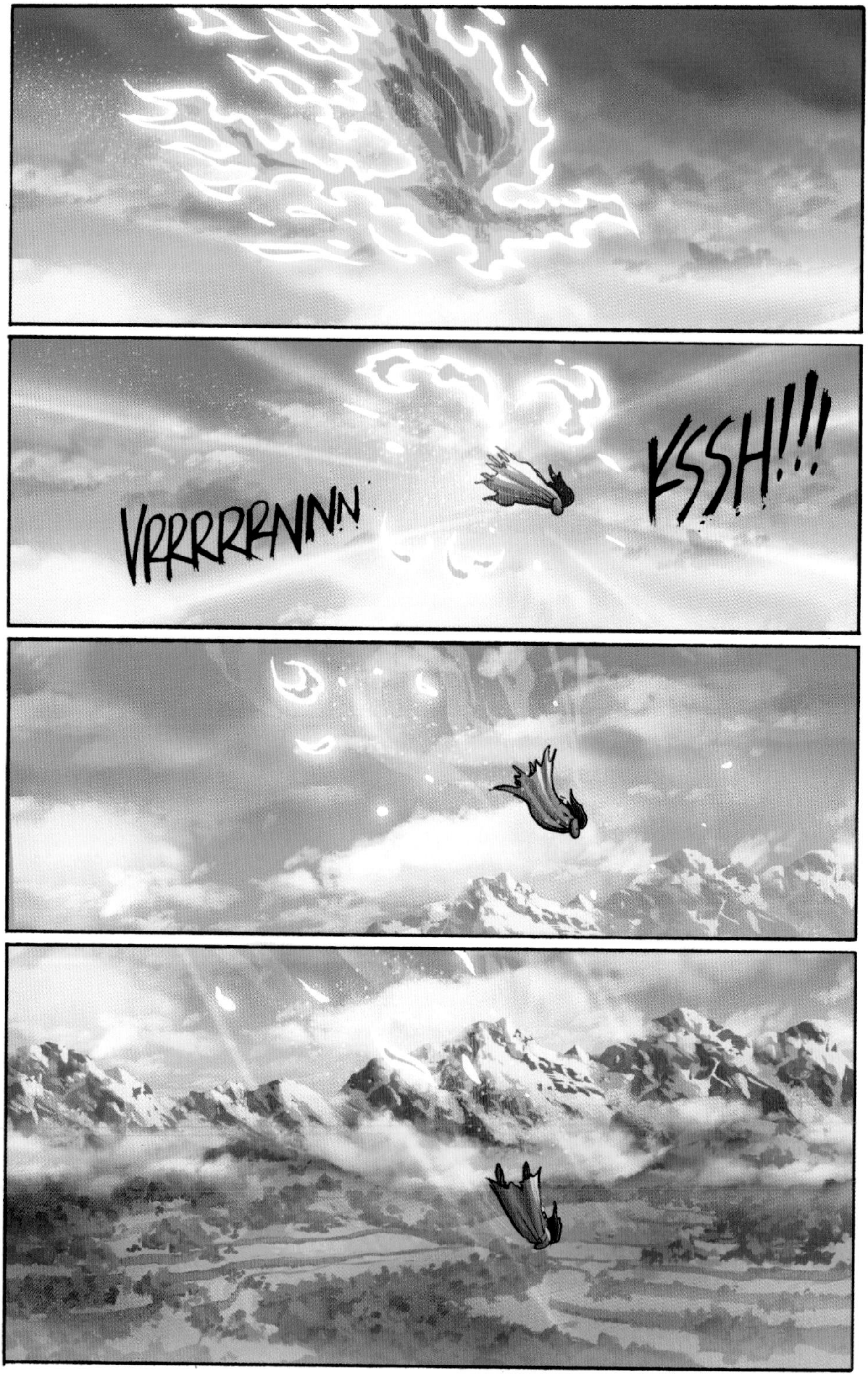
VRRRRRNNN
KSSH!!!

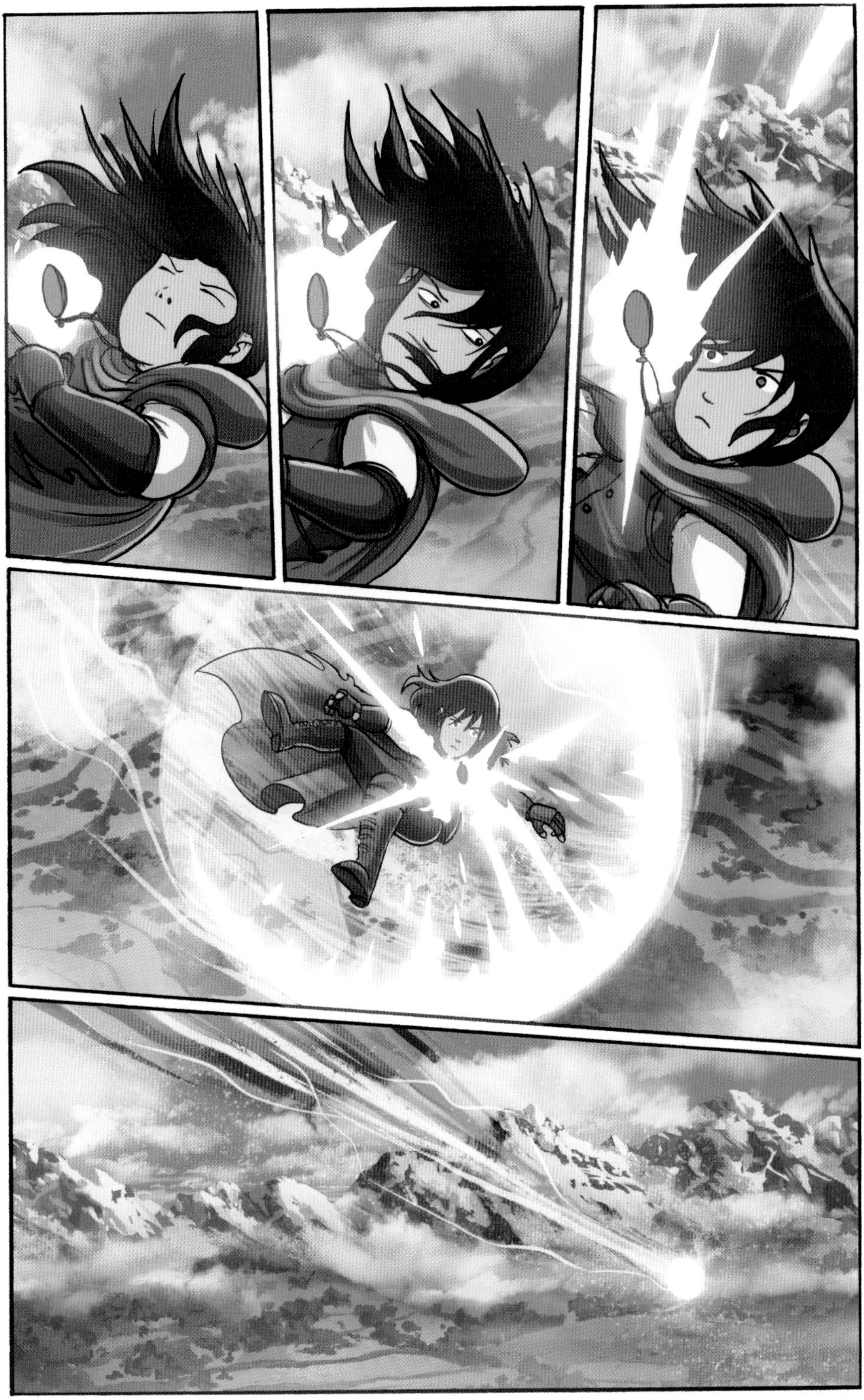

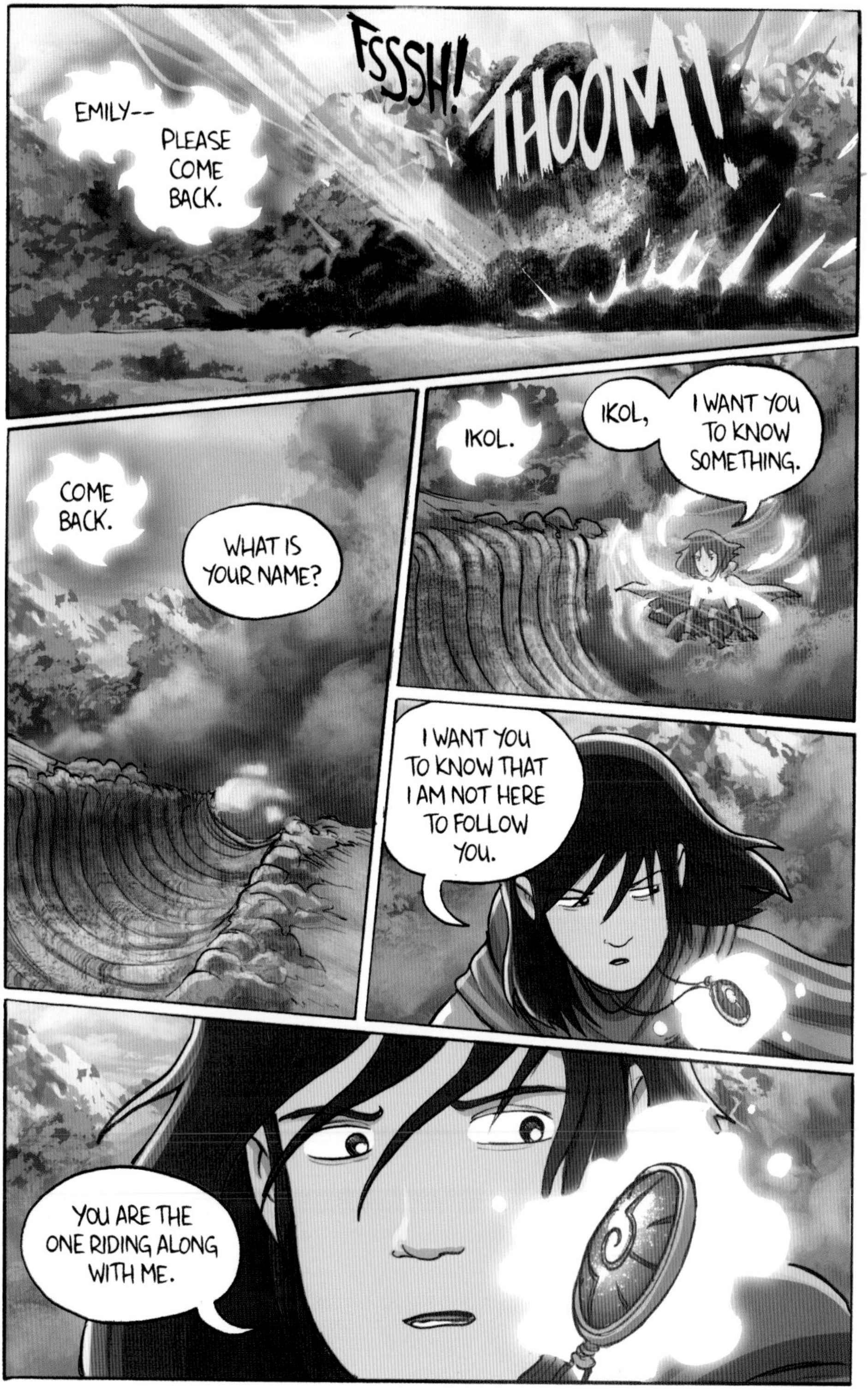
EMILY--
PLEASE COME BACK.
FSSSH!
THOOM!
COME BACK.
WHAT IS YOUR NAME?
IKOL.
IKOL,
I WANT YOU TO KNOW SOMETHING.
I WANT YOU TO KNOW THAT I AM NOT HERE TO FOLLOW YOU.
YOU ARE THE ONE RIDING ALONG WITH ME.

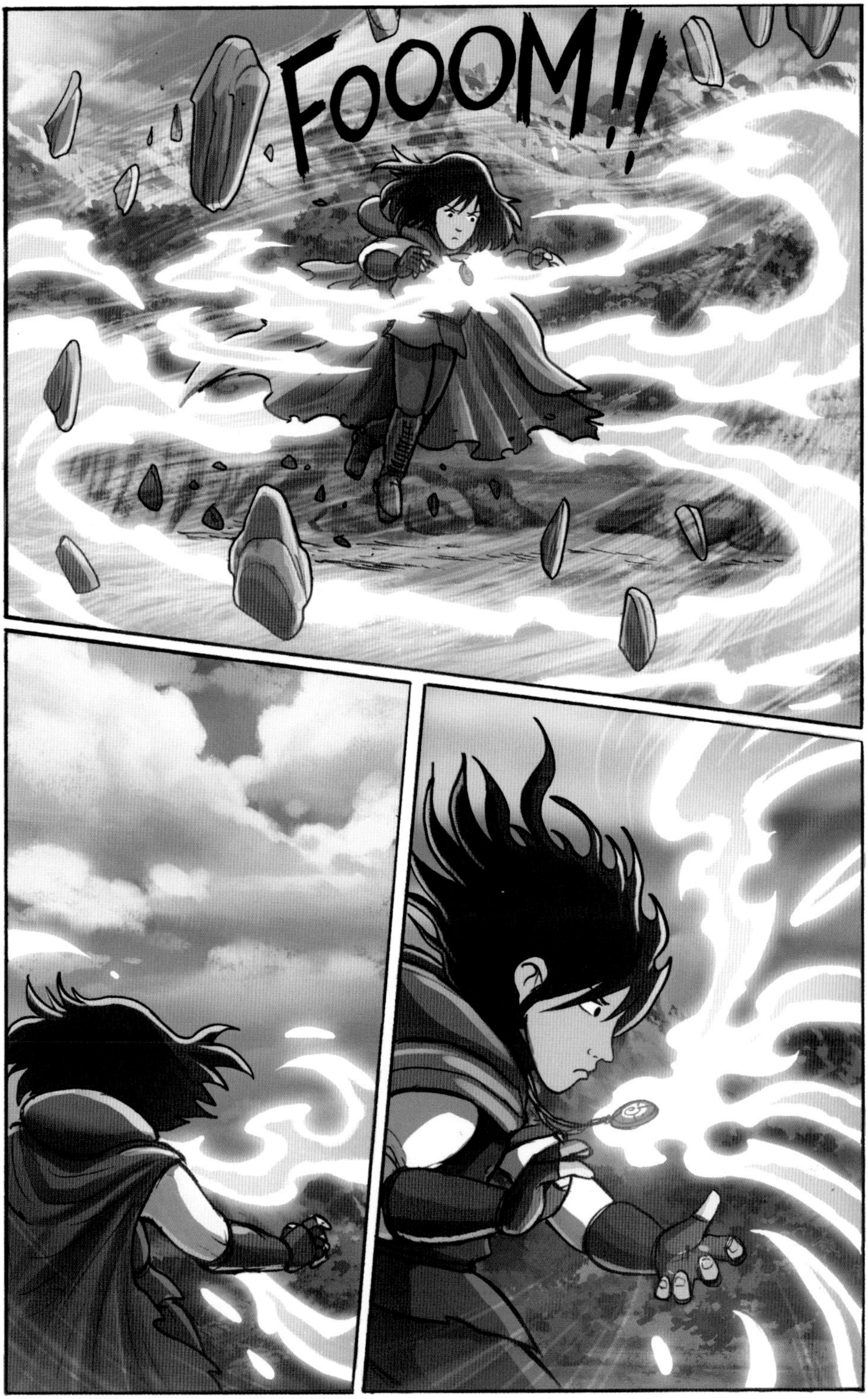
FOOOM!!

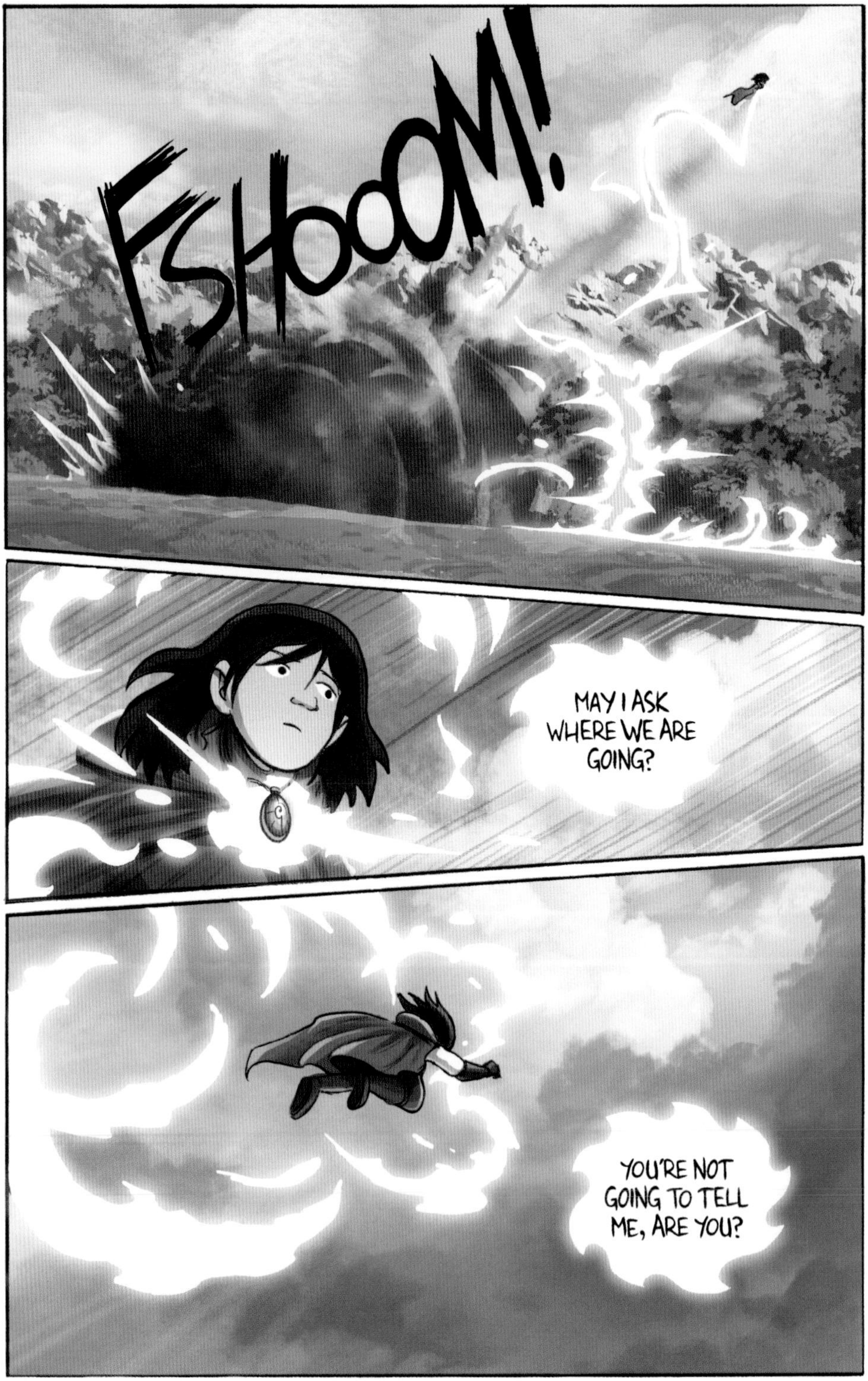
FSHOOOM!
MAY I ASK WHERE WE ARE GOING?
YOU'RE NOT GOING TO TELL ME, ARE YOU?

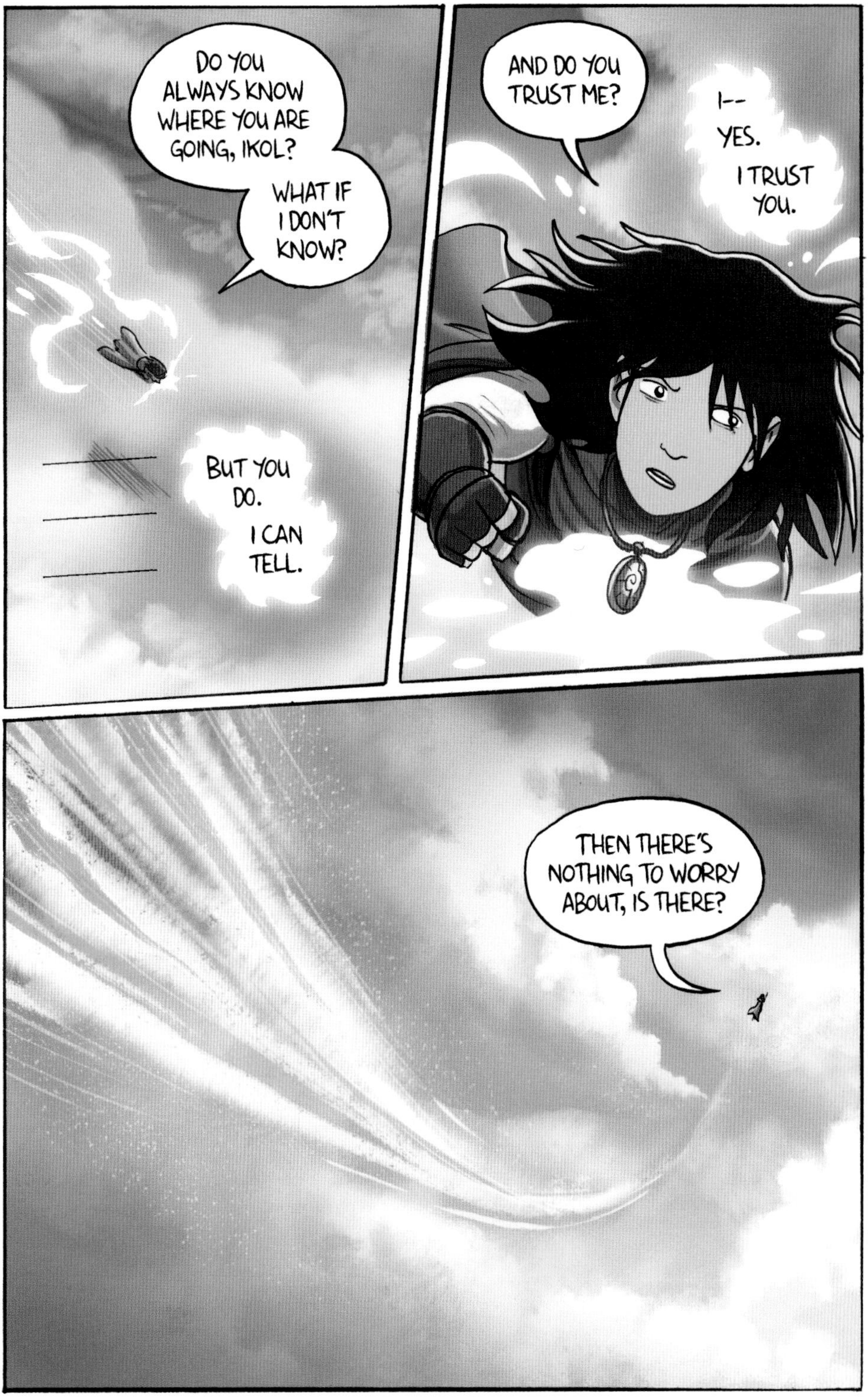
DO YOU ALWAYS KNOW WHERE YOU ARE GOING, IKOL?
WHAT IF I DON'T KNOW?
BUT YOU DO.
I CAN TELL.
AND DO YOU TRUST ME?
I--
YES.
I TRUST YOU.
THEN THERE'S NOTHING TO WORRY ABOUT, IS THERE?

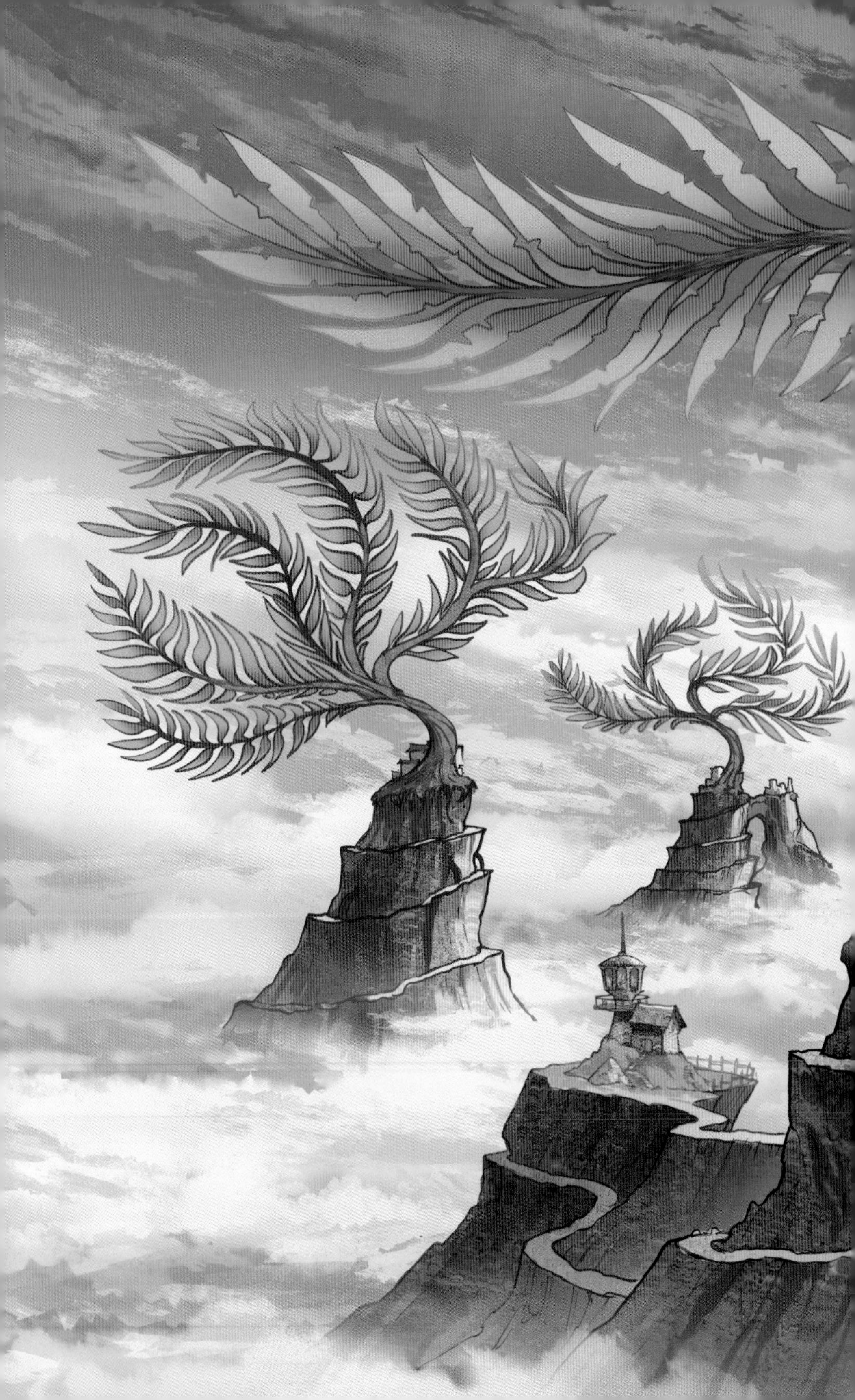

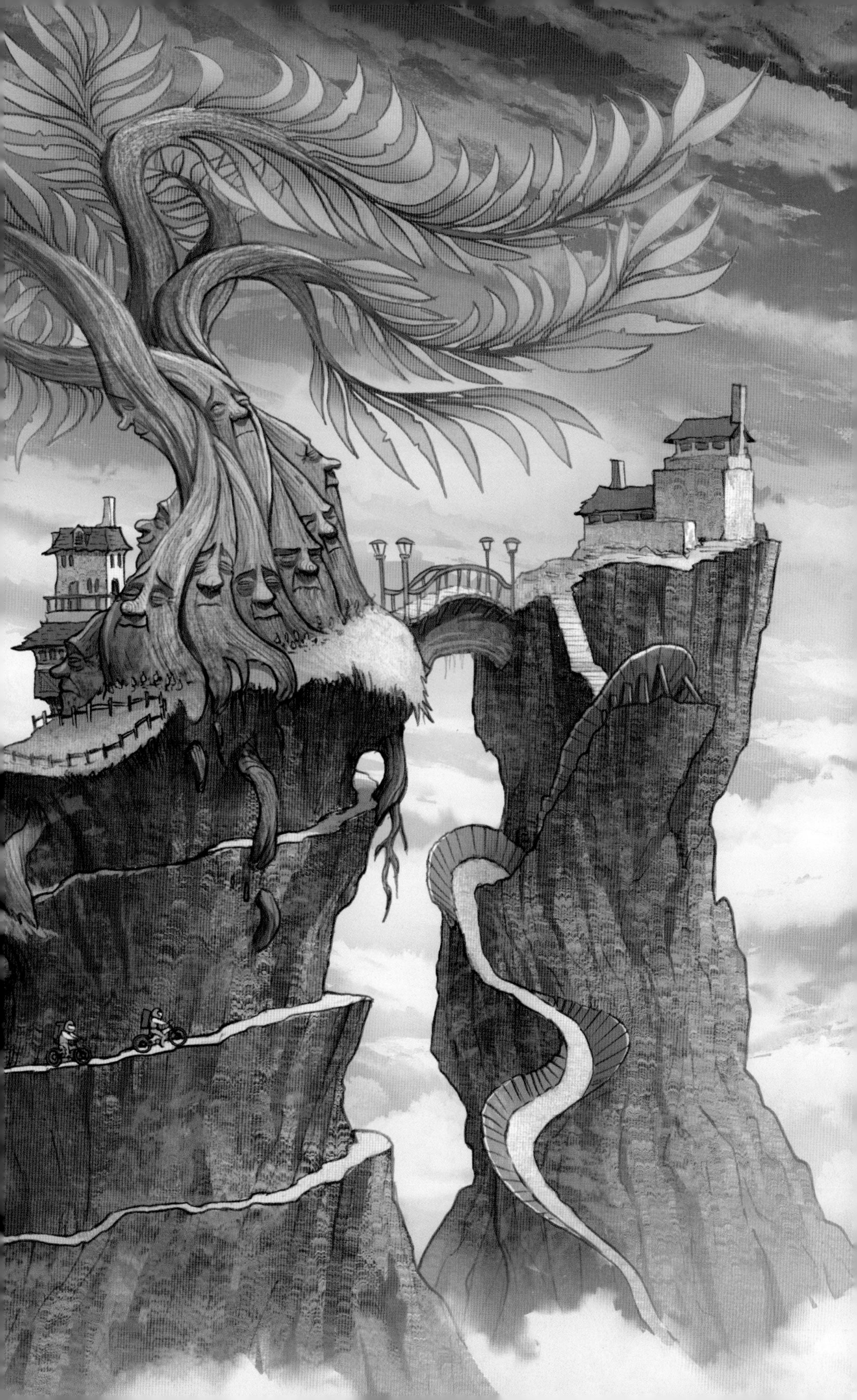

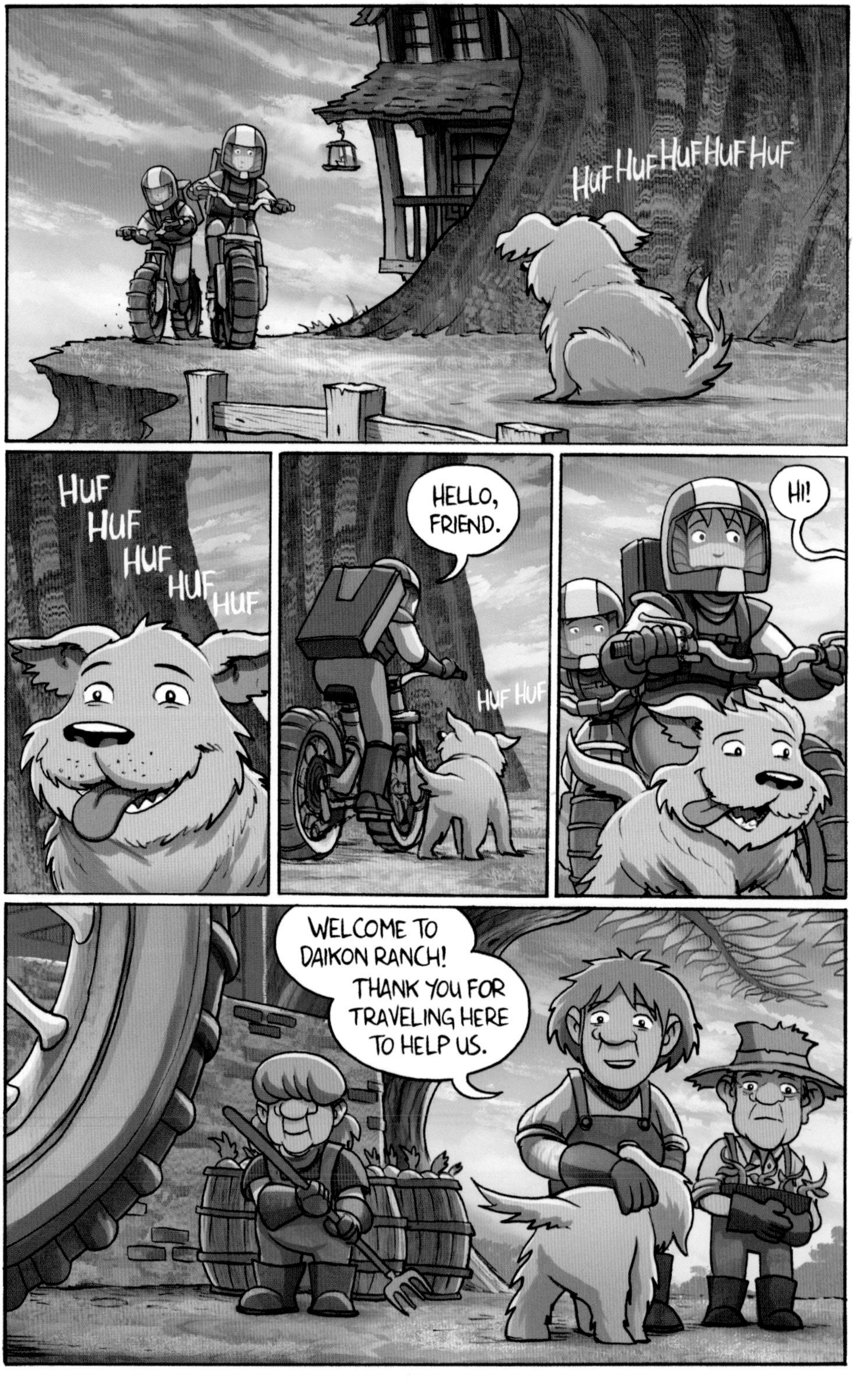
HUF HUF HUF HUF HUF
HUF HUF HUF HUF HUF
HELLO, FRIEND.
HUF HUF
HI!
WELCOME TO DAIKON RANCH!
THANK YOU FOR TRAVELING HERE TO HELP US.

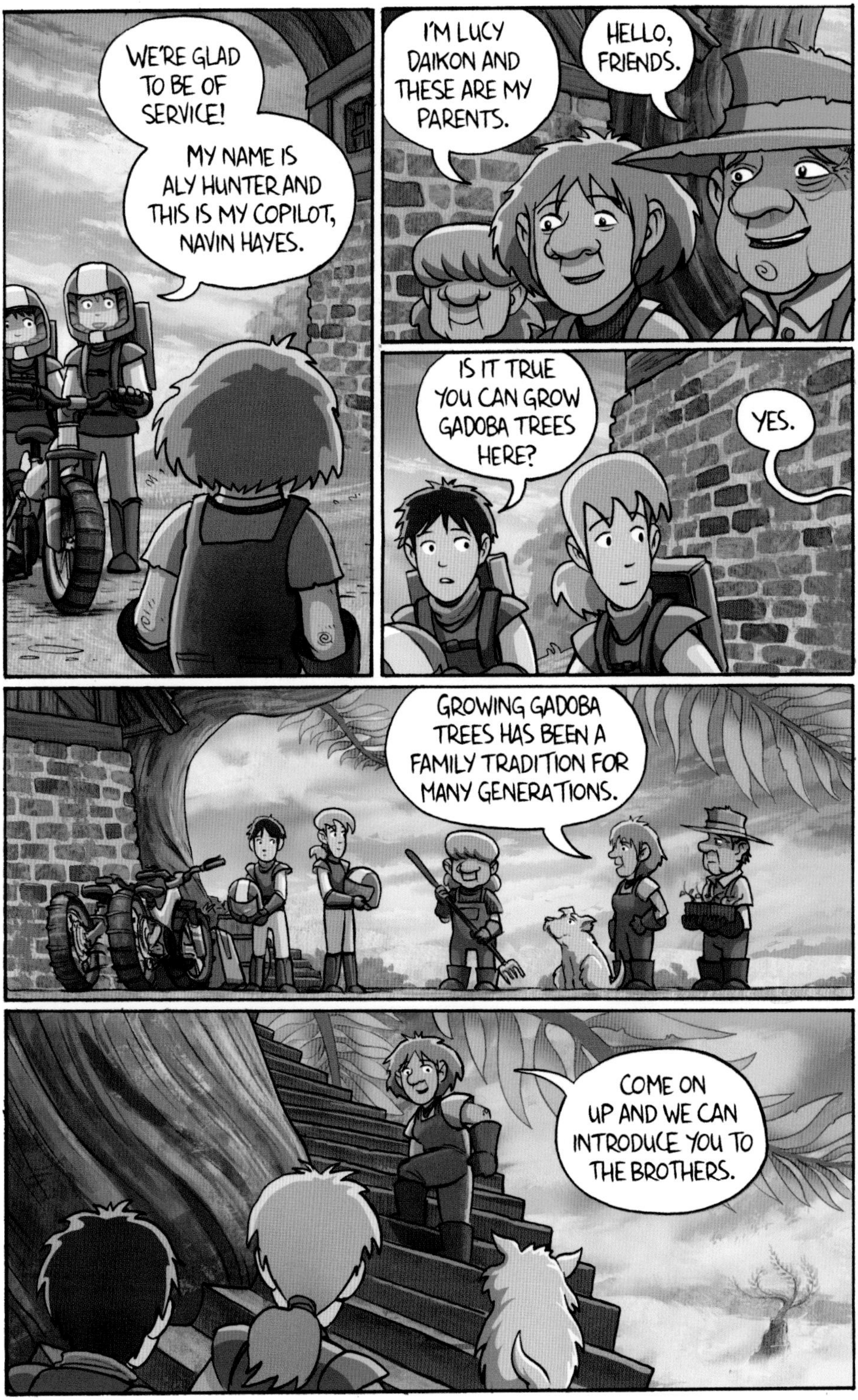
WE'RE GLAD TO BE OF SERVICE!
MY NAME IS ALY HUNTER AND THIS IS MY COPILOT, NAVIN HAYES.
I'M LUCY DAIKON AND THESE ARE MY PARENTS.
HELLO, FRIENDS.
IS IT TRUE YOU CAN GROW GADOBA TREES HERE?
YES.
GROWING GADOBA TREES HAS BEEN A FAMILY TRADITION FOR MANY GENERATIONS.
COME ON UP AND WE CAN INTRODUCE YOU TO THE BROTHERS.

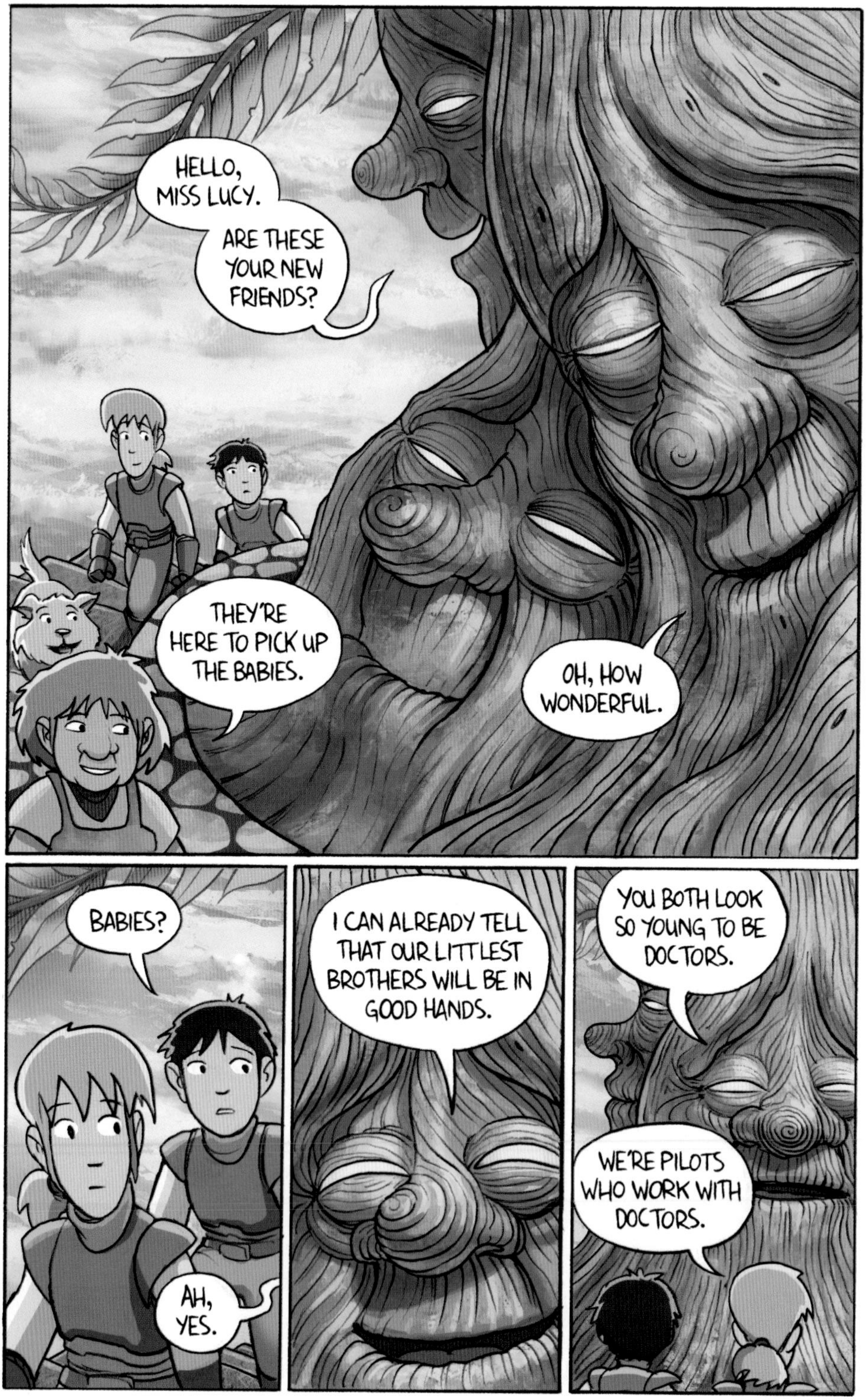
HELLO, MISS LUCY.
ARE THESE YOUR NEW FRIENDS?
THEY'RE HERE TO PICK UP THE BABIES.
OH, HOW WONDERFUL.
BABIES?
AH, YES.
I CAN ALREADY TELL THAT OUR LITTLEST BROTHERS WILL BE IN GOOD HANDS.
YOU BOTH LOOK SO YOUNG TO BE DOCTORS.
WE'RE PILOTS WHO WORK WITH DOCTORS.

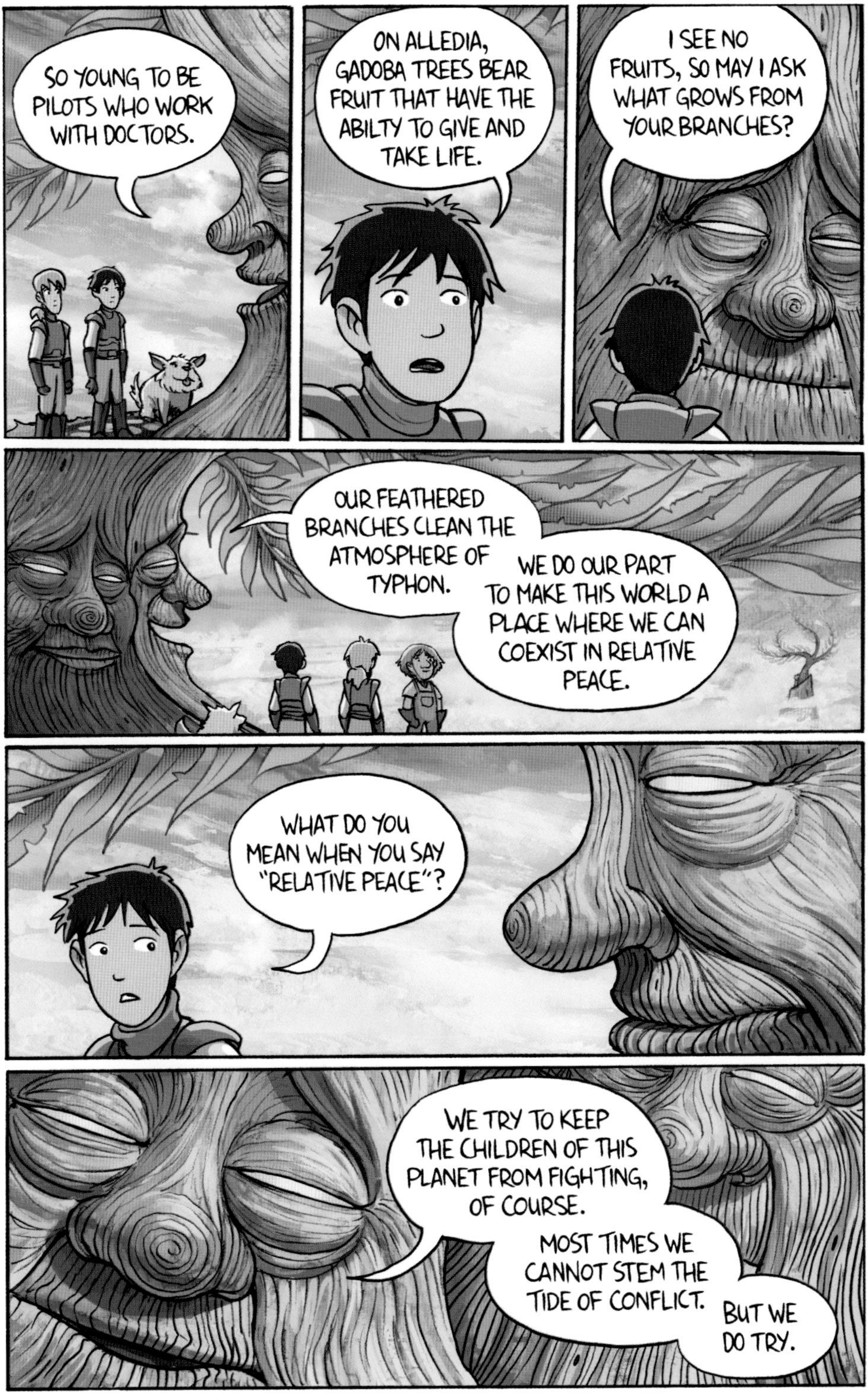
SO YOUNG TO BE PILOTS WHO WORK WITH DOCTORS.
ON ALLEDIA, GADOBA TREES BEAR FRUIT THAT HAVE THE ABILTY TO GIVE AND TAKE LIFE.
I SEE NO FRUITS, SO MAY I ASK WHAT GROWS FROM YOUR BRANCHES?
OUR FEATHERED BRANCHES CLEAN THE ATMOSPHERE OF TYPHON.
WE DO OUR PART TO MAKE THIS WORLD A PLACE WHERE WE CAN COEXIST IN RELATIVE PEACE.
WHAT DO YOU MEAN WHEN YOU SAY "RELATIVE PEACE"?
WE TRY TO KEEP THE CHILDREN OF THIS PLANET FROM FIGHTING, OF COURSE.
MOST TIMES WE CANNOT STEM THE TIDE OF CONFLICT.
BUT WE DO TRY.

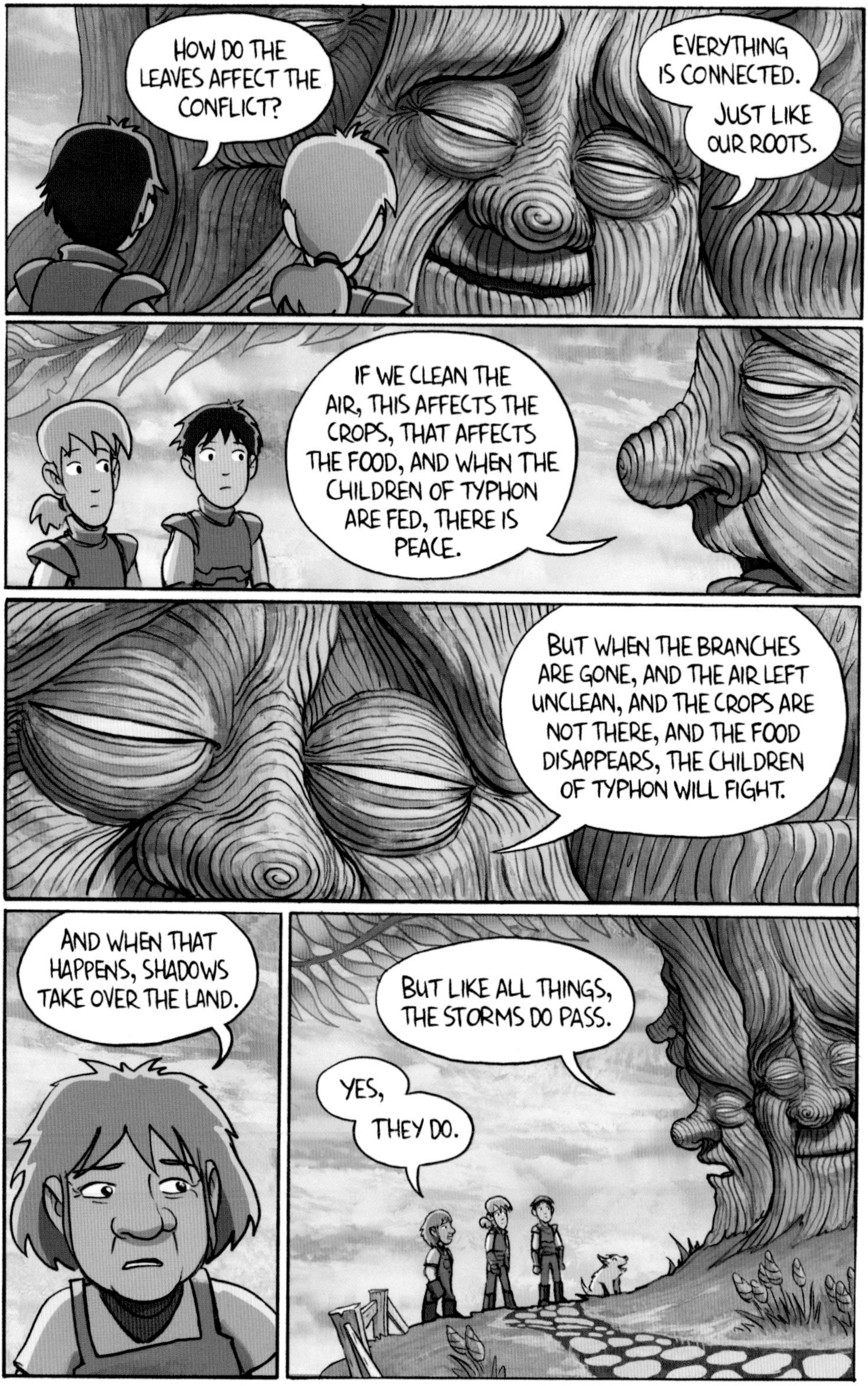
HOW DO THE LEAVES AFFECT THE CONFLICT?
EVERYTHING IS CONNECTED.
JUST LIKE OUR ROOTS.
IF WE CLEAN THE AIR, THIS AFFECTS THE CROPS, THAT AFFECTS THE FOOD, AND WHEN THE CHILDREN OF TYPHON ARE FED, THERE IS PEACE.
BUT WHEN THE BRANCHES ARE GONE, AND THE AIR LEFT UNCLEAN, AND THE CROPS ARE NOT THERE, AND THE FOOD DISAPPEARS, THE CHILDREN OF TYPHON WILL FIGHT.
AND WHEN THAT HAPPENS, SHADOWS TAKE OVER THE LAND.
BUT LIKE ALL THINGS, THE STORMS DO PASS.
YES,
THEY DO.

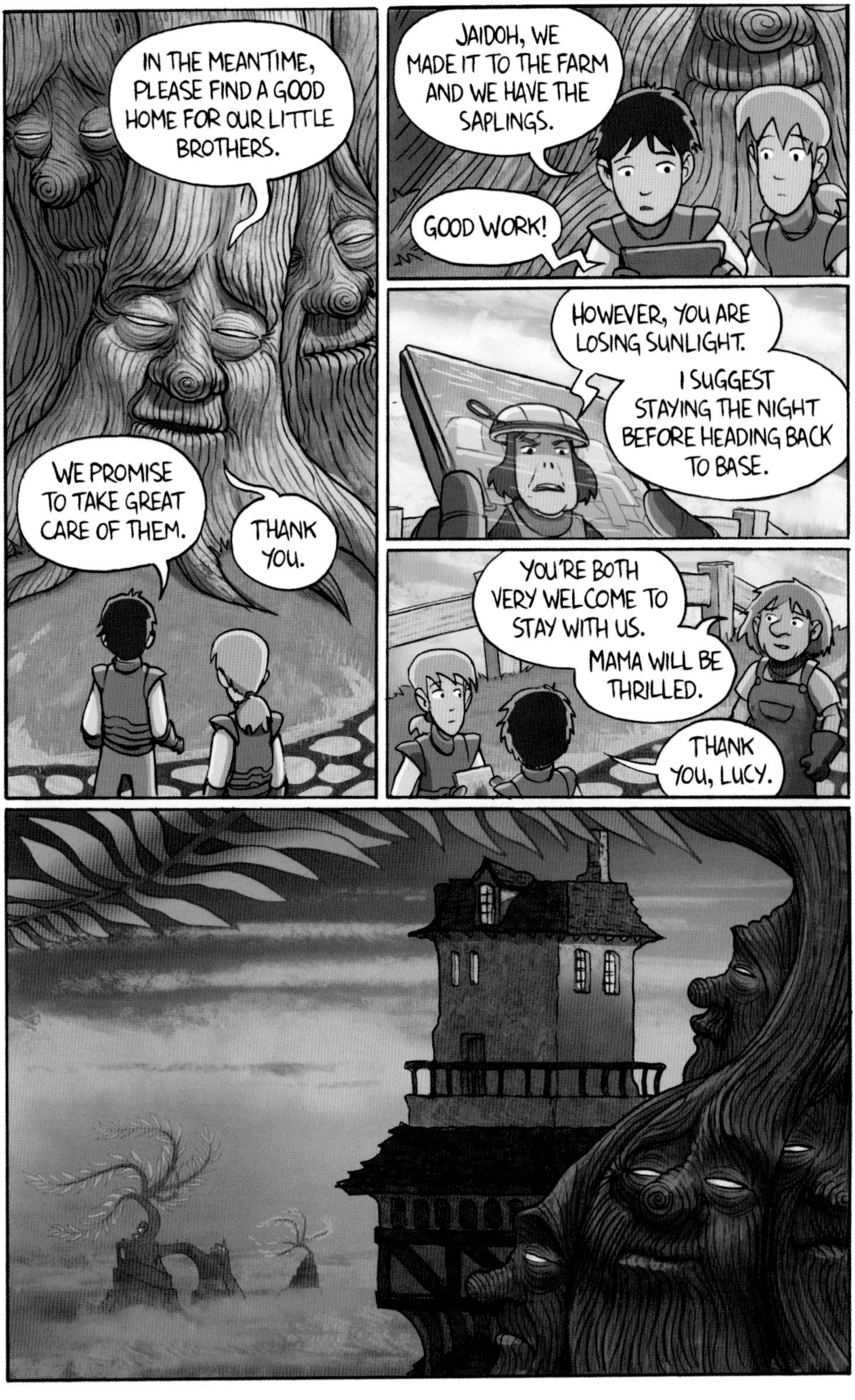
IN THE MEANTIME, PLEASE FIND A GOOD HOME FOR OUR LITTLE BROTHERS.
WE PROMISE TO TAKE GREAT CARE OF THEM.
THANK YOU.
JAIDOH, WE MADE IT TO THE FARM AND WE HAVE THE SAPLINGS.
GOOD WORK!
HOWEVER, YOU ARE LOSING SUNLIGHT.
I SUGGEST STAYING THE NIGHT BEFORE HEADING BACK TO BASE.
YOU'RE BOTH VERY WELCOME TO STAY WITH US.
MAMA WILL BE THRILLED.
THANK YOU, LUCY.

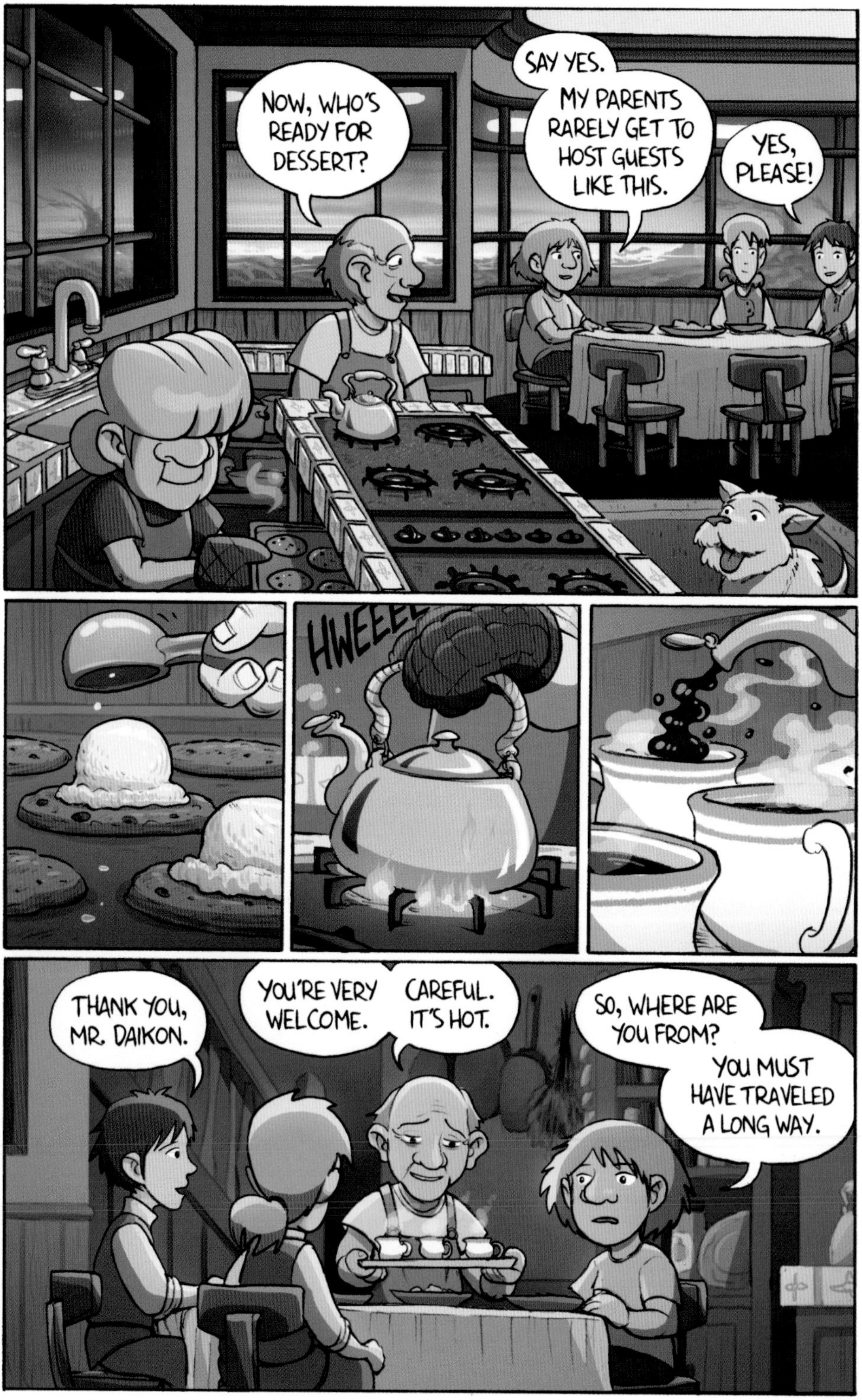
NOW, WHO'S READY FOR DESSERT?
SAY YES.
MY PARENTS RARELY GET TO HOST GUESTS LIKE THIS.
YES, PLEASE!
HWEEE
THANK YOU, MR. DAIKON.
YOU'RE VERY WELCOME.
CAREFUL. IT'S HOT.
SO, WHERE ARE YOU FROM?
YOU MUST HAVE TRAVELED A LONG WAY.

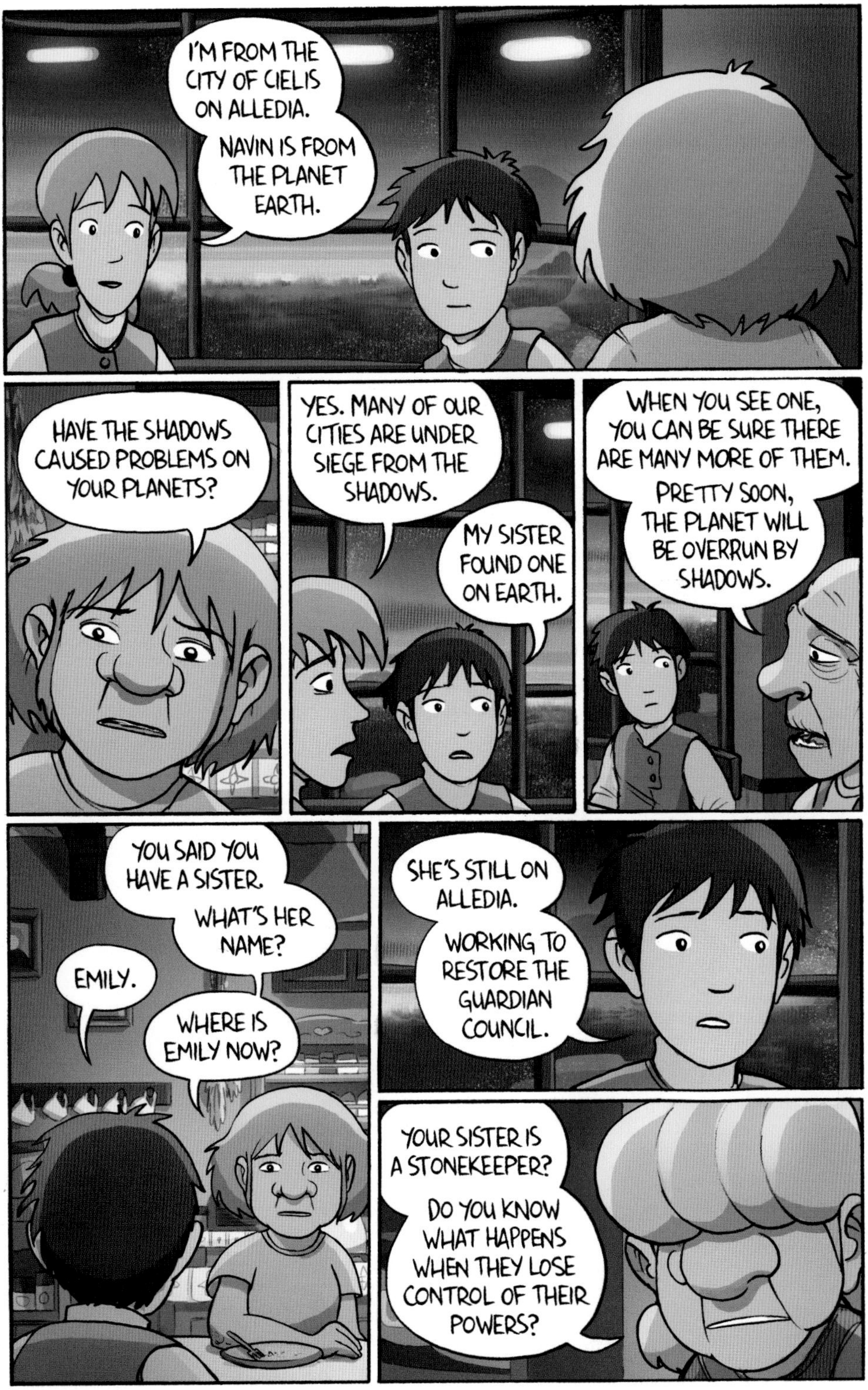
I'M FROM THE CITY OF CIELIS ON ALLEDIA.
NAVIN IS FROM THE PLANET EARTH.
HAVE THE SHADOWS CAUSED PROBLEMS ON YOUR PLANETS?
YES. MANY OF OUR CITIES ARE UNDER SIEGE FROM THE SHADOWS.
MY SISTER FOUND ONE ON EARTH.
WHEN YOU SEE ONE, YOU CAN BE SURE THERE ARE MANY MORE OF THEM.
PRETTY SOON, THE PLANET WILL BE OVERRUN BY SHADOWS.
YOU SAID YOU HAVE A SISTER.
WHAT'S HER NAME?
EMILY.
WHERE IS EMILY NOW?
SHE'S STILL ON ALLEDIA.
WORKING TO RESTORE THE GUARDIAN COUNCIL.
YOUR SISTER IS A STONEKEEPER?
DO YOU KNOW WHAT HAPPENS WHEN THEY LOSE CONTROL OF THEIR POWERS?

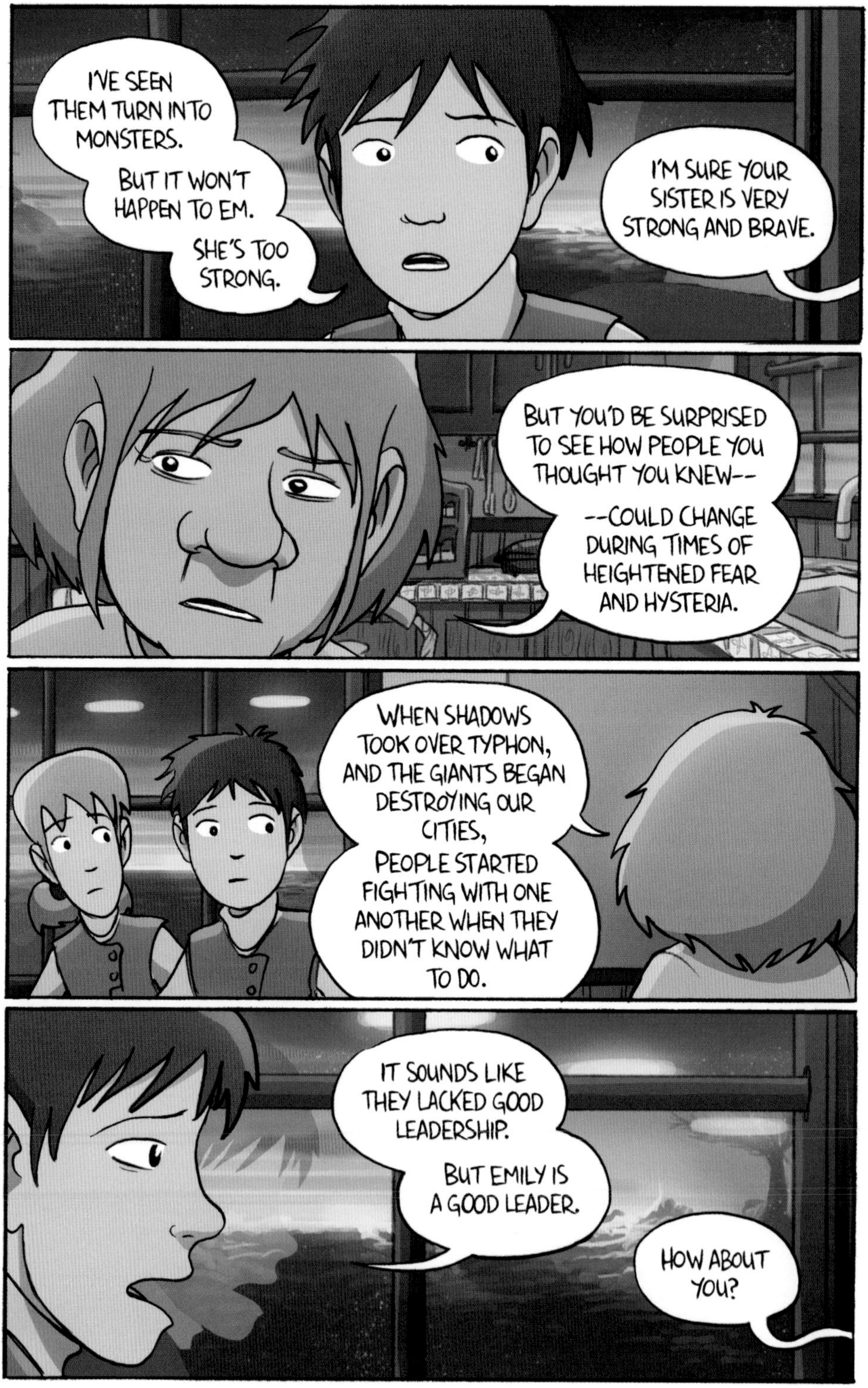
I'VE SEEN THEM TURN INTO MONSTERS.
BUT IT WON'T HAPPEN TO EM.
SHE'S TOO STRONG.
I'M SURE YOUR SISTER IS VERY STRONG AND BRAVE.
BUT YOU'D BE SURPRISED TO SEE HOW PEOPLE YOU THOUGHT YOU KNEW--
--COULD CHANGE DURING TIMES OF HEIGHTENED FEAR AND HYSTERIA.
WHEN SHADOWS TOOK OVER TYPHON, AND THE GIANTS BEGAN DESTROYING OUR CITIES,
PEOPLE STARTED FIGHTING WITH ONE ANOTHER WHEN THEY DIDN'T KNOW WHAT TO DO.
IT SOUNDS LIKE THEY LACKED GOOD LEADERSHIP.
BUT EMILY IS A GOOD LEADER.
HOW ABOUT YOU?

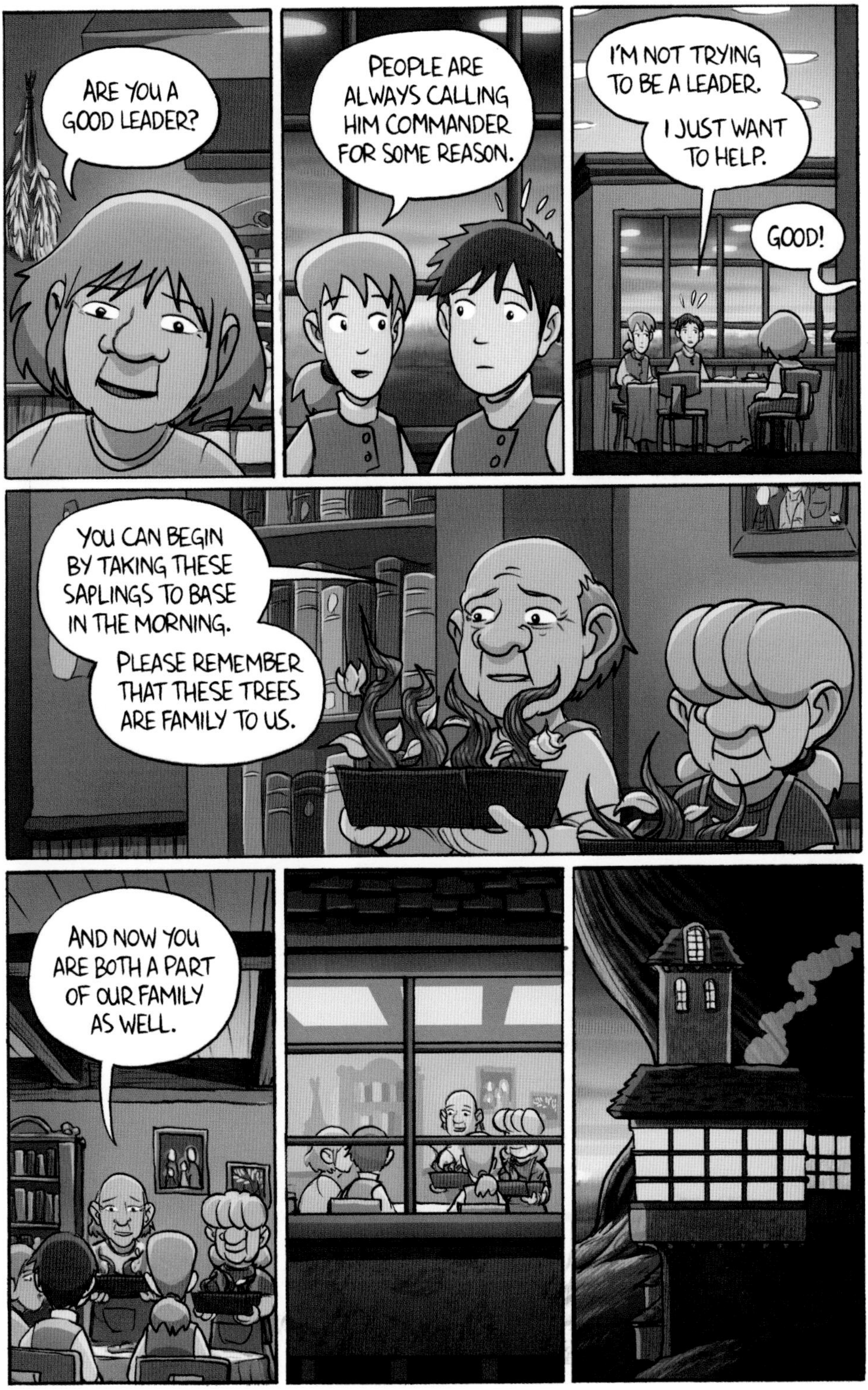
ARE YOU A GOOD LEADER?
PEOPLE ARE ALWAYS CALLING HIM COMMANDER FOR SOME REASON.
I'M NOT TRYING TO BE A LEADER.
I JUST WANT TO HELP.
GOOD!
YOU CAN BEGIN BY TAKING THESE SAPLINGS TO BASE IN THE MORNING.
PLEASE REMEMBER THAT THESE TREES ARE FAMILY TO US.
AND NOW YOU ARE BOTH A PART OF OUR FAMILY AS WELL.

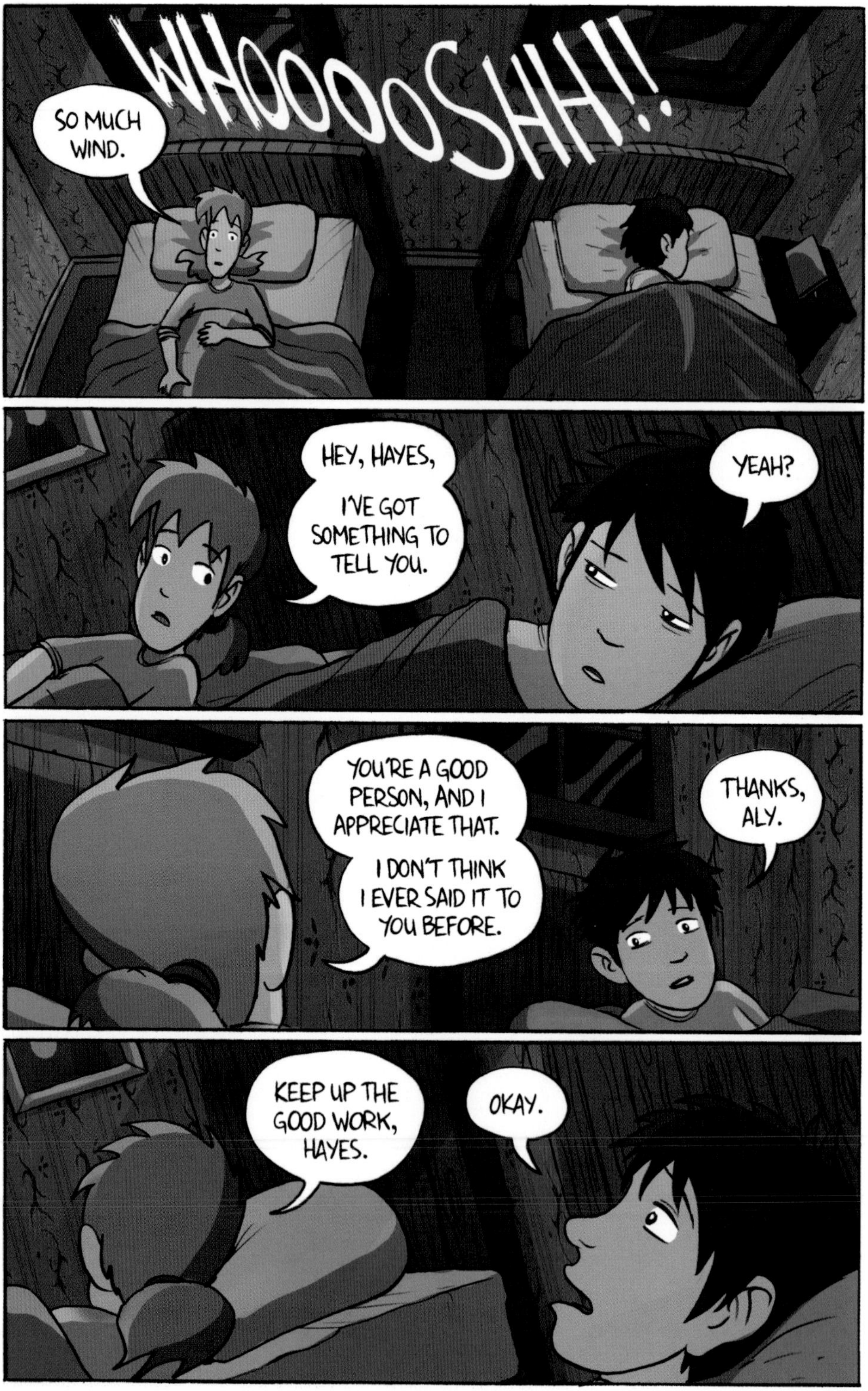
WHOOOOSHH!!
SO MUCH WIND.
HEY, HAYES,
I'VE GOT SOMETHING TO TELL YOU.
YEAH?
YOU'RE A GOOD PERSON, AND I APPRECIATE THAT.
I DON'T THINK I EVER SAID IT TO YOU BEFORE.
THANKS, ALY.
KEEP UP THE GOOD WORK, HAYES.
OKAY.

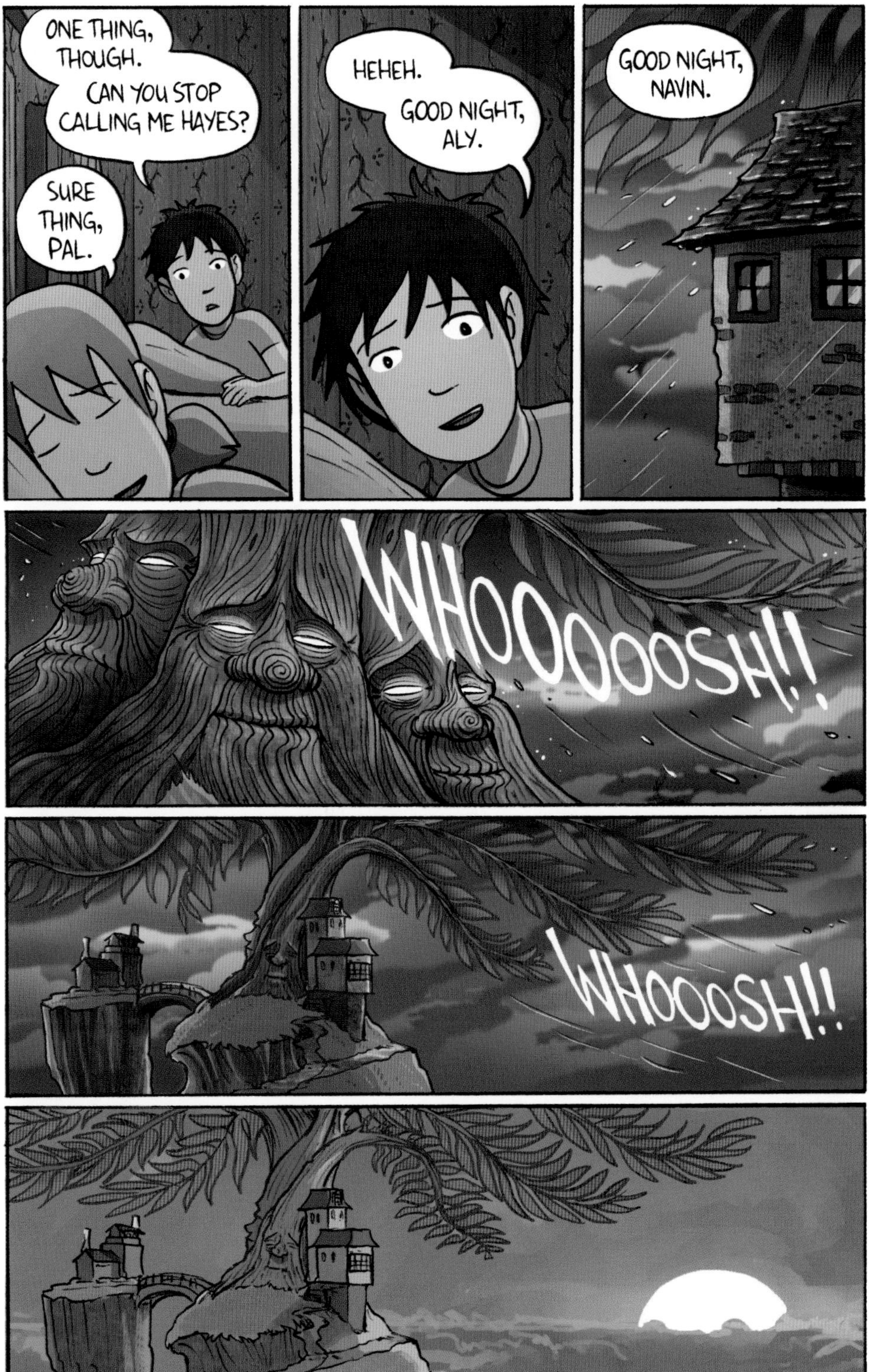
ONE THING, THOUGH.
CAN YOU STOP CALLING ME HAYES?
SURE THING, PAL.
HEHEH.
GOOD NIGHT, ALY.
GOOD NIGHT, NAVIN.
WHOOOOOOSH!!
WHOOOSH!!

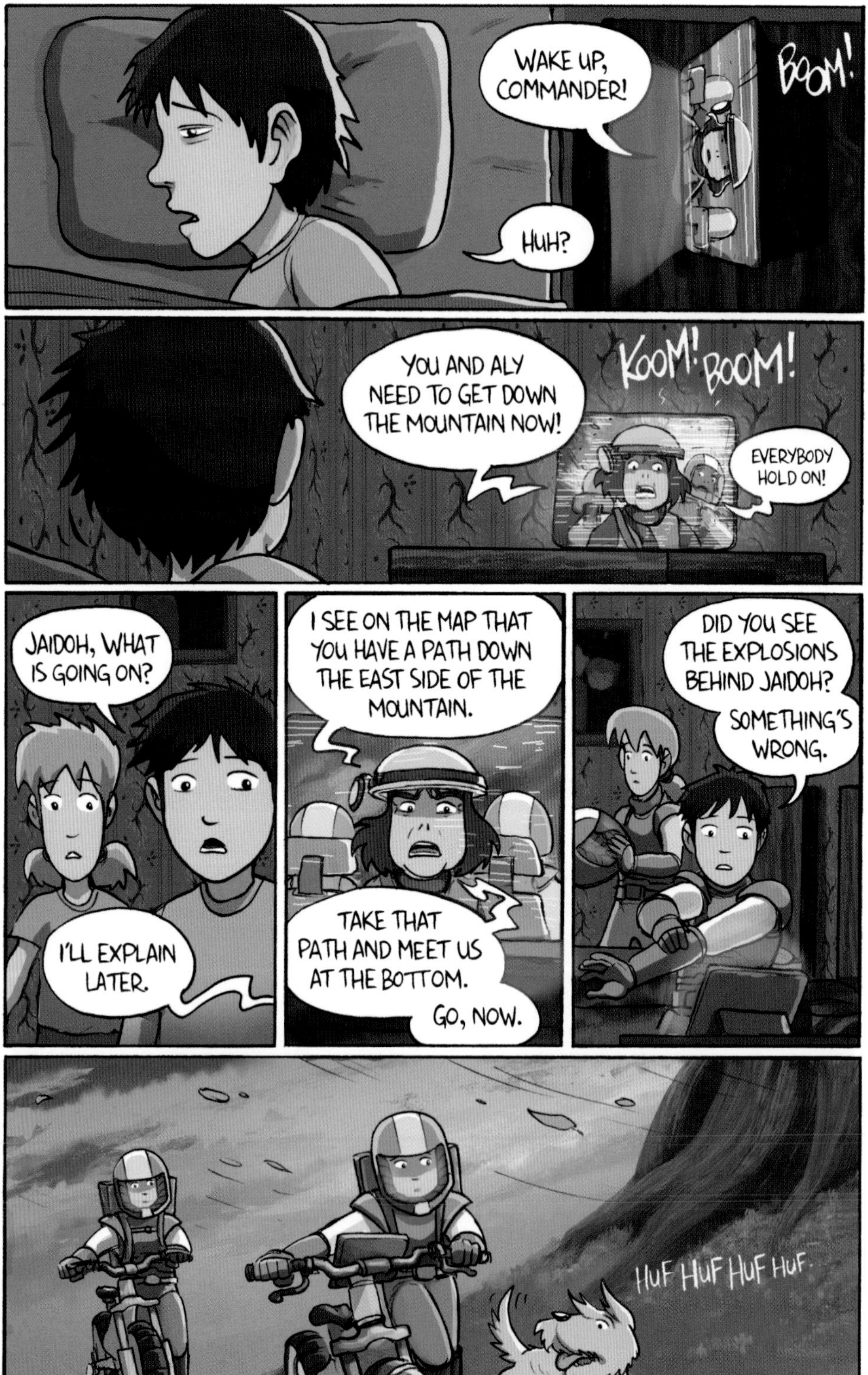
WAKE UP, COMMANDER!
BOOM!
HUH?
YOU AND ALY NEED TO GET DOWN THE MOUNTAIN NOW!
KOOM! BOOM!
EVERYBODY HOLD ON!
JAIDOH, WHAT IS GOING ON?
I'LL EXPLAIN LATER.
I SEE ON THE MAP THAT YOU HAVE A PATH DOWN THE EAST SIDE OF THE MOUNTAIN.
TAKE THAT PATH AND MEET US AT THE BOTTOM.
GO, NOW.
DID YOU SEE THE EXPLOSIONS BEHIND JAIDOH?
SOMETHING'S WRONG.
HUF HUF HUF HUF

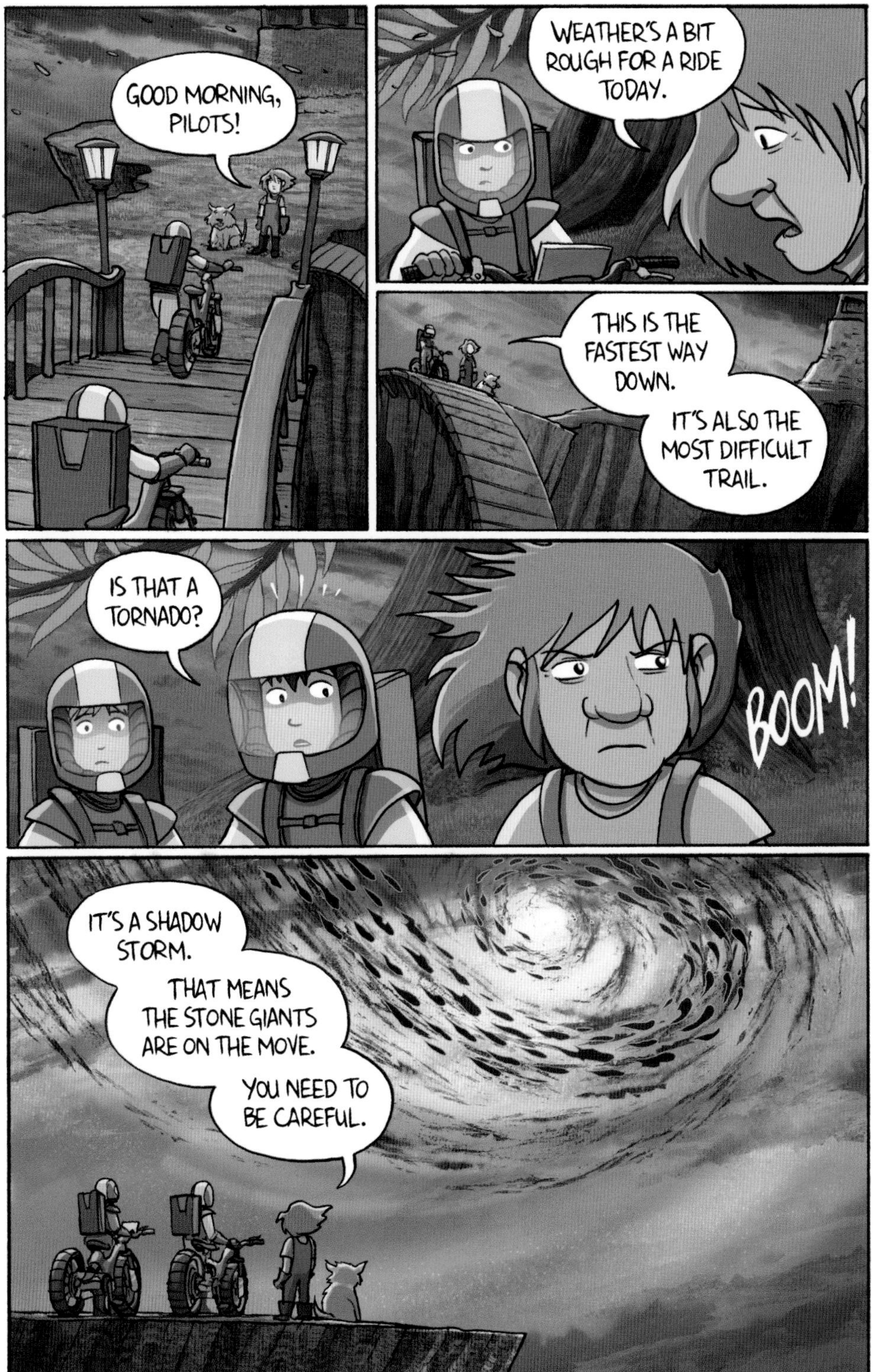
GOOD MORNING, PILOTS!
WEATHER'S A BIT ROUGH FOR A RIDE TODAY.
THIS IS THE FASTEST WAY DOWN.
IT'S ALSO THE MOST DIFFICULT TRAIL.
IS THAT A TORNADO?
BOOM!
IT'S A SHADOW STORM.
THAT MEANS THE STONE GIANTS ARE ON THE MOVE.
YOU NEED TO BE CAREFUL.

BEEP
BEEP
WHIRRRP

KSHT!

THE TREE SAPLINGS ARE SAFELY SECURED IN YOUR PACKS.

PLEASE TAKE CARE OF THEM.

WE WILL.

I'M VERY GLAD TO HAVE MET YOU AND ALY.

I HOPE OUR PATHS CROSS AGAIN!

I HOPE SO, TOO!

LET'S GO, NAVIN!

FOLLOW ME!

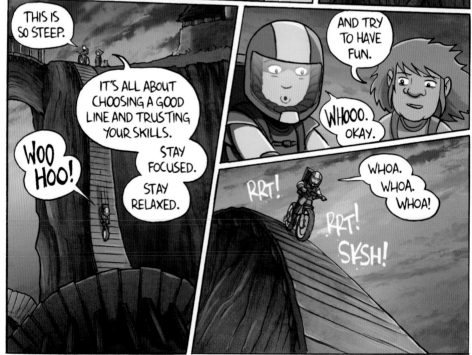

THIS IS SO STEEP.

IT'S ALL ABOUT CHOOSING A GOOD LINE AND TRUSTING YOUR SKILLS.

STAY FOCUSED.

STAY RELAXED.

WOO HOO!

AND TRY TO HAVE FUN.

WHOOO. OKAY.

WHOA. WHOA. WHOA!

RRT!

RRT!

SKSH!

160

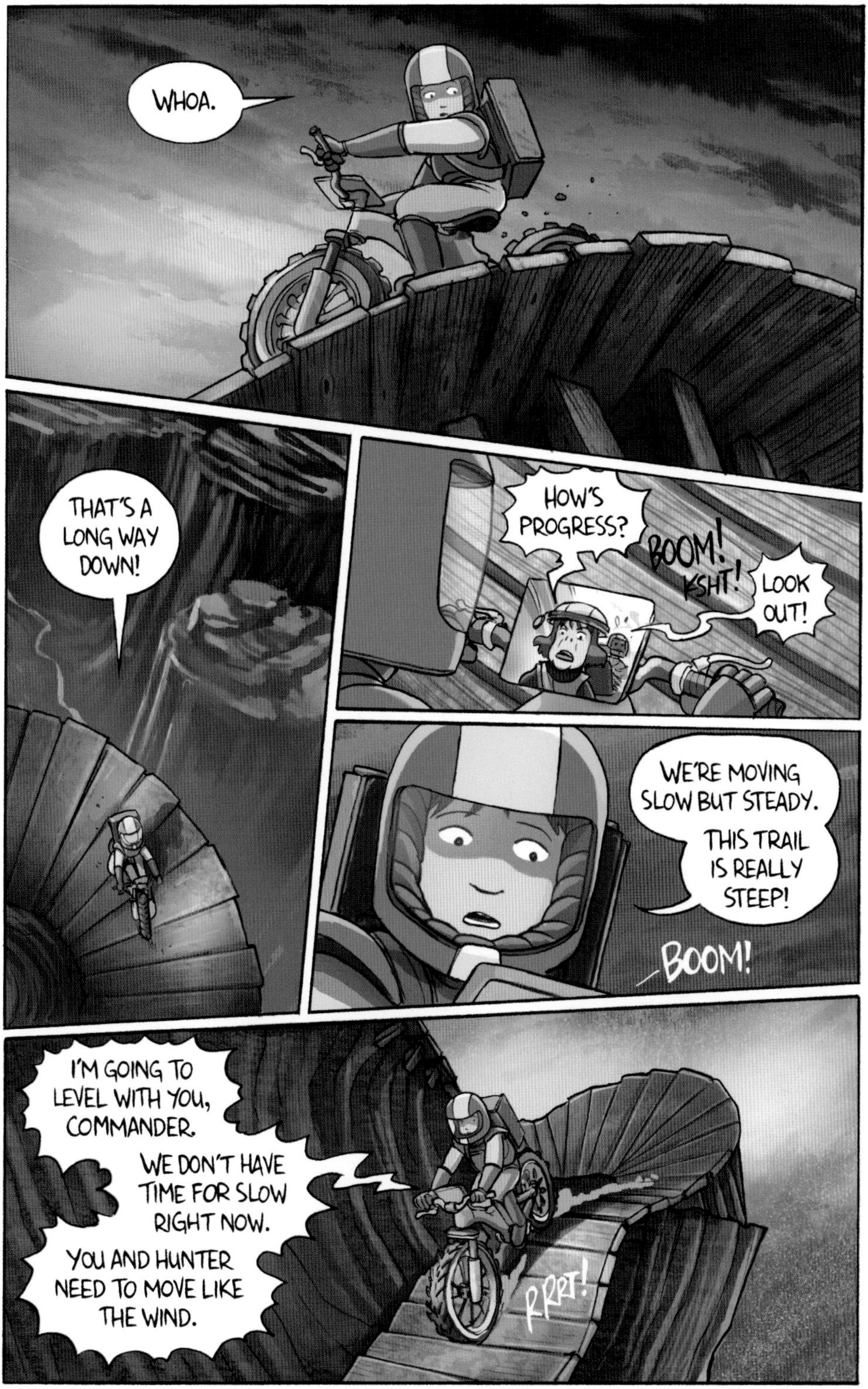
WHOA.
THAT'S A LONG WAY DOWN!
HOW'S PROGRESS?
BOOM!
KSHT!
LOOK OUT!
WE'RE MOVING SLOW BUT STEADY.
THIS TRAIL IS REALLY STEEP!
BOOM!
I'M GOING TO LEVEL WITH YOU, COMMANDER.
WE DON'T HAVE TIME FOR SLOW RIGHT NOW.
YOU AND HUNTER NEED TO MOVE LIKE THE WIND.
RRRT!

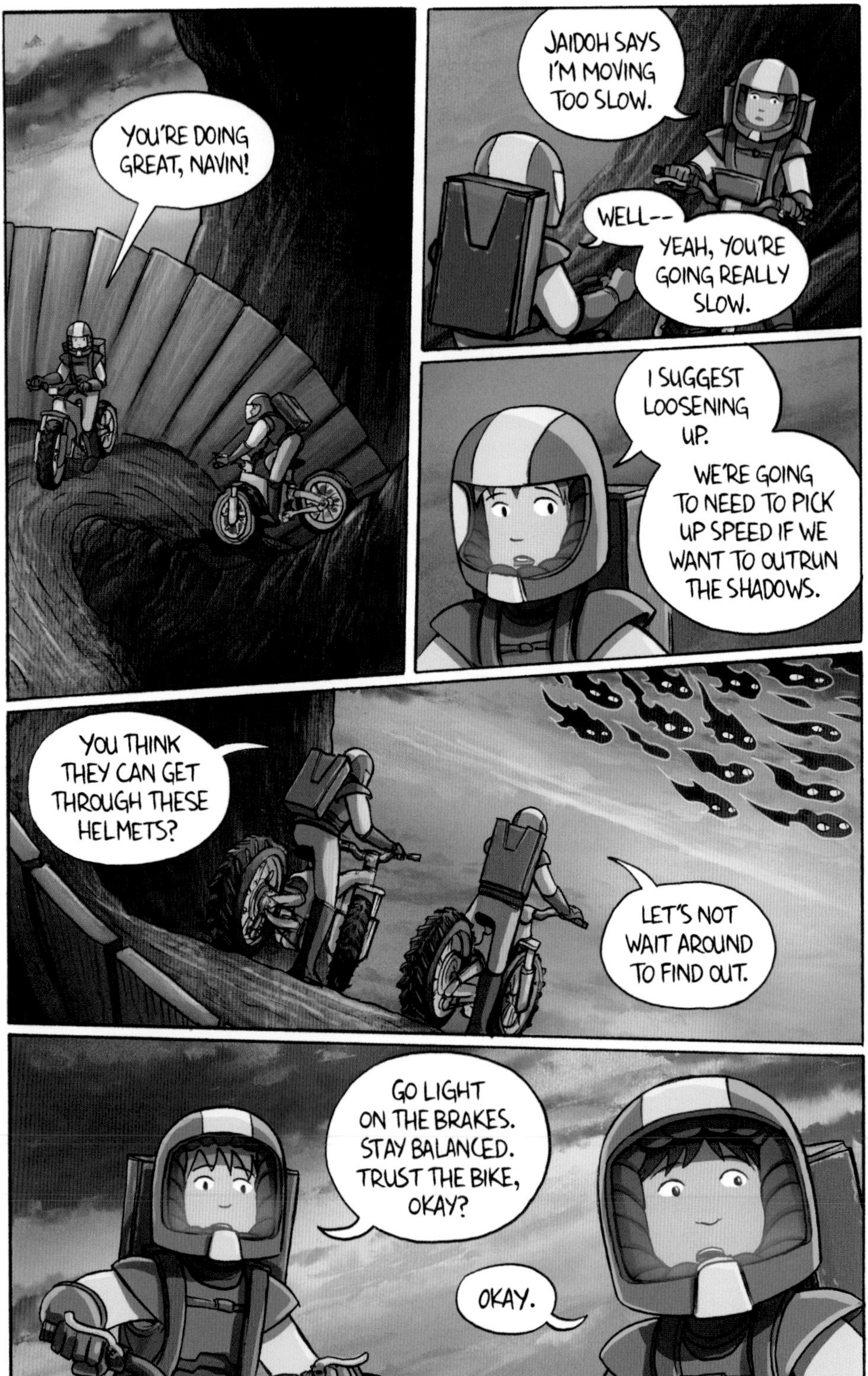
YOU'RE DOING GREAT, NAVIN!
JAIDOH SAYS I'M MOVING TOO SLOW.
WELL--
YEAH, YOU'RE GOING REALLY SLOW.
I SUGGEST LOOSENING UP.
WE'RE GOING TO NEED TO PICK UP SPEED IF WE WANT TO OUTRUN THE SHADOWS.
YOU THINK THEY CAN GET THROUGH THESE HELMETS?
LET'S NOT WAIT AROUND TO FIND OUT.
GO LIGHT ON THE BRAKES. STAY BALANCED. TRUST THE BIKE, OKAY?
OKAY.

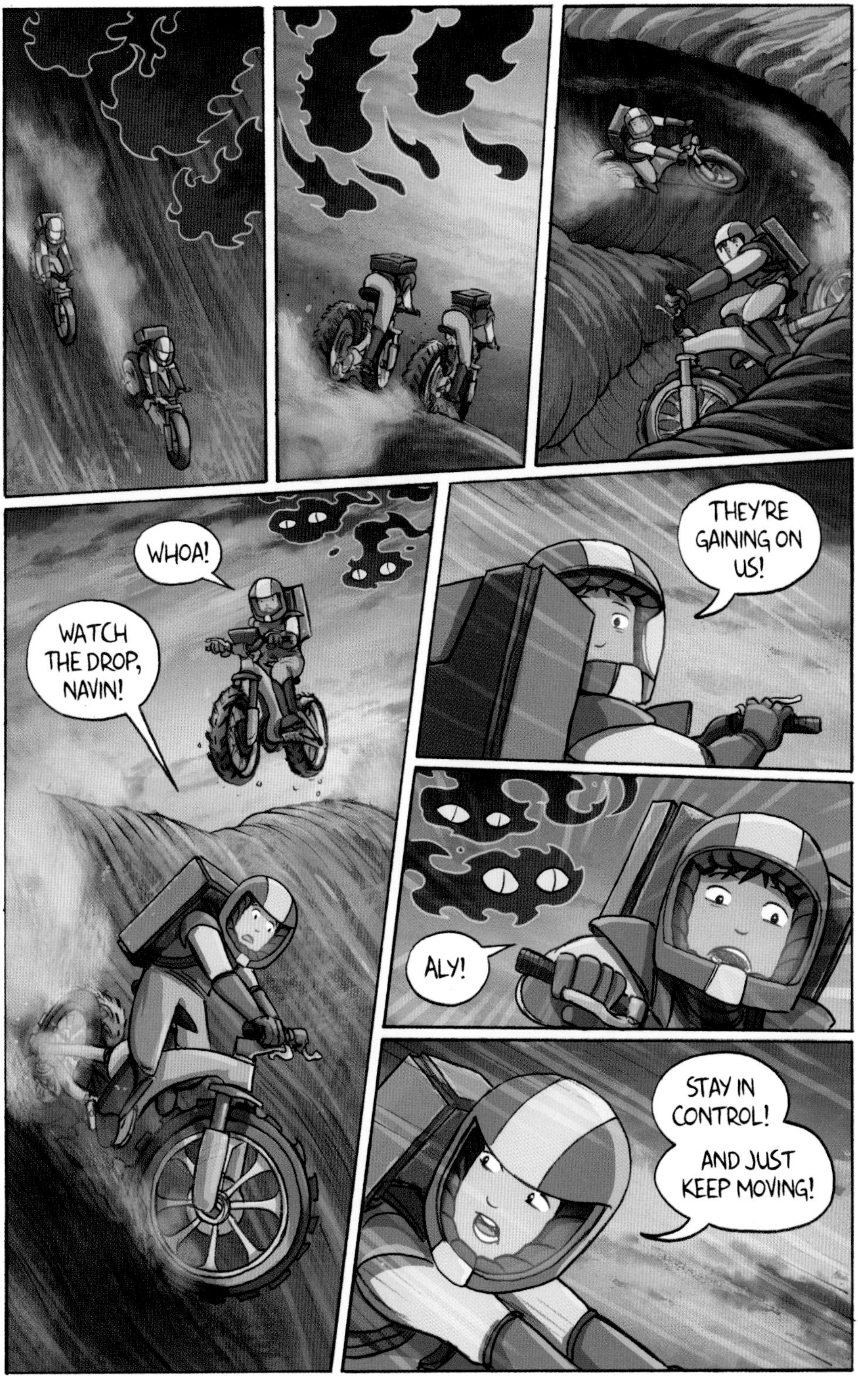
WHOA!
WATCH THE DROP, NAVIN!
THEY'RE GAINING ON US!
ALY!
STAY IN CONTROL!
AND JUST KEEP MOVING!

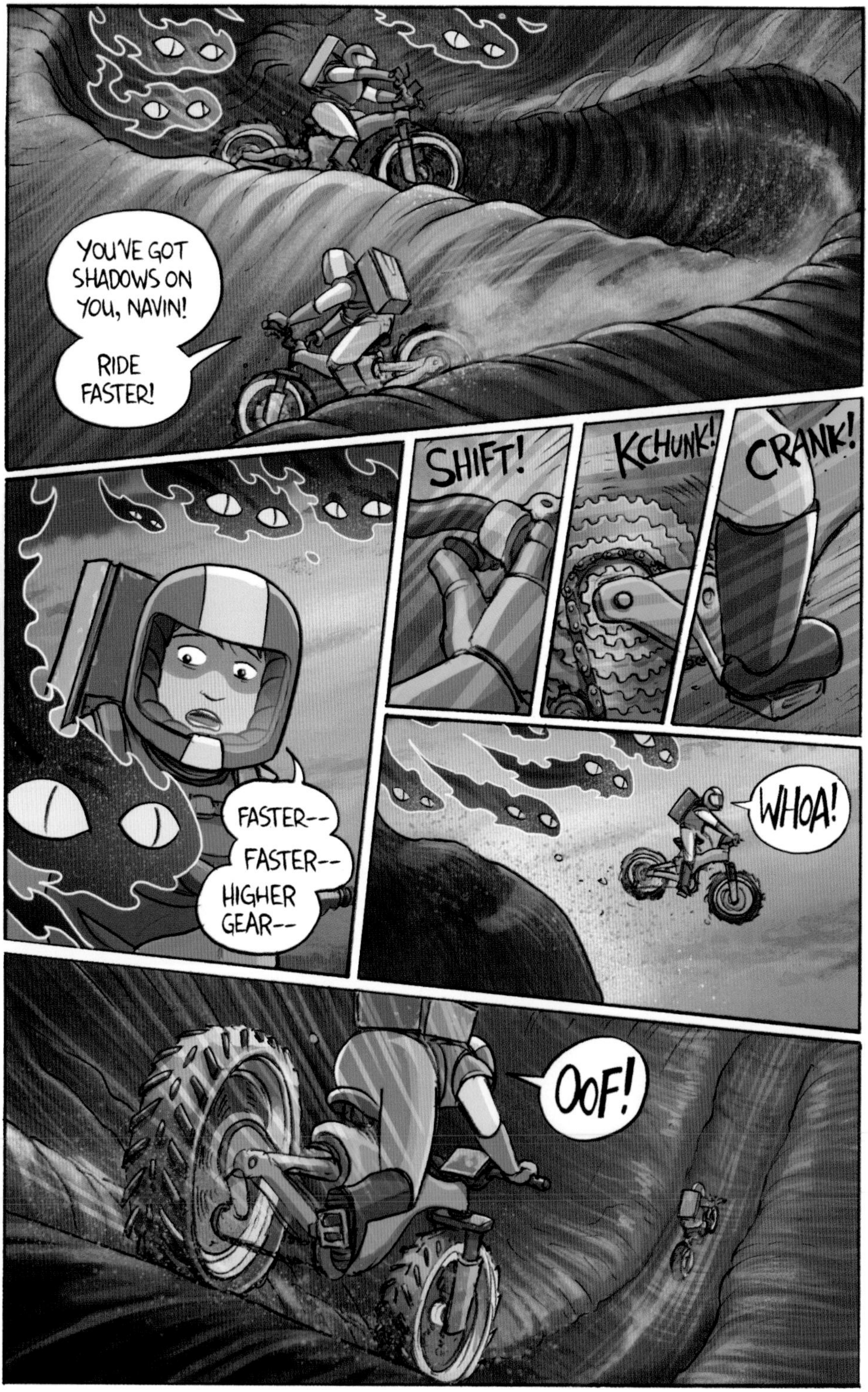
YOU'VE GOT SHADOWS ON YOU, NAVIN!
RIDE FASTER!
SHIFT!
KCHUNK!
CRANK!
FASTER--
FASTER--
HIGHER GEAR--
WHOA!
OOF!

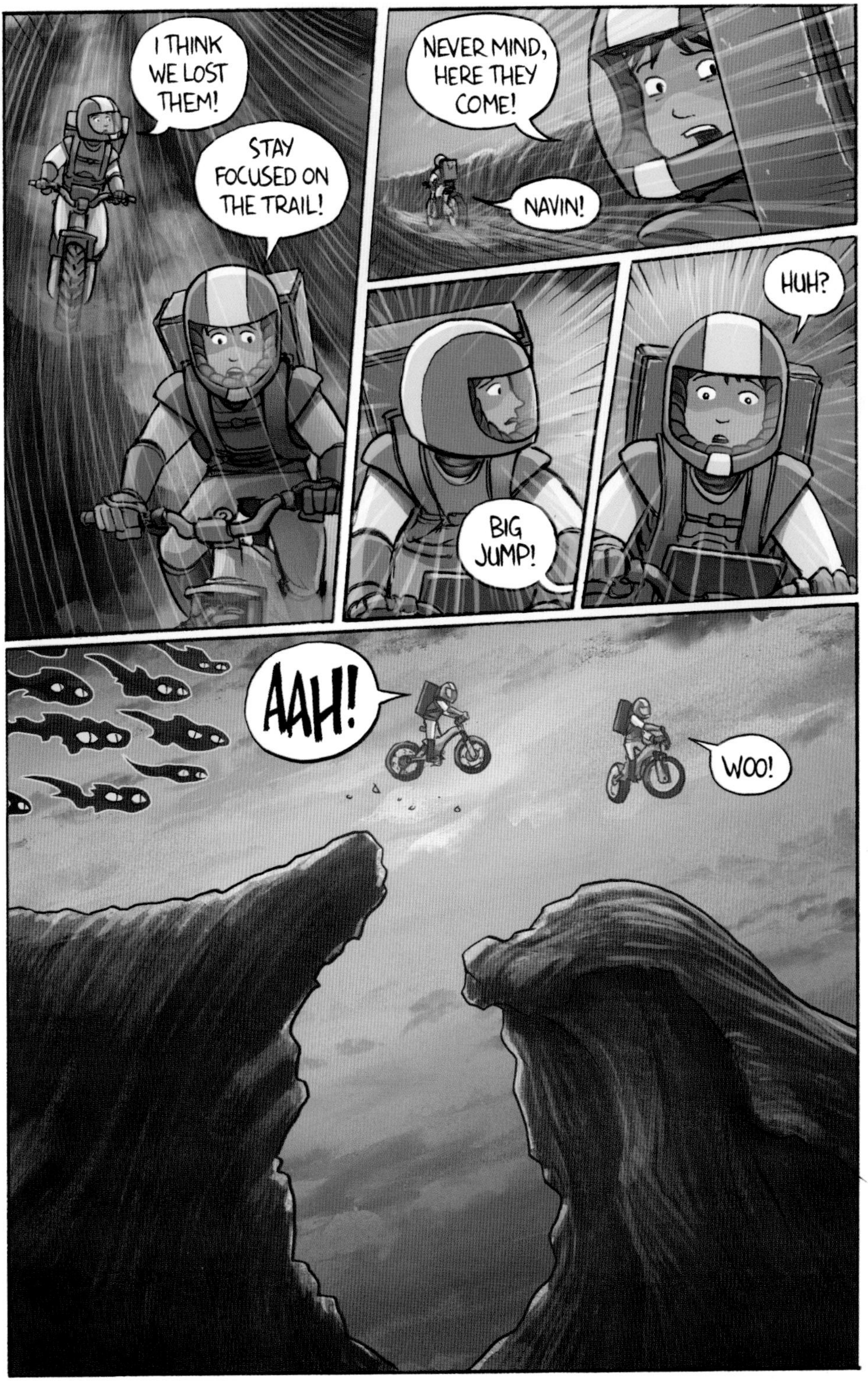
I THINK WE LOST THEM!
STAY FOCUSED ON THE TRAIL!
NEVER MIND, HERE THEY COME!
NAVIN!
HUH?
BIG JUMP!
AAH!
WOO!

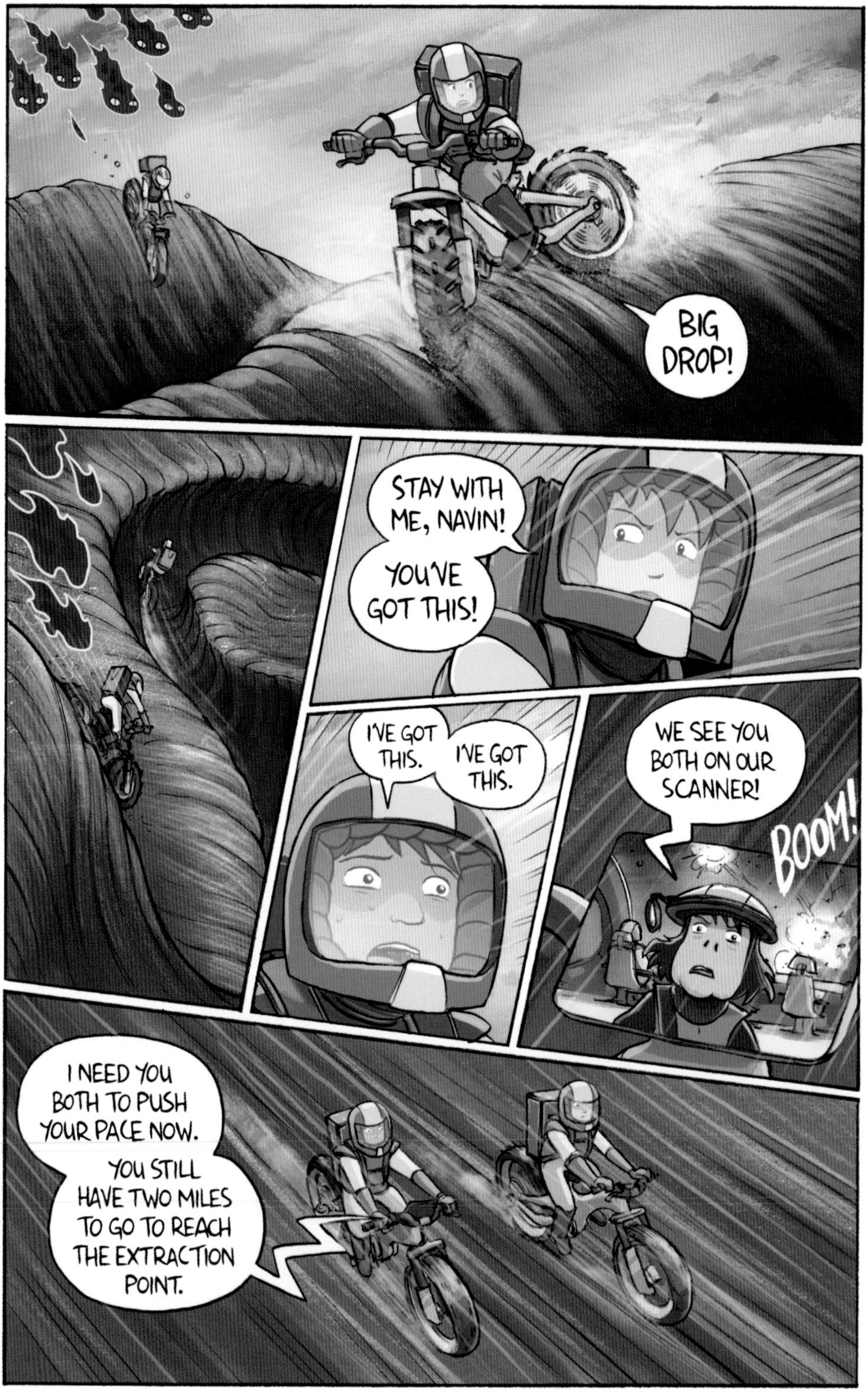
BIG DROP!
STAY WITH ME, NAVIN!
YOU'VE GOT THIS!
I'VE GOT THIS.
I'VE GOT THIS.
WE SEE YOU BOTH ON OUR SCANNER!
BOOM!
I NEED YOU BOTH TO PUSH YOUR PACE NOW.
YOU STILL HAVE TWO MILES TO GO TO REACH THE EXTRACTION POINT.

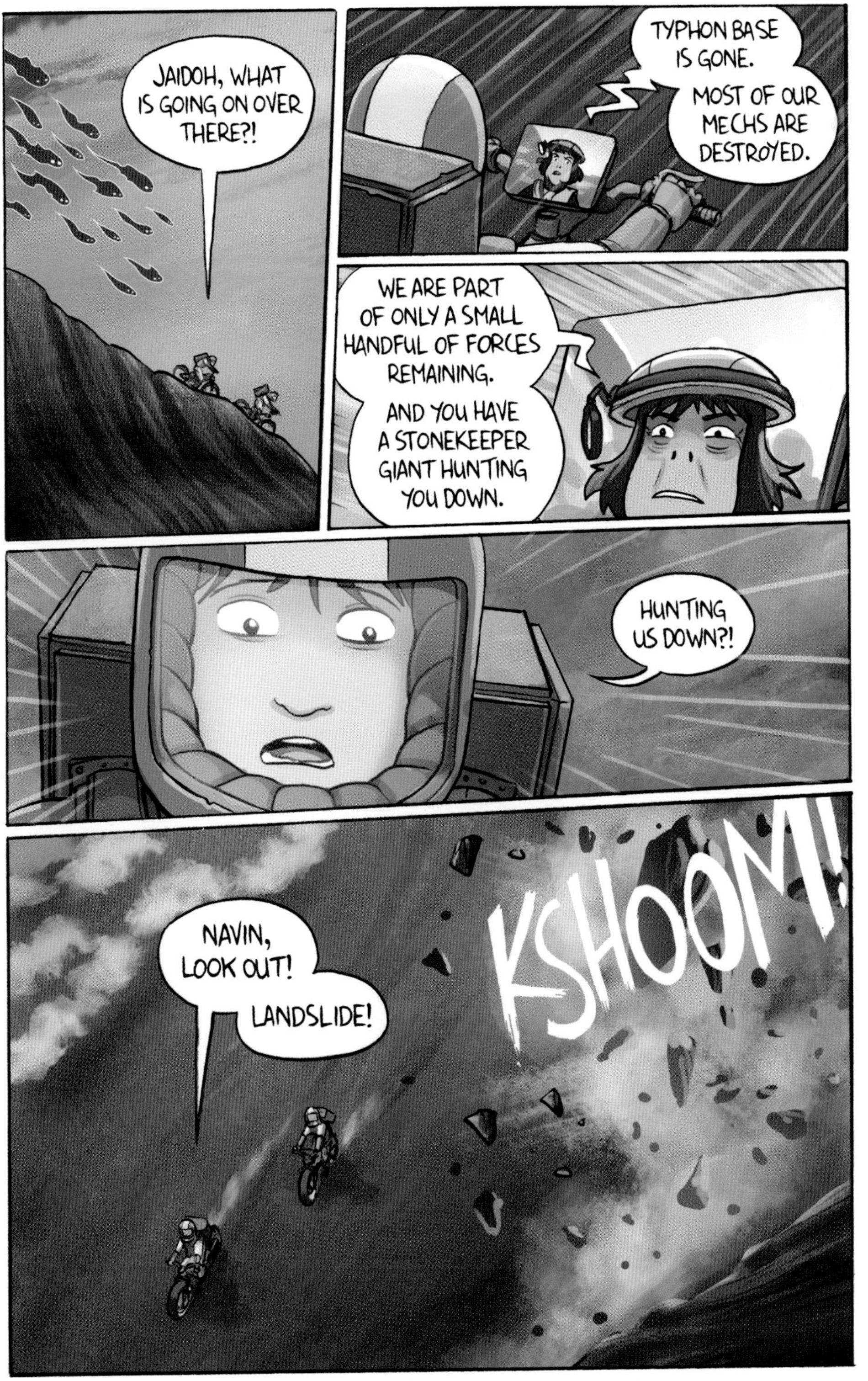
JAIDOH, WHAT IS GOING ON OVER THERE?!
TYPHON BASE IS GONE.
MOST OF OUR MECHS ARE DESTROYED.
WE ARE PART OF ONLY A SMALL HANDFUL OF FORCES REMAINING.
AND YOU HAVE A STONEKEEPER GIANT HUNTING YOU DOWN.
HUNTING US DOWN?!
KSHOOM!
NAVIN, LOOK OUT!
LANDSLIDE!

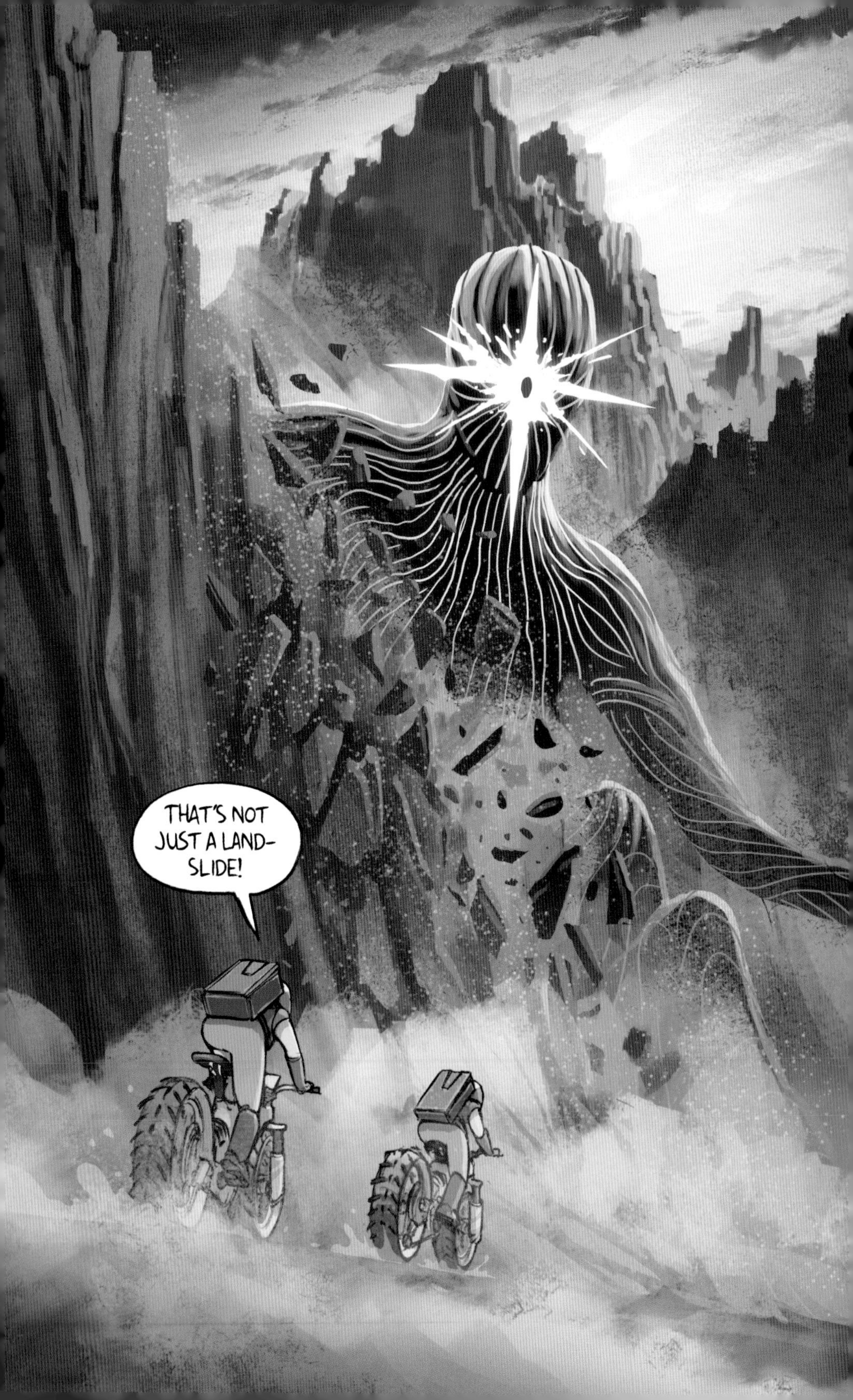
THAT'S NOT JUST A LAND-SLIDE!

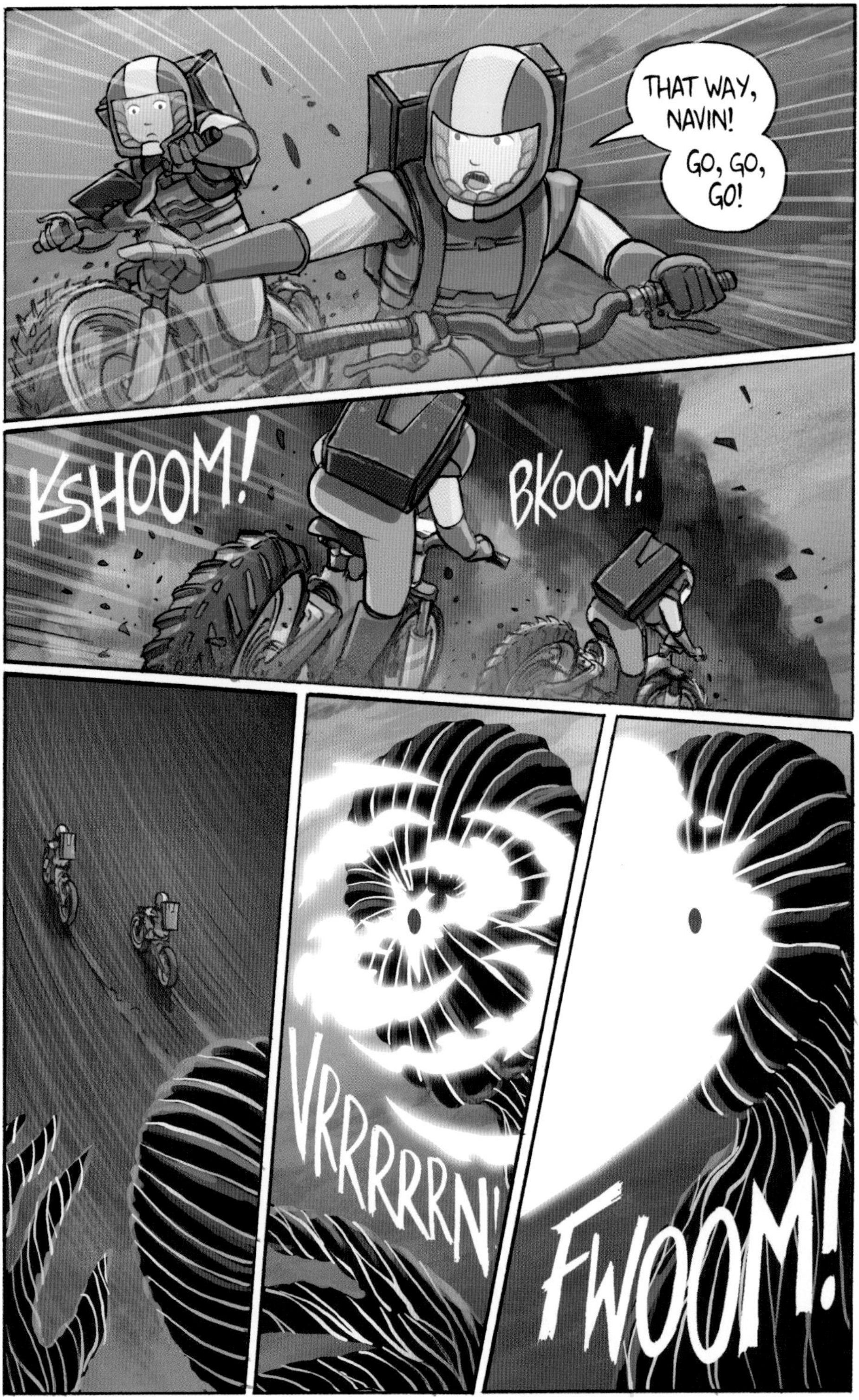
THAT WAY, NAVIN!
GO, GO, GO!
KSHOOM!
BKOOM!
VRRRRRN!
FWOOM!

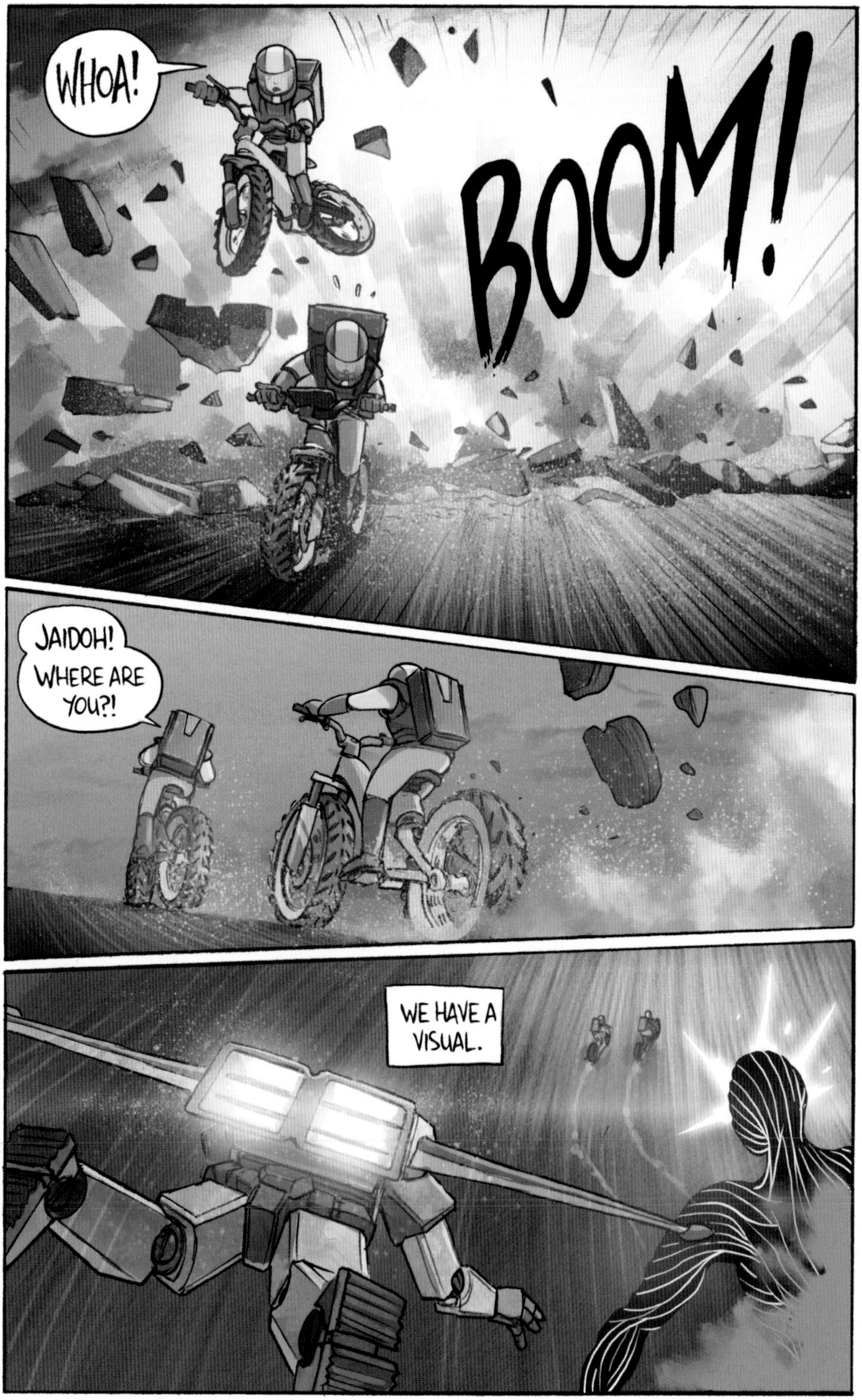
WHOA!
BOOM!
JAIDOH! WHERE ARE YOU?!
WE HAVE A VISUAL.

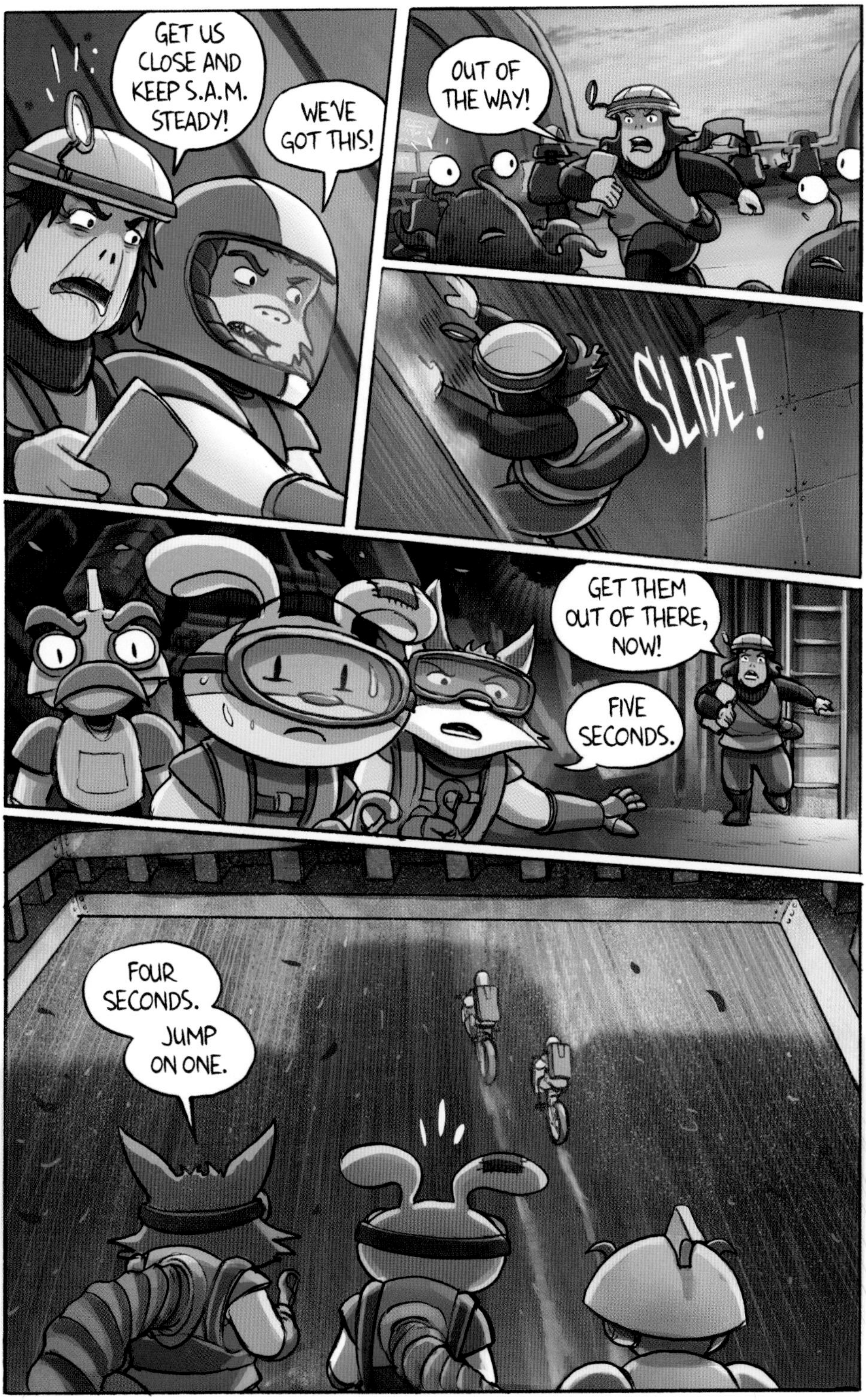
GET US CLOSE AND KEEP S.A.M. STEADY!
WE'VE GOT THIS!
OUT OF THE WAY!
SLIDE!
GET THEM OUT OF THERE, NOW!
FIVE SECONDS.
FOUR SECONDS.
JUMP ON ONE.

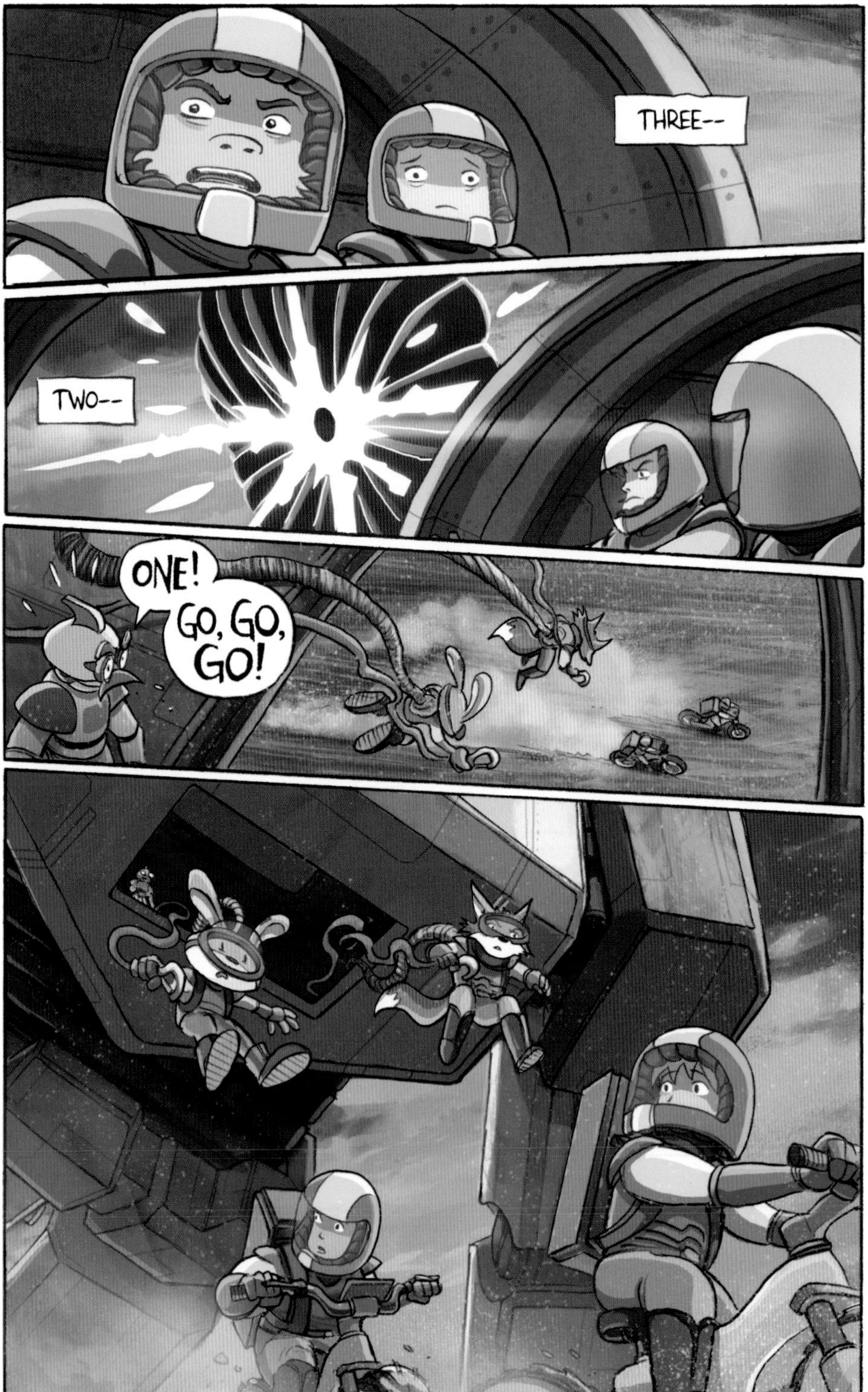
THREE--
TWO--
ONE!
GO, GO, GO!

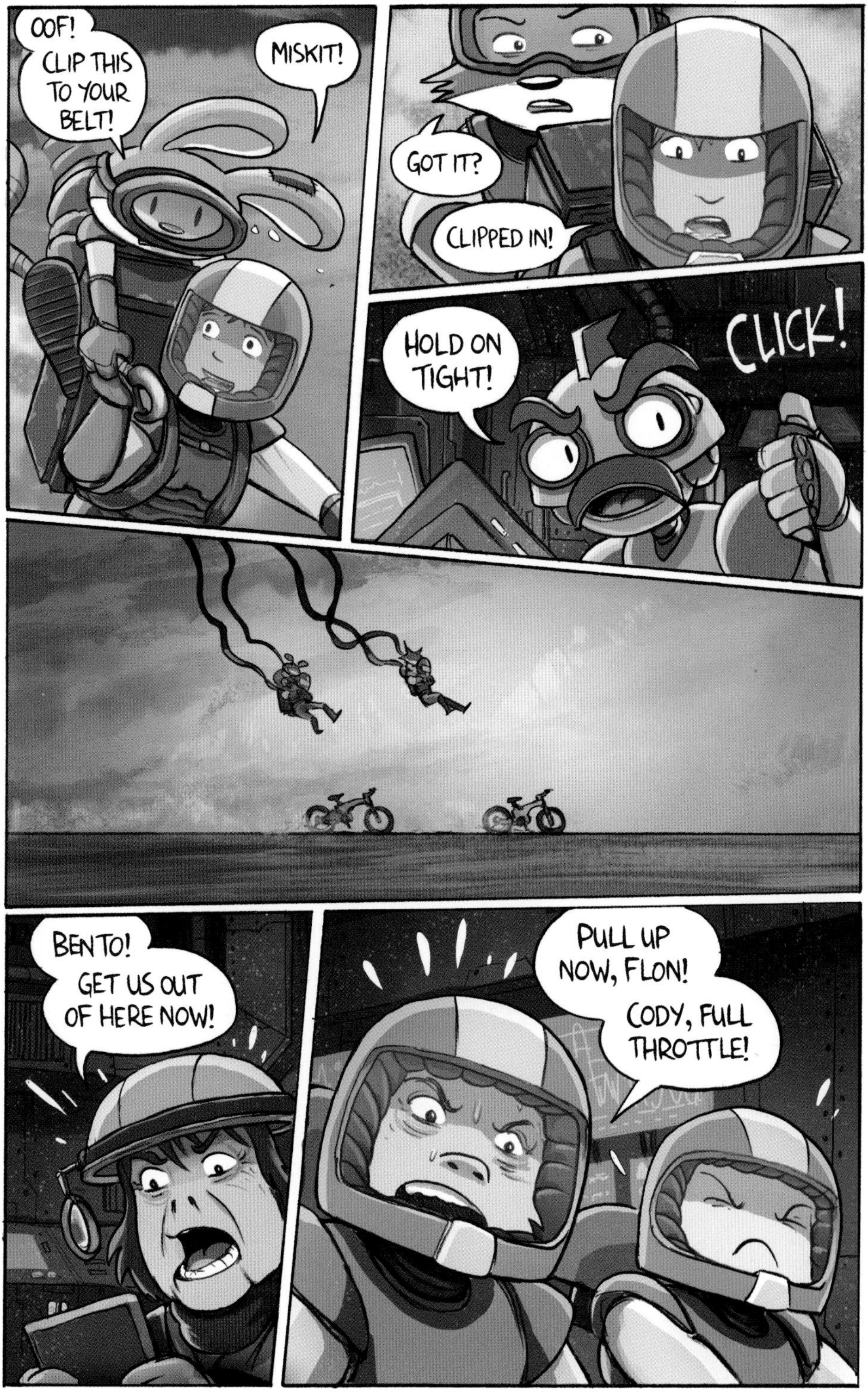
OOF!
CLIP THIS TO YOUR BELT!
MISKIT!
GOT IT?
CLIPPED IN!
HOLD ON TIGHT!
CLICK!
BENTO! GET US OUT OF HERE NOW!
PULL UP NOW, FLON!
CODY, FULL THROTTLE!

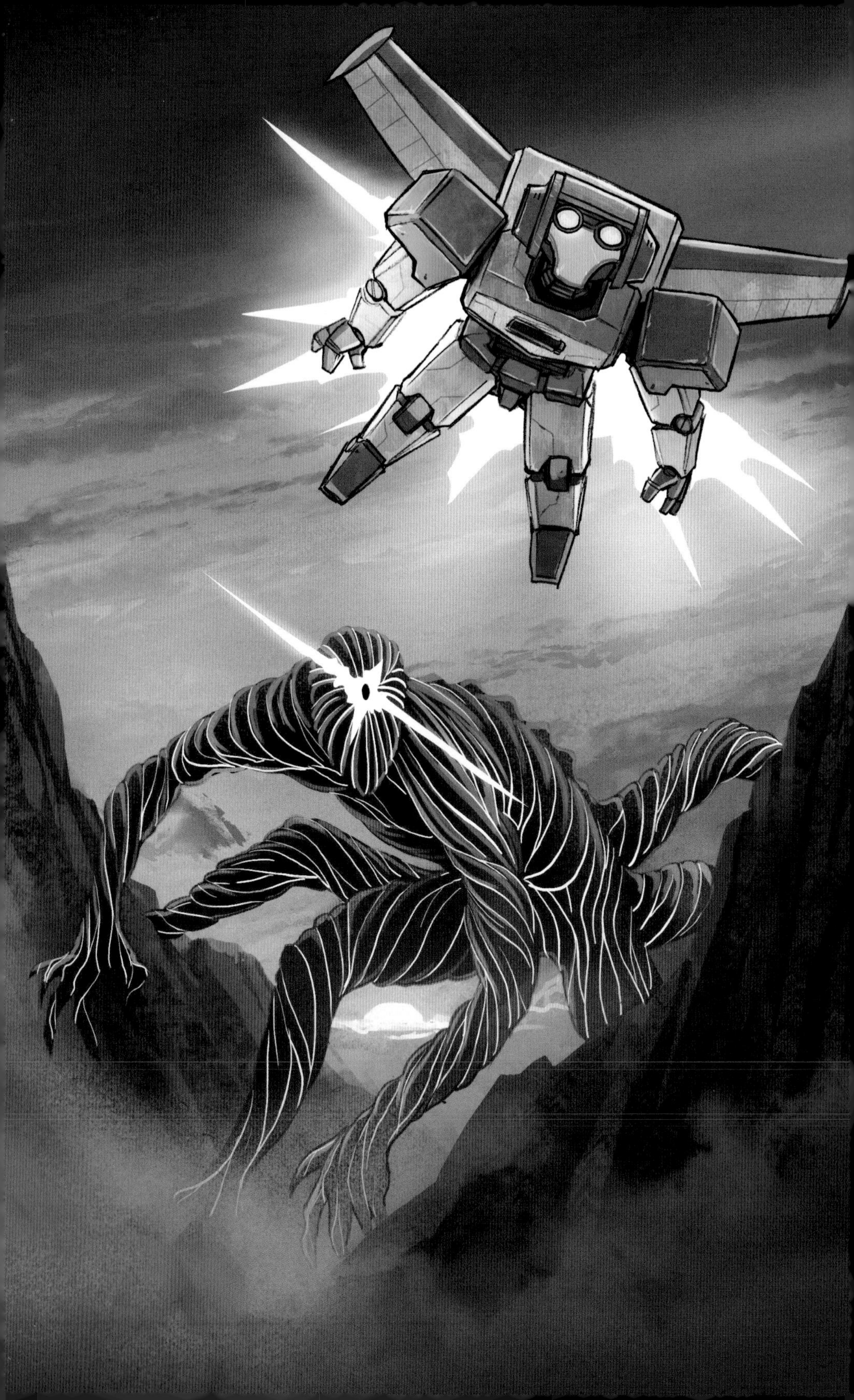

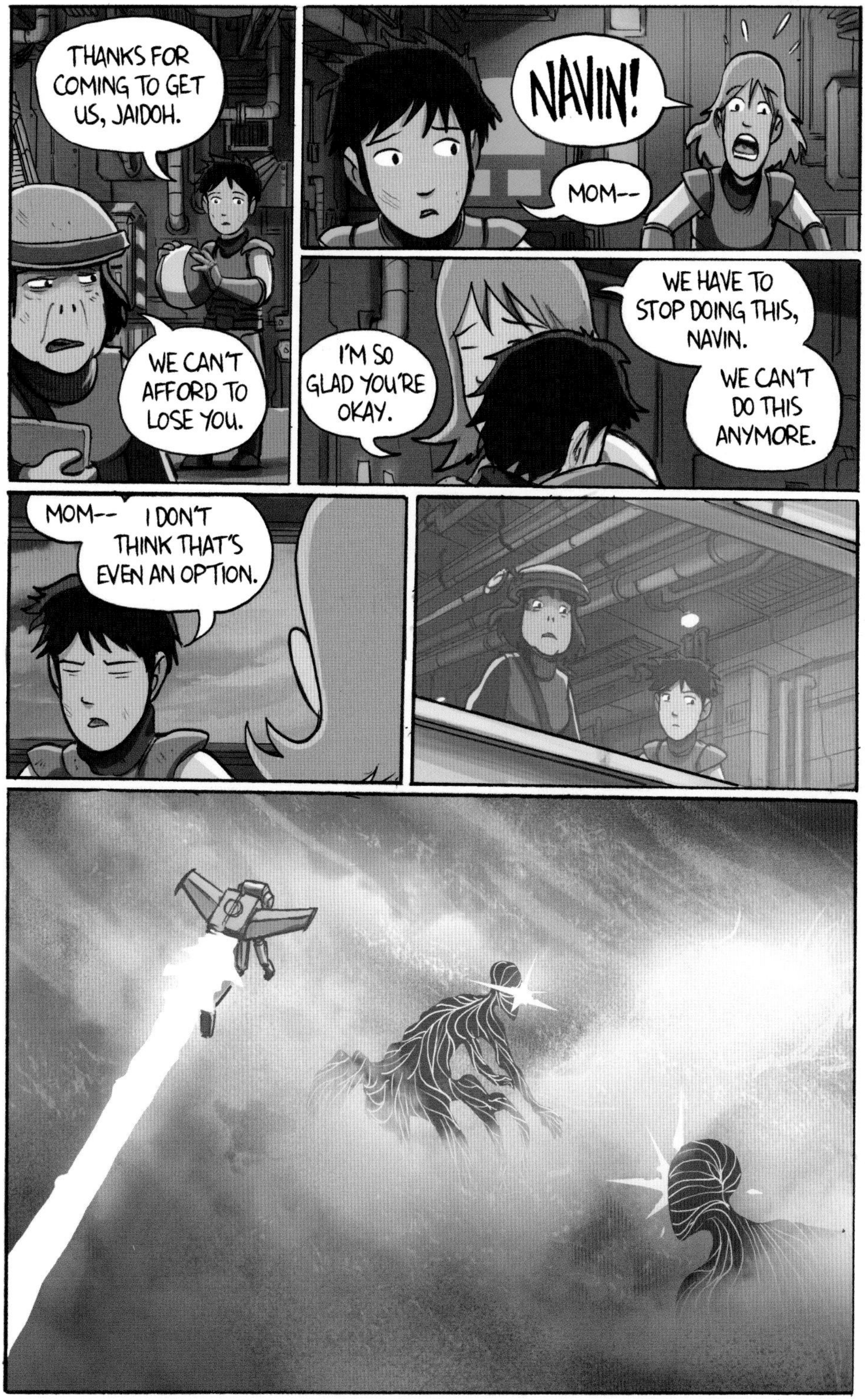
THANKS FOR COMING TO GET US, JAIDOH.
WE CAN'T AFFORD TO LOSE YOU.
NAVIN!
MOM--
I'M SO GLAD YOU'RE OKAY.
WE HAVE TO STOP DOING THIS, NAVIN.
WE CAN'T DO THIS ANYMORE.
MOM--
I DON'T THINK THAT'S EVEN AN OPTION.

WE ARE SIMPLY OVERPOWERED. OUR POWERS ARE CRIPPLED.

LEADERSHIP... ALL THE LEADERS ARE GONE.

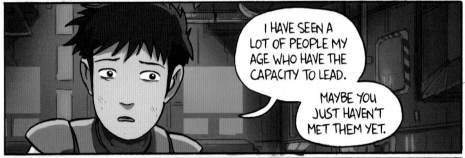

I HAVE SEEN A LOT OF PEOPLE MY AGE WHO HAVE THE CAPACITY TO LEAD.

MAYBE YOU JUST HAVEN'T MET THEM YET.

I KNOW THEY'RE OUT THERE.

THEY JUST NEED TO BE GIVEN A CHANCE.

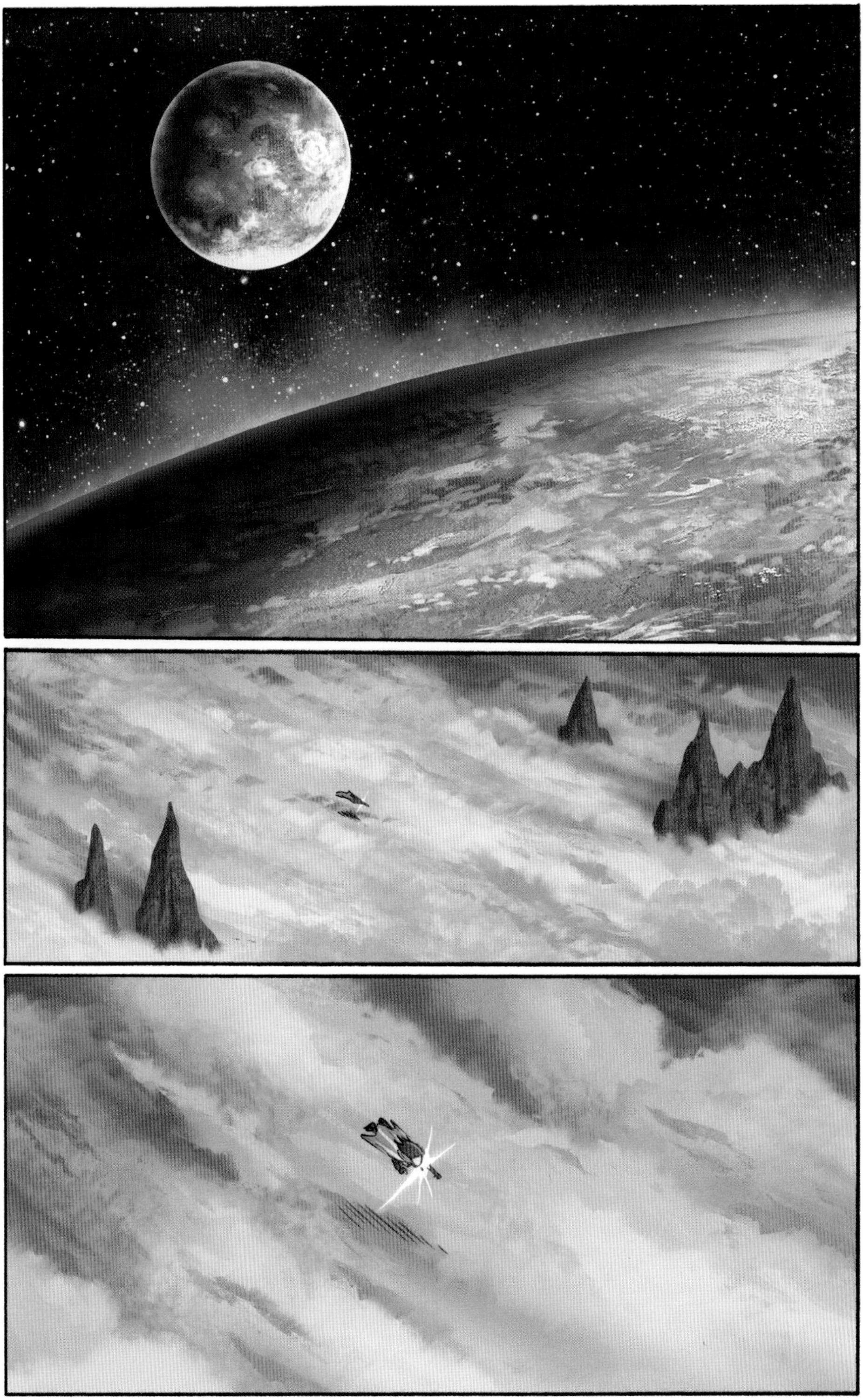

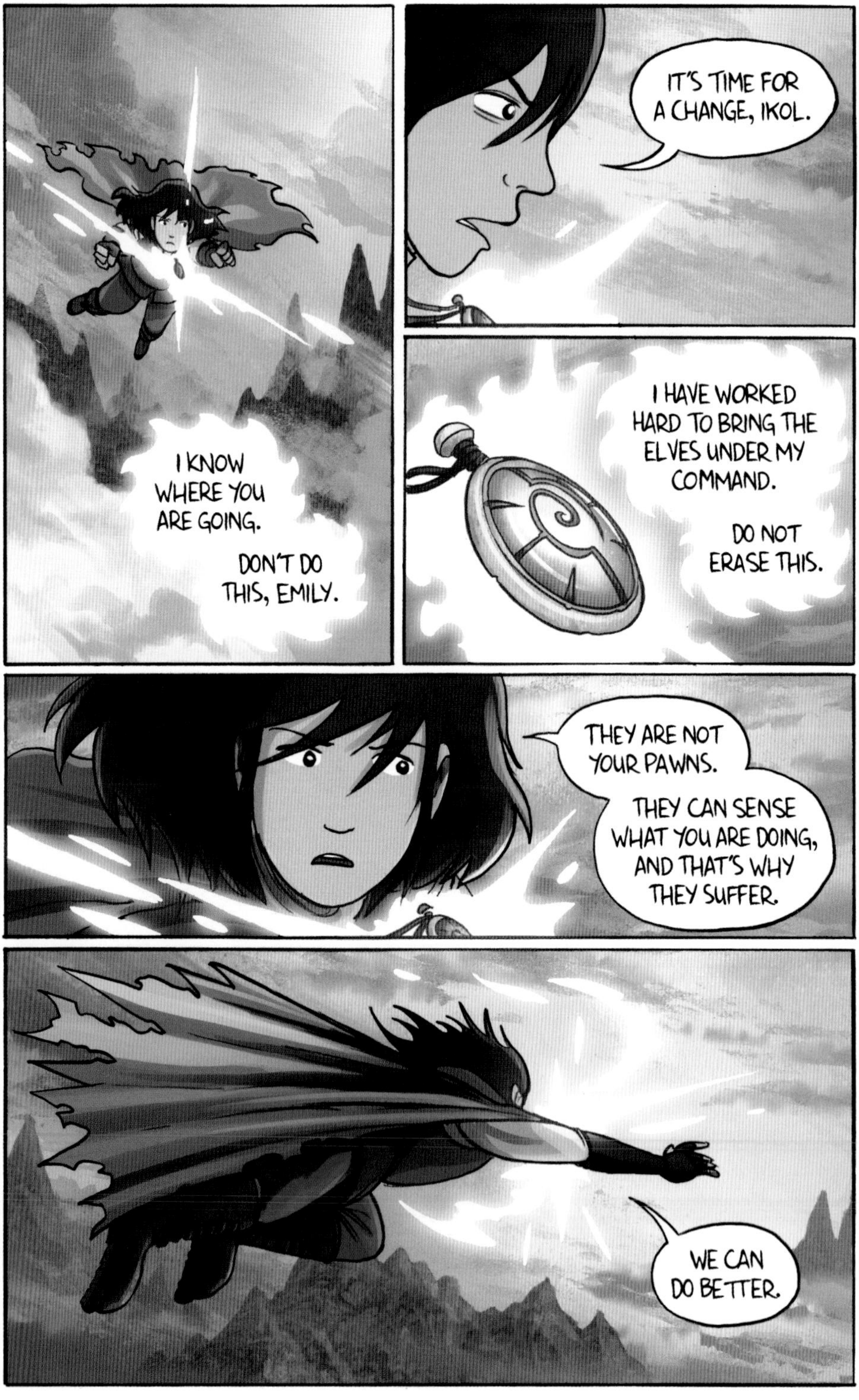

I KNOW WHERE YOU ARE GOING.
DON'T DO THIS, EMILY.
IT'S TIME FOR A CHANGE, IKOL.
I HAVE WORKED HARD TO BRING THE ELVES UNDER MY COMMAND.
DO NOT ERASE THIS.
THEY ARE NOT YOUR PAWNS.
THEY CAN SENSE WHAT YOU ARE DOING, AND THAT'S WHY THEY SUFFER.
WE CAN DO BETTER.

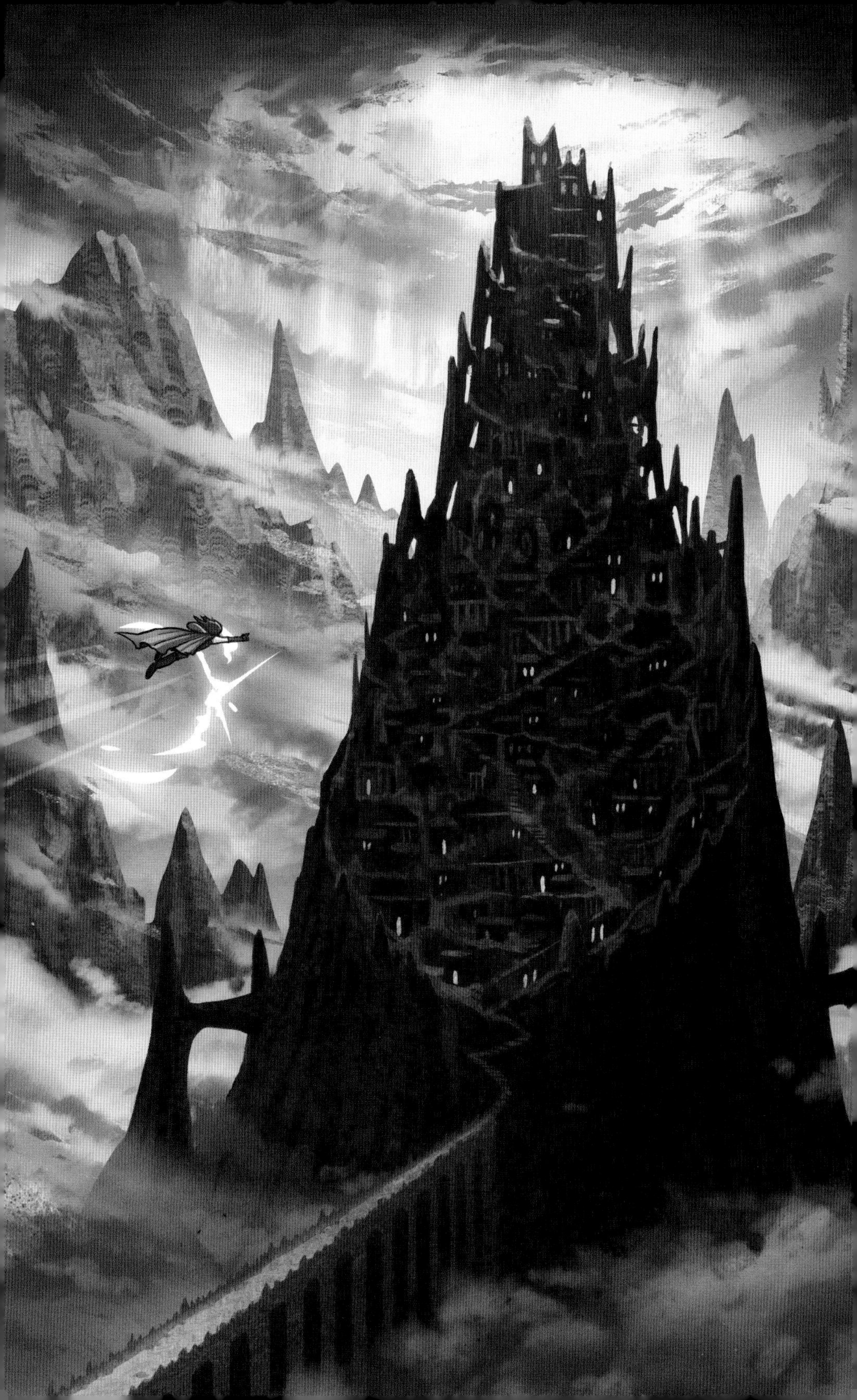

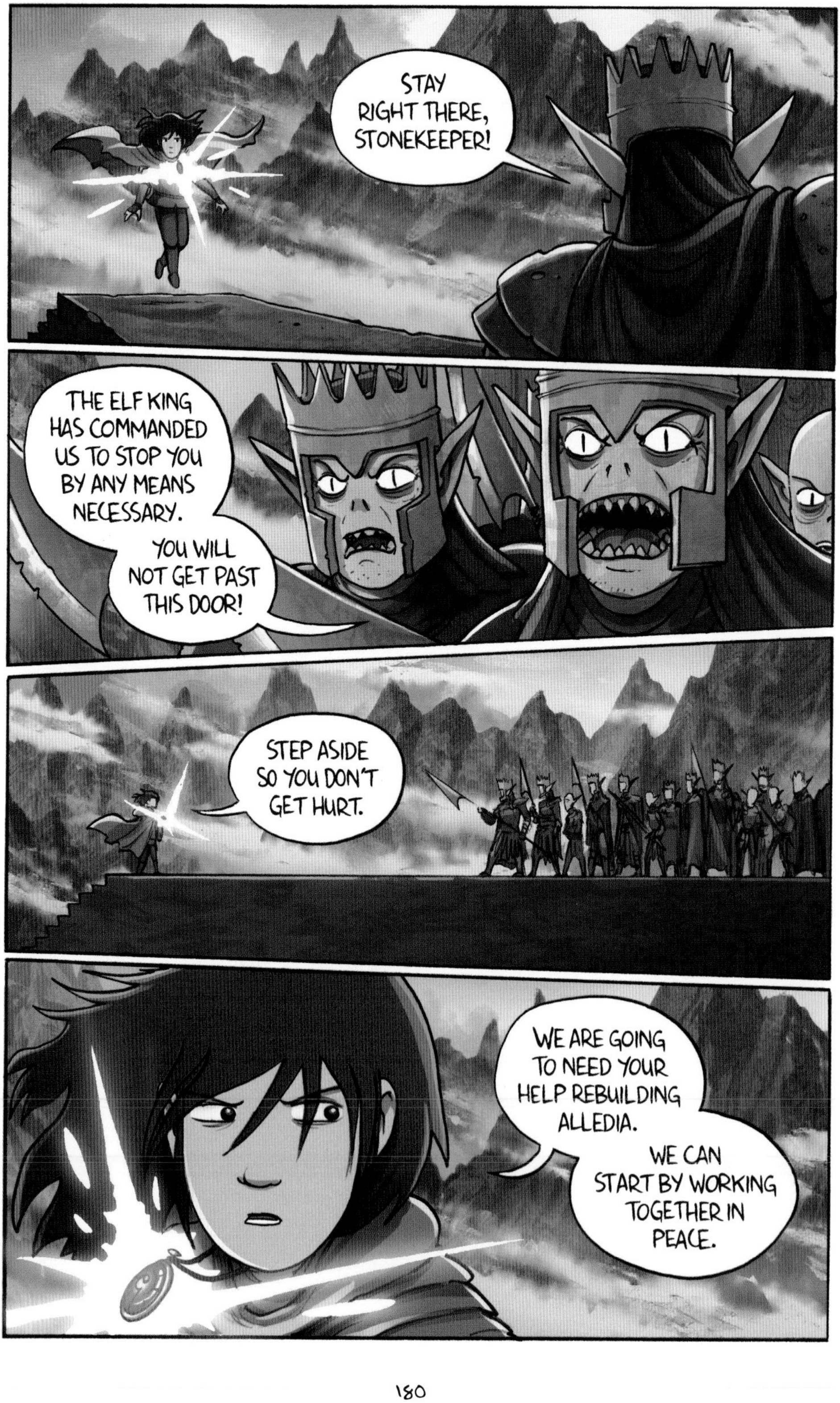
STAY RIGHT THERE, STONEKEEPER!
THE ELF KING HAS COMMANDED US TO STOP YOU BY ANY MEANS NECESSARY.
YOU WILL NOT GET PAST THIS DOOR!
STEP ASIDE SO YOU DON'T GET HURT.
WE ARE GOING TO NEED YOUR HELP REBUILDING ALLEDIA.
WE CAN START BY WORKING TOGETHER IN PEACE.

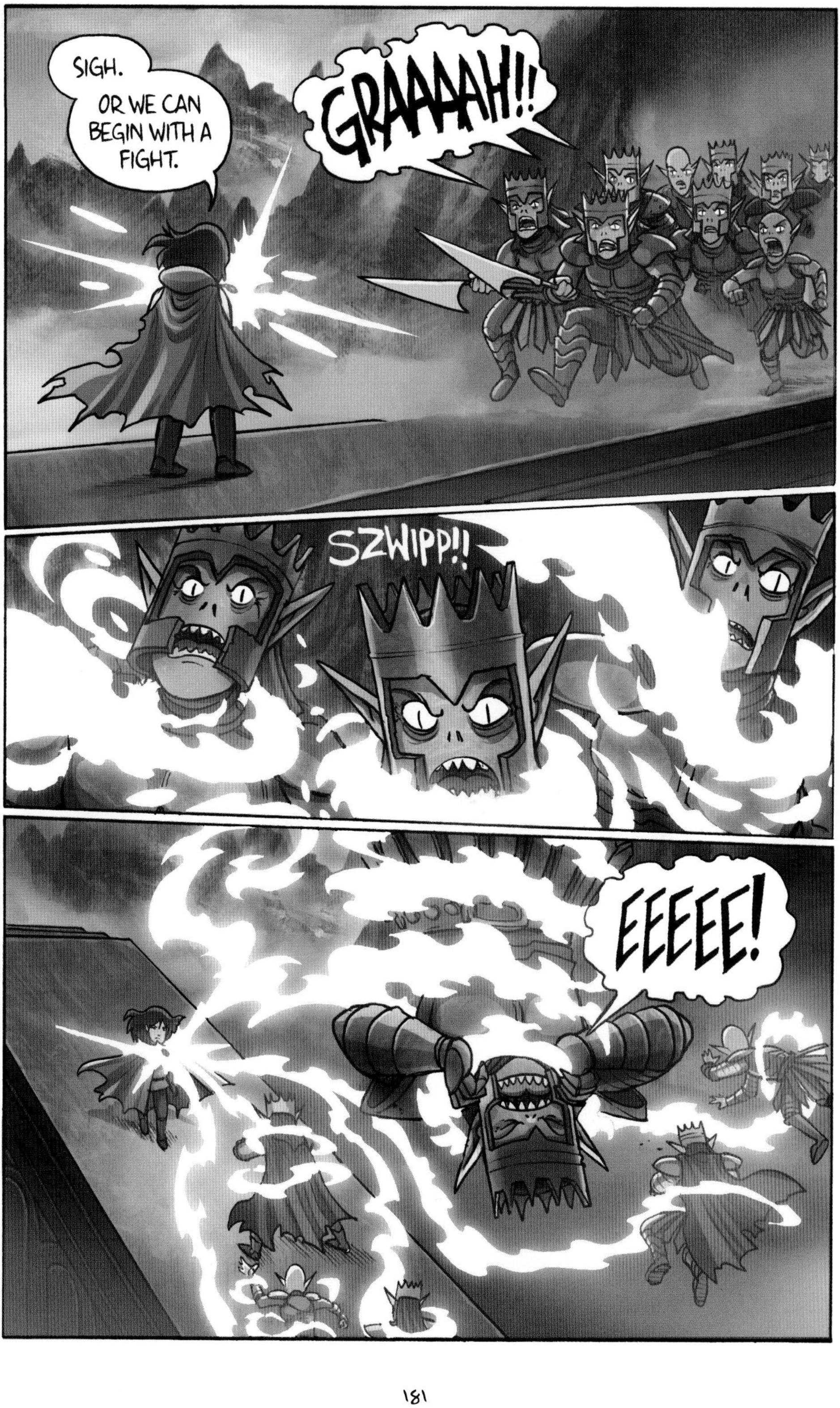
SIGH.
OR WE CAN BEGIN WITH A FIGHT.
GRAAAAH!!
SZWIPP!!
EEEEE!

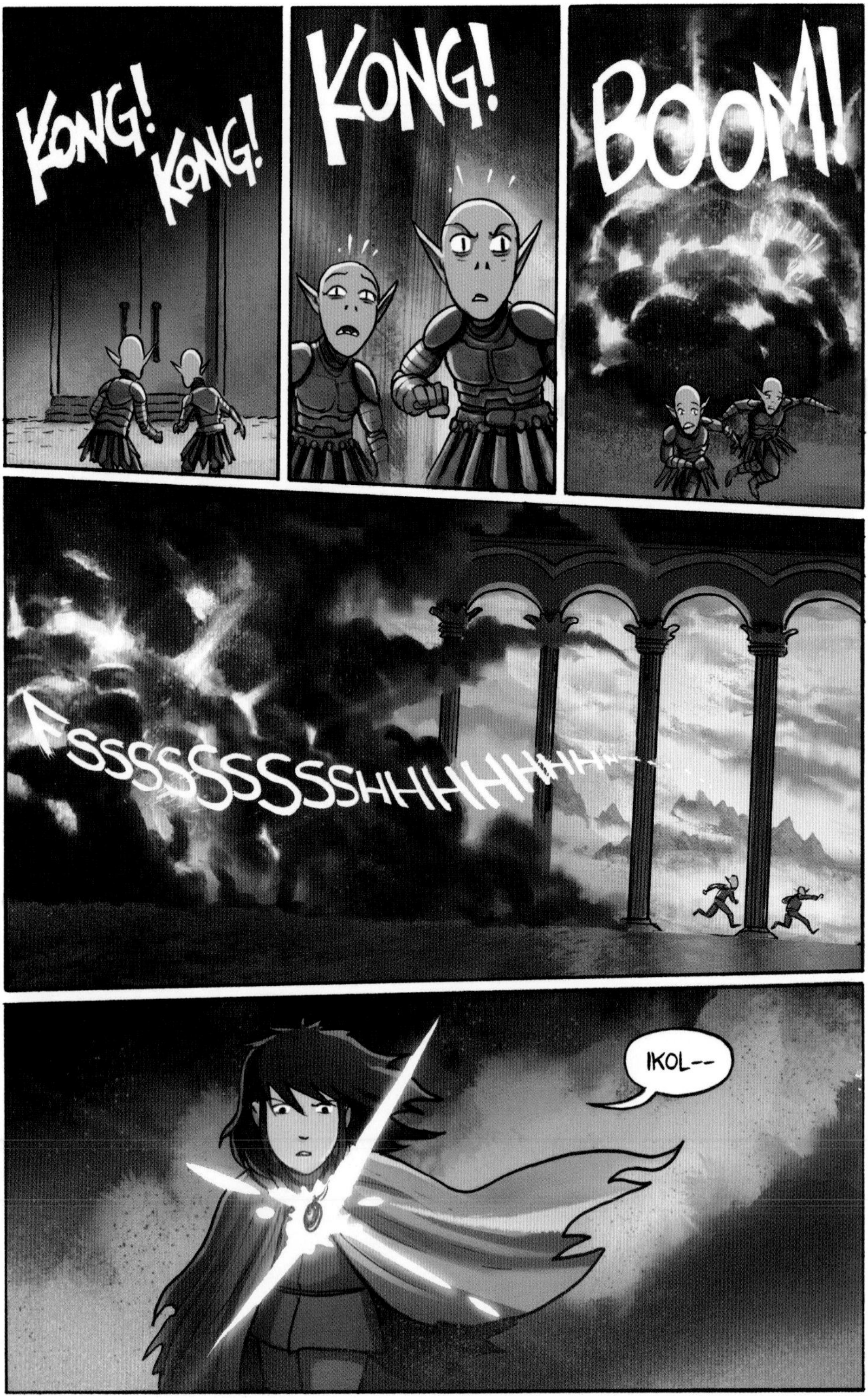
KONG! KONG!
KONG!
BOOM!
FSSSSSSSSSHHHHHH...
IKOL--

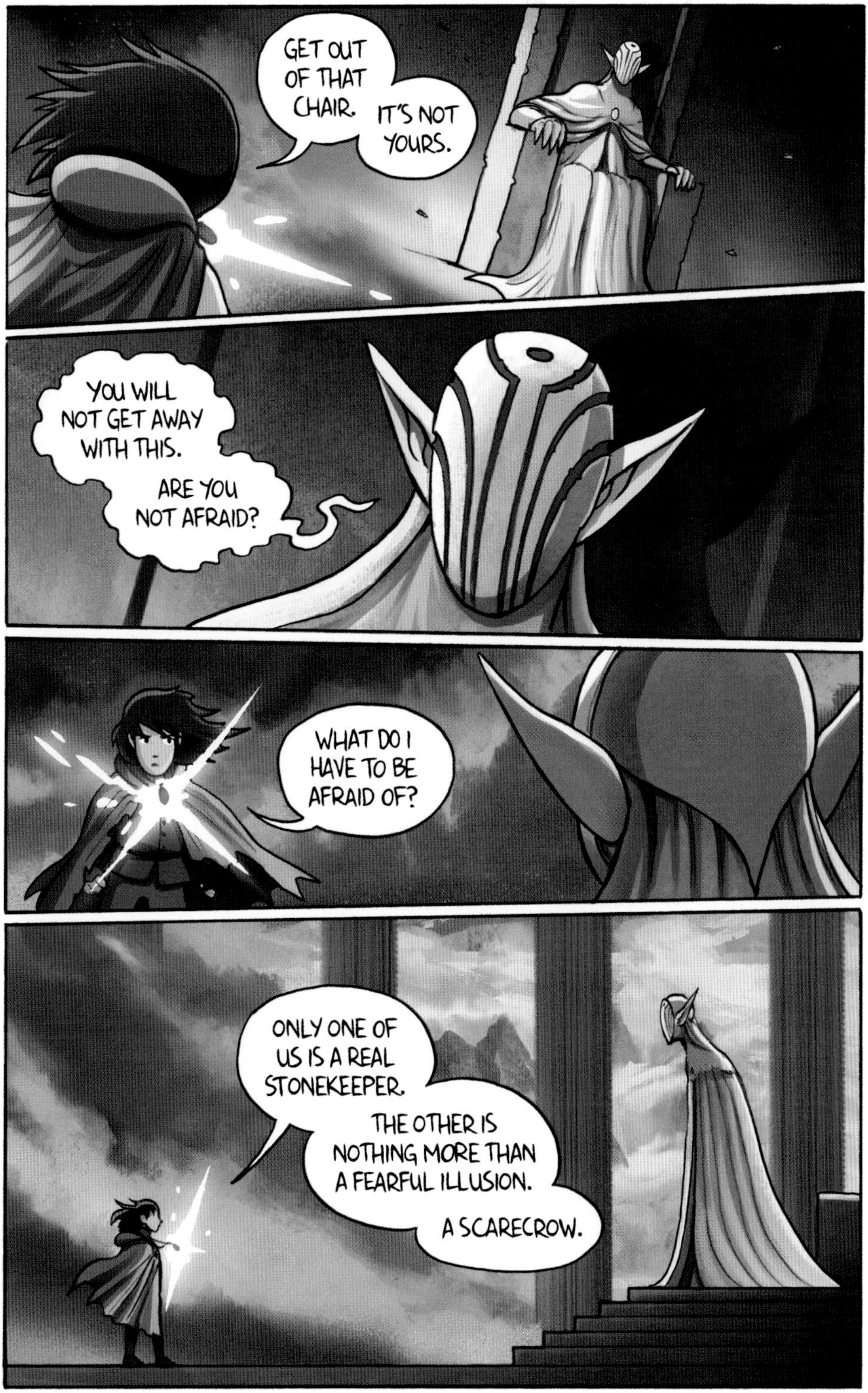
GET OUT OF THAT CHAIR.
IT'S NOT YOURS.
YOU WILL NOT GET AWAY WITH THIS.
ARE YOU NOT AFRAID?
WHAT DO I HAVE TO BE AFRAID OF?
ONLY ONE OF US IS A REAL STONEKEEPER.
THE OTHER IS NOTHING MORE THAN A FEARFUL ILLUSION.
A SCARECROW.

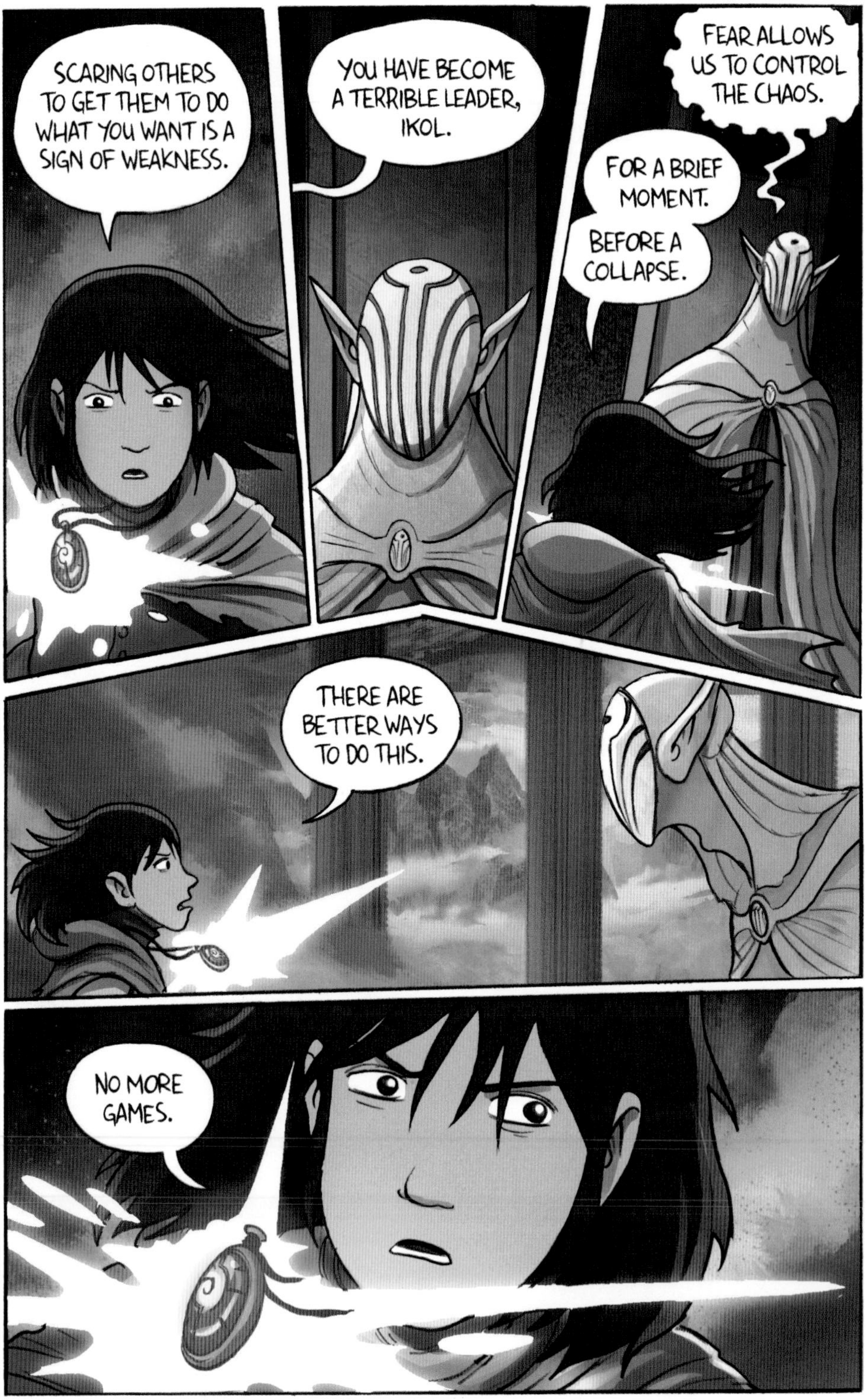
SCARING OTHERS TO GET THEM TO DO WHAT YOU WANT IS A SIGN OF WEAKNESS.
YOU HAVE BECOME A TERRIBLE LEADER, IKOL.
FEAR ALLOWS US TO CONTROL THE CHAOS.
FOR A BRIEF MOMENT.
BEFORE A COLLAPSE.
THERE ARE BETTER WAYS TO DO THIS.
NO MORE GAMES.

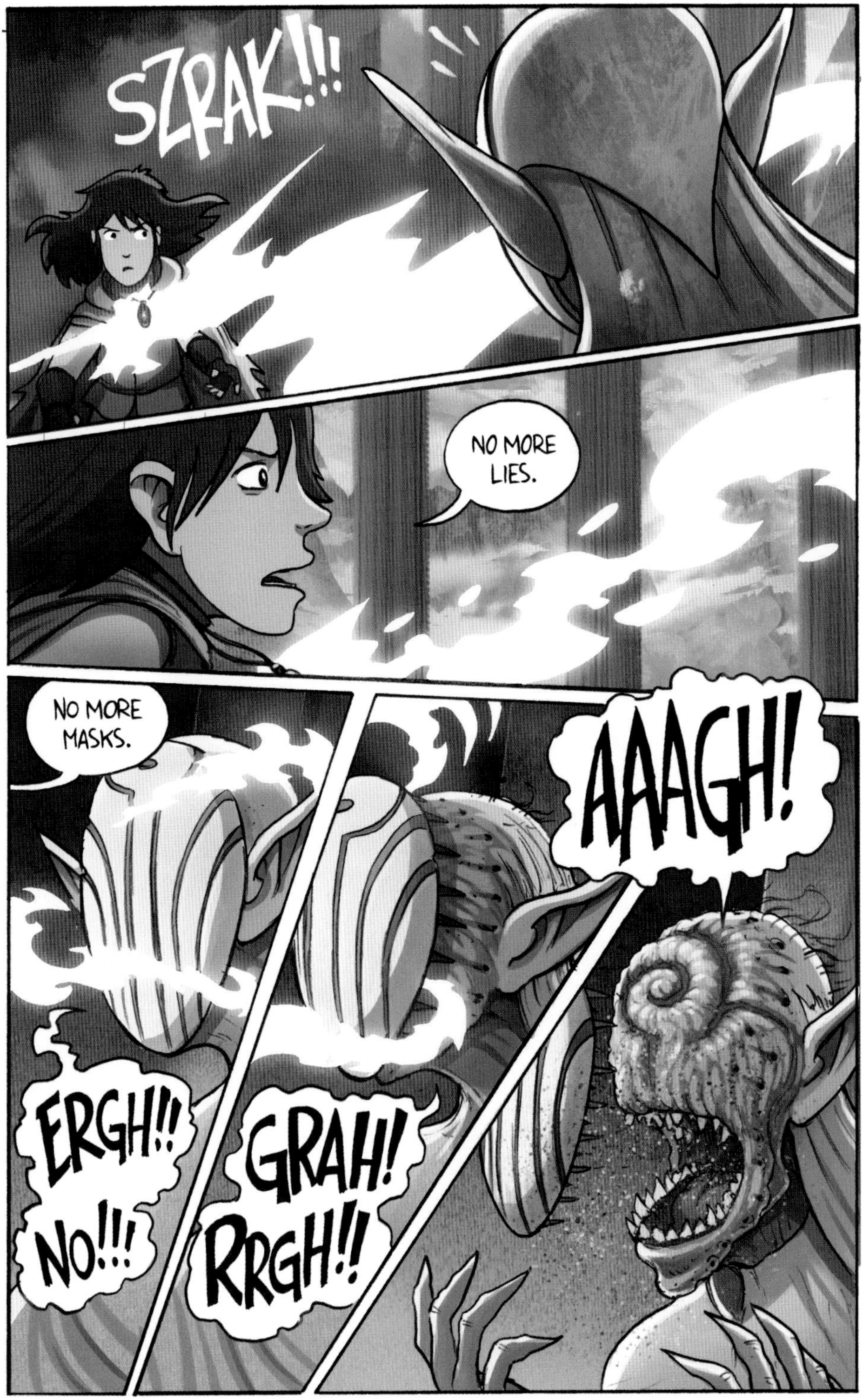
SZRAK!!!
NO MORE LIES.
NO MORE MASKS.
ERGH!! NO!!!
GRAH! RRGH!!
AAAGH!

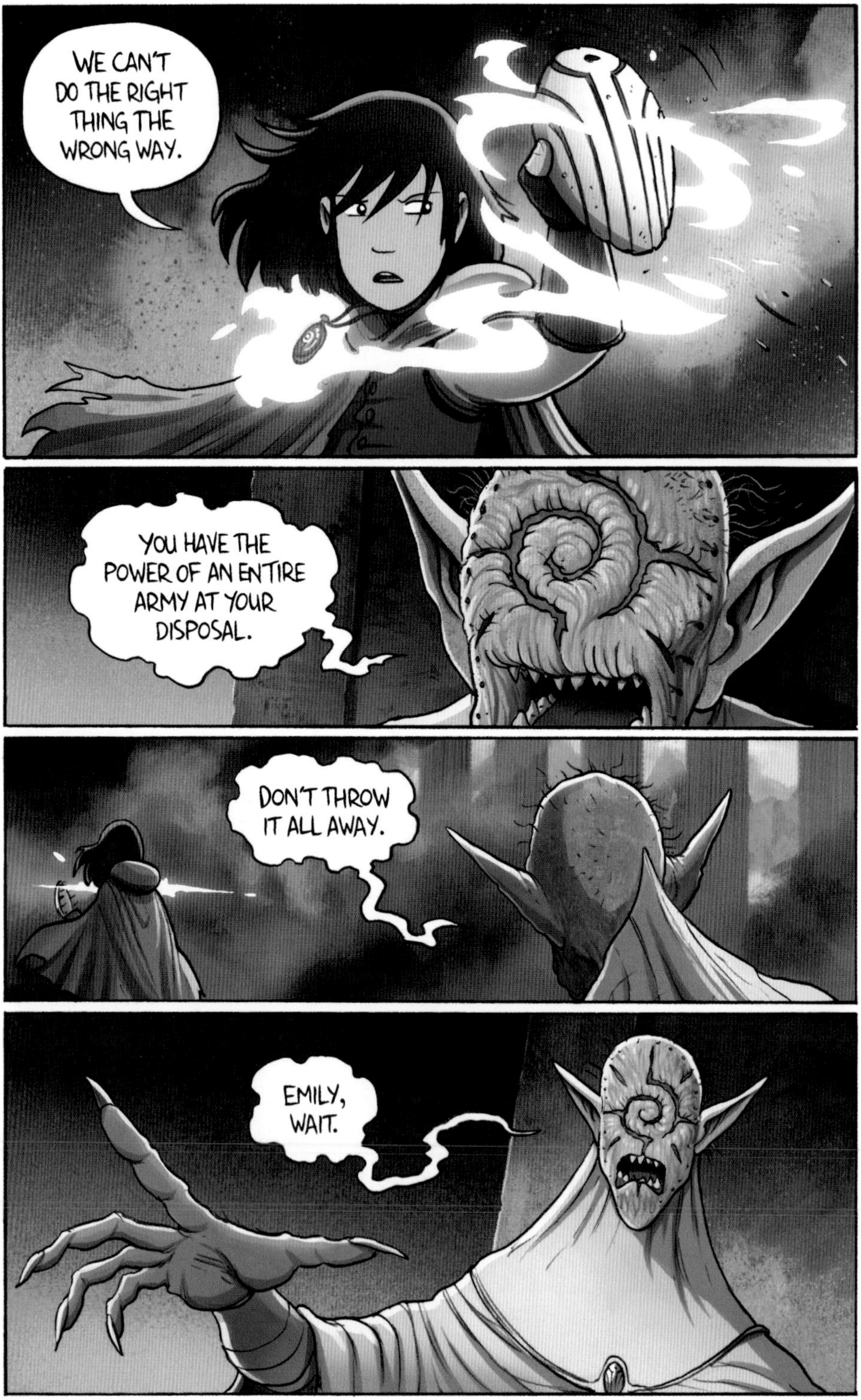
WE CAN'T DO THE RIGHT THING THE WRONG WAY.
YOU HAVE THE POWER OF AN ENTIRE ARMY AT YOUR DISPOSAL.
DON'T THROW IT ALL AWAY.
EMILY, WAIT.

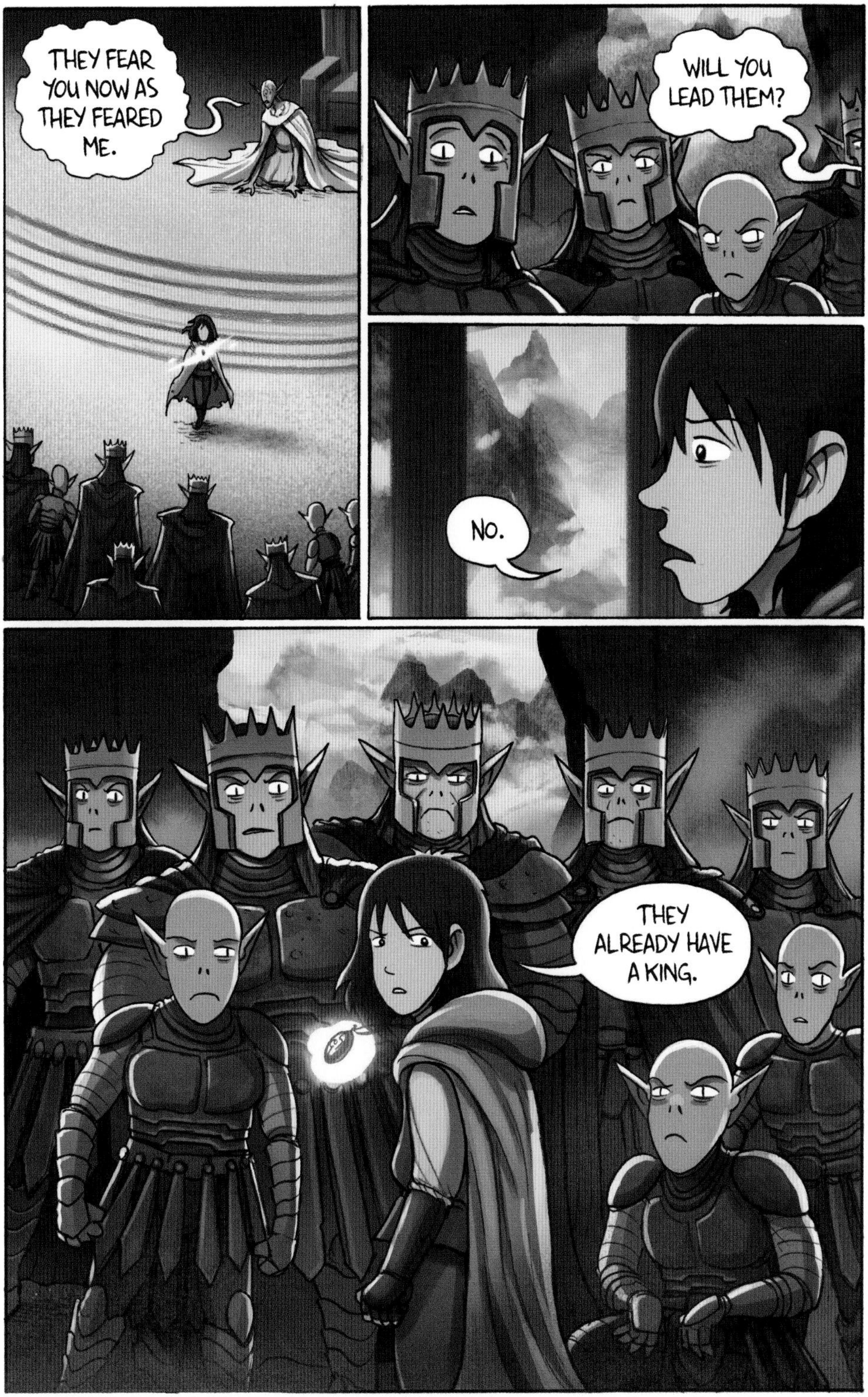
THEY FEAR YOU NOW AS THEY FEARED ME.
WILL YOU LEAD THEM?
NO.
THEY ALREADY HAVE A KING.

ZZZ.

HEY, TRELLIS.

ZZZ. SNORK!

TRELLIS!

HUH?

WE'VE ARRIVED.

CARE TO JOIN ME OUTSIDE?

OH, YES. OKAY.

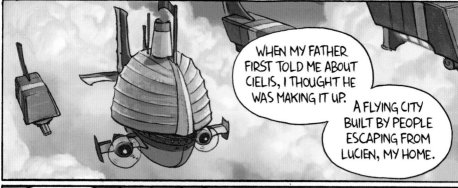

WHEN MY FATHER FIRST TOLD ME ABOUT CIELIS, I THOUGHT HE WAS MAKING IT UP. A FLYING CITY BUILT BY PEOPLE ESCAPING FROM LUCIEN, MY HOME.

THEY WERE RUNNING AWAY FROM MORE THAN JUST LUCIEN.

PERHAPS, BUT THE LENGTHS SOME PEOPLE WILL GO TO GET AWAY FROM WHAT THEY FEAR OR DON'T UNDERSTAND--

IT'S SOMETHING I DON'T THINK I CAN EVER RELATE TO.

CAUSE ANY MORE TROUBLE AND THE RESTRAINTS GO BACK ON.

GOT IT, LOGI?

YES, PRINCE TRELLIS.

THANK YOU, PRINCE TRELLIS.

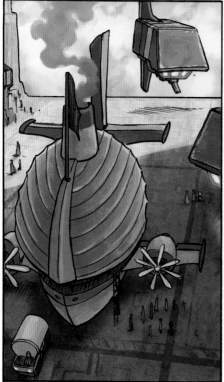

THE CIELIS GUARD WELCOMES THE RETURN OF THE GUARDIAN COUNCIL!

STONEKEEPER EMILY HAYES HAS BEEN AWAITING YOUR ARRIVAL.

EMILY'S ALREADY HERE?!

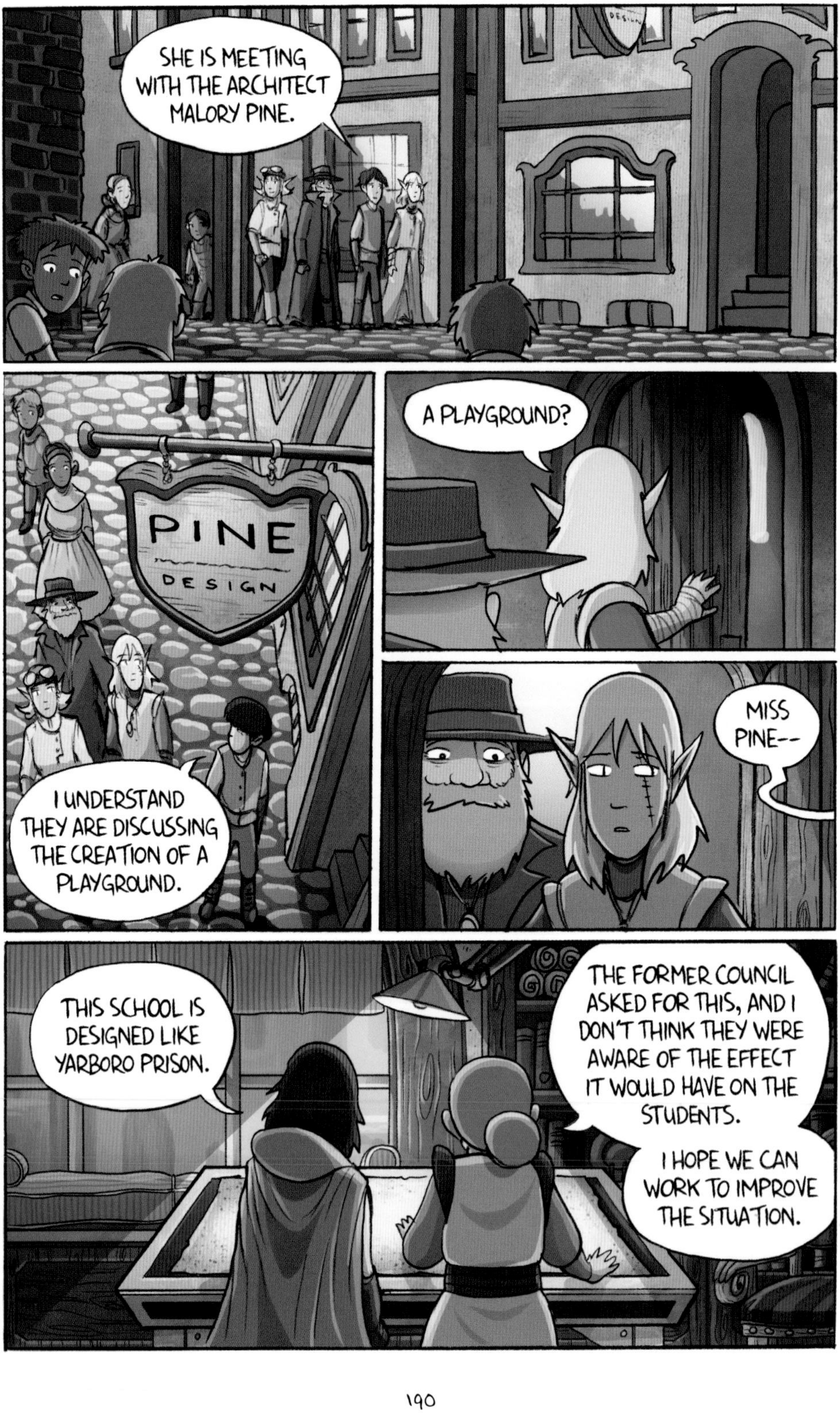
SHE IS MEETING WITH THE ARCHITECT MALORY PINE.
PINE DESIGN
I UNDERSTAND THEY ARE DISCUSSING THE CREATION OF A PLAYGROUND.
A PLAYGROUND?
MISS PINE--
THIS SCHOOL IS DESIGNED LIKE YARBORO PRISON.
THE FORMER COUNCIL ASKED FOR THIS, AND I DON'T THINK THEY WERE AWARE OF THE EFFECT IT WOULD HAVE ON THE STUDENTS.
I HOPE WE CAN WORK TO IMPROVE THE SITUATION.

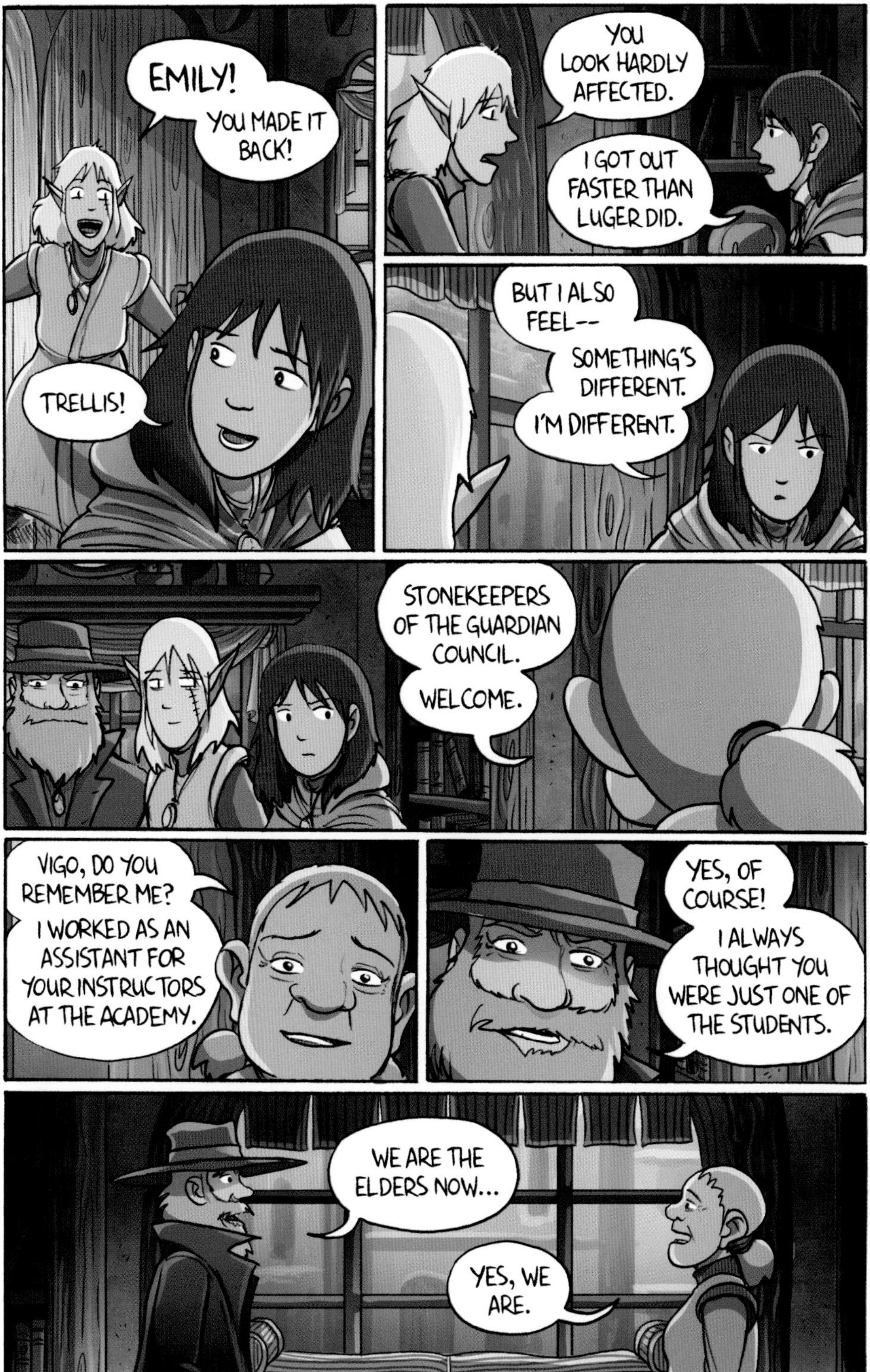
EMILY!
YOU MADE IT BACK!
TRELLIS!
YOU LOOK HARDLY AFFECTED.
I GOT OUT FASTER THAN LUGER DID.
BUT I ALSO FEEL--
SOMETHING'S DIFFERENT.
I'M DIFFERENT.
STONEKEEPERS OF THE GUARDIAN COUNCIL.
WELCOME.
VIGO, DO YOU REMEMBER ME?
I WORKED AS AN ASSISTANT FOR YOUR INSTRUCTORS AT THE ACADEMY.
YES, OF COURSE!
I ALWAYS THOUGHT YOU WERE JUST ONE OF THE STUDENTS.
WE ARE THE ELDERS NOW...
YES, WE ARE.

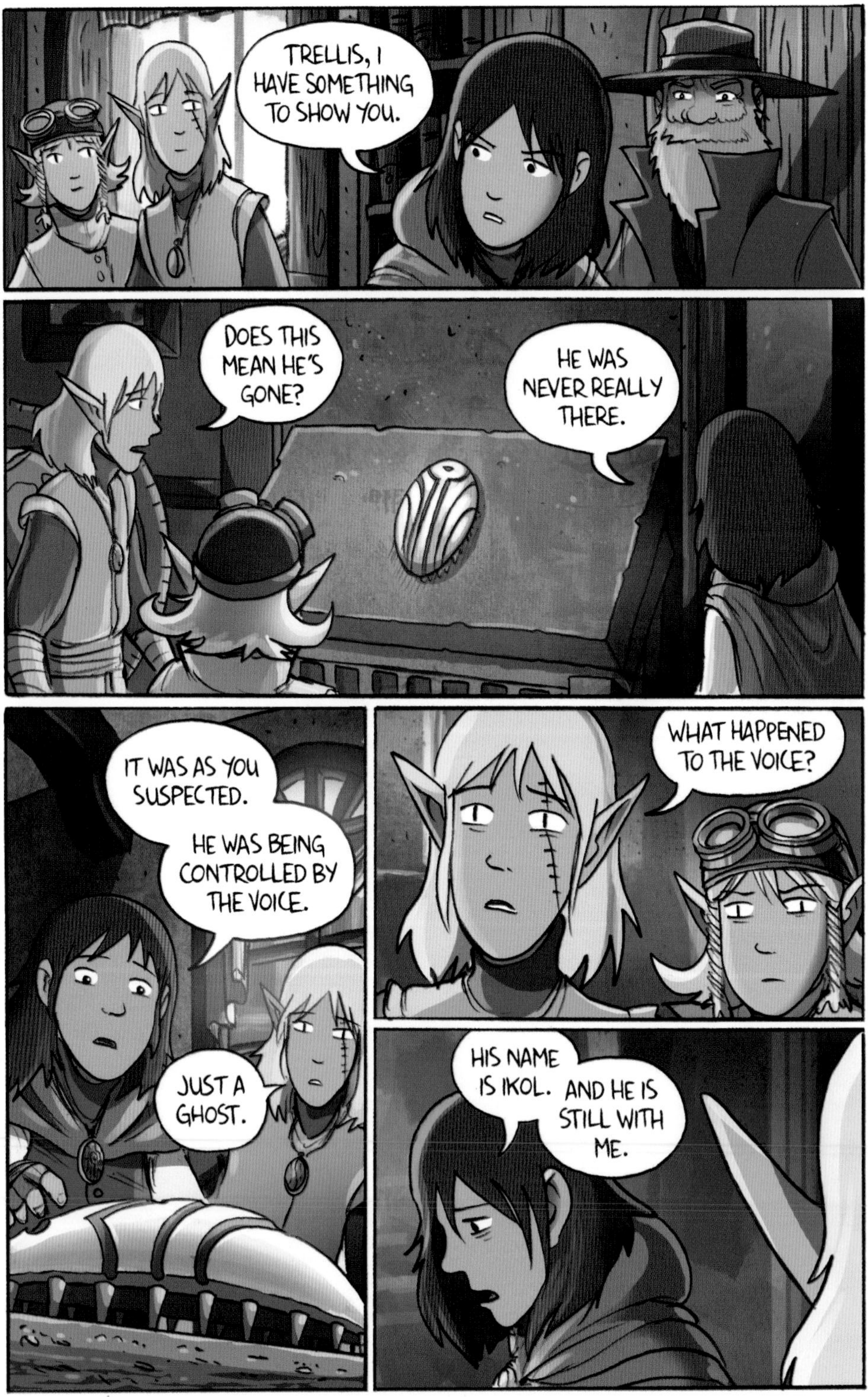
TRELLIS, I HAVE SOMETHING TO SHOW YOU.
DOES THIS MEAN HE'S GONE?
HE WAS NEVER REALLY THERE.
IT WAS AS YOU SUSPECTED.
HE WAS BEING CONTROLLED BY THE VOICE.
JUST A GHOST.
WHAT HAPPENED TO THE VOICE?
HIS NAME IS IKOL.
AND HE IS STILL WITH ME.

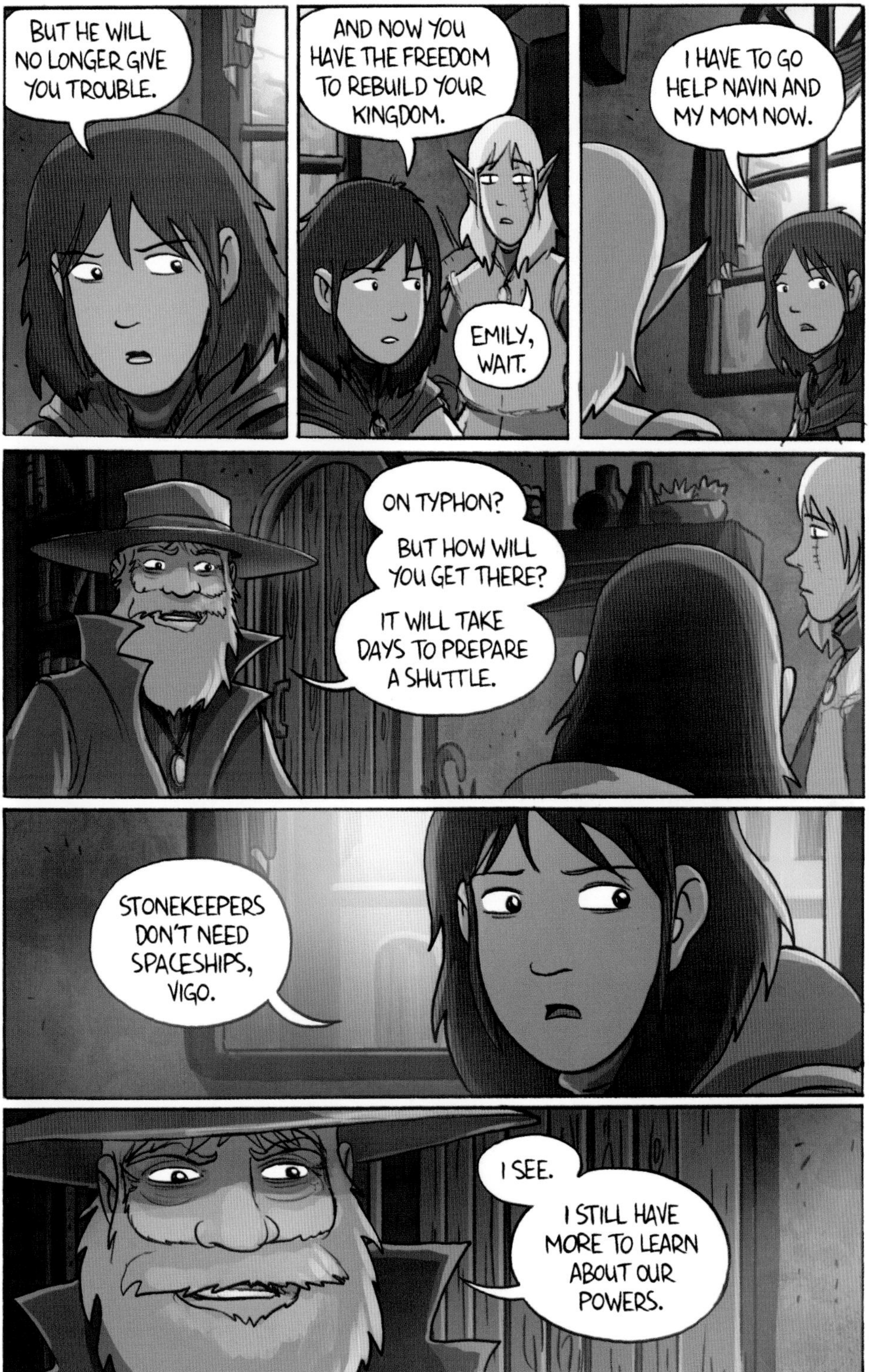
BUT HE WILL NO LONGER GIVE YOU TROUBLE.
AND NOW YOU HAVE THE FREEDOM TO REBUILD YOUR KINGDOM.
EMILY, WAIT.
I HAVE TO GO HELP NAVIN AND MY MOM NOW.
ON TYPHON?
BUT HOW WILL YOU GET THERE?
IT WILL TAKE DAYS TO PREPARE A SHUTTLE.
STONEKEEPERS DON'T NEED SPACESHIPS, VIGO.
I SEE.
I STILL HAVE MORE TO LEARN ABOUT OUR POWERS.

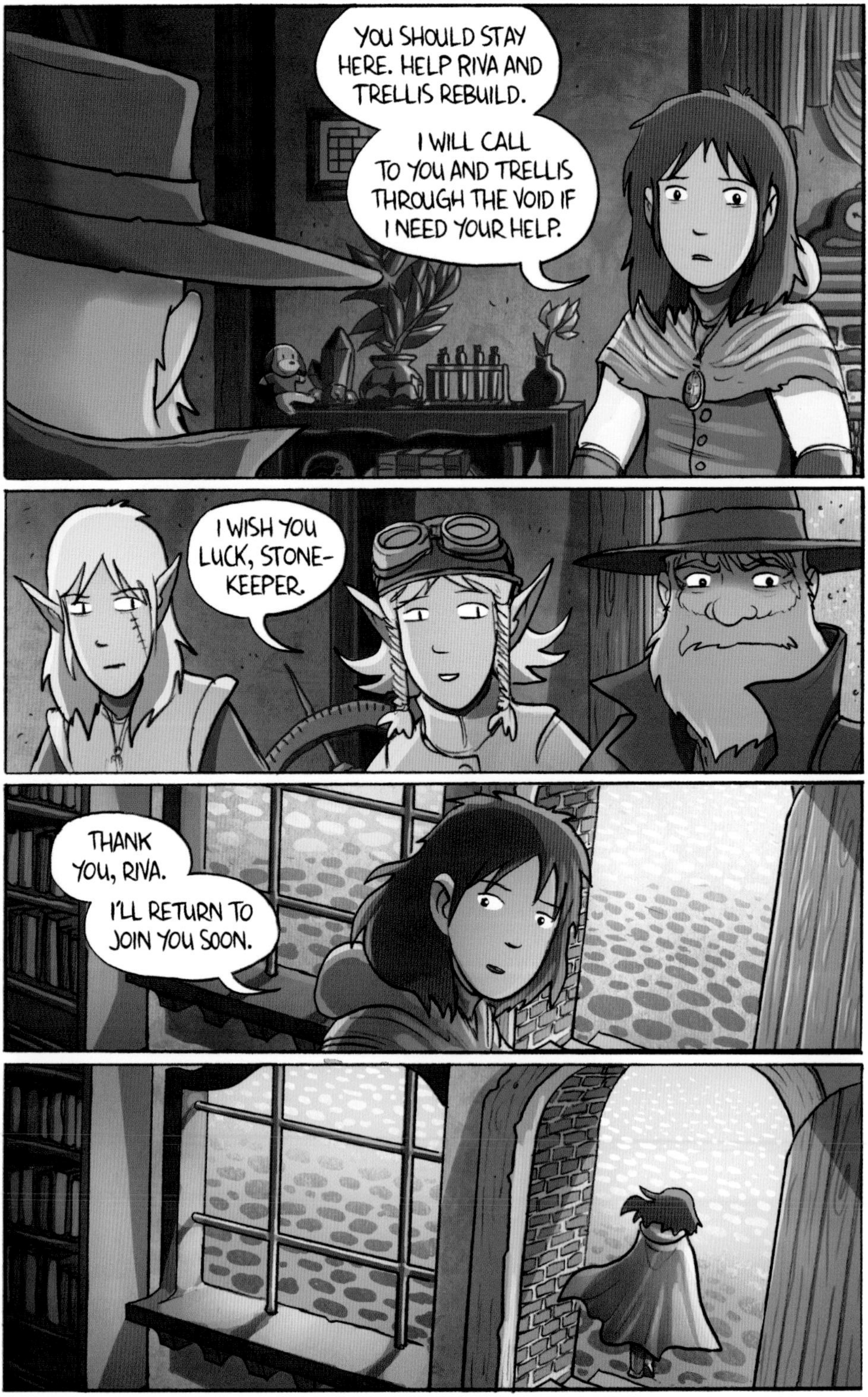
YOU SHOULD STAY HERE. HELP RIVA AND TRELLIS REBUILD.
I WILL CALL TO YOU AND TRELLIS THROUGH THE VOID IF I NEED YOUR HELP.
I WISH YOU LUCK, STONE-KEEPER.
THANK YOU, RIVA.
I'LL RETURN TO JOIN YOU SOON.

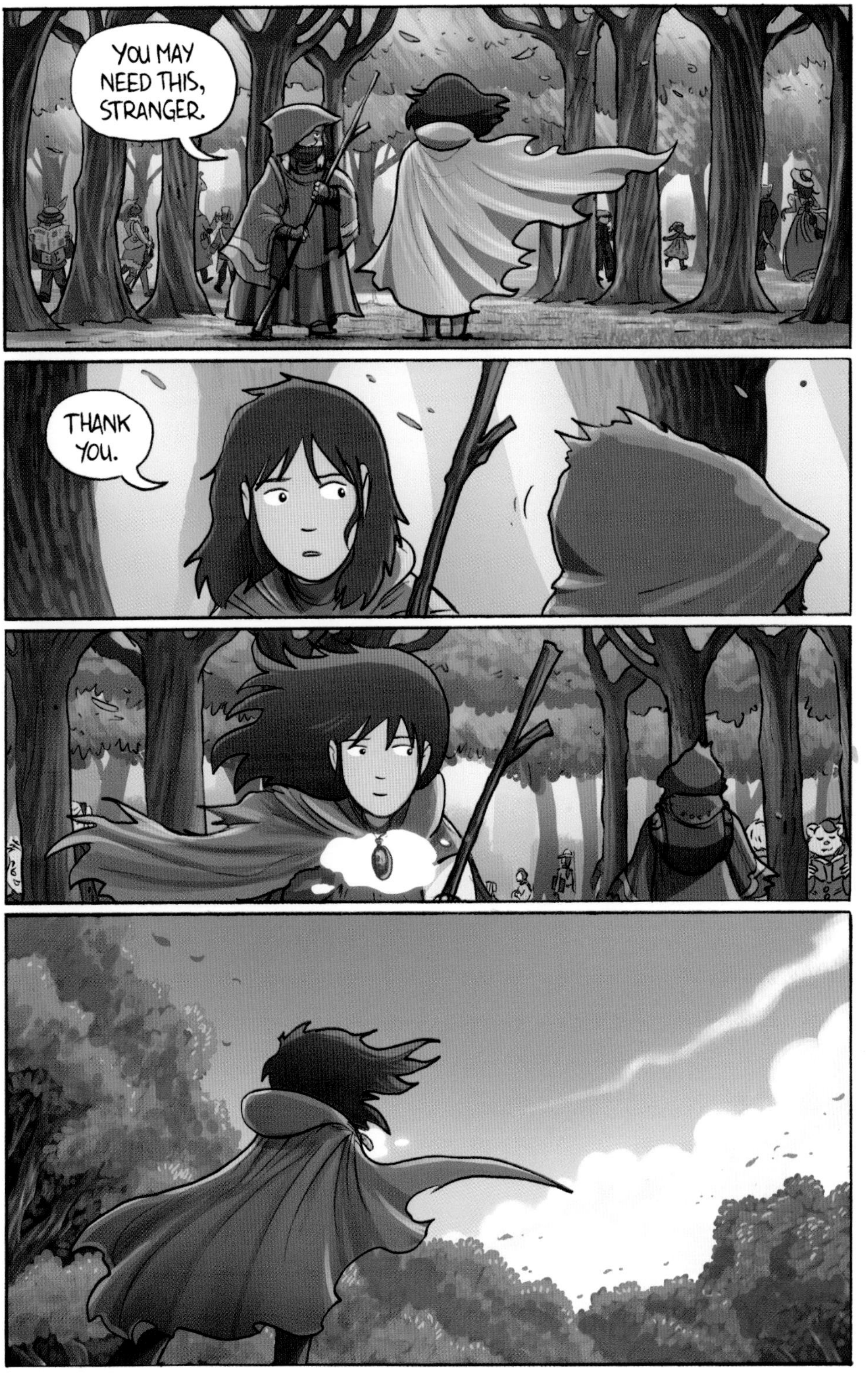
YOU MAY NEED THIS, STRANGER.
THANK YOU.

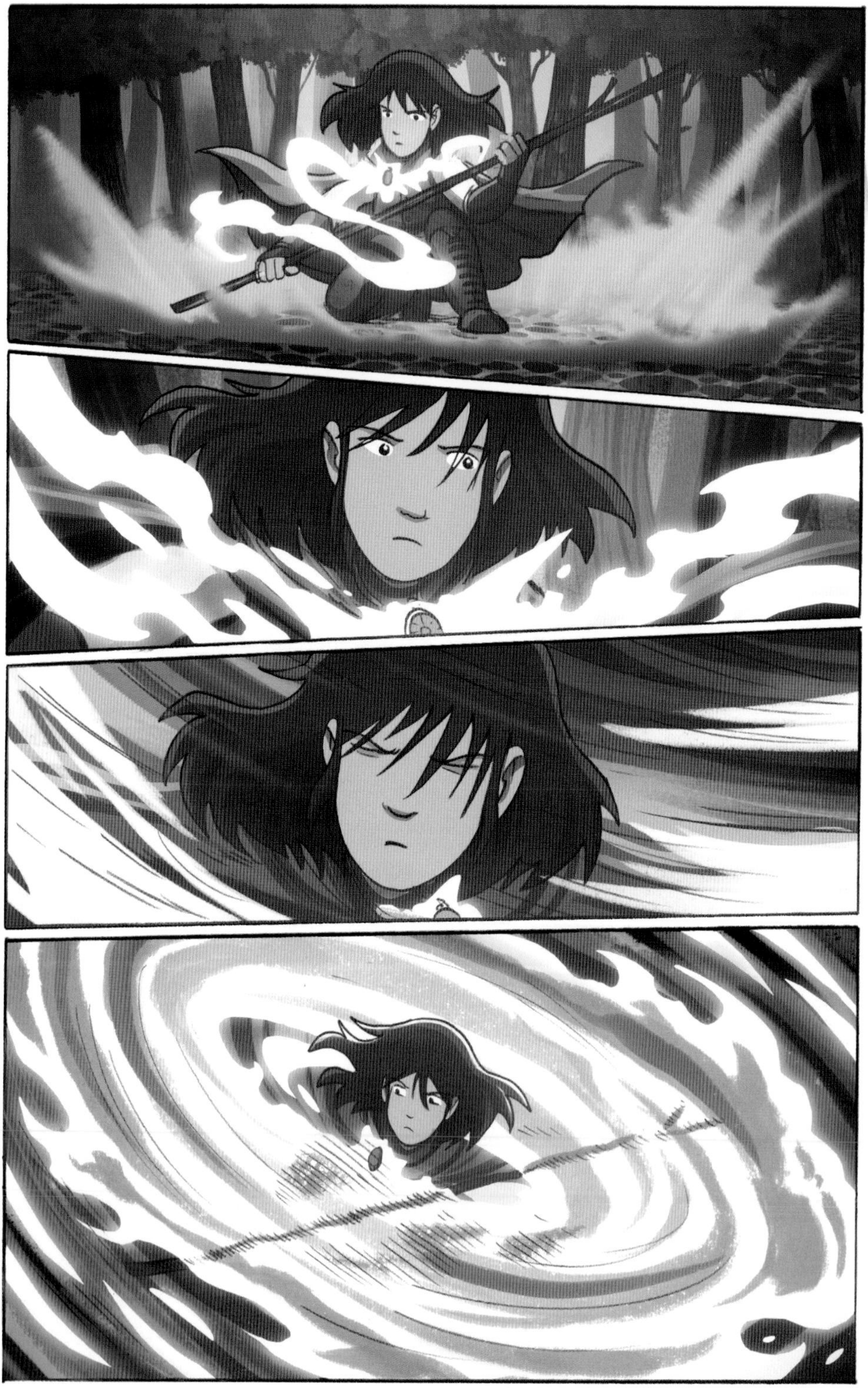

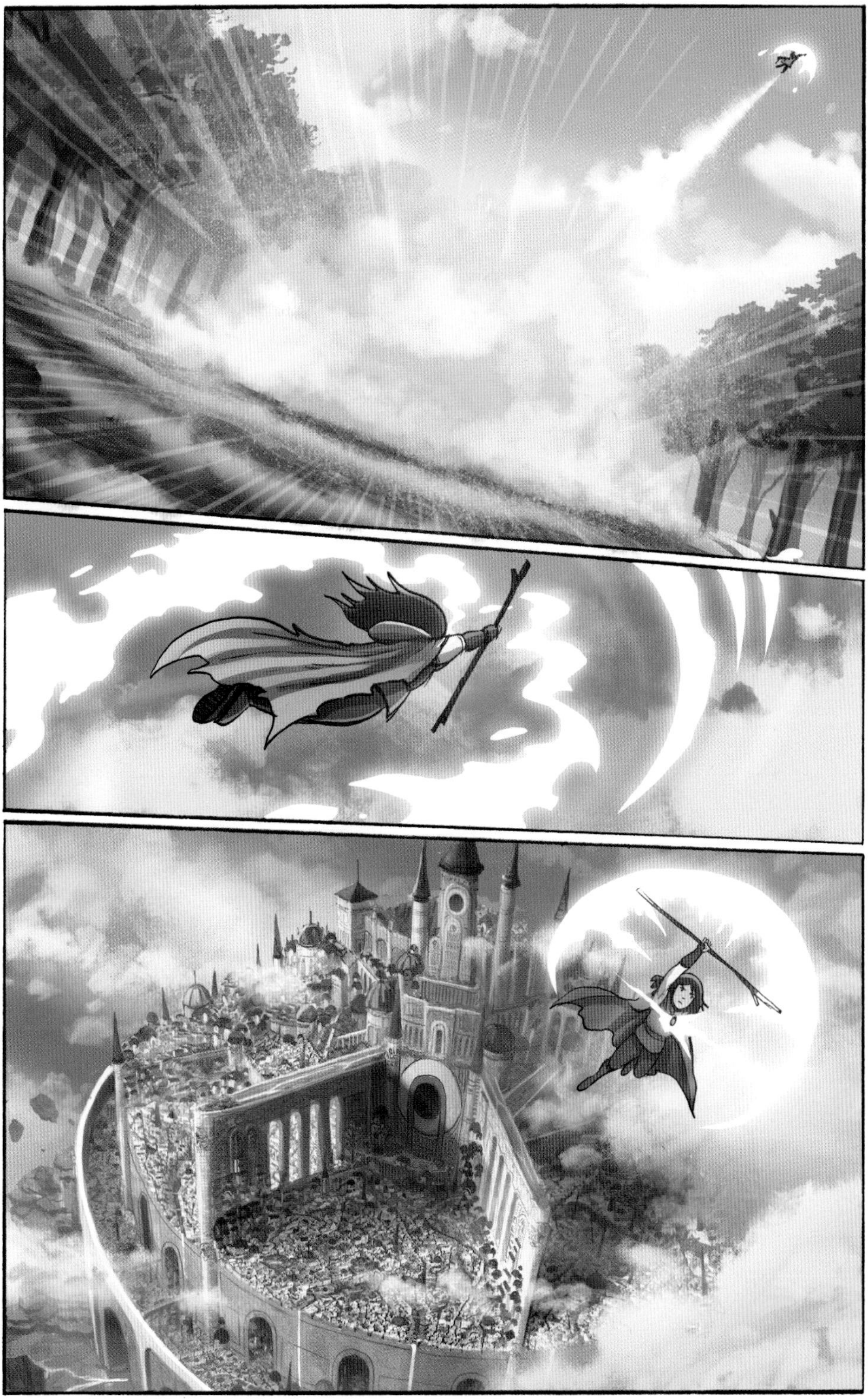

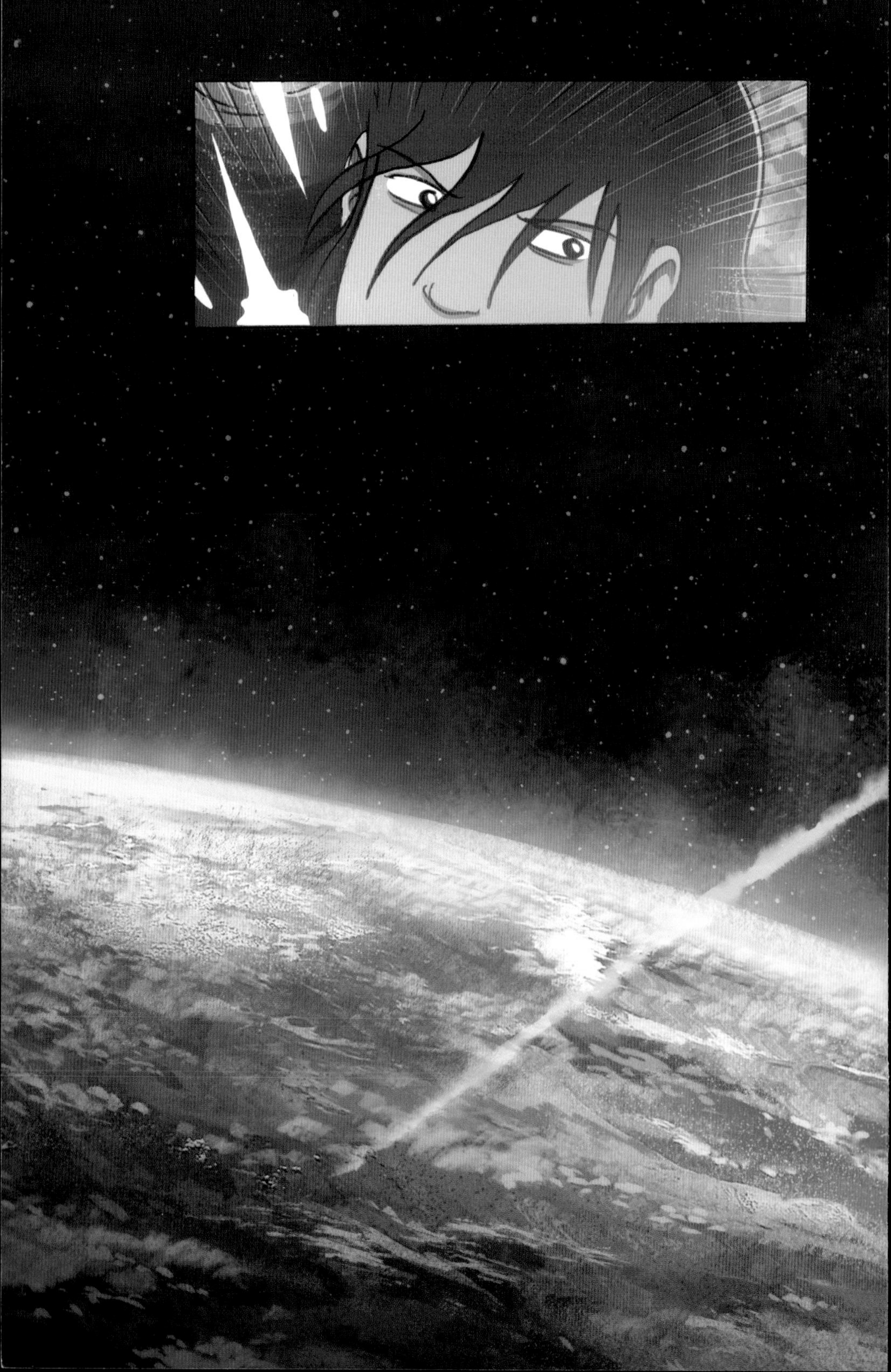

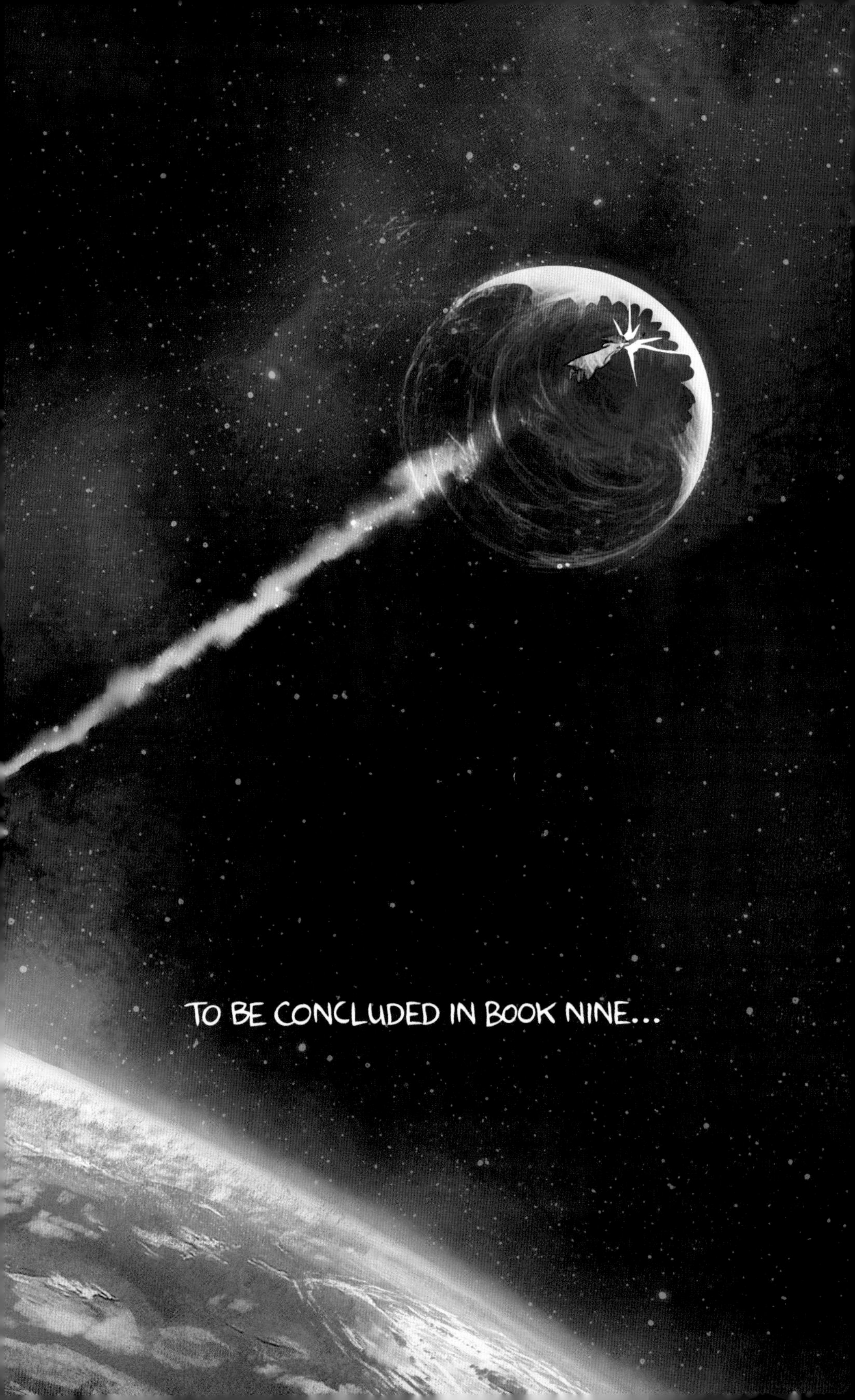
TO BE CONCLUDED IN BOOK NINE...

CREATED AT

BOLT CITY
PRODUCTIONS

WRITTEN & ILLUSTRATED BY
KAZU KIBUISHI

LEAD PRODUCTION ASSISTANT
JASON CAFFOE

COLORS & BACKGROUNDS BY
JASON CAFFOE
KAZU KIBUISHI
AMY KIM KIBUISHI
FORREST DICKISON
TIM PROBERT
POLYNA KIM
AUDRA ANN FURUICHI
DERICK TSAI
AMANDA JANE SHARPE
JOE MARQUIS
KELLY HAMILTON

PAGE FLATTING
CRYSTAL KAN
MEGAN BRENNAN
POLYNA KIM
JOEY HAN
AUDRA ANN FURUICHI
LINDSEY REIMER
PRESTON DO

SPECIAL THANKS

Judith Hansen, Cassandra Pelham Fulton, Phil Falco, David Saylor,
Nancy Caffoe, Juni & Sophie Kibuishi, Rachel & Hazel Caffoe,
Dan & Heidi Ullom, Moses Phillips, Bart Foutch, and Ryan Brown
and the Bicycle Centres crew.

Thank you to all the librarians, booksellers, parents, and readers
for whom this book was made.